THE DOWAGER'S GRAND TRIUMPH

A TENDER REGENCY ROMANCE OF SECOND CHANCES, UNLIKELY HEROES, FAMILY LOYALTY, AND LOVE STRONG ENOUGH TO CROSS CONTINENTS.

DOUBLE-DILEMMA ROMANCE
BOOK SIX

SUSANNE DUNLAP

The Dowager's Grand Triumph

First Paperback Print Edition: 2026

Published by Comfortable Prose Publishing

Cover design by 100Covers

eBook: 979-8-9938526-9-0; Paperback: 979-8-9960551-0-4

Every word of this book was written by the author. AI tools were used in a supporting role for research, analysis, and marketing.

CHAPTER 1

The Dowager Lady Lewiston thought she was well beyond the age of being shocked by anything she might receive through the post. But one morning just before the beginning of the London season of 1817, buried in her unread pile of invitations and notes from friends coming to London to fire off their daughters, was a letter that made her heart race, her temples throb, and her face heat in a raging blush.

She hadn't thought of him in years. No, that wasn't quite true. Belinda's courtship and marriage the year before brought him briefly to mind like a flickering point of light on a dark, starless night.

But that was all. Everything then had been too complicated for her to waste time dwelling on her own past. She had to get her daughter settled, not to mention the child whose very existence reminded her every day of her late husband's infidelity. Now, though, things were different. She lived alone in the London dower house on Park Street, not far from her son the marquess and her grandson. She had blessed solitude, the freedom to order her life however she wanted—and no distractions to prevent her unwelcome contemplation of the past.

She picked up the letter and began to read it again.

"My Lady, are you unwell?"

It wasn't like Fairing to make such a personal remark. Lady Lewiston quickly arranged her features to erase all evidence of emotion. "Perfectly well, thank you. You may clear away the breakfast things."

All she wanted when she moved her household to London, leaving the Cornwall estate to the steward and occasional residence by her son and his family, was a serene, untroubled existence. She wished the past to stay tucked safely away where it belonged. She sighed. It seemed there was no getting around it. Her unruly history would insist on intruding on her present. In fact, in less than a week it would actually come calling. It would do so, that is, if she consented to what Thomas—whom she had not seen for the twenty-nine years he had been in India—asked of her.

Why was he returning to England now, of all times? What would it be like to see him again? They'd been so young then. So young, and so in love. Caroline shook her head hard, wanting to clear all thoughts of that time out of her mind. How foolish to remember it at all! She was a sober old woman now, on the very shady side of forty. And she could discern no evidence of tender feelings in his letter. On the contrary, it politely and formally asked her assistance in a matter, he said, that he was wholly unequipped to manage on his own.

I know I presume much when I ask this of you, but would you consider introducing my daughter to society? I can think of no one better placed to act as her sponsor. She is genteel and accomplished, as well as having benefited from a superior education, and being of an age to make her come-out.

Before you make your decision, however, I feel it only fair to tell you that Anjali's mother was Indian, from a noble Bengali family. Her ancestry is illustrious—much more so than mine. I doubt that fact will weigh in London, unfortunately, and her parentage will no doubt make your task more difficult. Indeed, I am not entirely certain there is any possibility of success, of finding her a suitable match. But it was her late mother's wish that she take her rightful place in English society, and in honor of those wishes I humbly ask your assistance.

I would be grateful if you would send a note to me at The Clarendon, where we are staying until I find a suitable residence in town, telling me whether you are willing to take on this charge. If not, I fully understand. Nonetheless, I hope that, in fond remembrance of our former friendship, you will consent to act as chaperone for my poor motherless Anjali.

Your servant,

Thomas Ashcombe

Caroline rose from the table and walked slowly to the window that looked out over the small garden at the back of the house. It still wore its wintry brown, the lone lime tree devoid of leaves, although in the most sheltered spot she could see a few green shoots poking through the soil optimistically.

Why not? she thought, making an uncharacteristically sudden decision. She had no other demands on her time now that Belinda and Antonella were both married. The theatre and concerts, card parties and picnics, could only occupy so much of her life. She had thought of finding a charitable cause, something that would serve as a worthwhile focus for her restless energy. This young lady, Thomas's daughter, was not a charity case—not if they were staying at the Clarendon, certainly. But the task would truly be a challenge. If the girl was as accomplished and well born as Thomas intimated, the fact of her mixed heritage might be overcome. It would take all her social ingenuity to manage it, though.

Caroline whirled around and strode out of the breakfast room to the tambour desk in the drawing room, drew out a sheet of fine paper, and wrote an affirmative reply to Thomas's letter before she could think better of it. She was doing this, she told herself, not because it would give her an opportunity to see Thomas again, to spend time with him. That was well in the past. She simply felt it was the right thing to do, to help a worthy young lady with the cards stacked slightly against her to find a husband of the right sort who would secure her future.

She pulled the bell rope next to the fireplace. A moment later Fairing walked into the room. "Will you have one of the footmen deliver this letter to Mr. Thomas Ashcombe at The Clarendon?" she said, startling herself with the sensations that shot through her body simply because she spoke his name aloud.

CHAPTER 2

*B*ramble yelped and stretched his paws up to Julian's knees as his valet, Addison, helped the baronet into his greatcoat in preparation for their morning walk. "Yes, friend. Shall it be the Green Park today? I don't think I can face the *ton* before nuncheon." Bramble did not answer, but panted expectantly.

Coat on, Julian bent down causing Bramble to sit so abruptly, ears plastered back, tongue lolling, that it never failed to make him grin. Moments like these—and when he was actually asleep—were the only times the pup stopped wriggling or demanding attention. Bramble had learned early on that if he didn't stay still at this strategic point, the leash would not be attached and the much-anticipated walk would not occur. Of course, he never behaved so obligingly at any other time.

If only all the world could be as easily pleased, as uniformly cheerful, as quick to understand as Bramble, Julian thought. He encountered all too much deceit and prevarication in his chosen profession of law. Of course, the spaniel had no cares, no ambitions, no unmet needs or wants. He did not have to attend balls and routs and dress parties. The thought made Julian smile.

Other than Bramble's unruly conduct, Julian's life was quiet and sober. He conscientiously pursued his profession as a barrister. His father had thought him a bit eccentric to insist on having a career, but his mother championed his desire to do something more than idle away his inheritance and end up an indolent country gentleman. Neither of them expected him to choose the law, however, and were shocked when he was called to the bar soon after leaving Oxford.

"Are you in chambers today, sir?" Addison asked.

"I shall look in later. Bicknell has some briefs for me to examine. I'm in King's Bench tomorrow and I'll be dining out after, so would you..." He looked down into Bramble's adoring eyes and up with a sheepish smile at the elderly valet.

"As you wish, Sir Julian," Addison said with the faintest suggestion of a sigh.

Much to the dismay of Addison, in default of Julian the spaniel followed him around. Only late in the evening would Bramble's peregrinations stop while he sat patiently by the door, awaiting his master's return from his chambers at Lincoln's Inn or from dinner with friends at Brooks's. Then he would trail Julian through all his nightly ablutions, curl up at his feet while he read a book and sipped his port, and hop up onto the end of the bed as if he had every right to sleep there too. His loyalty might have been because Julian rescued Bramble from certain doom in a gutter in Covent Garden. But the truth was, as Julian well knew, that Bramble had rescued him. He'd been sunk in grief for the loss of both of his parents in a sailing accident a mere week before then. Suddenly, with a puppy to nurse and care for, his world didn't feel so empty, so pointless.

Before he left his lodgings that cold, sunny March morning, Julian put on his hat, pulling it as low as decently possible to hide as much of his head and face as he could. At that hour of the morning, few fashionable promenaders were about and the tradesmen with their young helpers were too busy preparing their establishments for shoppers to pay him much heed. The Green Park was a bit nearer his lodgings than Hyde Park so he didn't have to spend much time among pedestrians, and once inside the gated enclosure he could let Bramble off the leash and toss a stick for him not to fetch. The spaniel would dash after it enthusiastically, become distracted by something far more interesting, and forget why he'd run off in the first place. Spaniels were bred for one of two things: hunting or companionship. Bramble seemed to have got stuck somewhere in the middle of the two. Or perhaps there was some other blood mixed in that gave him a bit more independence of spirit. If so, Julian was glad of it.

As soon as they entered the park through the nearest gate, Julian unleashed Bramble, who set about nosing around for a likely stick as they wandered more or less together down the path that ran along Piccadilly. The park was nearly empty at that hour, save for a few nursemaids with their charges, and Julian began to relax his vigilance. They had gone no more than a quarter of a mile, however, when Bramble stopped, tail out, nose alert. Julian knew the signs. He'd better fasten him to the leash again, and quickly, before the dog raced off after some quarry—real or imagined. He ran forward, but too late. Bramble had found his scent and pursued it with the determination of a gun dog.

Although short of leg, at a full run Bramble would be impossible to catch. Nonetheless Julian ran after him, determined at least to keep him in sight.

Some way ahead he spied a heavily muffled female figure, doing her best to stop Bramble jumping up at her in apparent pursuit of something on her shoulder. When he was close enough to see more clearly, he discerned that the object on her shoulder was in fact a bird that flapped occasionally and ruffled up its feathers, but didn't seem otherwise much bothered by Bramble's yelps.

To Julian's astonishment, the lady stretched out a gloved hand, palm downward, and said in a commanding voice, "Sit!"

Although he'd never made much of an effort to train Bramble to respond to commands, the dog did just that, gazing alertly up at the lady's face. As Julian approached, the bird opened its yellow beak and—did he hear correctly?—said "Sit!" in exactly the same tone as the lady had moments before.

He was about to beg the lady's pardon and call Bramble to him when the bird launched itself from her shoulder and flew straight at his head. He ducked slightly, but not enough so that the bird couldn't knock off his hat, which rolled away through the grass.

His hands immediately went to try to cover his hair. Too late. The lady's deep brown eyes opened wide and stared. She was so muffled up against the cold that her eyes, nose, and lips were all he could make out of her. He let his hands drop to his sides. No point hiding the bane of his existence. His mop of red curls caught the morning sun and likely glowed like fire. "Sir Julian Meredith at your service, Ma'am. My apologies for my ill-behaved dog."

THE DOG WAS A BIT OF A NUISANCE, ANJALI THOUGHT, BUT clearly quite harmless. Even Kavi sensed it. Once it had barked itself into a slightly calmer state, Anjali did what she'd done with the dogs they had to leave behind in Calcutta and gave it a voice command accompanied by a gesture. Either the animal was well trained or simply responded to her tone, she couldn't tell.

She expected that the rather sweet, brown-eyed, floppy-eared spaniel mix must belong to a lady who had lost control of him on a walk. When instead a tall, well-dressed gentleman hurried toward her, she was somewhat astonished. He was well dressed, that is, aside from his hat, which he pulled unfashionably low on his head so it shielded his eyes. She couldn't tell whether his expression was angry or irritated or amused.

Then Kavi—not always the best judge of character—decided that something about the man was not to be trusted and flew at him, knocking the obscuring hat off his head.

At first, all she could do was stare. She'd never seen hair quite that color before. There were a few ginger-haired officers in the Company ranks, but none had that dark red mass of curls, the color of smoldering coals being brought to life by bellows. And his eyes! She wasn't certain what color they were exactly. Somewhere between green and brown. Or was it gold?

It took her a moment to realize he'd introduced himself to her. She curtsied slightly and said, "It is no trouble, Sir Julian. I must apologize in turn for my cheeky bird." She was about to offer to retrieve his hat, but the dog had anticipated her and scrambled after it, bringing it back to his master now crushed and damp.

"When I actually want him to fetch something he ignores it," Sir Julian said, grimacing at his spoiled hat.

For a moment they stood there like two saplings that had put roots down into the soil. Then Anjali said, "I think he believes he's done you a very great service," and smiled. She had no idea how she was supposed to respond to a chance meeting like this. Her father had warned her that there were very strict rules of propriety to be followed in London society. Already she'd disobeyed one by walking out alone before breakfast. She had Kavi to scare people off—although she soon realized that walking through London streets with a bird perched on one's shoulder wasn't exactly calculated to ensure no one noticed her.

"Forgive me, Ma'am. Your chaperone has wandered off—I shall not trouble you any longer." Sir Julian nodded and made as if to turn around then stopped and faced her again. "Please, before I go, would you satisfy my curiosity about three things? If you won't think me impertinent." His green-gold eyes met hers with frank interest and his lips stretched into a tentative, shy smile.

Oh no, Anjali thought. *He'll ask me where I'm from, and then treat me like an exotic specimen of some kind.* But he said he wanted to ask *three* things, which seemed oddly specific and made her curious. "Very well, Sir Julian. Ask what you will."

"First question: What is your name? You have had mine."

"My name is Miss Ashcombe." She decided to give him the minimum information necessary.

He bowed slightly. "Second question: What kind of a bird is that?" He did not point, only nodded his head in the direction of Kavi, who now sat placidly on her shoulder.

"Kavi is a myna bird." *Now he'll ask where Kavi came from and I shall be cast in the role of outsider, as no doubt he already has done without actually saying it!*

"Third question: How did you manage to make Bramble —that's this commoner's name—respond to your command?" He bent to scratch the now docile dog on the head. "I assure you, he's never done so for me. He only sits when it suits him."

It was Anjali's turn to smile. Was he really not curious about her? All bundled up in a warm pelisse, wrapped in two paisley shawls and carrying a fur muff when other ladies seemed to think the weather pleasantly mild; her skin a color matching that of no English person she had seen. Of course, very little of it was in view. "I cannot answer that question, because I honestly don't know. It is how we treat our dogs at home." Home. Was it still that? Would she ever see it again?

"I'm sorry," he said. "I have said something to upset you."

"Oh! No, sir. Not at all." She didn't realize her thoughts were quite so visible on her face, and smiled as serenely as she could.

"If you are certain. I am grateful for your answers. It's a hazard with me: unbridled curiosity. It's because of my profession. Bramble and I shall not intrude on your morning walk any more. A pleasure, Miss Ashcombe." He bowed, actually put his ruined hat on his head again, squashed it down as far as it would go, clipped a leash onto the spaniel's collar, and walked away.

She wanted to tell him that he needn't cover his head that way, that the color of his hair was so beautiful it made her want to bury her fingers in it. Instantly she berated herself. Could she be thinking such disloyal thoughts so soon? She might never see Nalin again, but she owed him so much. They owed him so much.

Nalin. All warm brown eyes and skin a few shades darker than hers. Not pasty like these English people. At least, that was what she could remember. Odd how hard it was to conjure up his image. It hadn't been so long since she had last seen him. Only the three months of the voyage.

She sighed. He was so far away. Kavi rubbed his beak against her ear and murmured, *sad sad sad*, which ironically always cheered her up. "Let's go back," she said. "If I can remember how I got here, that is." She thought she could.

The London streets were not nearly so haphazardly arranged as those in Calcutta, and she'd committed some landmarks to memory as she made her way south from the hotel.

South. The direction her thoughts continued to stray. How long would that be the case?

CHAPTER 3

homas believed his actions were honorable. Everything he was doing was right for Anjali as well as himself. His business in Calcutta had run its course. Conditions in Bengal had made it increasingly difficult to operate as an independent trader, to maintain his autonomy from the East India Company. And his beautiful daughter—who looked so much like her late, magnificent, beloved mother—needed a future worthy of her heritage. Even without the events that hastened their departure, it would have been the right thing to do.

The sooner Anjali became accustomed to life in England the better.

Those the change in the business climate and the need to establish Anjali in society would have been enough in themselves to justify this hurried move from Calcutta. The imminent Maratha war, which threatened to disrupt trade, added still more urgency to his move.

There was yet another reason, however. One that Anjali didn't know about, the one that was most pressing. Only Nalin, Thomas's chief clerk, was privy to the information he'd stumbled upon and that was contained in the documents he'd brought with him on the three-month voyage. He hadn't even told Nalin the whole of it. He could have let the matter lie. He could have turned a blind eye to actions that most of the British in India would not have questioned. But Thomas was certain that, had Shanta still been alive, she would have encouraged him to do exactly as he planned. And now, he must take care of it as soon as he possibly could, before other stories had a chance to circulate. Before anyone interested in preventing his actions could follow him to London.

"Papa, why are you frowning?"

Thomas grasped Anjali's hand. Together they sat in the new barouche, jolting over the cobbled streets behind a handsome team of bays. "Was I? I expect I'm still a little tired from the voyage."

"Are you worried about seeing Lady Lewiston? That she won't like me after all and refuse to sponsor me? If that is so, I assure you, I would be quite content not to become an English debutante." She gave his hand a squeeze and flashed a mischievous smile at him.

"Lady Lewiston will find you charming, I am certain. How could she not, *beti*?"

Anjali grimaced. "I can think of several ways in which I might fall short in her eyes, beginning with my very un-English complexion."

Anjali's skin was the most beautiful shade, somewhere between ivory and honey. Of course, it wasn't anything like the damask or peach of the supposed English beauties. And her large, luminous dark eyes rimmed by long, curling lashes were truly captivating. Just like her late mother's. Thomas couldn't blame her for being anxious, though. The *ton* could be cruel and very jealous of their rituals and conventions. He could only hope that her keen intelligence and insight would guide her—unscathed—through what was to come.

The carriage came to a stop in front of the home of Lady Caroline Holbrook, now the dowager Marchioness of Lewiston. The groom let down the step and opened the carriage door. Thomas climbed out first. When Anjali placed her slender, gloved hand in his, it shook. "Courage, my love," he whispered.

The house was elegant but not imposing. He wouldn't describe it as a mansion, but it was large enough to be unmistakably *quality*. That was like Caroline, he thought, nothing too overly demonstrative. He had such a clear picture in his mind of her at the age of seventeen. A true beauty, yes, but she was more than that. She had a quiet elegance that could not be taught. No doubt she'd made an excellent marchioness. Perhaps it had all been for the best.

"Well, my dear. There's no going back now," Thomas said as he lifted the brass knocker and let it fall against the large door, which opened almost immediately. Thomas suspected the butler—or more likely a footman—had been watching for their arrival. They were a curiosity, no doubt: the returning nabob with his half-Indian daughter. "Please tell Lady Lewiston that Mr. Thomas Ashcombe and Miss Ashcombe are here."

The butler bowed and plodded up the stairs to the first floor while a footman took Thomas's hat and driving coat. Another footman stood behind Anjali preparing to help her out of her warm cloak. She whirled around and glared at him as though he must be mad.

"My daughter feels the cold. She will keep her cloak on for the moment."

Poor Anjali's teeth had started chattering as soon as they stepped on shore at Southampton and she swore she would never get used to the damp chill.

They mounted the stairs and the butler announced them and ushered them into an elegant drawing room on the first floor. Four long windows, curtained in subtly striped silk, flooded the room with light. Thomas was relieved to see a fire crackling merrily in the hearth in the deceptively bright early spring.

"How do you do, Mr. Ashcombe, Miss Ashcombe?"

The warm greeting issued from a lady Thomas would have recognized anywhere, even though time had threaded her once brown hair with gray and fine lines fanned out from the corners of her still-bright eyes. She advanced toward them with her hands outstretched, the welcome of a dear friend rather than a casual acquaintance.

"My Lady," Thomas said, taking her hands and bowing. "I cannot express how grateful we are to you for your condescension in agreeing to sponsor Anjali." He let go of her and turned toward his daughter, whose quizzical gaze took in both of them at once. Remembering his manners, Thomas said, "I would like to present to you my daughter, Anjali."

Did he imagine it, or did Caroline—Lady Lewiston— stiffen slightly after he spoke to her? He didn't want to presume upon a friendship of so long ago and act more familiar than would be comfortable. But the open look in Caroline's eyes had now retreated, to be replaced with an expression of calm regard.

"I am delighted to make your acquaintance, Miss Ashcombe. Please come and sit closer to the fire. I imagine you are accustomed to much warmer weather."

Anjali smiled, revealing her straight white teeth and showing the good humor in her beautiful, candid eyes. "I see I am found out," she said as she curtsied gracefully to their hostess.

A look of approval lit Caroline's eyes. Caroline. He found when faced with this woman who had been his first love he could not think of her as the formidable Lady Lewiston. Yet that was who she came to be while he was in India. He breathed an inward sigh of relief that he will have placed Anjali in capable hands.

They spoke on polite, indifferent subjects for a few minutes. The butler returned with a silver tray loaded with tea things and a plate of cakes.

"I don't normally drink tea at this time of day, but I imagine you would appreciate something hot to drink. Perhaps it would enable you to shed your cloak, Miss Ashcombe," Caroline said, suppressing a smile.

Anjali stood at this and let the cloak drop to the chair behind her. The short, puffed sleeves of her muslin day dress revealed her slender arms, now covered in gooseflesh. Her cheeks reddened slightly and she said, "I expect I will grow accustomed." All of them laughed quietly.

Soon Thomas realized that his presence was not making things easier for Lady Lewiston and Anjali. It was an awkward situation, strangers that they were. "I should leave you two alone to get to know one another better," he said. "Shall I call back in half an hour?" He rose.

Caroline looked up at him and said, "No, I think not. In fact, I would be delighted if you would allow Miss Ashcombe to stay with me here, starting right now. That way I may ensure that she is prepared for the rigors of society. Our ways are likely a bit different compared to the ones you have been accustomed to in Calcutta."

He exchanged a look with Anjali. His was all relief. Caroline had not found his daughter wanting. Anjali's, on the other hand, contained a shade of panic. Thomas said, "That is most kind, My Lady. I took the liberty of having Anjali's things loaded into a carriage, hoping that you would extend such an invitation. Her trunks should arrive at any moment."

"And Kavi?" Anjali said on an anxiously rising note.

He did not answer, but gave her a tiny nod, which seemed to comfort her. He wondered what Lady Lewiston would make of the myna bird and hoped that she would not object. Without Kavi's company, Anjali would not consent to stay in Park Street.

Lady Lewiston rose and gave him her hand. He took it and raised it to his lips, then turned and left them.

ANJALI WATCHED THE DOOR CLOSE BEHIND HER FATHER AND then turned to face Lady Lewiston, who had come back and sat down to pour out the tea.

"Now, Miss Ashcombe, I think we need to understand each other if your season is to be a success. I won't pretend that there won't be challenges, but—"

"I don't want a season!" Anjali announced, fists clenched at her side, giving in to her frustration and anxiety. It had all been too much. The voyage had been difficult and uncomfortable. Everything was strange. "I mean, you should not go to such trouble for me. I am very grateful, but I do not see why you should help me in this way."

Lady Lewiston paused with the teapot tilted not quite enough to pour into the waiting cup and said, "That's as may be, but I told your father that I would introduce you to society. It appears to be what he wishes. I was not aware that you don't agree with him."

Anjali felt wretched. She didn't want to disappoint her father, not in the least. All this just wasn't anything she'd ever imagined she would do. "No, I want to do his bidding. I know he means it for the best. It's just …"

"It's just that you find yourself suddenly in a place you've never been before and expected to live with someone you never met before. I think that would try the endurance of anyone, let alone a motherless girl of nineteen. I suggest you drink a cup of tea and we become better acquainted. I have a daughter in town who is about your age. You will meet her."

Anjali had had what passed for tea in this country at the hotel, an insipid brew with no spices, and wrinkled her nose. And the daughter? She shivered to think what a marchioness's spoiled child would think of her. She feared she was being impolite, but she simply had no more energy for pretense. "I-I thank you Lady Lewiston. But I'm very tired. I'd be grateful if a servant could show me to my bedchamber." She would not meet Lady Lewiston's eyes. Let her father's old friend think what she would. Perhaps in the morning she could be persuaded to relinquish the whole idea, that now that she'd met Anjali, it was a mistake to even try. If they must remain in London, could they not live quietly, out of society? Anything to give her time to adjust.

"Of course, my dear." Lady Lewiston set the teapot down, rose, and pulled the bell rope next to the fireplace. "I'll have a tray sent up to you for supper later. Let us talk in the morning so that we can come to an agreement about what is to be done."

At last, Anjali looked into Lady Lewiston's eyes. They were not hard and haughty, as she half expected them to be. Rather they looked upon her with something like tenderness and pity.

Am I to be pitied? Not for the reasons this lady likely believed. Not because she wasn't a lily-white English damsel. Her life in Calcutta had been full and pleasant. No cause for pity there. Her father was wealthy, and she would never want for anything. Again, not a reason to be pitied.

That left only one thing. Lady Lewiston perhaps pitied her because of what she would face in the coming months. She was different. She didn't fit. Although in Calcutta she didn't quite fit either, there were enough others like her to make her not so obvious an outsider. And there, even the British respected her mother's high status.

Lady Lewiston herself showed Anjali up to her bedchamber on the second floor. So many stairs! And all on the one side of the house, although wide enough to give the impression of grandeur. There was another floor above that and, she guessed, attics too. Lady Lewiston opened a door partway down the corridor. "My apartment is a little farther down on the opposite side. I thought you would want to be near me."

Oddly, Anjali did. Lady Lewiston provided a connection —albeit tenuous—with her father. She stepped through the door of a very pretty bedchamber and looked up at the ceiling. No fans, of course. A fireplace, with a sizeable blaze crackling in the grate, warmed the room.

"This is Millicent. She will look after you," Lady Lewiston said as a maid in a simple green dress paused in her unpacking of Anjali's trunk and curtsied to her. "Unless this Kavi, as you said, is your abigail?"

"No, Lady Lewiston. I have no abigail here." She didn't explain. It would become clear soon enough.

"As you see, your things have indeed arrived. If you need anything at all, simply ask."

Anjali turned right around in a circle, peering into every corner. "Is Kavi not here?"

At that moment, a footman knocked on the open door. In one hand he held up a large circular birdcage swathed in black.

"Kavi!" Anjali ran forward, took the cage from the footman, and placed it on the table in the middle of the chamber. Then she whisked off the cover to reveal her myna bird. Her friend. The only living piece of India she was allowed to bring with her. The bird looked around and opened his beak a few times before ruffling his feathers in displeasure. "He shall remain with me. I will feed him and care for him."

At that moment, a sound of horses' hooves clopping on cobbles very nearby made Lady Lewiston walk over to the window to look out.

Anjali chuckled. "It's Kavi, My Lady. He imitates things he hears. He's a myna bird."

"Extraordinary," Lady Lewiston said with a suspicious glance at the bird.

She didn't immediately object, which Anjali took as a good sign. Instead she said, "Millicent, please continue unpacking Miss Ashcombe's things."

The maid had retreated to a corner when Anjali revealed the bird, and there she remained, hands gripped together in fear. "He-he's a demon!"

"Nonsense! He won't hurt you, I promise," Anjali said, and the maid stepped cautiously forward to resume her task— keeping as much distance between herself and the birdcage as possible.

The footman had remained just inside the door. "A remarkable bird, Miss," he said, bowing to her.

"I'll have a tray of supper sent up, Miss Ashcombe," Lady Lewiston said, flashing a slightly disapproving look at the young footman. "I understand your need to have a little time to yourself. We shall talk in the morning. Good night."

Her compassionate words almost broke down Anjali's resolve to be perfectly reserved. She forced herself to paste a shaky smile on her face and said, "Thank you, Lady Lewiston. You are most kind."

As soon as the door closed behind her, Anjali threw herself on the bed and burst into tears, joined by Kavi's very convincing accompanying sobs.

CHAPTER 4

What was she going to do with this child? Caroline had asked herself the question numerous times in the three days since Anjali's arrival. Unless specifically requested to attend some lesson in etiquette or dancing or some other ladylike accomplishment, Anjali spent most of her time in her bedchamber surrounded by books written in strange script that bore no similarity to English and caring for her odd bird. She was perfectly polite and amenable, but Caroline could tell her heart wasn't there. All her efforts to find out more about what interested her, asking her about her books and what she was writing, met with polite but distant civility. Anjali told her she was translating a volume of Urdu poetry into English. It was her way, she said, of keeping her knowledge of this language alive.

"Besides," Anjali said, "the poetry is beautiful, although very different from English verse."

Caroline didn't want to offend her or show a lack of sensitivity about what must be a wrenching change for her, but this was not a useful accomplishment, not if she hoped for a successful launch into society. Anjali's time would be much better spent learning how to play the pianoforte with more proficiency or perfecting her steps for the quadrille, but nothing Caroline said altered Anjali's practice.

At least the Indian languages weren't the only ones in which she was proficient. In addition to Urdu, Hindustani, and Bengali, Anjali spoke excellent French and read Latin fluently. Her breeding and education also showed in her grace and address. In fact, in a way, she was too reserved. No, that wasn't quite the right word. She was self-contained, as if she existed in some kind of vessel that kept her separate from everyone and everything around her.

Lady Lewiston cast a quick glance at the slender, straight figure seated next to her in the barouche. Her large, dark eyes rimmed by long curling black lashes so often seemed to be focused somewhere far distant. To all outward appearances she was looking out at the world, but Caroline had the sense that Anjali was, in fact, gazing inward. At that very moment, Anjali stared straight ahead rather than out of the windows on the short carriage ride from Park Street to Madame Pauline's in Curzon Street. Another nineteen-year-old come to London for the first time would be agog with wonder at all there was to see. Caroline could only imagine that London appeared a dreary, colorless place compared to Calcutta. Perhaps that was why Anjali didn't appear to derive joy from anything she saw.

The rout party, her first foray into society, was only a week away. Would it be possible to persuade her to emerge from behind her protective shield, at least for the evening?

They entered the modiste's shop a little before their appointed time. Madame Pauline was just finishing up with another young lady—the daughter of Lady Callender, Baron Callender's thin, ambitious wife, if she wasn't mistaken. A fair girl, pretty enough, but she would have a hard time standing out among the other come-outs that season. That was one thing Anjali didn't have to worry about, Caroline thought. As soon as she walked into a room, all eyes would be drawn to her. This could be turned to advantage—or it could be disastrous.

"Please, Lady Lewiston and Miss Ashcombe, Félicité will show you some of the silks that have just come from the mercer's while I help Adele finish with Miss Inchford," said Madame Pauline. The pert, clever modiste was always uniformly pleasant to her clientele, unlike some proprietors who measured out their respect depending on rank and importance. A solicitor's wife could come to purchase the one silk gown she would need for the entire season and Pauline and her staff would treat her as if she had come to order an entire wardrobe. That was only one of the reasons the shop was so popular. It couldn't fail to be, with the backing of the Countess of Bridlington, who, it was said, designed many of the gowns. Lady Bridlington managed to avoid the taint of trade by seldom if ever crossing the modiste's threshold, and never taking any credit for her work.

As Miss Inchford and her mother passed by them on their way out of the shop, the girl said in a voice just loud enough for Caroline and Anjali to hear, "Is that Lady Lewiston's maid? I can't imagine why she's brought her here."

Making sure the two ladies could hear her as well before they stepped outside, Caroline said to Pauline, "Miss Ashcombe requires an entire wardrobe for the season. You're to send the bills to her father, Mr. Thomas Ashcombe. He told me that we weren't to count the cost of anything." Caroline cast a sidelong glance at the departing mother and daughter—knowing that their estate was modest at best— and was pleased to see the blushes that indicated the pair had heard her comment.

Satisfying as their discomfiture was, Caroline had more

reason than that to say what she did. First, she knew her words would be repeated all through the *ton,* which would alert those who mattered to the presence of an unfamiliar heiress in Mayfair—an heiress with impeccable connections. And then, those same words ensured that the next time Anjali appeared among members of the *ton,* she wouldn't be mistaken for a maid—if it had been a mistake.

Madame Pauline drew their attention to the bolts of material and rolls of trimmings her assistant had chosen for them. "Do you have any preference as to colors? Or shall I simply show you what is in fashion this season?"

Lady Lewiston didn't hear Anjali's reply, because at that moment the tinkling of bells announced someone else entering from the street, and a moment later her daughter Belinda swept into the atelier. Like Miss Inchford, Lady Belinda was fair, but she was the sun to the other girl's distant star. Not just her beauty, but her radiant charm made her a leader of society without even trying. Of course, she was already married, so no competition for any of the marriageable debutantes that season. Thus the marauding mothers were pleased to invite her and her handsome, charming husband to all their parties. A connection with her would guarantee Anjali at least a foothold among her set.

"Please introduce me, Mama! This must be Miss Ashcombe, of course." Belinda walked up to Anjali with no ceremony and said, "You have just come from India, I hear, and your father is one of my mother's oldest friends. So of course, we must become great friends as well!"

"Lady Belinda," Anjali said and gave her a lovely curtsy. "I am honored to make your acquaintance."

Caroline had to confess, for all her odd ways the girl had a distinct air about her. She couldn't help wondering if the influence of her aristocratic mother had a hand in that quality. Thomas tended to be more informal. He was no high stickler. It was one of the things Caroline liked best about him.

"I'll let Madame fuss over you and measure you, but as soon as she's done we shall have a comfortable chat so I may get to know you better. What do you think of our London fashions?" She twirled around with her arms out, taking in all the sample gowns on forms and the shelves full of silks and muslins.

"I have hardly had time to look as yet," Anjali said as the assistant helped her step up on the platform so she could be measured. "Will you show me what you like?"

Caroline smiled at her daughter. Belinda brought out the best in most people, and she coaxed the first really genuine smile out of Anjali. Although Caroline had been confident that Belinda would treat Thomas's daughter amicably, that she seemed to have taken to her so quickly made her breathe a sigh of relief. Perhaps Belinda would be able to break through Anjali's reserve. She feared that unless someone did, the girl would never *take* that season. *I must not fail Thomas,* Caroline thought, although why such a possibility should disturb her so much she wasn't quite certain. It was more than a challenge. It mattered to her on a deep level she hardly dared admit to herself.

What would Shanta think?

Ashcombe couldn't shake the words out of his head as the estate agent led him through a handsome house in Blooms-bury a few days after he left Anjali with Lady Lewiston.

"Bloomsbury's not Mayfair, but very respectable. Professionals, you know. Businessmen and their families," he said with a rather oily smile.

Like me, Thomas thought. He'd forgotten how stratified

London was, how one had to be seen to be in one's place so that the *ton* could accurately assess one's worth. As if that was something measurable in any concrete sense. He was worth far more than this world would think he was. Not just in fortune, but in less tangible ways—ways that made sense in the very different world of India but that would likely remain obscure to the English. And that suited him. He had no desire to try to explain it to this grasping society.

That was Shanta's influence, this sense of intrinsic worth not dependent on the opinions of others. Not only her words but her thoughts had come through so clearly in her will. She'd left all her personal wealth in trust for Anjali and of course all her jewels. These were in a strongbox in the hotel, along with a copy of Shanta's will and Thomas's portfolio of personal documents. He'd had Nalin transcribe those documents from Hindustani into English so they could be understood by the officials he hoped to meet with. The only drawback to that was that it necessarily put Nalin in possession of facts that Thomas would have preferred to keep to himself.

With one more look around the newly papered walls and the painted wainscoting, Thomas said, "I think this will meet my needs."

"But Sir, you have not seen any other residences."

Thomas shrugged. "I look down these streets and squares and all the houses appear the same to me. Perhaps one is a little bigger than another, but it matters not."

By the end of the day, he had signed the lease for the house in Bedford Square and made arrangements for his few things to be moved there. It was sparsely furnished, but enough for his immediate needs. With Anjali settled in Park Street, he needn't hurry about that. Of course, he must hire servants. But he'd leave that for another day.

It was all such a dizzying contrast to the life he had left

four months ago: The bungalow with its open, airy rooms, colorful rugs and comfortable cushions. The heat, mitigated by the punkahs—the ceiling fans pulled by houseboys; the gardens overflowing with vibrant flowers; Indian servants padding quietly about; spices and dung scenting the air. It was his home.

He smiled to remember stepping off the ship in Calcutta as a young man full of angry determination to prove to everyone that he could succeed. And he did, with a vengeance, beginning in the textile trade and moving into more lucrative indigo. Through painstaking negotiations and constant work he bought goods from estates in Bengal and established routes to bring them safely to market—without the intervention of the Company—down tributaries and rivers to Calcutta, then onto ships bound for England and customers hungry for the various goods.

For ten years at the beginning of his time in India Thomas thought of little else aside from making his way. Then one day before the monsoons in 1797, he'd traveled to Murshidabad to negotiate a sticking point in one of his trade contracts with the zamindar there, but the translator he'd been provided with wasn't doing his job very well. By that time, Ashcombe knew enough Hindustani to pick up a few mistakes, although not enough to master the subtleties of trade contracts without help.

That was when the zamindar's young daughter emerged from deep in the house along with her maid. He could still see her in her saffron-colored sari shimmering with gold embroidery, a tranquil, self-possessed presence. She bowed and spoke to him in impeccable English. *I will translate for you now, Ashcombe sahib.*

He was struck dumb. He had never thought he would ever fall in love again after Caroline, but nothing could have prepared him for Shanta. She had something ineffable, something almost magical in her bearing. On that first day, the clerk she replaced bowed himself out as if retiring from before a deity.

Within a month, the contract he negotiated with the zamindar was for marriage rather than trade. The British in India looked askance at such marriages, but Thomas knew full well that Shanta was conferring a great honor on him, not the other way around. Among the Brahmin caste in India, women did not relinquish their status and become mere adjuncts of their husband's family, chattel to add to someone else's prestige. Shanta brought her noble quality with her, remaining his social superior—at least in the eyes of the Indians. When she gave him the gift of a daughter, he thought his life had reached the pinnacle of happiness.

And then, when fever took her from them five years ago, he had to muster all his strength not to succumb to deep despair. Only knowing that Anjali needed him kept him going.

Caroline's marriage to the marquess was clearly not a love match—how could it be, when her family forced her into it—but he hoped she found joy in other ways. He could not ask her about it, though. He had no right.

He also had no right to expect her help with his daughter, and yet he had done so. Establishing Anjali in society was only part of his reason for renewing his acquaintance with Caroline. She would give him access to a world he needed to become part of again if he wanted to accomplish what he'd come to London for. It had been so long since the events of their youth that he thought he would be able to face her with complacence. The feelings their meeting awakened in him took him by surprise. They were part resentment, part yearning, part hope. Hope for what?

Ashcombe sighed as the barouche took him back to the Clarendon. Whatever had been between him and Caroline almost thirty years ago must surely have died under the weight of time and life. And to be honest with himself, bringing Anjali to Caroline had been little more than a convenient excuse to make the necessary change in his domicile and business without raising suspicion that he had any other motive. Was he using her? Yes. But it was for a good cause. At least, he hoped so. Once it was all over and Anjali had had her season, perhaps he would purchase a small estate somewhere in the countryside and retire there to live quietly with his half-Indian daughter.

Of course, the other reason for bringing Anjali to London was to distance her from Nalin, his clerk. Nalin was like a son to him and had known Anjali since she was ten. He'd seen the signs of infatuation on Anjali's part as she blossomed into womanhood. As for Nalin—how could he help falling in love with such a pearl? Ashcombe did not blame him. The young man made a clean breast of it to him, a point of honor in someone of his stature. There was no doubt that he was a promising young man, but not for Anjali.

Nalin was well aware that Anjali must leave India with her father, and he must remain behind, at least for now. Besides that, Shanta would never have allowed the match.

Thomas chuckled drily to himself. He wasn't blind to the fact that in a sense he'd done to Anjali what Gareth Holcombe, Earl of Havering, and his own parents had done to him all those years ago. Perhaps they had been right. He couldn't imagine Caroline subsisting on his younger son's portion, or journeying to be by his side in India while he made his fortune.

Whatever the truth of it, this was their life now. He and Anjali were here, and Shanta was dead. He must do his best for Anjali. The difficulty, as Thomas saw it, was that finding her a husband who would see her as more than a way to prop up an encumbered estate was likely to be a challenge. Anjali was extraordinarily pretty, educated, and wealthy, to be sure. But she was more than that. He'd made a vow to himself before they left Calcutta that whatever else he had to do, whatever compromises he would be forced to make, he would not promise his daughter to anyone who couldn't see her true value. Anjali's husband would have to appreciate the rare jewel she was, outside and in, from her soulful eyes to her remarkable intellect, just as he had discerned in Shanta from the moment he met her.

He well knew how difficult a promise that would be to keep.

CHAPTER 5

The ordeal at the modiste's over, Anjali let her eyes close briefly in the carriage on the way back to Park Street. It wasn't that she didn't like beautiful clothes, both British and Indian. After all, their fortunes came from them. Her father's business fed the voracious appetite for elegant attire by means of the fine muslins, cambrics, and dyes he purchased from the Bengal estates and sent to market in Europe and England. It was simply what the clothes at Madame Pauline's represented that disturbed her. In a week she would be exposed to the *ton* at a rout party. Held up for inspection by people she neither knew nor respected. None of the ladies would have had the thorough education she had enjoyed. What would they talk about? To make matters worse, she knew well that the English *ton* disdained those engaged in trade, no matter how successful or cultured they happened to be.

She'd gone to a rout party in Calcutta and found it insufferable—the women all competing to be the most magnificently dressed, the men boasting of wealth and how they managed to trick the zamindars and subjugate the natives, everyone trying to pretend they weren't perspiring uncomfortably. Even the Company executives held themselves above people like her father. Weren't they the same? Or worse? They not only engaged in trade, but sent their military into regions to subdue the native communities so that they could control their actions, levy taxes, and create favorable trade agreements to the detriment of the Indians.

"Your gowns should be ready just in time for our first social events," Lady Lewiston said, dragging Anjali's thoughts back to the moment. "I'm hoping to procure vouchers for Almack's, although likely not right away. Lady Jersey will be at Lady Allston's rout party on Thursday, and I'll present you to her. I'm certain she'll be delighted with you and after a time will send me the vouchers." Lady Lewiston smiled and patted her hand reassuringly. Anjali perceived the uncertainty beneath Lady Lewiston's assertion. But she didn't share in the belief that such things were important. How could they be?

At that very moment, Anjali glanced out the window and a figure caught her eye. She sat up straight and leaned forward, tempted to lower the glass. "Lady Lewiston, may we stop the carriage please?"

"Whatever for?"

What could she say? That she saw a gentleman she'd met when she was out early in the morning unbeknownst to her father? That she was certain it was he, walking a silly, badly behaved spaniel on the flagway with his hat pulled low to cover as much of his hair as possible? He was tall enough that it was impossible for him to move through the crowded streets unnoticed, and many of those who walked past turned their heads to stare after him. He paid them no heed. Anjali smiled. "I thought I saw someone I knew. But I must have been mistaken." There was something about him. He seemed a little out of place, and the thought that there could be someone else in London who felt as out of place as she was comforted her—even if they never encountered one another again.

Lady Lewiston's next words only strengthened that feeling. "I wouldn't think you'd know anyone in London! You've been here less than a week and hardly stirred out of doors."

Anjali believed Lady Lewiston didn't mean to be critical. It must be hard for her to know what to do with someone as odd as she was. "Perhaps it was someone who bore a resemblance to an acquaintance in Calcutta." But she knew it wasn't. What she didn't know was why it should matter to her at all. Sir Julian was hardly the kind of gentleman she was drawn to. None of the British men in Calcutta had sparked the slightest interest in her heart or mind. To a person they were arrogant and unattractive. She still couldn't think what exactly it was about Sir Julian that lodged his image somewhere near her heart. It couldn't be his respectful treatment of her alone. Perhaps it was his acceptance of Kavi. What use was it to speculate? She would likely not see him again. He didn't seem the type to frequent balls or to enjoy a rout party. After all, he said he had a profession. Besides which, he clearly dreaded revealing his remarkable head of hair.

If only, Anjali thought, he would be at the coming party. They could be outsiders together. Their shared interaction, mediated by his dog and her bird, gave him at least a gloss of familiarity. She wouldn't then feel quite so entirely alone.

By that time they had reached the dower house, and Anjali accepted the footman's steadying hand as she climbed out. All she wanted to do was go to her room and write a letter to Nalin.

That idea was wrenched from her mind as soon as Fairing opened the door. A scene of total chaos greeted them. Inside the hall and up and down the grand staircase maids ran about, some screeching, others calling out that everyone should be calm. Stranger still, a footman ran from the back of the house carrying a net on a long pole.

"What is the meaning of this!" Lady Lewiston said, her eyes flashing.

Fairing cleared his throat. "It appears, My Lady, that Miss Ashcombe's bird has got loose and is evading capture."

Anjali guessed what had happened as soon as she walked through the door and surprised everyone by saying in a commanding voice, "Stay where you are! Stop yelling!"

Lady Lewiston looked at her with a shocked crease in her brow.

Anjali's heart plummeted. She was behaving rudely. This was not her house. "I beg your pardon, Lady Lewiston, but Kavi will not allow himself to be captured and is likely hiding somewhere terrified. The noise must stop!" She turned beseeching eyes to her hostess, whose brow cleared—although the kindness Anjali was accustomed to seeing in her expression had yet to reappear.

Lady Lewiston lifted her chin and addressed her now cowering servants. "Do as Miss Ashcombe says. Please return to your duties."

The house quieted but for some murmurs of petulance and frightened sniffs.

"Thank you, My Lady," Anjali said and then turned to Fairing. "Where did you last see Kavi?"

"I believe, Miss Ashcombe, that the bird flew into the dining room on this floor."

Without waiting, Anjali ran to the open dining room door, stood quite still, and said, "Ka-vi!" in a singsong voice. At first nothing happened. Then a moment later another voice echoed the call, and a flutter of brown wings brought the myna to Anjali's shoulder. She put up her hand to coax him onto her finger so she could grasp his talons and prevent him flying off again in fright. "If you will permit me, Lady Lewiston, I shall return Kavi to his cage."

Lady Lewiston said nothing, but nodded, lips compressed in a thin line.

What have I done? Anjali thought. She had assured Lady Lewiston that the bird would remain in her room, that he would not disturb anyone in the house. One of the footmen, young Andrew, was actually fascinated and had timidly asked if he could see Kavi, so not all the servants were afraid. Where was Andrew, she wondered? She'd had hopes of perhaps introducing him to Kavi so that he could share some of the care. Kavi liked company and needed to be entertained. And besides, she thought, he was probably feeling as out of place as she was—if a bird could have such a sentiment.

None of that mattered at the moment, however. What if Lady Lewiston decided it was too much to have Kavi in the house and wanted to send him away? He would fret and pine without her and likely die. No, if Kavi went, she would have to go as well. How would she explain that to her father? Although he tried not to put pressure on her, she was well aware that her success in London society was important to him, and without Lady Lewiston's sponsorship would be very difficult to achieve.

When Anjali approached her bedchamber, the mystery of Kavi's escape became clear. The door stood wide open, and she could see in to Kavi's cage on the center table. The wire that held the door of the cage closed was bent, making it no doubt an easy matter for the bird to nudge it open and fly free. She took Kavi to the cage and placed him on the swinging perch inside, then examined the latch. "You canny fellow!" she said, in a combination of vexation and amusement. "What made you decide to break out of your elegant prison?" She looked around the room until her eye spied what must have seemed temptation beyond endurance to Kavi. The plate with a small apple on it brought in by the parlor maid every morning with her cocoa was now empty of any such treat. The maid left it there when she took away the cocoa, perhaps believing Anjali would be tempted to eat the fruit later. She never did.

Anjali sighed. "What shall I do with you?" She took a bit of ribbon from the dressing table and wound it around the wires of the cage door, knotting it as securely as she could. "No doubt you'll have that open in a trice. But you mustn't, you know!"

"Bad bird!" Kavi screeched.

He must have got that from a maid, Anjali thought, because she never addressed him so. She could only imagine that Millicent had entered earlier to put her night clothes in order and seen the bird outside of his cage. That would be enough to send the girl into hysterics, no matter how Anjali tried to reassure her that Kavi would not harm her. Her carrying on no doubt startled and alarmed Kavi. Millicent likely fled and didn't bother to close the door behind her. Kavi would, of course, go off in search of his mistress—if she could be called that.

Kavi settled and she covered his cage. "You should sleep after your exciting adventure. I must go and have a lesson with the piano tutor." She'd learned the rudiments of that instrument in Calcutta, but pianofortes were so often in an unplayable state because of the weather—the humidity and heat cracking sound boards and making the strings swell up and lose their tuning overnight—that she dreaded having to sit down to it. Lady Lewiston's instrument was in much better repair as well as in tune, so at least it wasn't painful to her ears. She'd been considering begging off the lesson, but after Kavi's disruption, she decided that would be unwise.

She determined that she would make an effort the next

day to make it up to Lady Lewiston by trying harder to enter into the spirit of the London season. She had arranged to meet Lady Belinda in Hyde Park to promenade, something she really had no desire to do. However, Lady Belinda was kind and thoughtful. There was something candid and fresh about her. Anjali had the sense that despite being the daughter of a marquess and therefore very lofty in rank, she would answer her questions honestly. Questions such as how did Lady Lewiston know her father? What had been their relationship? Were they more than friends? Lady Belinda might not know, however. Anjali's father left England long before she was born. But perhaps she'd heard something.

And perhaps the next day would bring that mild spring weather she'd been assured was on its way. It couldn't come soon enough for Anjali.

CHAPTER 6

The case Julian would appear for in King's Bench later that day seemed simple on the face of it, so the solicitor, Bicknell, had told him.

"I'm giving it to you because you know that Davenant would merely glance at it and assume the gent bringing the suit was justified, that the other fellow owed him the money. But there's more to this, I guarantee, and you're the man to discover it."

He'd caught Julian on his way out at the end of a day when he was too tired to say anything other than, "All right." Today he would have to discover exactly what it was he had agreed to.

"You got yer 'ands full on this one, Mr. Meredith—or should I say Sir Julian?" Griggs gave a sly grin and a wink. The clerk performed an indispensable role in chambers, everyone's schedules planned to the minute and materials funneled to the right barrister in a timely way. This gave him some latitude to exercise a degree of impudent familiarity from time to time, and Julian merely smiled.

"That's as may be," Julian said, stretching out his hand for the brief.

"Oh no, gov. It's all on yer desk." He jerked his head toward the door that led into Julian's chambers and then scurried away.

As soon as he entered this inner sanctum, Julian groaned. Occupying the center of his desk was a wad of documents several inches thick tied together with twine. No doubt Davenant had been approached first and declined this civil case, and Bicknell had merely flattered Julian to get him to agree to it. With a sigh, he removed his coat, hung it on the peg, rolled up his shirtsleeves, and untied the bundle. Within minutes he'd entered that state of keen concentration that his opponents in the courtroom were learning to fear, the concentration that absorbed every minute detail of a case and stored it away to use at the moment of greatest impact.

Though it took him the better part of three hours, Julian found what he was looking for and began feverishly to write notes. Twice while he was doing it, Griggs poked his head in to hurry him along. The second time he said, "Your hack's below," and surveyed the mess of scattered documents. "You'll likely lose this one, so I hear, so takin' all this trouble won't pay no toll."

Griggs had control of the practice finances as well as everything else, and did his best to squeeze optimal results from all the junior barristers. More than once, Atticus Chiselhurst, senior barrister and head of chambers, had to leap to Julian's defense when he took longer than Griggs thought necessary to prepare his notes and opinions. This was one case, Julian thought with a glow of satisfaction, that would upend Griggs's certainty. Julian had found the flaw buried in the avalanche of papers.

"Just finishing," Julian said with a smile, collected up all the documents, and stood. Griggs nodded and left Julian to get his robes from the press and his carefully preserved wig in its box out of the cupboard. Papers and court garments in hand, he raced out in the direction of the Strand to jump into the waiting hackney to Westminster.

The afternoon traffic was heavy and it took longer than it should to get to King's Bench. Julian rushed into the robing room minutes before the appointed time. He asked the porter, "Who's sitting?"

"Lord Ellenborough today, Mr. Meredith."

That's good, Julian thought. Ellenborough appreciated a hidden truth coming to light through diligence.

The porter watched Julian take his robe out of the bag and shake it out and gave a disdainful tsk. Yes, Julian thought, it had been a while since he'd had it brushed. But it wasn't actually dirty.

The wig was another matter. Shooing the porter away, Julian approached the box and reverently lifted its lid, reaching in to release the powdered, carefully curled wig from its form. Other junior barristers chafed at being forced to adopt this outmoded dress. Not Julian. In point of fact, the wig had been one of the primary reasons he decided to become a barrister. He settled it gingerly on his head, faced the small mirror, and ensured that every last strand of his red hair was concealed. Then he drew himself up, smiled at the porter, collected his papers and strode through to the courtroom.

meet, by the pond where the children sailed their boats. It was the only place she was certain she could find.

"Miss Ashcombe! Isn't the day lovely? It's finally starting to feel like spring. See, the crocuses are already blossoming."

She pointed to a small patch of little flowers, some yellow, some purple, some white.

Anjali struggled with the temptation to compare this pathetic little showing of color to the feast of vibrant hues that made gardens in India intoxicating and lovely. She managed a smile and said, "Yes, indeed."

At first, it was difficult to have much of a conversation with Lady Belinda as they wandered agonizingly slowly along the footpaths in the park. She seemed to have a vast acquaintance, most of whom happened to be either walking or riding in the park that afternoon. Belinda made a point of presenting Anjali to all her friends, but every single one of them peered at her in varying degrees of curiosity or suspicion. Anjali tried to ignore her growing discomfort and simply smile and nod, stand tall, and say little. The only one whose name Anjali remembered was Lady Henrietta Vaughn. She had given her a look of dismissive condescention when they were introduced, and said, "How quaint! You're from India. Beastly hot there, so I hear," as if that was the only feature of the entire subcontinent worth commenting upon. Anjali felt a surge of indignation and struggled not to snap at her, remembering her father telling her that ignorance is not the same as stupidity. The one can be overcome with education. The other—well, that was inborn. She wondered which of those qualities Lady Henrietta had revealed to her.

After she strolled off with her little group of friends, all trailed by their maids, Lady Belinda said, "Don't mind her. It's her third season. She's received several eligible offers, but she's an heiress, and her father has turned them all away accusing them of being basket scramblers."

"What?" Anjali said. It was a term she'd never heard.

Belinda laughed. "It's a rather unkind way of referring to fortune hunters."

When at last they'd reached a part of the park less populated by *ton*ish strollers, Anjali decided it was time to ask Lady Belinda some of the questions that had been bothering her. "Lady Belinda, might I ask you some things about London? We came here so quickly and my father's London is from thirty years ago. I don't know what's different now, if anything."

"First of all, Miss Ashcombe," Belinda said, squeezing the arm that was threaded through hers, "Please just call me Belinda. That's what my friends call me. The *lady* part is for servants and casual acquaintances, and even then I find it rather pretentious."

Only someone who had grown up in a position of unchallenged superiority could say such a thing, Anjali thought. But she said, "I will do so if you will call me Anjali."

"With pleasure! It's such a lovely name. Does it mean anything? My name means *lovely,* apparently." She blushed.

"An apt description. Anjali is an offering, a reverence. In India we often greet each other with the *Anjali mudra.*" She demonstrated by putting her palms together and bowing her head over them.

"That is beautiful," Belinda said. "Now, ask me whatever you wish."

Where to start? How to introduce the principal subject on her mind? She certainly didn't want to talk about the weather, which seemed to be the preferred topic of conversation among these people. She decided the direct approach would be best. "I'd like to know something about the post."

Belinda's bemused expression told Anjali that what she asked was not at all expected. "The penny post? Have you acquaintances you would like to write to?"

"Not that, no. I should like to send a message to a friend I left behind in India, only I have no idea how to go about doing so."

They walked along in silence for a few moments before

Belinda said, "I know nothing about your life in Calcutta. I should like to know more. You had friends there, of course, and I gather they have remained behind."

Friends. Remained behind. How to convey the deep sense of loss she experienced? She couldn't. Not at that moment, at least. "Yes, a few."

"Are they English friends? Or Indian? Your mother was a native, so my mama told me—I hope you don't mind me being so forthright." Belinda's cheeks reddened slightly.

Anjali smiled at her. Of course she must feel awkward too. No doubt Belinda had never met anyone quite like her before. Anjali sent a silent thanks to Lady Lewiston for raising her daughter to be polite and kind. "I don't mind at all. Anyone need only look at me to understand that I am not fully English. My mother was the daughter of a very powerful Indian man, a zamindar of the highest caste. She brought great honor to my father's family."

"Are you a princess?" Belinda asked, eyes growing round.

"No, not exactly. I can't explain it in English terms. It's different there. But my mother's family owned land and plantations nearly the size of the whole of Scotland. Please don't tell anyone though! I'm not saying this to boast, only to make you understand. If you are truly to be my friend, you must do so."

Belinda gave a short laugh. "And here I was feeling apologetic about the ten-thousand acres my brother owns!"

"Shall we agree not to speak of it again?" Anjali said, stopping and turning Belinda toward her.

"Of course. But you haven't really asked me any actual questions yet."

Anjali thought carefully about how to put her inquiry to Belinda in a way that would not raise any suspicions. "My question has to do specifically with the post to Calcutta. I have a particular friend who would wish to know that I have arrived here in safety."

"A particular friend?" Belinda turned eyes of dawning understanding to Anjali. "And you cannot ask your father, or my mother, how you may convey this message to—him, I presume?"

It was Anjali's turn to blush. "Yes. Please do not say anything. I know nothing will ever come of it, but you see, we were—are—very dear to each other." She decided not to explain the more complicated reasons she felt compelled to write to Nalin. Reasons that became less clear to her with every passing day, but which nonetheless remained.

Belinda's eyes shone. "But why? Not why are you dear to each other, but why must nothing come of it? Is he handsome? Wealthy? Or perhaps of more humble origins. A soldier!"

Anjali could see that she had inadvertently ignited Belinda's romantic imagination. She must try to explain that it was all so much more involved than anyone in this country would ever understand. "Please believe me when I say I have reconciled myself to the fact that Nalin and I could never be more than just friends."

"Nalin—that's his name. It's musical. Just like Anjali."

How was she to rein in Belinda's fantasy? "He is a respectable gentleman from a good family. But he is Indian, and not of the same caste."

"People who belong to different classes wed here all the time! Why, just last month—"

"It's not the same!" Anjali's voice was harsher than she intended, and she regretted causing the flash of hurt that showed in Belinda's eyes. "I'm sorry, truly. I cannot explain millennia of traditions and practices to you in a few minutes, so you must simply believe me that even if I had remained in

Calcutta, such a marriage would never have been sanctioned."

Belinda's mouth quirked into a smile. "Here, there are ways to achieve marriages that are, as you say, unsanctioned. They mostly involve traveling north and crossing the border into Scotland."

This naive young lady—a little older than Anjali was in years, but, having only her experience of life in England on which to base her judgements, so much younger in other ways—would never believe that to do such a thing in India would risk the severest retribution by her grandfather's family. "No doubt," Anjali said. "But you must trust me that it is not so in India. All I wish to do is send a letter to Nalin. We parted without a proper goodbye."

"Of course," Belinda said, her eyes now moistening with sympathetic tears. "But you won't be able to send it through the regular post without the knowledge of my mother. The expense would call attention to it, for one thing. And then, if you simply put it with the outgoing post, the servants would see it too."

"I see," Anjali said. Not only that, she thought, but she would fear that her mail might be intercepted and read. Although her father did not confide in her, she knew enough from talking to Nalin to guess that their furtive departure must have raised some suspicions in the East India Company's officers—who were desperately trying to control all trade in India, something her father opposed. Nalin had not explained it all, but enough for her to realize that a desire for her to be presented to the *ton* was not the only—or even the biggest—reason for their move.

"Perhaps I can ask Hector—my husband, Mr. Gainesworth—if he knows how it might be accomplished."

"No!" Again, Anjali regretted her sudden vehemence. "I

mean, I'd rather keep this between ourselves for now. Is that all right?"

Belinda showed signs of being a bit confused and put out, but she continued to smile.

"You must think me so impertinent," Anjali said. "I humbly beg your forgiveness. I haven't yet learned all the English proprieties. Shall we talk of something else? Tell me what I can expect at my first rout party."

It was information she needed anyway, and Anjali could tell that Belinda was much happier discussing such things. Anjali had done her best to deduce what Lady Lewiston was anxious about on her behalf, and she thought that looking at it through Belinda's eyes might make it a bit clearer. She did not want to disappoint her chaperone, even if she had no intention of succumbing to the imperative to marry well. It seemed that the important thing was not to call undue attention to herself through her words and actions. She would be attracting enough unwelcome attention by virtue of her physical appearance. Lady Lewiston and the modiste had called her beautiful. Was that not enough? Must she be pretty in a particular way?

She could do nothing to change her birth. And she wouldn't want to. But her father had impressed upon her the importance of making a life in this cold, dreary country. More than her happiness was at stake, as Anjali knew. So, much as she dreaded it, she would face the *ton* for her father's sake. Perhaps there would be more people like Belinda than she expected, and fewer like Lady Henrietta. And perhaps, a little voice said inside her, there would be more gentlemen like Sir Julian. The heat that climbed into her face surprised her, and she hoped Belinda did not notice it

Just as they were about to start back to Park Street, Anjali heard her name called out. Not loudly, not as though someone were hailing her, but as if it was simply an observation unwittingly uttered aloud. She looked toward the source of the interruption and recognized the red hair of the very man whose image had been in her mind only a moment before. His dog clearly recognized her too, or at least associated her with some memory.

"Who is that extraordinary looking man?" Lady Belinda murmured into Anjali's ear without altering her polite smile.

"That is Sir Julian Meredith," she said, struggling to sound uninterested. "We met a few days ago, very briefly." She didn't explain more, for Sir Julian stood immobile, clutching the leash of his straining—but fortunately not very powerful—spaniel. They walked toward him, and his eyes never strayed from hers.

JULIAN EMERGED VICTORIOUS FROM THE TRIAL. THE MERCHANT who would have been ruined if he had been forced to pay the sum he claimed never to have agreed to grasped Julian's hand and pumped it vigorously up and down, calling him a fine chap, a regular right 'un, a rare cove.

The day was fine, and Julian was in a good mood after his small triumph. He directed the hackney to take him back to his lodgings—despite what he'd said to Addison earlier—so he could leave his robes and wig and then go for a walk in Hyde Park. Some of the glow remained with him for hours whenever he argued a persuasive suit, and in a burst of self-confidence he felt equal to facing the stares of the *ton*. He must show himself this season, now that the mourning period for his parents was at an end, and he might as well start with an innocuous stroll rather than turning up out of the blue at a fashionable rout party.

"Come Bramble! Another walk!" he'd said, immediately sending the spaniel into a fever of ecstasy. He supposed he ought to have left the dog at home, but somehow he didn't feel quite brave enough to participate in the hour of the strut entirely alone.

It had been a long time since he'd dared to mix with the promenading fashionables in the park. Thank heavens the season had yet to truly begin, he thought, regretting his decision to go out almost as soon as he passed through the gate into the park. He could not let Bramble run free in that place and at that time, and the dog strained on his leash, causing several ladies to cast disapproving glances in his direction.

The usual discomfort began to creep back into his body. He hoped he would soon reach a point within the park where it would be reasonable for him to turn around and return home, but the sight of all the people brought out Bramble's sociable side, and the dog kept pulling him onward. When Bramble suddenly tried to surge forward in a very decided direction, Julian looked up to see what had attracted him so strongly, and his face flamed.

It was she. The lady from Green Park, though now without her bird, and not so buried in clothing. How he recognized her when he'd seen only bits of her in her covered up state he couldn't say. Only he was not mistaken.

And he was transfixed. She was utterly magnificent. Something about her made him think of sunshine and endless skies. She was not a typical English lady—especially when compared with the pretty blond she stood talking to. A pretty blond who was just like every other debutante in town.

Miss Ashcombe.

It seemed that he hadn't merely thought her name, because she turned toward him, a puzzled expression in her remarkable eyes transforming to one of dawning recognition.

Before he knew it, she and the other lady were walking

toward him. "Sir Julian!" she said, a smile illuminating her face and making it even more radiant. "And Bramble, if I remember correctly."

He regained control of himself quickly enough to touch the brim of his hat and bow to them. Miss Ashcombe introduced him to her friend, Lady Belinda Gainesworth.

"You have not brought your bird," Julian said, immediately kicking himself for such a clumsy beginning to a conversation.

Lady Belinda turned quizzical eyes to Miss Ashcombe.

"I'm afraid my myna bird took exception to Sir Julian's hat the other morning in the Green Park," she said by way of explanation.

"Your what?" Lady Belinda asked.

Julian felt more and more foolish standing there and his neck prickled as if all eyes were staring at their little conversational group. As Miss Ashcombe was explaining what a myna bird was to Lady Belinda he interrupted rather clumsily and said, "I'm afraid I cannot stay. I only came out to give Bramble a walk, and I'm already late."

He bowed to them again, and when he straightened, met Miss Ashcombe's eyes, expecting to see pique or disapproval in them. Instead, they were soft and deep, full of compassion. *Oh Lord!* he thought. I'll likely never see her again, and perhaps that's just as well.

His face and neck heated uncomfortably as he turned away, pulling Bramble to him.

CHAPTER 7

homas pulled his pocket watch out and looked at the time. He was early. Her note had said half-past ten, and it was only a little after the hour. He remembered very clearly the last time they met in Kensington Gardens. The memory was certainly bittersweet. Had she chosen this spot because she remembered as well? Or had she forgotten what to him was still a vivid, painful memory?

He chuckled. He was ascribing sentiments to Lady Lewiston she likely didn't have. Why would she have given him a thought once they parted all those years ago?

"Thomas! Mr. Ashcombe!"

Caroline came toward him arrayed in a slim walking dress of violet Jaconet muslin with a twilled silk spencer jacket. A modest chip hat and a lace parasol completed her ensemble. As she drew closer his expert eye discerned the quality of the materials. The fine cloth came from India. Was it one of his? He smiled to think it. Her exquisite taste was still very much in evidence. "Good morning, My Lady," he said, offering her his best courtly bow.

She looked to left and right as she approached. "There is

no one nearby to hear us. I wish you would not be quite so formal with me here. Seeing you like this takes me back to a time when …" Her voice trailed off and she looked down. "Well, when we did not feel the need to put such distance between us."

Thomas put his arm out for her to take and they began to walk together. The feel of her hand tucked in a place that seemed made for the purpose made him catch his breath. He swallowed and said, "I have found a house. In Bedford Square."

"Bloomsbury?" She was clearly shocked.

He smiled down at her. "You surely didn't expect me to be your neighbor in Mayfair. A little above my touch, I'm afraid." She needn't know that he stayed away from the most fashionable district by choice rather than necessity. And perhaps it was right to give Anjali a little distance from him as well.

"I didn't mean—I don't know what I meant. Only I understood that your business has been successful. That you made quite a go of it. Muslin! And some kind of dye?"

She was babbling. Could she be nervous? "It's no matter. The house is adequate to my needs. Do you think it will make any difference to those who might take an interest in Anjali?"

Caroline pursed her lips and cast her eyes upward, as if she might find the answer in the canopy of pale green budding twigs above them. "I think not. They won't expect you to be entirely conformable. You are a prosperous merchant who happens to be the younger son of a baron. An odd enough combination to excuse any eccentricities."

Yes, it was an odd combination. Although younger sons were expected to pursue a profession, trade was not among those considered genteel enough. "I hope you know I'm very grateful to you for taking Anjali under your wing. It has been hard to know how to advise her since her mother died. There's only so much a father can do for a girl." He didn't know quite why Caroline had requested this meeting, but he assumed naturally enough that they must discuss what was to be done with Anjali now that she had become a little better acquainted with her.

Fortunately, Caroline took the lead in the conversation. "Your daughter is extraordinary. I would expect nothing less. She is lovely and has good manners. I can see why you think she could have a brilliant future."

"But?" Thomas said. "I sense you have reservations."

She pulled him to a halt and expelled a sigh. "She is a strong young woman, and extremely smart. Those are not qualities which are highly prized in the *ton*, I'm sure you are aware."

He had feared as much. The *ton* he remembered disdained many of the attributes he prized in his daughter and her late mother. Those qualities were submerged beneath propriety in English ladies. Yet he had confidence that Anjali would perform her role well, if she could be persuaded that it was in both of their interests. "Anjali is high spirited, but she also understands what is required."

"Required by you? Or does she have any desire of her own for a successful come-out?"

Thomas knew too well that Anjali would as soon not brave the *ton*. But he needed her to follow through with the plan for his own reasons. "She is unsettled as yet. Our departure was a bit sudden, and she loves India." How to explain it to Caroline in a way that would not make Anjali sound obstinate? And what if his spirited daughter had already said or done something to alienate Caroline? "She wants this in her heart, I feel certain. She knows it is her only practical option. She has not given you cause to regret your offer to help her?"

Caroline drew him along the path again. "No, not at all.

As I said, she is a taking young lady. Yet not in the usual way of come-outs. Because of this I cannot guarantee that I will be able to achieve what you wish for her."

She stopped speaking, but Thomas had a distinct feeling that she had more to say to him about Anjali, and remained silent.

"Tell me, Thomas, why did you uproot yourself and Anjali from a place where it's clear that you both prospered?"

He'd rehearsed different answers to this inevitable question and gave the first one that came to mind. "I wanted Anjali to know England, to have as much of a connection to this side of her heritage as she has always had to her mother's."

Caroline looked up at him with that skeptical tilt of her chin he remembered so well, and it gave him a pang of regret. "Forgive me, but that does not seem reason enough. You must have had to work hard to persuade her to agree to this. I know as your daughter she is in your power and must do as you say, but I also know you. You would not force your will on her for such a paltry reason."

"What can I—I fear there is much I cannot explain to you, at least not yet. All I can say is that it was time. For one thing, the Company is consolidating its control not only of Bengal, but westward into Pune. This makes everything more difficult for independent traders like myself." Thomas hoped that would be enough to satisfy Caroline's probing mind.

"And for another?"

He sighed. "The India I loved, and that Anjali considers home, will soon be no more."

She cocked her head to the side and peered into his eyes. "I want to know about that India, the one you loved. But I can see that this is not the time for you to tell me about it. More important is what is to be done for Anjali."

Thomas listened as Caroline told him of the myna bird's

disruption the day before, citing it as an example of things that must change about Anjali's life. Nonetheless, they both laughed about it.

"She won't be parted from that bird," he said. "I know he's just a clever mimic, but she swears he understands her, and if it comforts her to think that, I haven't the heart to separate them."

Caroline nodded. "She assures me that she will take steps to ensure the bird does not escape from her room again. I certainly hope he doesn't. It's hard enough to keep good servants!"

They shared a congenial chuckle and after that, Caroline explained her plan for launching his daughter into the *ton.* Thomas only half listened to the details, enjoying the sound of Caroline's voice. All he knew was that what Caroline hoped for would not be easy, despite the fact that his lineage was impeccable enough for the most fastidious stickler. The true irony was that, although Shanta's heritage was much more noble than his, Anjali would be looked upon askance by many because of it.

"It is of the greatest importance that Anjali do all she can to conform to the proprieties, to make herself appear the same as any other come-out, if she is to have a hope of making a suitable match."

They had reached the farthest point of their promenade and turned to go back. Thomas could hardly imagine Anjali conforming to anything, if by conforming Caroline meant hiding that Indian side of herself. Anjali had a fierce, uncompromising pride in her homeland and Indian family. "If she does not have a success this season, I am certain it will be no fault of yours," he said. Had he asked too much of her?

"I think, Thomas, it would be helpful if you would speak to her. It is important that she believe you want this for her."

"Of course she must know that!" he said.

"Does she? Well, next week is the rout party where she will have her first foray into society. I assume you will attend as well. I have a card for you."

Thomas supposed he must. Much as he welcomed the opportunity to spend time in Caroline's company, he wasn't ready for the possibility that he would see many people who knew him from before and be forced to make polite conversation. Despite his need for introductions to influential men so he could act expeditiously, he quailed at the thought. Would he ever be ready? "Of course, My Lady," he said with a mock-serious bow. "At what hour shall I call for you and Anjali at Park Street?"

njali had never seen that expression on her father's face before. He'd come to fetch them for the rout party, and when she walked down the stairs in her evening gown of pearl satin with an amber gauze overdress, her hair in a top knot with artful curls dangling down by her ears, his eyes had tears, but he wasn't sad. He said, "I see your mother in you, my dear," and kissed her cheek.

"In a gown like this?" Anjali said in an effort to lighten the tone. "My mother would never have worn such a thing."

"Perhaps not. But she would have been proud to see you do so. She always knew this was your future."

Lady Lewiston came down the stairs a moment later in her sable-trimmed evening cloak. Once again, Anjali could not decipher the expression in her eyes when she looked at her father. Belinda hadn't been able to tell her anything about the relationship between them beyond that they had been friends in their youth. Yet from what she had seen the few times they were together, Anjali was starting to believe something more connected them. She wished she could ask her father, but they had not had a moment alone together since the day she moved into the house in Park Street.

The drive to Berkeley Square was not long, but there was some delay entering the house due to the press of carriages discharging passengers. Once they were finally inside, Anjali and Lady Lewiston left their cloaks in the ladies' retiring room before rejoining her father to make the majestic climb up the grand stairs to greet their hostess.

"If you intend to dance this evening," Lady Lewiston murmured in Anjali's ear, "remember that you must stand up with any gentleman who asks you, unless you choose instead to sit out and chat. This isn't a ball, but Lady Allston's parties are always lively. She hires an excellent ensemble and everyone comes and the young people always dance."

If she meant her words to be reassuring, they failed to achieve their object. Although Anjali was an accomplished dancer—she'd learned all the country dances, the waltz, the cotillion, and the quadrille before she left Calcutta—the idea of putting her skills to the test in this potentially hostile environment made her shiver.

Taking a deep, steadying breath, Anjali forced her lips into what passed as a smile and followed Lady Lewiston and her father up the stairs. Aside from a few whispers from people behind them in which she thought she heard someone say *Ashcombe* and *rich nabob*, the introductions went smoothly. Lady Allston, a contemporary of Lady Lewiston with hair that had already turned almost completely gray, rather watery pale blue eyes, and a silver crepe evening dress trimmed with blond lace, appeared unsurprised by Anjali's appearance.

"But you are enchanting!" she said. "Dear Caroline has told me so much about you and I'm delighted you and your father could favor my gathering with your presence this evening."

Anjali was about to respond with humble thanks, but Lady Allston had already turned to greet the next guests in line.

After that, Anjali hardly knew how she ended up with a glass of lemonade in one hand and a dance card around the wrist of the other. Nor did she know how she lost sight of her father. Likely he'd gone to find the card room, she thought—not because he liked gaming, but probably because there he would be out of the press of strangers and could sit and enjoy a glass of brandy. Lady Lewiston had wandered away to greet a friend on the other side of the room, and so Anjali found herself alone in an undulating sea of strangers. Where was Belinda? And where was … Anjali couldn't help glancing around and hoping to see telltale red curls peeking up among the heads of the gentleman guests.

She was about to give up and seek refuge in the retiring room again when an elegant, dark-haired lady dressed in the very kick of fashion approached her. "You must be Miss Ashcombe." She held out her hand. "I am Mariana Thorne."

"How do you do," Anjali said, a puzzled crease in her brow.

"Of course you have no idea who I am!" Mariana said, her violet-blue eyes dancing. "I know you because my dear friend Lady Bridlington described the gown you are wearing, saying I should look for you at the party because you might not know very many people."

Still none the wiser, Anjali was about to ask her outright what she meant when Belinda swept over to her, a very handsome gentleman in tow. Anjali let her shoulders drop in relief.

Belinda said, "Lady Mariana! I'm delighted to see you. And this, as perhaps you already know, is Miss Anjali Ashcombe, my wonderful new friend. She's staying with my mother."

Ah, so it's Lady *Mariana.* "Forgive me," Anjali said, "How did Lady Bridlington know anything about my gown?"

Belinda said, "You remember, I told you she's the real designer behind Madame Pauline's." She turned to Mariana. "Is Lady Bridlington coming tonight?"

"Alas no! Both her little ones have the measles."

"Show me your dance card, Anjali," Belinda said, abruptly changing the subject. Without waiting for permission she grasped the card so she could inspect it, dragging Anjali's wrist along with it. "As I suspected. Completely blank." She turned to the gentleman behind her. "Miss Ashcombe, may I present Mr. Gainesworth—my husband. I shall permit him to dance with you despite the fact that if we were not friends I might worry that he would instantly be smitten by your unique charms."

Gainesworth smiled apologetically. "I would be honored to stand up with you, Miss Ashcombe." To Lady Mariana he said, "Is Jeremy not here this evening?"

"Alas no. A late sitting. There's a heated debate over some bill about which he feels very strongly. Something to do with *habeas corpus*," Lady Mariana said before beaming her friendly smile once more on Anjali. "I've always wanted to see India."

"It is a unique place," Anjali said. "Calcutta is quite a contrast to London. Much hotter, to say the least!"

Lady Mariana grinned. "And you have only been here a short time, I gather. Not long enough to accustom yourself to our English weather. You must be quite bemused by it all. Not that it shows. You look perfectly at home here."

By this time, a small knot of guests had gathered around them and Anjali suddenly felt ridiculously conspicuous, despite what Mariana had just said. These interlopers seemed uninterested in introductions, simply standing near enough to hear their conversation and staying angled away.

After a time, one of the young ladies in that group spoke loudly enough to be heard quite clearly. "I find that Denmark lotion is quite effective to whiten the skin. Although it does not work on a truly brown complexion, it can brighten a dull one."

And then Lady Henrietta walked up to them, greeting Belinda like the fondest of close friends, and nodding briefly to Anjali. "There's no one here," she said, sweeping the room with her gaze.

Anjali was about to contradict her—the room was nearly as full as it could hold with guests—when Gainesworth took her hand and said, "I believe the orchestra is preparing to play the first dance, if you will do me the honor?"

So it was starting. As they made their way through to the ballroom following the strains of an excellent ensemble, Anjali felt the hot gaze of dozens of eyes, measuring, assessing, and no doubt finding her lacking.

She and Gainesworth took their places in the parallel lines. Anjali prayed that the music and the movement of the dance would distract her from her excruciating discomfort. She wanted nothing more than to run out of the room and all the way back to Park Street.

But that would be cowardly. *Mama would be ashamed of me if I did that.* All at once an image of her mother, clothed in a vibrant silk sari and draped with gold and jewels, moving through the world with the knowledge that no lady deserved more consideration than she did, gave her courage. She lifted her chin and resolutely smiled, curtsying to Gainesworth, who winked at her quickly and entered into the spirit of the dance.

After that, Anjali found herself dancing nearly every set. Some of the gentlemen she was certain only asked her to stand up with them out of curiosity. The conversations were vapid and general by and large: the weather, carriage horses, upcoming parties. Only two gentlemen asked any questions at all about her or displayed any curiosity about India. One who did so believed that it must be easy to get good servants there, with so many poor and ignorant souls to choose from. Anjali clamped her teeth together and resisted the temptation to give him a set down.

When there came a break in her stream of dance partners, Belinda found her and said, "Come and meet someone. The most remarkable coincidence! He has also recently come from Calcutta."

Something made Anjali wary, although she could not have said exactly why. She dutifully followed Belinda to the gentleman. Of course he was not a native, but a paunchy Englishman with half-closed eyes and a bulbous nose latticed by fine veins.

"Mr. Heatherington, this is Miss Ashcombe. She was born in Calcutta and has recently moved to London with her father."

Heatherington widened his eyes and arched an eyebrow upon seeing her. No doubt he expected her to be purely English as well and wasn't adept enough to hide his discomfiture. "Ashcombe, you say. I don't know of any Ashcombe in the Company."

Of course. It stood to reason that he had been associated with the East India Company. "My father was an independent exporter," Anjali said, hoping to find an excuse to get away as quickly as possible.

The gentleman pursed his lips and rubbed his chin. "Ah, yes, I seem to recall … Married a native, as I remember. Not the thing. Is he here?"

Had he really just said that aloud to her? Her stomach clenched. She was tempted to tell him that yes, he had, and that she was the result of that loving marriage. But this was not the place, so she simply answered, "I'm afraid I have not laid eyes on him since shortly after we arrived." How was she to end this uncomfortable conversation? "But you remind me that I must seek a particular friend who is here somewhere." She curtsied and walked away, soon followed by Belinda.

"Is something wrong, Anjali?" Belinda asked.

"Did you hear what he said?"

"No, I was talking to someone else." How could she explain the parochial attitudes of the English in Calcutta, and why that man might be the very worst person Belinda could have introduced her to?

In the end she didn't have to. Belinda suddenly grasped her wrist and whispered into her ear, "Look there! Isn't that the fellow we saw in the park? What was his name?"

Across the room, standing a few inches taller than everyone else and thereby revealing his tousled red curls, was Sir Julian. His eyes met Anjali's at that same moment, causing a flood of relief to course through her body. He excused himself from talking to the much smaller gentleman standing next to him and started in Anjali's direction. At last, she thought, someone she knew. Someone she wanted to see. Yet how could she say she knew this baronet she'd encountered only briefly on two occasions? And what exactly was it about him that made her wish for his company?

"Ah, Miss Ashcombe! I have brought you someone who wishes to meet you."

Anjali whirled around at the sound of Lady Lewiston's well-modulated voice and found herself standing in front of a man of above-average height and neat build wearing the requisite evening attire, but its embellishment with several gold fobs and a dazzling diamond tie pin proclaimed him a dandy.

"Lord Dawlish, this is Miss Anjali Ashcombe," Lady Lewiston said.

"Charmed, Miss Ashcombe," Dawlish said and bowed over the gloved hand she extended to him.

"How do you do?" Anjali said. He looked every inch the exact kind of Englishman she would have expected to meet at such a party. He said all that was polite and put his name on her dance card, then bowed and wandered away.

"Lord Dawlish has recently returned from an extended sojourn on the Continent, where he remained after selling out from being an officer in the army of occupation," Lady Lewiston said. "That, my dear, is perhaps the reason that no one has as yet secured him. He is one of the most eligible bachelors of the season," Lady Lewiston murmured in her ear, pretending to twitch a bit of lace at the edge of Anjali's sleeve into place.

Anjali barely heard her. She scanned the room for Sir Julian, but he was not to be seen. Had he left so soon? It wasn't late, not even midnight yet. "I should like to find my father," Anjali said, and before Lady Lewiston could stop her, threaded her way through the guests, most of whose eyes followed her with frank curiosity.

She passed quickly through the saloons and drawing rooms, then descended to the entrance floor thinking perhaps Sir Julian had gone to the dining room, where a lavish spread had been provided for the sustenance of the revelers. But he wasn't there. She perused her dance card. Lord Dawlish had put his name down for the dance that would be starting soon, the boulanger. She would have to go back up. Her feet were already sore where her new evening slippers chafed. Perhaps she might persuade Lord Dawlish to sit down. On second thought, something about him made her think a conversation with him wouldn't be very enjoyable. And then she realized she would far rather speak with Sir Julian. But she couldn't find him anywhere.

With a last glance around, she put her foot on the bottom step to return to the ballroom.

"Anji!" Her father's voice reached her ear and she turned to see where it had come from. A door that had been closed and which Anjali assumed led to a family apartment or office opened slowly, and her father emerged, wearing his hat and evening cloak and looking cautiously around him.

"Papa!" she cried and ran to him. "Why are you wearing your cloak?"

He put his finger against her lips. "Hush my dear. I must leave. There is no need for you to do so, but would you kindly make my apologies to Lady Lewiston?"

"What shall I say?"

"Tell her, please, that I am indisposed. The headache or something. Perhaps a touch of a malady I picked up in India. I shall take a hackney back to Bloomsbury." He squeezed her hand.

"But why? Papa, Lady Belinda introduced me to a man who has come from Calcutta. I think he's with the Company, but I didn't talk with him long enough to know for certain."

"Yes. It's Heatherington. I was afraid he might be here. It is he whom I wish to avoid. Anyone of his stripe, really. I cannot explain it all now. Please convey my message to Lady Lewiston."

With that, he kissed her cheek and left.

CHAPTER 9

All the young gentlemen who danced with Anjali left cards and posies the next day. That was as Lady Lewiston expected.

But when she sat next to her charge in the drawing room after breakfast going through them with her, hoping to gain some insight into the girl's sentiments concerning her first rout party and whether there was anyone who struck Anjali particularly, she was destined to be thrown off balance.

"Are you telling me honestly, my dear, that you don't remember dancing with any of these gentlemen?" She felt certain Anjali must recall Lord Dawlish, since she herself had introduced him, but he had not sent a card—much to Caroline's surprise.

Anjali turned her wide eyes to Lady Lewiston and said, "I had never met any of them before. We spoke so little. And there were so many of them!" She laughed.

Anjali had a delightful laugh, the kind that made everyone around her have to join in her merriment—all the more so because she laughed so seldom. Caroline was not immune to that power, and chuckled helplessly. "It is true that gentlemen in evening dress do have a tendency to look very much the same as one another."

"Unless, of course, they have done something outrageous to make themselves stand out, as did Sir Ponsonby. He did not ask me to dance, and yet I remember him so clearly." Anjali's eyes were alight with mirth, and her giggling deepened until it became laughter that took hold of her entire body.

"Oh, oh!" Caroline said, in a paroxysm that had her pressing her hand to her stomach. "Th-that absurd waistcoat! And the rows and rows of ruffles on his shirt!" It was unseemly of her to react so unhandsomely to the poor fellow's mistaken fashion choices, but it felt delightfully freeing not only to utter the words, but to do so without restraint. She couldn't remember the last time she laughed so hard. It made her realize that she had been holding a great deal of worry and anxiety inside ever since receiving Thomas's letter. She was self-aware enough to know that the reasons for her stress were complex. There was no question that she felt her responsibility for his daughter very keenly, but what had the girl done to deserve her anxiety? Nothing. She was in all ways a delightful young lady—except for that inescapable reserve. Even their shared merriment opened only a tiny chink in Anjali's closed-off mind, and Caroline expected that as soon as the moment had passed, she would once more retreat behind her veil.

While it lasted, this moment of high humor was delicious. They were only barely in control of themselves again when Fairing cleared his throat at the door and said, "Lord Dawlish," then stepped aside to bow the peer into the drawing room.

Anjali and Lady Lewiston rose. Caroline fought against the urge to laugh anew at the serious expression on Dawlish's face and his obvious confusion upon seeing the two ladies with their cheeks flushed and eyes moist with tears of laughter. "My Lord, how good of you to call," Caroline said, her inbred propriety finally winning the battle. "Won't you be seated?"

He did not immediately take the offered chair, but approached Anjali and held out a large posy to her. She curtsied prettily, and Caroline was glad to see that she had erased all hint of hilarity from her face, leaving behind a bright, engaging expression that—she felt sure—could not fail to be alluring to the eligible peer.

Once they were all seated and Fairing had brought in a tray with a decanter of sherry and a pitcher of lemonade, Lord Dawlish said, "I felt it incumbent upon me to pay this call after you so kindly introduced me to Miss Ashcombe, Lady Lewiston."

"You're very good to do so, My Lord," Caroline said, hoping he had come equipped with more conversation than that. When the silence lengthened, she finally broke it by saying, "Town is still very thin of company. I wonder if there will be anyone here to attend the first Almack's assembly?"

She intended her words to mean nothing in particular, but Dawlish opened his eyes wide and then swept them toward Anjali, who was occupied with examining the pattern on the carpet as if it were the most fascinating thing she'd ever seen. "Almack's? Has Miss Ashcombe been given vouchers? I didn't suppose—" He broke off, perhaps realizing his faux pas.

How foolish of her to speak without considering the very real possibility that Anjali would never cross the hallowed threshold of the jealously guarded marriage mart. Assuming her most top-lofty expression, Caroline said, "Lady Jersey assures me these will be forthcoming. However, before then, I plan to give a ball to welcome Miss Ashcombe to London. A masquerade ball."

Caroline's words had the effect of making both Anjali and Lord Dawlish jerk their heads in her direction and stare open-mouthed for just a moment. "A masquerade?" Anjali said, something kindling in her eyes.

"I realize this isn't the usual way to introduce a debutante. But Miss Ashcombe isn't the usual debutante." Caroline desperately tried to think of a way to explain her sudden, completely spontaneous announcement. And she had said it would occur *before* the first Almack's assembly. Was she mad? Of course, the celebrated patroness had been noticeably discouraging about the vouchers. Lady Jersey escaped responsibility for any slight by claiming that it would be Mrs. Burrell who would likely object.

Once more, the conversation died. Caroline exhumed it by saying, "I hear you are a keen sportsman, Lord Dawlish. A Melton man? Did you hunt on the Continent as well?" If he was addicted to hunting, that would get him talking.

"The Quorn, in fact. Yes, I take every opportunity to go to my hunting box during the season," Dawlish said, taking the glass of sherry Fairing had placed on the table at his elbow and sipping it appreciatively. "I did not find good sport in Germany, however."

"What do you hunt, My Lord?" Anjali asked.

Her question was so unexpected that Caroline had no time to leap in and say something witty to mask the revelation of her naivete.

"Why, foxes, of course! What else would one hunt in Leicestershire?"

Anjali turned startled eyes to Lady Lewiston—startled, or rather, disingenuously shocked—and said, "Do you eat fox meat? I had not heard of that practice. In India we hunt wild boar for meat, and tigers if they threaten our cattle."

Dawlish looked appalled for a moment, then he broke into a broad smile. "Ah, I see! The foxes are like your tigers.

Nuisances that raid the hen houses. So no, we don't eat them."

With a perplexed frown, Anjali said, "Is hunting them the only way to keep them from the hens? It would seem to me that better houses could be built instead."

"I suppose," said Dawlish, "But then we wouldn't have such good sport, would we?"

At last Caroline caught Anjali's eyes and gave a quick, barely perceptible shake of her head, even as she struggled to suppress the smile that wanted to spread across her face. It was remarkable, she thought, how those otherwise inscrutable eyes could hold such a light of impudence in them. Anjali was making a joke at poor Lord Dawlish's expense.

"How is your dear mother, My Lord? Please tell her I look forward to playing whist with her again this season." Caroline steered the conversation in a safer direction, and after a few more minutes of it, Fairing entered again.

"Mr. Thomas Ashcombe," he said.

Anjali's face brightened immediately, and Caroline was aware of a flutter in her stomach. He had left the party early without telling her he was going, although he sent a message through Anjali. Still, it felt a little like a rejection. Why she couldn't say. She had no particular claim upon him, except that of a shared history of disappointment.

A moment later he walked in, and by then Caroline had schooled her expression to be pleasant but bland. "Mr. Ashcombe! How lovely to see you."

Anjali hardly waited for him to enter the room and ran to him, kissed him, took his face between her palms and said, "I've missed you, Papa. I want to hear all about the house."

"You've missed me? But we just saw each other last night."

"Yes, but I didn't *talk* to you," Anjali said and drew her father further into the room.

Caroline cleared her throat and said, "Thomas, I don't believe you are acquainted with Lord Dawlish."

Dawlish had stood as soon as Ashcombe entered and scrutinized Anjali's warm greeting with an expression that was difficult to interpret. He didn't frown. He appeared perplexed, if anything. "How do you do," Dawlish said, taking the hand Ashcombe held out to him as he strode across the room.

"Are you feeling better?" Caroline said to Thomas.

Thomas looked blank, then suddenly he said, "Oh! Yes, much better. Turned out to be just a headache."

"You have come from Calcutta, so I hear from Miss Ashcombe," Dawlish said. "With the East India Company?"

"Yes to the first, no to the second," Thomas said. "I was an independent trader."

Dawlish knitted his brow. "Why would you choose such a course, if I may ask? I know little of India, but I have heard it is a savage place outside of the areas controlled by the Company." His gaze shifted to Anjali, who by then had pulled her father down to sit next to her on the settee and held his hand between both of hers.

Was this true? And how had Lord Dawlish obtained this particular view of the place? Caroline surreptitiously watched Thomas to see how he reacted. He was too well-bred to respond defensively, she hoped. But how could he not defend the world in which his daughter was born and flourished?

"In my experience, people—perhaps especially the English—are quick to label as savage any customs that deviate from their own," Thomas said, avoiding a direct accusation. "I assure you, although the Indian culture has many aspects that appear incomprehensible to us, they are a people who value education and heritage above perhaps any others I have known. No doubt your view of the matter has been acquired from men who have no experience of India."

Dawlish sat up straighter. "I assure you, Mr. Ashcombe, that I have some experience of the world, having spent years among foreigners, some of whom have become my greatest friends."

"Ah yes. I mean no discourtesy, but they were still European. Any differences cannot be measured against the vast gulf that exists in a country with different religions and millennia of history largely separate from the Christian world."

Dawlish had the good grace to nod. "I cannot help believing, sir, that what the East India Company is doing to bring civilization to the natives is to be applauded. So again, I ask why you are not associated with them."

Caroline was about to intervene and say that this was hardly appropriate conversation for a social visit when Thomas spoke again.

"When I went there almost thirty years ago, the situation was very different. Remaining independent, steering my own course, was the logical way for me to go about things."

Caroline worried that the conversation might soon become awkward. She wanted to save Thomas from potential insult, and to prevent Anjali—whose expression had darkened as Dawlish spoke—from leaping to a hot defense of her father. She made a point of glancing at the clock on the mantel.

As she hoped, Dawlish noticed. He rose and said, "I respect the choices you made, Mr. Ashcombe. And I am certain you wish to have private conversation with your daughter, so I will take my leave." He turned to address Anjali. "Before I go, I wanted to offer … What I mean to say is that I would be honored if you would permit me to take you out driving, Miss Ashcombe. If you are a horsewoman you will like my chestnuts. Got them at Tattersall's at the end of last season."

Caroline sent a look in Anjali's direction. For a moment, it seemed as if she was going to refuse, but Thomas gave his daughter's hand a twitch and sent her a surreptitious wink. Anjali smiled. "I would be delighted, Lord Dawlish."

"Would tomorrow afternoon suit?" Dawlish asked.

The appointment set, he bowed to them and left.

He hadn't danced with her. He hadn't even spoken with her. So why was he standing outside the house on Park Street—where he'd discovered Miss Ashcombe was staying with the dowager Lady Lewiston—looking for all the world like a loitering tradesman? Well, perhaps better dressed than that. Tradesmen did not wear fawn pantaloons, Weston-tailored green superfine coats, and highly polished Hessian boots.

He examined the absurdly perfect posy clutched in his gloved fist. What kind of flowers were they? He didn't ask when he purchased them. He'd left Bramble in his rooms so he could actually go inside like any other morning caller. So what was preventing him walking up the steps to the door and using the knocker for its intended purpose? *Julian!* he said to himself. Come, man! You face down hardened criminals, obliterate opposing counsel, and stand before the bench without flinching. All that was true, he thought, but somehow it didn't carry over to everyday life. He'd spent too many years feeling utterly incapable of any social niceties and being mercilessly teased and ridiculed for his startlingly red hair. Ridiculous really. He had complete confidence in his ability to construct compelling arguments, his command of great quantities of facts, and his exhaustive knowledge of the law.

He had absolutely no confidence, however, in his ability to say two sensible words to an attractive young lady.

And he was most definitely attracted to Miss Ashcombe. She was beautiful, but that didn't do her justice. It implied that only her appearance had the power to draw him to her. Although he had barely spoken to her that first time in the Green Park and then in Hyde Park, he glimpsed something in her, something hidden deep within her wide, dark eyes. He encountered her the previous evening for the third time, and after seeing her there amid so many vapid come-outs was more certain than ever that he must find a way to become better acquainted with her. Miss Ashcombe stood out against the crowd like a rare gem glittering up from the sea floor. He wanted so desperately to go to her, to ask her questions and find out more about her. Then Lady Lewiston had led Dawlish over to meet her, and the moment passed.

He had hoped he might have another chance to speak with her later that night, but soon after that moment Thorne had drawn him into a heated discussion about the act that Parliament had passed that same evening, the suspension of *habeas corpus*, a law that gave the Home Office the ability to arrest and confine someone without a shred of actual evidence, only reasonable suspicion. No trial, no hearing, no charges were necessary.

But this was not to the purpose. It was all too easy for him to seek refuge in contemplating some legal problem rather than confronting the reality of an innocent morning call. Julian drew himself up, took a few slow breaths to still his racing pulse and climbed the stone steps to the door.

Just as he raised his hand to lift the brass knocker, the door swung open, throwing him off balance. He scrambled to keep his footing and reached for the iron railing by the stairs, crushing the posy against it and sending a torrent of colorful petals fluttering to the ground. He looked up in consternation to see the person for whom the servant had opened the door staring at him, eyebrows raised, as Julian made a feeble attempt to pick up what remained of his flowers.

"I do beg your pardon, sir," the gentleman said.

"The fault is mine, please excuse me." It was Dawlish. Of course. How had he not foreseen it? Clearly some arrangement was afoot, and he would be too late to have a chance with Miss Ashcombe. A chance of what, though? The sight of the eligible peer made Julian want nothing more than to simply go back down the steps and return to his lodgings, but he had been seen, and that would be impolite.

Lord Dawlish touched the brim of his hat and walked past Julian to the street where a curricle drawn by a matched pair of chestnuts awaited him. With an air of perfect ease, as if he knew his place in the world and believed it was unassailable, the gentleman took the reins, called to the groom to step away from the horses' heads, and gave them the office to go without another glance at Julian.

"Are you wishful of entering the house, sir?"

The butler's voice startled Julian. "What? Oh! Yes, of course. Sir Julian Meredith. Is Miss Ashcombe at home?"

He'd done it. There truly was no going back now. He stepped across the threshold and gave what remained of the posy to a nearby footman, who waited to take his hat and cane from him.

The butler led him up to a handsome saloon on the first floor. In it, three people were arranged as if frozen in some strange tableau. Lady Lewiston sat on a gilt chair, an older gentleman he did not recognize occupied a settee opposite her, and Miss Ashcombe stood apart from both of them. She'd been facing away, but turned toward him when the butler spoke his name. He thought he saw a flicker of something like delight, or perhaps it was only relief in her eyes before she schooled her countenance to something more reserved.

Move, Julian! he thought, feeling utterly stupid standing rooted to the spot a few feet inside the door, on the outer edge of a gorgeous Axminster carpet. Before he could persuade himself to take a step forward, the gentleman—with whom he was unacquainted—walked up to him with his hand out.

"Thomas Ashcombe. Your servant, Sir Julian."

The man's warm grip and genuine smile reassured him. Miss Ashcombe's father. He bowed slightly to Mr. Ashcombe and then more deeply to Lady Lewiston. "My Lady," he said, "I hope you are well this morning."

An amused smile lit her face and she said, "Very well, thank you Sir Julian. I knew your mother. We were at school together. I'm so very sorry for your loss. Have you met Miss Ashcombe? She is lately come from Calcutta with her father."

He fixed his attention on Miss Ashcombe and caught her widening her eyes and tiny shake of her head, as if she wanted to send him a message. What was it? "We have not been formally introduced," he said, hoping he guessed correctly and that she wouldn't be offended and think he had forgotten her. How could he ever forget her? "How do you do, Miss Ashcombe?" He bowed again.

She came forward and held out her hand. "I believe I saw you at Lady Allston's party last night."

"Yes. Yes I was there. I saw you, but was called away before I could stand up with you. I fully intended ... And so I thought I would call ..."

He ran out of things to say and looked helplessly at Miss Ashcombe.

Just as he had responded to her subtle signal, she seemed

to understand what he needed from her and said, "Although we had not yet properly met, I believe I saw you in the park the other day, and I hoped to have a chance to talk to you last night. I'm delighted that you are here."

Julian smiled. "Yes. I am not much in the habit of attending parties."

"Won't you sit, Sir Julian?" Lady Lewiston said.

Sit? Somehow it seemed disrespectful to do so.

Again as if she'd seen his discomfort, Miss Ashcombe took a seat on a small settee and nodded toward the empty place next to her. Could he sit so close to her without bursting into scorching flames? That was fanciful, of course. But it was the only thing that came to mind when he thought of being near enough to her that he could reach out and touch her, or accidentally brush against her.

She raised an eyebrow at him, and he took three quick steps to the settee and sat abruptly, very upright, not angled at all toward her. He could sense her next to him but didn't dare look in her direction.

"You are in chambers at Lincoln's Inn, if I recall correctly, Sir Julian," Lady Lewiston said, breaking the uncomfortable silence.

"Yes," Julian said. He knew he should say something more, but every idea he ever had fled from his mind like so many dandelion seeds in a stiff wind.

This time, Mr. Ashcombe came to his rescue. "I know it's not the accepted topic of conversation in a drawing room, but is it true, what I heard this morning, that Parliament has enacted a suspension of *habeas corpus*? I imagine such a thing could complicate the lives of the legal men like you."

Julian cast a quick glance in Lady Lewiston's direction, thinking she must be desirous of changing the subject. But she sat in eager silence, searching his eyes for something, so he answered, "I cannot say how it will change things, but it will make it more difficult to protect people from untrue accusations of a certain kind." Mr. Ashcombe and Lady Lewiston exchanged a glance.

But it was Miss Ashcombe who surprised him by saying, "I thought that in returning to England we would have left such capricious laws behind. I'm afraid to say, Sir Julian, that we are all too familiar with—"

Before she could finish what she was saying, Mr. Ashcombe broke in. "Of course, Anjali is not familiar with the law here. You must forgive her assumptions."

Julian at last turned so that he could look directly into Miss Ashcombe's alive, intelligent eyes. *Her name is Anjali.* There was no sign of a simper or any bashful fluttering of the lashes. She did him the courtesy of steady, intent regard. She wanted to know more. "Not assumptions at all. Miss Ashcombe is very astute to be concerned about the implications of such a law to anyone who says anything that could be construed as seditious or revolutionary. It flies in the face of one's freedom of thought and speech."

"How so?" Ashcombe asked.

"Why, supposing in the privacy of this drawing room, or in my club, I complained that the poor were being unfairly taxed and observed that their rights were under attack. If someone overheard me and chose to interpret my words as evidence that I held revolutionary opinions, I could be informed against and imprisoned."

"Surely not!" Lady Lewiston said. "Who would do such a thing?"

Julian shrugged. "I no doubt see a different side of humanity in my work than you do in the the drawing rooms of the *ton*. But it is my experience that men—and women—are fully capable of harboring destructive ill will that sometimes results in real harm to their fellows."

Miss Ashcombe breathed in sharply, and Julian was

suddenly aware that he had spoken quite fluently in the presence of a lady. And most assuredly he had said nothing pleasing. "However, I would far rather hear about your life in India and what you think of London, Miss Ashcombe." *Feeble.* Still, at least it was something.

Miss Ashcombe sighed. "Our house in Calcutta was surrounded by lush gardens, and the birds—so many colorful varieties. I miss them most of all." She turned to gaze out of the window at a leaden early spring sky.

"But you have—" Julian stopped himself. They weren't supposed to have met that first time, when she had her myna bird with her. She must have been out without permission. "—such a lovely way of describing it."

A laugh came into Miss Ashcombe's eyes and she pressed her lips together to suppress a smile. Such very kissable lips.

Julian stood abruptly. He mustn't think such things! "I fear I must leave. I have an appointment. I must go to chambers today. Forgive me."

After the briefest of farewells, he all but fled from the house, berating himself for his clumsiness, and hoping he hadn't put Miss Ashcombe off for good.

CHAPTER 10

*I*t took Anjali longer than she thought it would to write the letter she knew she must to Nalin. She and her father had left India in haste nearly four months ago, and the reasons he had given her for something that seemed unlike him did not satisfy her. Why would he—scrupulous to a fault over anything to do with business or the household—announce one morning that they were going to England a mere week later? It left them barely enough time to see that all the servants were given their wages and had new positions to go to and to decide what to bring to England and what to sell or give away. To her repeated questions he said only that it was time, that another Maratha war might soon start, and that it had been her mother's wish that her daughter take her place in English society. This could not be all. Being in the metropolis in time for the season before she was twenty was in no way as important as her father tried to make her believe it was.

In the days before they left Calcutta, Nalin and her father spent many hours closeted together going over books and making other arrangements. She tried to get Nalin to tell her what they were doing, but he simply smiled at her sadly and shook his head. *It is best like this,* he said. *You will make a great debut in society.*

It was true. It made her sad, but in a curiously remote way. Anjali had spent the last two years gradually falling in love with Nalin—at least, she assumed it was love. She always looked forward to seeing him, would rather talk to him than anyone else, and dreamt of holding his hand, of letting him kiss her. Of course, he never did. He was familiar and kind, and although he had never said anything about it, a soft expression came into his eyes when he looked at her.

That would not have been enough, though. No matter how respectable, educated, intelligent, and handsome he was, he was first of all her father's clerk—which placed him on a lower social rung by British standards. As to her Indian relations, there he was also not quite up to her rank. They didn't consider him exactly unsuitable. Just not quite suitable enough. He was *Kayastha,* not Brahmin like her mother's family. A very fine distinction, but a distinction nonetheless, and a marriage with him would never have been sanctioned.

Now here she was in London where it was assumed she would find a husband who *was* suitable. Nalin knew that would happen, of course, but Anjali felt she owed it to him to express how important he had been, to receive his blessing, in a way. It was probably silly, but the idea of him hung over her and prevented her from entering into the spirit of Lady Lewiston's efforts to introduce her to society.

And there was that other reason for writing to him. Now that they were safely in London she hoped he would reveal what he knew, what he wouldn't tell her before they left. Of course, assuming she could get a letter to him, his reply would take just as long to get back to her, and who knew what might have happened in the interim?

Her letter-writing efforts were somewhat thwarted

because she couldn't let Lady Lewiston know she was doing it. To admit to sending a letter to India would raise questions, certainly. To admit that the recipient was a young man would open her to censure and likely force Lady Lewiston tell her father. So she composed the letter only after Millie had left her settled for the night, when she could use the excuse of reading before bed.

Although she would write the direction in English because no doubt she would have to find an English vessel sailing to Calcutta to take the letter, the body of it she wrote in a mix of Hindustani and English, making sure that the English parts were innocent enough—inquiries into the health of Nalin's family, requests to send her affectionate greetings to her grandparents if Nalin were to journey to Murshidabad for any reason, and other such commonplaces. In Hindustani she asked him to tell her honestly what made her father so nervous that they had to virtually flee India. She asked him in his reply to copy her method and write anything that might be interpreted as sensitive in Hindustani or Urdu.

His reply. Of course, she could not tell him to send it to her in Park Street. Who could she trust to receive it who would not tell either Lady Lewiston or her father? She didn't know. But until she did, she could not send her letter. The proprieties were so inconvenient! So she folded and sealed it and tucked it in the false compartment at the bottom of her jewel case, then slipped between the sheets and tried to go to sleep.

She lay down, but her eyes refused to close. The letter wasn't the only thing that kept her awake that night. In a way, the day after the rout party had been more memorable than the party itself. Aside from the strange custom of leaving cards and small bouquets of English flowers and Lord Dawlish's visit—which Lady Lewiston had obviously expected—Anjali could not stop thinking about two things. Uppermost in her mind was Sir Julian arriving when he did, without the excuse of having danced with her the night before. Something about him had appealed to her from the beginning, even before she'd said more than a few words to him. He had a rather un-English curiosity and was not afraid to ask questions. She guessed his profession had cultivated that in him.

It was more than that, however. His peculiar combination of shyness about his very noticeable red hair and the self-possession that made him unashamed of walking what amounted to a lady's lap dog in London's public parks made him—different. Perhaps it was simply that. What else could it be?

Sir Julian wasn't handsome in the way of Nalin, or even Lord Dawlish, whose crisp, clean Englishness would no doubt appeal to many young ladies. Not Anjali, however. She took the measure of Dawlish after a single conversation and suspected he saved his deepest thoughts and greatest consideration for his stables. But Sir Julian ... Anjali had a feeling the barrister-baronet had hidden qualities and capabilities he was too reticent to expose to the merciless judgment of the *ton*. What made her think that? Something in his eyes. Their color changed every time she saw him. She knew it was a trick of the light, of course, but they took her by surprise nonetheless and gave him a quality she could not define.

Just before she blew out her candle, determined to fall asleep, Anjali remembered the other remarkable thing about that day. Lady Lewiston was to give a debutante ball in her honor. And not just any ball. A masquerade. Why had she not mentioned it to her before? *More to the point*, Anjali thought, *what costume shall I wear?* The idea of such an event appealed to her much more than a simple ball. After all, it seemed that these English were careful to keep their masks on in public even when they weren't supposed to be in costume. It was possible an actual mask might inspire many to reveal more of their true selves.

Belinda would help her with a costume. Anjali chuckled softly. Poor Belinda! Little did she realize what hazards there were in being so friendly to a stranger of her ilk. Sweet, amiable Belinda would find herself involved in Anjali's affairs whether she liked it or not. *I shall find a way to thank her,* Anjali thought.

THOMAS WAS RELIEVED AND CHEERED BY THE FACT THAT Anjali seemed to have made a bit of an impression at Lady Allston's rout party—enough to have received numerous cards and flowers and to have two eligible gentlemen come calling. By any objective standards she was surpassingly lovely. But the *ton* was not known for its objectivity.

Although she didn't say anything to him directly, Thomas got the impression that Lady Lewiston thought Lord Dawlish would be a good match for his daughter. He wasn't quite so sure. The fellow seemed very proper and polite, was good looking and apparently from an excellent family. He was the ninth baron, so she told him.

But he thought that Anjali looked upon Dawlish with little—if any—interest.

The other fellow who arrived late, the barrister, was a different matter. He sparked something in Anjali's eyes. Whether it was attraction Thomas couldn't say. He knew his daughter well enough to attribute it to interest at the very least. The gentleman, a baronet apparently, seemed extremely ill at ease at first. But once he started talking about the law, his whole demeanor changed.

Odd that he sought Anjali out even though he hadn't

danced with her at the party. It seemed their acquaintance was quite slim—a brief greeting in the park and attendance at the same event. To Thomas, the baronet's unusual behavior in paying the call betokened more than passing interest in Anjali.

He'd had no chance to speak privately with his daughter to ask her how she felt about either of the gentlemen. Perhaps after she had her drive in the park with Dawlish would be a better time for that, when she came to know him a little more. As to Sir Julian—he did not make any arrangement to see Anjali again as far as Thomas was aware.

All this was going through Thomas's mind when he arrived at his club, Arthur's, in St. James's Street. His father had belonged to Brooks's, but Thomas had no appetite for trying to fit into that particular social set. Since he also had no taste for cards and certainly no desire to gamble away his hard-earned fortune, membership in Brooks's held little attraction for him. He doubted he could even be elected to it anyway. He carried the taint of trade, despite his old family name. The newer and less exclusive Arthur's was more to his taste. It offered a place to be among his peers in a quiet, congenial atmosphere, where he could arrange to meet the men who might be able to guide him to the successful conclusion of his business. He would be very relieved when all of that was taken care of, and he would have only Anjali's future to concern himself with.

He handed his hat and cane to the man at the door, who nodded to him in recognition and said, "Are you to dine with us today, Mr. Ashcombe?"

"No. I'm here to meet Lord Jeavons."

"The viscount is in the library, sir," the porter said.

At the rout party the other night, before he left to escape having to talk to Heatherington, Thomas had seen William Hawkridge, Viscount Jeavons, whom he knew from Harrow.

They had bonded at the time over a shared love of exploration and maps, devouring histories of the great explorers' voyages: Magellan, Columbus, Cook, and others. Together they dreamed of sailing around the world and visiting the mysterious East. Since Jeavons—then simply the Honorable Billy—was an eldest son, he was unlikely to be able to pursue his dream in any other place than his imagination. That didn't diminish their enjoyment of the planning and plotting. It took their minds away from the bullying Jeavons suffered while he was in school. Very small for his age and with a slight stutter, he was the butt of many pranks. Thomas defended him several times, earning his undying gratitude— and the wrath of those who sought enjoyment from tormenting boys weaker than they were.

They had not seen each other for more than a score of years, and Billy wanted to know all about India—more than just the polite snippets served up as social conversation. So the two men agreed to meet at Arthur's. Thomas was somewhat surprised that the viscount was a member of his club, imagining him more likely to be found in the hallowed precinct of White's. But Jeavons said he liked Arthur's because it *wasn't* White's, where he would most likely run into people he'd rather not see. People like Lord Crumhorn, one of his chief tormentors from school days.

Thomas spotted the viscount as soon as he entered the book-lined library, looking every bit the immaculate middle-aged peer, dark hair graying at the temples, a Prussian blue superfine coat over a striped waistcoat, jonquil pantaloons and shining Hessian boots—no doubt a product of Hobe's artistry. His friend rose, a joyful smile lighting his face. It had never been a handsome one—it was a bit too round and his light brown eyes sat a bit close together above a snub nose— but Jeavons was a good-natured, jovial man with a sparkling wit, ready conversation, and manners and address to match.

He'd outgrown his diminutive stature, tamed his stutter, married an heiress who was also the daughter of an Earl, and promptly attended to the business of engendering a numerous family. Lady Jeavons would soon be launching their eldest daughter into the *ton* and had brought her to London to gain a little pre-come-out polish.

"I was dashed pleased to see you at Lady Allston's," Jeavons said, once they were both seated with glasses of Madeira in front of them. "I felt sure you'd live out your days in India. When you left you said such a final goodbye. I understood, friend. You were devastated. But India! Was it really as glorious as it sounded in our books? And in your letters?"

Thomas smiled. Despite growing older, Billy hadn't changed. "It was. The people are wonderful and in most ways so very different from the English. Learning is prized there—much more than here. There's no such thing as a woman being too educated, too 'blue.' A good thing, since my late wife was one of the most erudite and intelligent people—man or woman—I ever had the privilege to know."

"Ah, yes. I'm so sorry for your loss, old man. Is that why you've come back?"

Thomas wondered how much he should tell his old friend. His instinct was to trust him. They had shared all their deepest thoughts as boys. But people do change. Life overlays its expectations and disappointments and what once would have been natural suddenly is freighted with complications. Whether or not Jeavons had changed, he himself had. No longer the impulsive firebrand, dealing with the Indian merchants had taught him patience and subtlety. In the end he decided to hedge a little, for the moment. "Not directly. I've brought my daughter here for her come-out. Lady Lewiston is sponsoring her into the *ton*."

Jeavons's eyes widened and he gave a low whistle. "So

that's how it is. I say, you do carry a torch for a long time, don't you?"

He should have anticipated that response, but it rattled him nonetheless. Billy had been his confidant during that tumultuous time and knew how deeply distressed he had been, how he'd railed against Caroline's grasping, ambitious parents who only wanted her to marry a title, not a man. In the end, she apparently accepted their view of what her life should be. She never wrote to him, never sent a plea for him to fight. "Don't read too much into it, Billy. That all ended long ago. I loved my wife very much, you know."

Jeavons raised one eyebrow but said no more. Clearly he was not convinced. "So your lovely daughter is your sole reason for braving the *ton*. If that's what you say I shall not question you more. Others might, although I daresay most don't remember what happened in '88. Flora and Caroline were thick for a while, until Caroline retired to Cornwall and Flora became so busy with all the children. I come up to London for Parliament, and she spends a month here as well, but until this year she preferred to remain in the country the rest of the time."

"And you? Are you content with being the lord of the manor?"

Jeavons smiled. "I am rather. There's good sport much of the year, and I've amassed quite a library. Old maps too. You should come and see them."

Thomas believed his friend. He was not the type to have mistresses or carouse around town. "I should like that, once the season is over. I must get Anjali launched before I can rest on my laurels."

After a considering pause, Jeavons said, "Really, Tom, I have to say I'm a bit surprised that Lady Lewiston agreed to sponsor your daughter—Anjali is her name? You'd think after how Lewiston behaved she would want nothing to do with a child who wasn't her own."

"What do you mean?" Thomas asked, leaning forward and lowering his voice. He never read the gossip printed in the British papers that made it to India months after the events they hinted at had happened. What had he missed?

Jeavons signaled for the waiter to bring them more Madeira, telling him to leave the bottle on the table. "I'm surprised you don't know. Although I hardly expect she would have told you. It all came out last year. You know she had twin daughters, I assume."

Thomas said, "Yes, I did hear that. One of them, Lady Belinda, has befriended Anjali. And so?"

"Well, it turns out they weren't twins, even though they were born at almost exactly the same time." He paused to sip his wine.

What was this? Thomas curled his fingers around the stem of his glass. He knew Lewiston had not been in love with Caroline. But he didn't believe him capable of harming her, of dishonoring her.

"No, apparently Lady Antonella wasn't hers. When it came out, they put it about at first that she was an orphan, a poor relation taken in out of charity. Turned out she was in truth Lewiston's by-blow. He foisted the infant on his wife, and she raised the girl alongside her own daughter, never giving anything away until they were about to make their come-outs."

Something twisted in Thomas's stomach. That was who Caroline's parents thought would make a better husband for their daughter than he would? And she had borne it. Of course. He stared at the ruby liquid in his glass, noting the way the flame of the candle on their table danced in it. Blood. That was what they cared about. Not happiness. Why did Caroline not say anything to him? Why didn't she refuse his request to sponsor Anjali? "I didn't know," Thomas said in a barely audible voice.

"Water under the bridge, old chap. She's made her peace apparently. The by-blow managed to catch a baron for a husband and lives in Cornwall. I don't know the entire story of how that came about, but it seems to have satisfied Caroline. Flora knows more than I do."

Thomas's head was in a whirl. Should he say anything to Caroline about it? No. It would be up to her if she wanted to confide in him. He had no right to expect any confidences. Or perhaps she thought he knew. What must she think of his asking her so brazenly to sponsor Anjali if that were so?

He was so caught up in his thoughts that he didn't pay any attention to the conversation at the next table over until Jeavons nudged him and said, "I say, there's something about India under discussion behind me. I daresay they don't know what they're talking about, but it sounds serious."

Thomas yanked himself out of his musing and listened. Someone he didn't know, but who spoke as if he had first-hand knowledge of the situation, said, "What's this about the Pindaris? These dispatches you speak of are months old. By now if I know anything about Hastings he must surely have acted against them and restored order."

Another said, "Yes, but the papers claim it's just a police action, that there's nothing widespread about it. Probably the natives making trouble for the Company again."

They repeated news that Thomas had lived through just before he left India. Very likely the newspapers had traveled from Calcutta to England for the same several months as he had. And Thomas knew that Hastings wasn't interested in small actions to preserve order. There was much more afoot, and some of it was related to what he hoped to accomplish in the next short while. Thomas sent a speaking glance to Jeavons, who responded by raising an eyebrow. Leaning forward,

Thomas said in a low tone that he assumed only Jeavons could hear, "Hastings does nothing by halves. Every move he makes is toward controlling more territory, with or without the cooperation of the Indians."

Thomas really wanted to question his old friend more about what had happened to Caroline during the years he'd been away, but once he heard those men who knew nothing at all about conditions in India pontificating as if things were clear cut and rational, as if whatever that monster Hastings saw fit to do was perfectly fine, it was all he could do to stay seated. After all, the Indians were godless people with filthy habits and pagan customs, so they asserted.

"Steady on, Ashcombe," Jeavons murmured, resting his hand on Thomas's forearm. "Best not to get involved. They don't know what they're talking about, as you said."

"If this is what people here truly believe, then there is no hope for India." Thomas tossed back the remaining half of his glass of Madeira, stood, and approached the table.

This caught the attention of the group and all three of them rose. One of them, looking every inch the dandy, lifted his quizzing glass and glared through it at Thomas, who did not shrink, but kept his gaze focused on that large bloodshot eye.

"I thought perhaps you gentlemen might prefer to gain some insight into affairs in India from one who has been there these nine and twenty years."

They stood frozen in their circle around the table until one of them stepped forward with his hand out and a welcoming smile. "Baldock. Pleased to make your acquaintance, Mr …."

"Ashcombe. Thomas Ashcombe," Thomas said, ignoring Billy's gentle tug on his arm. "And this is Viscount Jeavons."

"Of course. We know Jeavons. How d'ye do."

"We were just leaving," Jeavons said after returning this

acquaintance's greeting. "Come, Thomas, I believe you have a pressing appointment."

Thomas shook him off and continued facing the three men, all of whose color had heightened at his basilisk stare. "Hastings hides behind the authority of the government and the Company to justify abuses by those beneath him," he said.

"But he's part of the EIC, correct? As I gather you must also be, if you have been in India for so long." A puffy, pallid man who'd stood slightly back from the others kept his gaze fixed on Thomas.

"I am nothing to do with the EIC. I never have been and never will be. If you knew of the atrocities committed in the name of the Crown, you would understand why. This news is months old. Heaven only knows what Hastings has seen fit to do since then." After he said this, Thomas squared his shoulders and bowed to each of the men in turn. "Your servant," he said, and strode away.

Jeavons followed him out. Once they were on the street, he said, "You know, Tom, it's not wise to speak so openly against a man—and an organization that just happens to have its own government-sanctioned army—who has the backing of the Crown."

Thomas shook his head. "As far as I know in this country a man may speak his own mind without fear of reprisal. I find it deeply disturbing that apparently none of the news of the abuses perpetrated by Hastings and his underlings is being reported here." The papers he had brought with him, although they didn't directly relate to Hastings, were damning enough.

"All the same, my friend, take care." Jeavons told the porter to call his curricle around from the stables.

Thomas huffed out a long, frustrated sigh. While they waited for the vehicle, he asked, "I don't suppose you know who in the government is most closely involved with matters in India?"

Jeavons rubbed his chin while he thought. "Of course, Canning's the president of the Board of Control. He's hard to get to, though. Why do you want to know?"

"Oh, I need to ask some advice on a financial matter related to my estates in India." Thomas had already decided that he would use that as an excuse, hoping it would lead him to the right person.

"Then I think you just need to go to Leadenhall Street. I expect there are plenty there who could help you."

No doubt, Thomas thought. He wasn't certain he could trust anyone employed by the Company itself, however. He would have to ask someone more closely involved with the government. "Of course."

A groom brought the curricle up to where they stood. "Where are you racked up? Can I take you home?" Jeavons said.

"I'm in Bedford Square. But I think I prefer to walk."

"You can't walk all the way to Bloomsbury!"

The look of horror on Billy's face made Thomas grin. "I can and I shall. Oh! By the way, Lady Lewiston is to give a masquerade ball for Anjali. I'll see that you and the viscountess receive cards."

"Handsome of you! But we already have them. I'm well acquainted with Harry. He's younger, but we're both founders of the Philharmonic Society." Billy then climbed into the curricle and drove away.

Thomas relished a walk through the twilit London streets. It gave him ample time to consider all he heard while at Arthur's. The attitude toward India, although infuriating, was no more than he expected to find. And he was no closer to discovering how best to accomplish his task.

At the moment, though, the information about what

Caroline had suffered was more deeply disturbing, and not what he expected. How could she have borne it? To know a child she had raised from infancy was the product of her husband's thoughtless dalliance? From the moment he was married to Shanta, Thomas had no thought of being involved with any other woman. Among his Indian associates and friends, there were households that included more than one wife or sometimes even concubines. Yet none of them would have placed a woman in such a humiliating position.

One thing he decided before he arrived home: he would not question Caroline about it. Perhaps it was better if she assumed he didn't know. Better for him, at least. Otherwise his appeal to her to patronize his daughter would seem callous in the extreme. The last thing he wanted was to hurt or embarrass the woman who had been his first, all-consuming love.

Already things in London had turned out to be so much more complicated than he'd hoped. He should have anticipated it, and mentally kicked himself for being so naive.

CHAPTER 11

The letter hidden in Anjali's jewel case, although important, was not her most pressing concern, for the simple reason that she was powerless at that moment to do anything with it. No, she had to participate in the activities deemed suitable for a girl making her come-out, and because of her father, those must take precedence.

At breakfast on the day after Lord Dawlish and Sir Julian had paid their calls, Lady Lewiston said, "You're driving out with Lord Dawlish this afternoon, aren't you?"

"Yes," she said, a knot of unease in her stomach. "That is, he invited me, so I suppose he'll come." Anjali still wasn't certain of how the members of the *ton* saw her, and half suspected she was a curiosity that they'd soon tire of.

"Strange girl! Of course he'll come. He's a gentleman, and gentlemen honor their commitments." She paused to sip her coffee. "I think you should seriously consider Dawlish as a possible suitor. He's not only well born, he is well to pass financially, so he wouldn't be courting you for your fortune."

Anjali couldn't help wondering what else he might be courting her for. She would hardly be the mate to keep his bloodline pure, and she was tolerably certain he was not smitten with her. She certainly felt no stirrings of affection in his presence. "Are you telling me this for the simple reason that no one else you think suitable has shown any interest as yet, My Lady?"

Lady Lewiston choked slightly on her swallow of coffee and said, "You would think after more than a week I would be accustomed to your forthright way of speaking. I suppose it is not to be wondered at."

Why? Anjali thought. Did she think she'd been brought up to be bold and brazen? Hardly. Her mama would have scolded her for saying such a thing, which was partly why she felt free to do so now. The arrangement of her future was too important for her to hold back in expressing her wishes or asking questions, especially when her father was not easily at hand to support her. In a sense, she believed she must ask the questions her mother would have, had she been there.

After another pause, Lady Lewiston continued her previous line of conversation. "He is appropriate, too, because he has shown himself to be loyal and steadfast. He was a captain of dragoon guards, you know, and he fought at Waterloo."

"Indeed," Anjali said. "I did not know. Although perhaps I might have guessed he had a military background. He was very stiff and correct."

"He is respectful and polite, my dear," Lady Lewiston said, correcting her. "I think it's hard for most young gentlemen to know exactly how to make themselves agreeable to ladies within the bounds of propriety."

"Is he young? I thought you said he was over thirty." And if so, she thought, he must have some experience of making himself agreeable—if not to ladies, at least to women of a certain sort.

Lady Lewiston took a deep breath, flared her nostrils, and

smiled. "Your new driving dress with the villager hat and a parasol will do nicely for your drive."

Naturally. The trouble was, Anjali was not at all certain she felt comfortable being driven in an open carriage in public. Clearly one was meant to be seen, thus Lady Lewiston's interest in her dress. In Calcutta, if she wanted to go somewhere it would be in her father's closed *palki* with bearers to convey her quietly, swiftly, and privately through the crowded streets. Although the British in India kept some open carriages, they rarely used them for daily transportation. How could she make herself feel less uncertain about this? No doubt she'd think of something. It was some hours until Dawlish was due to arrive. Before then she had another pianoforte lesson and the Italian tutor was coming later as well.

She enjoyed learning Italian. It was like Latin, but with more nuance and musicality. Her teacher, an elderly Italian gentleman, likewise found it refreshing to teach so eager and able a student—Anjali knew this because he told her, and made her a present of a handsomely bound copy of *Rime scelti di Petrarca* printed in Venice. It pleased her to compare these western verses to the Urdu she was translating.

However, she suspected that Lord Dawlish had little interest in verse of any kind. Could she abide a husband who did not share her delight in the inventive combination of thoughts and words that comprised true poetry? It occurred to Anjali to wonder if Sir Julian turned his imagination to anything aside from the law. Something told her that there was much left to explore in the baronet's character, and the thought warmed her.

W HEN D AWLISH ARRIVED PROMPTLY AT FOUR O'CLOCK, A NJALI was already dressed and on her way down the elegant stair to the hall. She had made a surprising decision for this, her first venture at being on display in an open carriage. After considerable thought, she realized there was simply no point in trying not to be noticed. The entire purpose of such outings was to be viewed, after all. And so her bang-up-to-the-mark driving costume was completed not only by the elegant hat Lady Lewiston mentioned and a frivolous lace parasol that would do absolutely nothing to shield her from the sun, but by Kavi, seated quietly and proudly on her right shoulder.

At first, Lord Dawlish didn't appear to notice the bird. He was busy examining Anjali's attire through his quizzing glass. When he reached her shoulders, he dropped the glass, letting it swing on its silk cord, and stared open-mouthed at her.

Lady Lewiston, who had emerged from the drawing room to greet Dawlish, saw this strange start of Anjali's and quickly said, "Ah, I see Miss Ashcombe wishes to introduce you to her Indian myna bird. A privilege indeed." Then she called down the hallway to the back of the house, "Andrew!"

The footman who had shown interest in Kavi on Anjali's first day had indeed become her helper when it came to caring for the bird. Anjali interpreted Lady Lewiston's words to mean that she expected her to relinquish Kavi to Andrew, once the bird had astounded Dawlish with a few tricks. Kavi did this without prompting, calling out "Andrew!" in exactly Lady Lewiston's tone of voice. Anjali pressed her lips together in a vain attempt not to grin.

Dawlish only looked even more dumbfounded. "What an odd pet for a lady," he said, his voice betraying disapproval.

Andrew appeared and approached Anjali with his finger out for Kavi to perch upon, but Anjali said, "No, thank you Andrew. It's a beautiful day, and Kavi has been confined for too long. He will accompany me on this drive." She shifted her gaze to Lord Dawlish. "With My Lord's permission, of course."

Lady Lewiston emitted a nervous titter that was quite unlike her and said, "Miss Ashcombe is fond of a joke now and then."

"I'm not joking now, My Lady," Anjali said and smiled, knowing that Lady Lewiston could not argue with her in front of a suitor.

"Of-of course, Miss Ashcombe," Dawlish said, putting his arm out for Anjali to take.

She stole a quick glance at Andrew, who barely stopped himself from smiling wickedly. She didn't dare meet Lady Lewiston's eyes, though. No doubt she would receive a scold later.

As Anjali predicted, the presence of her myna bird made everyone in the park stare at them as they tooled around in Lord Dawlish's smart sporting curricle. Or rather, they stared past her at Kavi. She felt much less exposed with the exotic bird drawing attention away from her. Dawlish made a concerted effort to keep his eyes focused straight ahead, no doubt highly embarrassed by this odd behavior on Anjali's part. Better he should know what to expect from her if he was indeed a serious suitor, she thought. She had no intention of relinquishing all her Indian ways just because she was destined to live out her days in England.

But it was impolite to sit in stony silence: that Anjali knew. So she said, "I was quite surprised the first time I walked into the park with Lady Belinda to see so many ladies seated upon horses."

This made him steal a quick sidelong look at her before saying, "Riding well is an accomplishment desirable in any lady of consequence."

"My father taught me to ride, but only on our own

grounds, away from prying eyes. And not seated sidewise. Indian ladies generally do not ride horses for exercise."

"You mean, you rode astride?"

"Yes. But never in public. I admit, I'm sure it was a great deal easier than having to arrange one's limbs as the English ladies do. How do they keep from falling off? And how do they signal the desired gaits with their legs on only one side of the horse?"

Dawlish didn't appear to have an easy answer to that and made no attempt to continue this topic of conversation. "Has the date of your masquerade ball been fixed?"

"Yes. It is to be the week after next. You are, of course, invited. Shall you come in costume or simply wear a domino? I'm told that many gentlemen are loath to make themselves look ridiculous. I think that doing so is a wonderful way to show people who you really are, beneath all the manners and fashions. To give oneself a sense of freedom." Anjali was aware of Dawlish stiffening next to her. What had she said? Surely revealing one's true nature would be desirable if one were seeking a suitable wife.

Just at that moment, Kavi gave a squawk and flapped, drawing Anjali's attention away to the promenaders on the path near the carriageway. "Oh look!" she said. "It's Sir Julian and Bramble!"

"Is it?" said Dawlish, making no movement to slow his horses.

"Mightn't we stop and chat with them?"

The peer couldn't ignore such a direct request, so he pulled his pair up and over to the side so that other vehicles could pass him. Before Anjali could call out to Sir Julian, Kavi took this cessation of movement as his cue to fly off Anjali's shoulder. She called after him, "Kavi!"

At this, Sir Julian looked up and, before the bird reached him, he'd clamped his hand down on top of his hat, squashing it slightly. With his other hand he was trying to control Bramble who, remembering this fierce bird who had attacked his master, set up a series of barks and yelps no doubt meant to communicate menace.

Anjali laughed merrily and watched, amazed, as Kavi—rather than trying to knock Sir Julian's hat off his head—alit on his hand where it lay protecting the curly brimmed beaver. "You needn't keep holding your hat. Kavi likes you, I see," Anjali said, and nimbly climbed down from the curricle unassisted.

Helpless to stop her with no groom up behind to take charge of the horses, Dawlish watched as Anjali joined Sir Julian on the footpath. As she approached, Bramble—recognizing the voice of authority from the last time he saw this lady—stopped his complaining and sat at Sir Julian's feet. Anjali curtsied and invited Sir Julian to come closer to the curricle and greet Lord Dawlish.

The two gentlemen nodded to each other. The contrast between them could not have been greater. Dawlish sat rigid and stern, making no attempt at being pleasant. Although Sir Julian could not have been said to acknowledge Dawlish with anything beyond politeness, his tentative smile at Anjali opened something within her. She took Kavi from Sir Julian's hand and said, "You're privileged! Kavi is very particular about who he'll trust." Once the bird sat on her shoulder again, she said, "I gather you two are acquainted," and nodded in Lord Dawlish's direction.

"Yes," Dawlish said, unsmiling. "Sir Julian argued a case against one of my footmen, who was wrongfully accused of assaulting one of the maids at Dawlish House."

When Sir Julian did not follow up this information with anything else, Anjali thought about inquiring more closely, but a quick appraisal of the rather mulish expressions on each of the gentlemen's faces decided her against it. "Well, Sir

Julian is not in court now, and I hope he'll come to my debut masquerade ball." She turned her appealing gaze to the baronet. She was pleased to note that his hat wasn't rammed down on his head as it had been the first time they met, and his glorious red hair curled out under the brim. She smiled her approval at him, and he answered a smile that brightened his lovely green eyes.

Anjali was about to engage Sir Julian in conversation when Dawlish said, "I would not want to detain you, Sir Julian. I don't wish to keep my horses standing."

Although Anjali was not well educated in the niceties of curricle driving, she could see that the fine pair harnessed to the vehicle were stamping and fretting a bit. She put out her hand to shake Sir Julian's, but instead of doing so and letting it go, he kept hold of it and led her to the curricle, helping her up the step and into her seat. He had a firm, confident grip in contrast to his somewhat diffident demeanor, and she found it surprisingly comforting. Comforting and a little thrilling. "Thank you," she said.

Before she could once more remind Sir Julian that she expected to see him at her ball, Dawlish had urged his horses to a brisk trot.

For the rest of the drive around the park, Dawlish kept his horses moving quite swiftly. Anjali realized he was doing it because, contrary to wishing to be seen in her company, he wanted to avoid any more scenes with Kavi. That suited her. She found this driving around with no destination rather pointless, and could sense that Kavi was growing weary as well. He shifted lightly back and forth between his two feet and muttered indistinct noises into her ear.

She did, however, catch sight of Lady Henrietta promenading. They were too far away from each other to exchange greetings, but there was no mistaking the glowering look on her face. Anjali wondered what she had done to deserve it, and then realized that likely Lady Henrietta had her eyes on Dawlish as a suitor. She was welcome to him, Anjali thought.

After what was no more than half an hour but felt much longer to Anjali, they arrived back at the Park Street house. "I would walk you to your door, Miss Ashcombe, but I cannot leave my horses unattended."

Anjali smiled kindly, knowing she had discomposed Dawlish and feeling a little guilty about it, and said, "Thank you for a delightful drive, My Lord," and once more climbed down from the curricle unaided.

By the time she was at the door, Fairing had opened it, an unusually cheery smile on his face. "Good evening, Miss Ashcombe. The most delightful surprise. Lord and Lady Atherleigh have arrived from Cornwall!"

OF COURSE HE INVITED HER OUT TO DRIVE WITH HIM, JULIAN thought as he watched Dawlish's curricle disappear around a bend in the carriageway. He couldn't imagine Miss Ashcombe with that pink of the *ton*. In fact, what little gossip he had heard implied that a betrothal was imminent between Dawlish and Henrietta Vaughn, who was in her third season and, despite having a handsome fortune, had not had any offers that her father considered suitable. It was widely accepted that she was holding out for a title. Julian could easily imagine the spiritless baron with that lady. She was pretty enough, but as far as he could see cared only for what benefited her. In fact, she and Dawlish seemed admirably suited to each other. So what could have made Dawlish suddenly set his sights on Miss Ashcombe?

"Meredith! I say!"

Julian turned to see who was calling his name and saw Lord Jeavons striding purposefully toward him. The viscount was considerably older than he was, but the two of them struck up a casual friendship over the years through occasionally sparring at Jackson's Boxing School. Julian appreciated the science of boxing—the juxtaposition of balance, force, and speed—more than he enjoyed actually hitting people. And Jeavons—who had taken up the sport as a youth in the spirit of self-defense—appreciated an opponent who had no desire to give him a leveler. Jeavons was more thoughtful than most of the nobility, as far as Julian could tell, and seemed more to respect Julian for pursuing a profession than disdain him for it, as many did. In fact, the older man went out of his way to include Julian in social occasions he thought might be beneficial to his career.

"Hullo, Bramble," Jeavons said when he reached Julian, and gently pushed the importunate spaniel back down to the ground, scratching him behind the ears before straightening up. "Who was it Dawlish had up beside him?"

The two men continued walking on the footpath as they spoke. "Oh, that was Miss Ashcombe."

"Ashcombe?" Jeavons said.

"Daughter of—"

"Yes I know who you must mean. Thomas Ashcombe. One of my oldest friends as it happens, although I hadn't seen him for nigh on thirty years until this past week. So, do you have an interest there?"

Julian felt the heat rise into his all-too-readable cheeks. "We met by chance a little more than a sennight ago. I hardly know her." He didn't have to look at Jeavons to know that he wore a skeptical smile.

To Julian's relief, Jeavons resisted the no-doubt-strong temptation to tease him and said, "She's a beauty, to be sure. Although she'll have a hard time of it in London. Her mother was Indian."

"I know," Julian said, thinking not that this was necessarily a disadvantage, only that it made Miss Ashcombe so much more intriguing than all the other debutantes he'd studiously avoided during the past five seasons.

When he said nothing more, Jeavons said, "You *are* taking an interest, aren't you? Thomas is full of juice, I believe. Made his fortune in the textile trade, but not as part of the Company. He's playing it very close, though."

Julian wanted to say to Jeavons that it made no difference to him whether Ashcombe had a fortune or not. He was well enough to pass and in any case he had his profession. But he knew the viscount was only reflecting the preoccupations of the *ton.* It was not those words that caught his attention, but the last part of what Jeavons said. "How do you mean, *playing it close?*"

"Oh, I don't know exactly. He's taken a house in Bloomsbury when he could very likely afford something in Mayfair. I got the impression when we spoke at Arthur's yesterday that something was weighing on him. Something to do with what happened while he was in India."

Julian shook his head. "It's very difficult to know exactly what the EIC is engaged in there. As you say, Ashcombe was not part of that. Perhaps he left because the climate disagreed with him."

"Perhaps. But that wouldn't really account for what I witnessed at the club."

It seemed that Jeavons wanted to tell him something about Ashcombe. It could have nothing to do with him, and because of his growing feelings for Miss Ashcombe he feared too much unwelcome knowledge might put him in an awkward position. He'd only met Ashcombe once. But Julian's innate curiosity once again triumphed over his discretion. "And what would that be?" he asked.

"When a few know-nothings started talking about India as if they could judge all on the basis of months-old news he became almost irate, contradicting them and implying some kind of misconduct on the part of the Company. He spoke rather intemperately, I'm afraid."

Jeavons, Julian knew, was a conscientious peer who attended the House sittings and took part in many votes, at least the important ones. No doubt he had been present for the recent suspension of *habeas corpus* vote. It wasn't a great leap of understanding to detect that the viscount was uneasy about something Ashcombe had said, perhaps thinking he might have expressed sentiments that could get him in trouble. "Did anyone important hear him?"

"I think not, although I wasn't acquainted with all three of the men there. But I sense that Ashcombe's a bit of a powder keg. A very worthy man, sharp as whip, but he has, shall we say, ardently democratic ideas."

It was as Julian suspected. Ashcombe's friend wanted to protect him from potential difficulties, and for some reason appeared to have decided that Julian could possibly help. "I'm certain all will be well. As I understand it, the *habeas corpus* measure was enacted primarily to protect the industrial magnates in the north, as well as to give the Crown more teeth when dealing with seditious gatherings." He said it more because he wanted to reassure Jeavons than because he actually believed it presented no danger to people like Ashcombe.

"I expect you're right. Still, Thomas has been away a long time and likely isn't quite up to snuff socially and politically yet. If you know what I mean."

Julian did know what he meant. "As I said, I don't know the gentleman at all well. But if you—or he—are in need of my advice at any time, I'll gladly give it."

"You're a good fellow, Julian. So is Ashcombe. He'd make a kind and generous father-in-law." Jeavons nudged him playfully with his elbow.

I really must learn to make my face more inscrutable, Julian thought. He opened his mouth to deny any such ambition then thought better of it. Not that he really supposed there was any hope. But Dawlish! She couldn't be thinking of him. Could she?

"I assume you've received a card from Lady Lewiston for Miss Ashcombe's masquerade ball?" Jeavons said when Julian did not respond to his previous teasing.

"Yes. I don't know if I'll go, though."

"But you must! I'm convinced it would be the very thing for you. Masquerades, you know, provide a certain atmosphere free of inhibitions. It would also give you an opportunity to speak more with Ashcombe."

"I'll think about it," Julian said before the two men parted at the Stanhope Gate.

CHAPTER 12

t first, only a bandbox on the floor of the hall gave any evidence of visitors. But a moment after Fairing closed the front door behind Anjali, the door of the drawing room on the floor above burst open and a small figure flew out of it, all wide brown eyes and bright, rosy cheeks, sporting a dazzling smile that revealed even white teeth. Words bubbled out of her as she tripped lightly down the stairs. "You are Anjali! Belinda wrote to me. Atherleigh was already planning to be here for the House sitting, but as soon as I heard about you I decided I must come up to London as well."

She stopped abruptly as she reached the hall and gazed admiringly at Kavi. The myna had spread his wings in alarm at the sudden flurry of movement, but Anjali stroked his breast lightly and murmured, "It's all right, Kavi."

"Your bird—you called it Kavi? Is it a male or a female? What kind of bird? Aunt Caroline said something about a pet bird, but I expected him to be in a cage. May I come closer?"

Anjali remembered what Belinda had told her about her half-sister and her hawks and falcons. Those fierce creatures were not very like Kavi, but people who appreciated birds generally found something to like in most species. "Yes, of course. He's quite tired. We've been out for a drive in the park."

"Oh, I'm sorry I'm being so rude! I'm Lady Atherleigh. But you must call me Antonella."

"Not Lady Antonella?"

She shrugged her shoulders. "Apparently not! But I expect you've heard all about that."

Belinda hadn't said very much, only that she and Antonella had been raised believing they were twins, only to be told on their eighteenth birthday that they were not. She seemed anxious not to have to explain it all, and at the time Anjali didn't press her to give her any more information. "Kavi is an Indian myna bird. They are cheeky scavengers, eating mostly bits of fruit or egg, sometimes small insects. Not hunters, not meat eaters, like your raptors." She nudged Kavi onto her index finger and said, "Say hello to Antonella, Kavi."

After an introductory squawk, Kavi said *how d'ye do* all run together, but unmistakable nonetheless. Antonella grinned.

"He's a mimic." Anjali held Kavi out toward Antonella, who raised her hand. After a brief hesitation, the bird hopped over to her waiting finger, cocked his head to the side, then hopped back to Anjali's hand.

"Did you have to train him to speak? Did you raise him from an eyas—or a chick? I want to hear all about Kavi. He's so different from our hawks and falcons! They are not tame. They only tolerate us."

Anjali privately thought Kavi was no more tame than any other bird, but that he simply preferred his easy life with her. "Are birds ever truly tamed?" The two girls had started climbing the stairs together, and already Anjali felt as if she had met a kindred spirit in Lady Atherleigh. "Let me put Kavi back in his cage to rest, and then I'll come join you in the drawing room with Lady Lewiston. Kavi likes you!" Anjali could tell that Antonella was comfortable around birds, and Kavi sensed it too. Quite a relief after Dawlish's unease. "Soon he'll be saying your name."

Antonella laughed before leaving Anjali to continue up to the bedroom floor. Yes, it was apparent from the first instant that Kavi had nothing to fear from Antonella. Nor from anyone in that house, in fact. While not all the servants were as enthusiastic as Andrew, even Millie was growing used to Kavi, albeit still cautious. How could she tell Lady Lewiston that there was no likelihood that she would ever marry a man Kavi didn't like?

Not long after, Anjali entered the drawing room to find Lady Lewiston and Antonella seated side-by-side on the small sofa, clutching each other's hands and gazing at one another in what could only be described as joy. Never very expressive, Lady Lewiston had been transformed. Her eyes were wide and moist with tears, and her smile was broader and more unrestrained than Anjali had ever seen before.

"Anjali, I have had the most wonderful news. Lady Atherleigh is with child!" Her voice broke slightly at the end.

"How wonderful!" Anjali said and took a seat in the chair nearest to them. No wonder they were so happy. "This is not your first grandchild, I gather, My Lady. Lord Lewiston has a son, so Belinda told me."

"Yes," Lady Lewiston said. "And he's a fine, lusty infant. But there's something about one's daughters expecting that is somehow different." She lifted a hand and stroked Antonella's cheek.

Anjali was confused. Belinda had told her that Antonella wasn't Lady Lewiston's child. Without being given the entire story, Anjali deduced—since Belinda referred to her as her half sister—that they had a father in common. And since the two girls were of an age, clearly Antonella was the product of an illicit affair on the part of the late marquess. And yet, Lady Lewiston appeared to hold her in great affection. It was extraordinary. Only a moment before she had referred to Antonella as a daughter. Which, since she raised her from infancy, she must have been in all ways but one. Things in the *ton* certainly were a muddle.

"You've yet to meet Atherleigh—Malcolm, my husband," Antonella said once they'd finished chatting about the tedious journey from Cornwall and she shared some news about a former governess who was now married. "He went out immediately to the House. He says there's a very important debate at the moment, but that he hoped they would at least break for dinner and he would return. That's why I'm here instead of at Lewiston House. We'll go there together later."

"It's great good fortune that you have arrived today," Lady Lewiston said. "I haven't yet told Miss Ashcombe, but Harry and Olivia will be coming this evening, along with Belinda and Hector. Oh, and I thought that Mr. Ashcombe might as well join us and meet everyone at the same time."

Anjali could have sworn the dowager's cheeks grew a shade pinker when she said this last. "I would love nothing more than to be a guest at such a family gathering," she said. In truth, although she very much liked what she'd seen of Belinda and Antonella, Anjali had yet to meet the marquess and marchioness and was a little nervous. She was glad her father would be there. It would make her feel a little less like a jay in the nest of that noble family.

After another half hour of pleasant chat, they went upstairs to change for dinner. Change for dinner! And it wasn't simply a matter of freshening up, or adorning oneself a little more elegantly, perhaps with finer jewels, as it was in their home in Calcutta. She was expected to put on an entirely different sort of gown, one that was lower cut, had more embellishment perhaps and a demi train. Not to mention changing the arrangement of her hair. It was exhausting, this constant alteration. Morning dress. Walking dress. Carriage dress. Evening dress. Fortunately, Millie was well versed in all the niceties of a *ton* wardrobe and would not let Anjali leave her dressing room inappropriately garbed.

That evening, since it wasn't just herself and Lady Lewiston in the austerely formal dining room but all the Ambletons and their spouses who were in London, and therefore more of an occasion, she let Millie fuss more than usual with her hair and insist she wear some of the magnificent jewels she inherited from her mother. When she went down to meet the rest of Lady Lewiston's family, she would be decked in an emerald-and pearl-studded collar and bracelets and matching hair clips, and an amber silk gown that set off her creamy skin to perfection.

What she thought of these very British customs did not matter. She was in London now and, for her father's sake, she must do her best to fit in.

~

CAROLINE HADN'T SEEN THOMAS SINCE THE DAY AFTER THE Allston rout party and she was oddly nervous about entertaining him with her family. As far as she could tell, none of the children or their spouses knew the details of her history with him.

What she feared was that Thomas's return to England might awaken the gossips, ever on the lookout for something that would titillate the *ton*. The Ambleton family provided them with plenty to talk about last year, so she hoped greedy eyes were now focused elsewhere. With luck they would not remember that their names—hers and Thomas's—had ever been linked in any way, however unofficially. Her highly advantageous marriage had wiped out the recollection of other suitors, she hoped. No one would ever have suspected her of forming a lasting passion for the younger son of a younger son, however smart, imaginative, sensitive, and loving. Most members of the class she belonged to would be entirely incapable of understanding that she would have thrown her reputation to the winds if she hadn't believed that Thomas had forsaken her—for whatever noble reasons.

In her despair, she had agreed to the arranged marriage. It was just like so many others in the *ton:* relatively bloodless if not a love match. Only she knew that it had not been bloodless at all, that it tore her heart out and made her feel as if she could never be a whole human being again.

She'd buried all those painful memories and made the best of her life, no matter what Lewiston did to degrade her. But that wasn't fair. He did no more than so many men who believed that marriage was a duty, not an occasion for love.

Caroline gazed into her dressing table mirror as Falk brushed out her hair. She made a conscious effort to erase the frown that threatened to carve a permanent line between her eyebrows. The fact remained that despite all Lewiston's efforts to make her feel badly used, the small, mercurial creature who was more at home in the woods and with her birds than in a drawing room had worked her way into her heart. When the slip of a girl chose to potentially sacrifice her own happiness and reputation to protect Caroline's—in that dramatic moment on a Cornwall beach—she proved herself more than worthy of that regard and, yes, love.

Falk had laid out one of her evening gowns from last season, no doubt assuming that as it was just a family party she had no need to wear anything new. "That one?" Caroline said, standing and surveying the serviceable gown of puce satin with a silver sarsenet overdress. "In truth I'm a bit tired of it. I don't know why, but I thought I might wear the new pomona green lace and crepe, the one with the beading and the demi train."

"Are you certain, My Lady?" Falk asked. "You was thinking it might do for a dress party."

Caroline looked over her shoulder at her aging abigail, who had been with her from the beginning of her marriage and seen her weep into her pillow so many times. Their eyes met. Caroline said, "Yes, I'm certain. Besides, I can still wear it to a dress party. No one there will have seen it."

The gown in question was new and had been a bit of an extravagance. Although Caroline had enough money to live comfortably she was by no means wealthy. Her dowry had been tied up so it couldn't be gambled away, and the jointure was locked into the original settlement, so she had that income. Although sufficient to her personal needs, it had not been adequate to creditably launch the two girls into society with sufficiently handsome dowries. Her conscience pricked her from time to time when she recalled her manner of halving the projected expenses. Poor Antonella might have ended a spinster, a paid companion, had it not been for the good fortune that brought Atherleigh to Cornwall.

That, in part, was why it had been a point of honor for her now that she was on her own not to hang on her son's sleeve. Nevertheless, she justified the purchase of that luxurious gown because, as Anjali's sponsor, she would be attending more parties than she originally thought. It had nothing to do with Thomas, she assured herself.

By the time she entered the drawing room a half hour later, everyone else was already assembled, including

Thomas. He stood, immediately drawing her gaze as if he was the fulcrum around which the room revolved.

He stepped forward and bowed. "You look just like the seventeen-year-old girl I knew—except perhaps not quite as nervous."

"I think your eyes are beginning to fail you, Mr. Ashcombe!" she said, with a playful smile. Caroline might also have said that, despite all appearances, she was, in fact, nervous. The difference was that she had learned since her girlhood how to hide it better.

Once greetings had been exchanged all around, the nine individuals naturally divided into smaller groupings. The four young women soon formed a little conversational knot —something Caroline would have discouraged in any other setting. Let them be girls together for an evening, she thought. Even Olivia, who could hold herself a bit aloof— more out of reticence than any sense of superiority—talked animatedly and laughed with the others. That was as it should be. Anjali could use all the allies she could get as she embarked on the serious business of finding an appropriate match despite her disadvantages.

"They look as if they've known each other for a lifetime." Thomas's warm, deep voice startled Caroline out of her reverie.

"Yes. Who could have foreseen such a thing all those years ago." She turned to him, intending to simply strike up a light conversation, but something in his expression stopped her. "What is it?"

He shook his head. "It's of no moment. I was just thinking about a conversation I had at the club earlier."

"Oh? About what?" Caroline asked, but she wasn't certain she would want to know about anything gentlemen said to each other between the walls of those bastions of masculinity.

"India," Thomas said—and then, as if regretting revealing even this much, continued in a softened voice, "You really do look lovely this evening."

Before she could still her pulse enough to say anything coherent in reply, Fairing came to the door and announced dinner. Thomas put his arm out for Caroline to take, but precedence wouldn't allow her to do so. She smiled apologetically and took Harry's instead. Olivia and Atherleigh followed, but after that the precedence broke down. Belinda should have been next, but there was no other gentleman of rank to escort her in, and it wouldn't do for her to link arms with her own husband.

In the end, Thomas escorted Belinda and Hector took both Anjali and Antonella through to the dining room. Had there been any outsiders there it would have been awkward. But there weren't, and soon everyone was seated at the table conversing quietly with their neighbors and enjoying the feast Caroline's excellent chef had prepared.

Everything was going along well until Belinda asked, "Mr. Ashcombe, I don't think I ever heard the story of how you came to know Mama."

Silence engulfed the room. What would he say? Pray the Lord he would be discreet. Caroline studiously avoided looking at him.

Thomas smiled and cast a quick, reassuring glance in Caroline's direction. "It was a long time ago. Your mama was the undisputed diamond of the season. Of course I was smitten with her. But I was a distant star among so many, and the marquess naturally won her."

Belinda glanced curiously at her mother. Caroline did her best to present an unaffected countenance, and said, "Mr. Ashcombe is much too kind. My suitors were not so numerous, and there were many prettier girls making their come-outs that season."

"Besides," Thomas said, perhaps sensing that his uninformative reply hadn't satisfied anyone's curiosity, "I was heading to India and had no intention of leg-shackling myself before I went off to make my fortune!" A chuckle went around the room, and then he said, "I loved the Indian food, but the cooks out there couldn't do justice to any European dishes. Your chef deserves the highest praise for this meal."

No one pursued the matter after that, being too well bred to continue a line of conversation that was clearly not welcome.

THE AFTER-DINNER CONVERSATION WAS LIVELY AND interesting. Thomas found himself agreeably surprised by the current marquess as well as by Mr. Gainesworth and Lord Atherleigh, the husbands of Caroline's daughters. Of course Lady Atherleigh was more an adopted child, but Caroline treated the two of them equally well, not making any apparent distinction.

Indeed, the news that Lord and Lady Atherleigh were in expectation of a blessed event seemed to put Caroline in high gig, and was loudly celebrated by all.

Gainesworth was an affable fellow, very wealthy and of good family, but content to spend his days bringing pleasure to those he loved while at the same time enjoying himself immensely.

Atherleigh, on the other hand, was more self-contained, more serious. He'd been a military man until the wound that maimed him on the Peninsula, which Thomas assumed must have been what caused his relative withdrawal from society. That, along with the predilection for training and hunting hawks and falcons on his estate in Cornwall gave him the air of a relative outsider in the *ton*. Nonetheless, he took his responsibilities as a peer quite seriously. Although he didn't remain in town all through the session, Caroline told him that he traveled back and forth for the important debates and votes.

Everyone declined the offer of cards and games after dinner. They were far too engrossed in conversing to do something designed to fill a gap in social intercourse. Thomas was glad. He was far more interested in improving his acquaintance with Lord Atherleigh than in playing cards, for a number of reasons. Thomas was eager to discover whether Atherleigh had any direct contacts to the Board of Controllers and might help him gain an interview with one of them. But it would be a social solecism to bring up politics with all the ladies present, so he was at a loss concerning how to broach the subject.

Instead, once Anjali had done the honors of the tea tray, he sat down next to Atherleigh on one of the sofas and said, "Tell me about your mews, Atherleigh. Who takes care of the hawks while you and Lady Atherleigh are in London?"

"I have a most excellent falconer," he said, raising his cup of tea to his lips and sipping it.

Thomas thought for a moment. "I imagine that is not an easy position to fill in these times. Gone are the days when every estate worth its name possessed hunting birds. Now it's all shooting and riding to hounds."

Atherleigh chuckled softly. "As you say. But Rafiq has been with us since I was a boy. I hardly remember a time without him."

"That's an Indian name, I perceive. What is his history? His family?"

Thomas assumed the fellow would have been someone's servant on a short sojourn in India, part of an extended grand tour perhaps, so what Atherleigh said surprised him.

"He came from India to bring a rare falcon from the Punjab. My uncle had something to do with the East India Company —before it was established, mind, when the French were still fighting us for control of the region. He did a great service for a Mughal prince, I believe, and was given both the bird and the falconer as a gift."

The Punjab was many, many miles away from the India that Thomas knew. It was far to the west, in an area ruled by hereditary princes, and so far not under the administrative jurisdiction of the Company. "His name?"

"Ah, yes," Atherleigh said. "Rafiq Mirza."

Mirza! Thomas thought. That was no ordinary surname. Although he had never been to the Punjab, Thomas was familiar with the names of the noble families there. Could this humble falconer in fact be a near princeling himself? How odd to have agreed to uproot himself and take on a lowly position in the inhospitable English countryside. The service Atherleigh's uncle performed must have been very great indeed.

"You look as though the name means something to you," Atherleigh said.

He's perceptive, Thomas thought. "It does, although I am not personally acquainted with the family. Mirza is a very noble name among the great Muslim princes."

A broad grin spread over Atherleigh's face. "That doesn't surprise me in the least. Although in title Rafiq is my servant, he holds himself in high regard and expects the greatest respect from us all. Which, of course, we give him. He has an extraordinary way with the raptors."

"Has he never expressed a wish to return to India?" Thomas asked.

Atherleigh shook his head. "Not to me, at any rate. He's extremely fond of Antonella, although he does his best to hide that fact. Me, he tolerates. My wife can do no wrong where he is concerned."

"I'm curious, My Lord," Thomas said, shifting his position slightly. "Forgive me for raising this at this moment, but I don't know when we'll next have a quiet moment to talk. I'm hoping to make some connections with a few British merchants who have experience with the transfer of funds from Calcutta to London. I don't suppose you know anyone on the Board of Control who could tell me how best to make the right contacts at Leadenhall Street?" The last thing Thomas wanted to do was make Atherleigh suspect he had something potentially explosive to impart, and seeking financial advice seemed the best way to couch his inquiry.

"I'm afraid I cannot help you. My advice would be simply to go to India House and inquire there. Surely that would be the easiest course of action."

Easy, but dangerous, Thomas thought. Although he was tolerably certain he must have arrived in London before anyone involved had a chance to warn the London directors that he was in possession of information that could do material damage—to the Company itself as well as the government's view of it—he knew that time would be at an end sooner than he would like.

He wasn't ready to give up on finding a more direct way in, however. Anjali's ball was less than a week away. There would no doubt be many influential people there. If he didn't make a useful contact at the ball, he would risk turning up at India House, and hope he could find someone trustworthy there.

CHAPTER 13

The house on Upper Brook Street that was the home of the marquess and marchioness of Lewiston was much, much grander than Lady Lewiston's dower house. Double-fronted, with a galleried staircase, several large saloons, two drawing rooms, and Anjali didn't know how many bedchambers. It seemed rather ridiculously enormous to her. But when Belinda explained to her that Harry had bought it for Olivia because it had a ballroom that could be converted to a small opera house, which would give her opportunities to stage her own operas, she thought instead that it was a thoughtful tribute to his wife's love for music as well as his love for her.

"Someday I'll tell you that whole story. Antonella and I were in Cornwall when it all happened, but I promise you, it was quite a drama!"

It was in this elegant theatre that the girls met: Anjali, Olivia, Belinda, and Antonella, with the addition to their number of Lady Mariana and—to Anjali's immense surprise—Lady Bridlington. Surely they didn't need such a crowd to figure out what they would wear to the masquerade. One of the reasons they met there was because behind the stage was a warren of small rooms that included not only dressing rooms, but a larger chamber given over entirely to costumes. Anjali assumed they would each select something and then a seamstress would make the necessary adjustments to whatever they chose.

Apparently not.

Lady Mariana quickly took charge of everything. She had them sit on the benches at the front of the small pit while she stood on the stage and addressed them.

"Now, one or two of you may know that Lady Bridlington and I once attended a Covent Garden masked ball—not, I hasten to add, that I'd advise any of you to do the same—but it was at the beginning of our deep friendship, and I believe that evening was material in bringing my brother and my dear friend together. There is magic in a masquerade, to be sure, but only if you choose your disguise carefully.

"All of you know that Augusta—Lady Bridlington—is the talented designer behind Madam Pauline's modiste establishment. It seemed to me that it would be a shame not to make use of all the resources at our command for this delightful event. And because this is Anjali's big debut in London, Augusta and I have agreed that we must make it as memorable as possible."

At that point, she turned to face the curtain behind her, and a pretty young woman came bustling out accompanied by two footmen bearing not gowns, but bolts of silks in different colors and patterns, which she proceeded to lay out on the floor of the stage.

"*Bon! Eh voilà!*" the young woman said in a decidedly French accent.

"Thank you, Félicité," Mariana said, her face glowing with what Anjali could only describe as wicked glee. "What only Olivia knows is that Félicité was a dresser at the King's Theatre, and had the honor of costuming Olivia when she appeared there as the countess in *The Marriage of Figaro*."

Olivia hardly seemed like someone who would be comfortable standing on stage in front of thousands of people. Anjali turned to Belinda, a question in her eyes.

Belinda whispered, "She wore a mask," as if that would explain all.

Mariana waited for them to quiet and said, "I should like all of you to come up here and choose the materials that appeal to you, whatever the colors or designs. Don't worry about what they will be made up into yet. I have already selected mine, as has Augusta, but it doesn't matter if more than one of us chooses the same colors. Select at least two. Better three."

Casting puzzled glances at each other, the four younger ladies did as requested. It was like looking at a rainbow that had somehow been pinned to the earth. Anjali hadn't seen colors so rich and vibrant since visiting the bazaar in Calcutta. With a frisson of delight, she found herself drawn to the golds and oranges, adding a contrasting pink gauze with a tiny flower print to her selection. The combination reminded her of the sunset over the lake in Murshidabad.

After Belinda chose a palette of blues—from vibrant sapphire to the palest hint of a spring sky—Olivia selected ruby and emerald, and Antonella fixed on a varied combination of robin's egg blue, brown, and vibrant yellow, they all stood next to the bolts that the footmen had moved for them and waited expectantly for Mariana to say more.

"Now," she said, "Anjali, I need you."

Lady Mariana had a natural ability to command. Anjali went to her—she had no thought of not obeying.

"I believe the Indian women, such as your late mother,

wore very elegant garments of silk draped around them and beautifully adorned."

"Saris, yes," Anjali said with a sudden sinking feeling in her stomach. Did Mariana intend her to be put on display as a Hindu lady? She loved dressing in those whisper-soft clothes, but had no desire to stand out so obviously from the other guests, who would no doubt be wearing gowns from the previous century and fanciful concoctions from mythology. She wouldn't do it! It wasn't at all fair. How could she prevent this embarrassment? She screwed her courage up and said, "Lady Mariana, I beg you."

"What is it, Anjali?"

"You cannot expect me to dress as if I don't know how to go on in London society, but insist on clinging to the traditions of India. I don't think that Lady Lewiston would be at all pleased to have me attired so." Best to blame it on her sponsor, Anjali thought.

Mariana came to her, fixed her dark blue eyes on her and placed her hand gently on her cheek. "No, of course not! But we need you to instruct us about how these saris are worn and show Félicité how to construct them."

Anjali wrinkled her brow. What could she mean?

Mariana looked up and addressed everyone. "Félicité will make something superb and European for Anjali. The rest of us will attend the masquerade wearing saris."

Everyone started talking and laughing at once. Anjali said a silent thank you to the English God and to Ganesha for delivering her from what she thought would be an unpleasant situation, and smiled at Lady Mariana. If they'd had to leave Calcutta in unseemly haste without being able to adequately prepare for such a change, how fortunate she was to have ended up just here, in this circle of remarkable ladies. It was like her father to have the most thoughtful friends. Anjali couldn't help thinking that he and Lady Lewiston would have made a fine couple—although she was very glad her father chose her mother.

For the next two hours, Anjali imparted everything she knew about making a sari—which garment was at heart merely a long expanse of silk wound around the body in a way that was both alluring and modest. She pointed out that they would also need elaborate trimmings, and ideally gold bangles for their arms and hoops for their ears. She wouldn't suggest anything like nose rings or toe rings. Anjali imagined they would create quite enough of a stir as it was looking like a Hindu court set down in a proper British *ton* party.

She'd been anxious and apprehensive about the masquerade at first. Now she looked forward to it with enthusiasm, wondering what the French seamstress would concoct for her to wear.

But could all this be accomplished in less than a week? Somehow Anjali believed that Mariana could do almost anything she tried, and she smiled.

JULIAN WAS TEMPTED TO GO TO MISS ASHCOMBE'S masquerade ball wearing his robes and wig. Unfortunately, such things were frowned upon at the Inns of Court. Making light of the serious business of the law could be seen as provocative, to say the least.

This left him with a conundrum. Should he rely only on a domino and a mask, as no doubt many gentlemen would? Or should he try to think of some other costume, something that would truly disguise him so that he needn't be embarrassed. He could leave before midnight and avoid the unmasking.

Or he could simply not go at all. A younger Julian might have made that decision without a backward glance. Likewise a Julian who had not yet met Miss Ashcombe. There was the rub. Unlike the first time he saw her at a party, he had now been introduced to her, and therefore they could dance together. If he did not allow his identity to be known, would he be able to do that? Who could he ask?

Griggs. The chief clerk of his chambers seemed to know everything about everything and everyone. He was a stickler for etiquette as well, despite his assumption of familiarity with the junior barristers, and was forever taking one to task over a badly tied cravat or a slightly askew wig.

So although Julian had no cases pending that day, he left his lodgings in St. James's Street and went to the nearest hackney rank. "Holborn," he said to the jarvie, "Lincoln's Inn Fields."

At that hour the traffic was quite heavy, so it took longer than the usual fifteen minutes to get to his chambers. When he arrived, he was startled to find no one there. Normally one or two of the junior barristers were about, waiting for their solicitors to bring them cases, and certainly being the clerk, Mr. Griggs would be in his office with his door open, alive to the possibility of work for any of the barristers.

But none of this was in evidence. At last Julian spotted Kit Dawes, a runner, living up to his job description by scurrying down the corridor. "Dawes!" he called.

Without stopping, Dawes craned his head around. When he registered who it was, he came to a screeching halt. "Yes, Sir Julian," he said with a quick, deferential duck of his head.

"Where's everyone gone?" Julian asked.

"They've all gone down the Grecian," he said, not waiting to explain more, and before another moment had passed he disappeared around a corner.

He had said enough, however. The Grecian was a venerable coffee house in Devereux Court where the legal fraternity often gathered to discuss matters in an informal setting.

Although he didn't know for certain what had sent his entire chambers out at that hour, Julian could guess.

He left as quickly as he'd come and soon found himself seated on a hard wooden bench along with the three junior barristers, Griggs, and Chislehurst himself. As he predicted, the topic on everybody's mind was Parliament's passing of the Suspension of Habeas Corpus Act.

"What's at issue here is that it changes how we are empowered to act should one of our clients come afoul of this ridiculous law," Chiselhurst said with uncharacteristic vehemence.

Davenant, who in his usual way lounged negligently with one leg over the other, said, "I don't see that we have any clients who would be affected. I say it's a necessary step to thwart sedition and riot. Our merchants and pickpockets would hardly be likely to be seen as a threat to national security."

The other junior barristers chuckled, and there was a noticeable easing of tension in the group. Then Julian said, "Yes, but what if one of those pickpockets laid his hands unknowingly on a pamphlet deemed inflammatory by someone? Or if one of our merchants, especially those with foreign connections, found that his money had passed through an intermediary also employed by an insurrectionist faction, or that one of his innocuous letters had been misinterpreted? Worse, what if his enemies used the act for retribution of some kind? What then? How could we defend him if he is wrongfully arrested and no charges are brought?"

"As usual, Meredith, you have delved right to the nub of the issue. We can't. All we could do in such an instance would be to write opinions and petition the Home Office to review the case," Chiselhurst said, casting a sobering pall over the gathering.

Of course, Griggs was never one to remain silent. "Seems

to me, Mr. Chiselhurst, it's best we find out—or get our solicitors to find out—which of their clients might be most at risk here, so's we can be prepared in advance if they're nicked."

Peter Brackenbury, the youngest of the barristers and still keeping terms, cleared his throat nervously before saying, "And what, if I may ask, are the factors likely to put someone who is otherwise acting lawfully at risk of coming afoul of this act?"

"I think that's the question we must all ask. I put it to you that every one of us should write an opinion—just for the chambers, mind you—about the different things that might throw suspicion on the kinds of men we normally defend." He took a long pull on his pipe and blew out a plume of smoke before saying, "Once we have that, we can then start working on how we would go about defending them if the worst were to happen."

Julian's mind was whirring already, the words and sentences forming themselves before his eyes. Something struck him so forcibly about those who might be at risk because of this legislation that he almost forgot why he had come to seek Griggs out.

The conclave was breaking up, so Julian said to Griggs, "Walk back to chambers with you, old chap?"

Griggs narrowed his eyes at him. "What is it you want?"

"Only a bit of advice." Julian flicked his eyes around at the assembled company, hoping to convey that he'd rather other people didn't hear what he was going to ask.

They walked slowly back, and Julian put his question to the clerk.

"Why are you in such a fuss about this? Just wear a domino and be done with it," Griggs said, flicking a bit of dust off his sleeve.

"I suppose I could. But I was hoping for something a little more … a little less …"

"So, do you want people to know who you are or do you want to be the mysterious stranger? It's not like you to put yerself out in society, so I'd guess it's the other one." They walked on in silence for a bit. "Who is she?"

Julian wanted to deny all possibility that there was any question of a female in the case, but his ever-responsive complexion would have made him a liar. "I-I'd rather not say."

"What, is the shy, confirmed bachelor Sir Julian Meredith contemplating becoming a tenant for life?"

Julian looked around quickly. The clerk had spoken uncomfortably loudly. "No! I don't know. She wouldn't have me anyway."

His obvious panic made the clerk soften his tone. "Ye're the most brilliant barrister in this chambers, if you just knowed it. It's beyond my powers of comprehension to understand why you think so ill of yerself. Be bold! What do you think the lady would like? Is there sommat about her that's unusual?"

"She's half Indian."

Griggs gave a low whistle. "Well. I hope she's worth it. But there's yer answer. Get yerself up like a pasha, or a mogul, or one of them."

"Do you really think so?" Julian was doubtful, in part because he couldn't imagine himself being so bold, in part because something inside him suspected that to do so would belittle Miss Ashcombe's heritage.

"Course I do! Get yerself to the costume warehouse and see what they can furnish. Ye'll bowl her out."

They parted, but Julian was not entirely certain he'd been given any useful advice. Oh well, he thought. Perhaps Griggs knows best.

CHAPTER 14

*H*er daughters had been very quiet about what they planned to wear to Anjali's ball. All Caroline knew was that they had the help of Lady Mariana and Lady Bridlington—a fact that both reassured and alarmed her. The two women had impeccable taste. They had also engaged in some rather scandalous hijinks before they were married. She was too busy with all the other arrangements to concern herself overmuch with that one aspect, however. All the organization fell on her shoulders—which was appropriate. Anjali was her protégée, after all. And her daughter-in-law was preoccupied with her little boy, aside from the fact that Olivia was never much of a one for planning parties—other than the theatricals and musical events that gave her and Harry such pleasure.

Besides, if Anjali's costume was anything to go by, then she was genuinely eager to see how they would all appear. Lady Bridlington had titled Anjali's dress *Aurora*. It fell in layers of silk of different textures and degrees of translucence—sarsenet, gauze, crepe, satin—in shades that mimicked the morning sky. The layers began just below her bust and ended in the demi-train that whispered along the floor when she moved. The tiara she wore was one that Thomas had brought over from his strongbox, all gold filigree with amber beads set into the points. It was from her mother's family. Although it was unlike a traditional British tiara, it was every bit as impressive and it completed the effect. Anjali was the image of the sunrise on a beautiful morning. Breathtaking.

Lord Dawlish had sent a bouquet to Anjali for the evening—a polite act, but rather inconvenient. As it was made up of pale pink flowers, she could not carry it to the ball. It would look terrible with her gold and amber. It would be for Caroline to smooth things over with him without giving any offense.

Caroline's "costume" could be loosely interpreted as representing the Roman goddess Juno. The choice was a subtle one. She wore rich blue silk, her diadem was trimmed with a peacock-feather jeweled motif, and she carried a peacock feather fan. Standing next to Anjali at the top of the stairs, she felt as if she served as the quiet backdrop to the girl's magnificence. If the guests weren't awed by this self-possessed, beautiful young lady, who unapologetically managed to be exactly who she was, then they weren't worth knowing.

Of course, Caroline was well aware that the surprising number of acceptances had arisen in many cases out of sheer curiosity to see who was this Indian—half Indian—girl sponsored by a lady accustomed to moving in the first circles. What did that signify, after all? Were there second circles, or third circles? It made her world sound like Dante's hell. In all honesty, existing in that elite circle had at one time become a sort of hell for her. At least, it had not made her happy in any real sense.

But she was being melodramatic. She was content

enough, and found fulfillment in fostering the lives of her children. That was adequate. It was all any lady truly had any right to hope for.

The stream of guests flowing into the masquerade gradually dwindled to a trickle, just before Caroline thought her hand would be shaken off her wrist. It was time for her to release Anjali to the party so she could open the ball with Lord Dawlish, who had arrived in a conventional domino and half mask, all smiles and artificial mystery. Anjali responded politely to his attempt at playfulness, but Caroline could tell her heart wasn't in it.

And still Caroline had not seen her daughters or daughter-in-law. They had told her that they all planned to dress at Lewiston House so she knew they would not be arriving through the front door. Yet where were they? It was high time for them to join the guests. Lady Mariana and Augusta Bridlington were also notably absent. This strange delay began to make Caroline a little uncomfortable. What had they planned?

She and Anjali entered the large saloon where Mr. Ashcombe, who had been conversing with Atherleigh and Gainesworth, soon joined her. His simple domino and mask did little to disguise his identity, so Caroline greeted him with no pretense.

Lord Dawlish had seen them enter and was making his way through the crowd to reach them. Anjali saw this at the same time as Caroline did and said, "Excuse me, My Lady, but I find I must adjust one of the layers of my costume. I shall go and find Félicité, the seamstress, to help me. She will be in the ballroom, as the dancing hasn't started yet."

"Of course, my dear, if you must." Why was she running off just now, when her only viable suitor clearly wanted to speak with her? "But don't be long. I believe the dancing will start soon. Your dance card, I see, is already quite full!" It had pleased Caroline to see how many of the young gentlemen they'd greeted on the stairs asked for the favor of a dance. Dawlish claimed the first and one other, but no one had yet put their names to the waltzes or the supper dance—or, she suspected, had been allowed to. Perhaps Anjali didn't want to waltz. But she must have someone to take her in to supper.

Not long after Anjali left her with Thomas, Fairing—who had come from the dower house to swell the ranks of the servants for this important event—announced in his deep, resonant voice, "The presence of all the guests is requested in the ballroom." He then stood by the open door and waved people through. When a knot of chaperones continued sitting in the corner and chatting, he went to them and quietly said, "If you please, ladies."

They looked at him as if he must be mad, but something —Caroline guessed curiosity—made them obey his thinly veiled command.

The ballroom/theatre was large, despite the fact that the stage and the rooms behind it took up about a quarter of the space that was originally there. Even so, it took some doing to fit all the guests in, since normally at least half of those invited would not be dancing, either out of inclination or lack of opportunity.

The room had been designed with the ear as much as the eye, and conversations that would have been muffled in a drawing room filled the space with noise. Caroline turned to Thomas and asked, "Whatever can be happening here? I never suggested we do this." She was becoming irritated. It seemed rather impolite to cram everyone into one room at a party of this size.

In addition to its quality as an acoustic jewel, Olivia had insisted on an innovation for her small theatre, one which the large public theatres had not adopted. Beyond being able to lower a scenic backdrop behind the singers in her intimate, private operas, she had had a heavy velvet curtain installed not at the back of the stage, but at the front. This curtain would remain closed until the beginning of a performance, thus creating a spectacular moment of revelation when it was opened on an opera's setting.

At that moment, Lady Bridlington walked out from the side of the stage to stand in front of the curtain. Everyone gasped. She wore not a typical masquerade costume—no figure from history or mythology, no shepherdess or milkmaid—but instead she had on a garment of magnificent embroidered silk, wound skillfully around her form and draped over one shoulder and her head. She slightly extended one slim leg to reveal close-fitting pantaloons above delicately jeweled slippers before addressing the audience. Caroline was aware of Thomas stiffening as he stood next to her.

"In honor of this occasion, the ladies of the house of Lewiston would like to present a living picture."

At that, she backed away to the side and gestured a lavishly bangled arm toward the center of the stage. Unseen by the audience, lackeys pulled the ropes that opened the curtains.

A unified gasp went up from the guests, followed by an immediate buzz of conversation. The parting curtain revealed a tableau of rising steps leading to a painted structure with arches and minarets behind them. Antonella, Belinda, Lady Mary, and Olivia were posed at separate levels on these steps, Belinda at the base, looking down and smiling at something below her, trailing her hand as through water, which had been cleverly represented by a muted expanse of blue silk that was being gently undulated from either side by the lackeys who had opened the curtains. The others were similarly frozen in attitudes of suspended action, for all the world as if they'd been painted there.

Lady Bridlington held up her hand and waited for the chatter to die down.

"Behold the Steps at Benares, on the Ganges River, adorned by Lady Belinda, Lady Atherleigh, Lady Mariana Thorne, and the Marchioness of Lewiston. They await the arrival of Miss Anjali Ashcombe, who has traveled far to grace us with her presence."

At the end of this short speech, the ladies parted to reveal Anjali climbing up behind them until she stood on the top step, taller than everyone else, and after standing still for a breath, she sank into a graceful curtsy, head modestly bowed. The lights at the foot of the stage imbued the entire scene with a magical glow, and everyone in the room began to applaud.

Caroline wasn't certain whether to be thrilled or deeply shocked. The English ladies were all garbed as Lady Bridlington was, in diaphanous, clinging silk wraps with pantaloons underneath, their limbs, ears, and hair lavishly adorned with jewels. The only one of them not wearing a costume that might have come off the ship from India was Anjali herself. *How clever,* Caroline thought. No doubt the evening would be the talk of the town tomorrow.

Talk, she realized, that could go one way or the other. She hoped against hope that this display of warm support for Anjali's position in society by five young women at the very heart of the fashionable world would incline the *ton* to be charmed and entertained rather than scandalized. She cast surreptitious glances around, and to her relief, smiles predominated. In the back of the crowd she briefly spotted Lord Dawlish. He wasn't smiling. But then, Caroline thought, he was rather a dour person generally. Still, she wondered what effect this open embracing of Anjali's distinct heritage would have on a gentleman everyone knew to be a bit of a high stickler. To be honest, Caroline wasn't completely certain why the baron was attempting to court Anjali. Although he would make an eminently suitable husband, something told Caroline that having someone like Anjali as a wife would not suit *him*.

By then, all four ladies had descended the stairs and begun to mingle with the other guests, and the quintet in the balcony began to tune their instruments for the first dance.

"I love to watch Anjali dance, but I find I am rather nervous. Would you accompany me to the saloon, Lady Lewiston?" Ashcombe said quietly into her ear, his warm breath making her shiver.

She smiled up at him and took his arm. "If at least half the guests don't leave this room there will be no space for dancing! Shall we lead the way?"

After he opened the large box that had just been delivered to his lodgings and saw its contents, Julian seriously considered not attending Miss Ashcombe's masquerade ball at all. The attendant at the warehouse assured him the costume would be just the thing to make him look like a *proper eastern gent*. Julian had tried to convey more specifically what he wanted, stressing that it should be authentically Indian in nature, but the fellow simply winked at him and said, "Don't you worry about nuffin' guv! Ye'll be all the crack—I got just the thing fer ye."

What had made him take the man at his word? He stared down into the box at something that looked like it was designed for a clown at Astley's Amphitheatre. Somewhere in its conception, he supposed, was a passing nod to an Indian gentleman, but the vague outlines had been explosively exaggerated to include a gaudy, spangled knee-length coat of rather tarnished-looking gold cloth that winged out absurdly on the sides, and a turban that was so large and had such an enormous jewel pinned to its front that—aside from the fact that it nearly overbalanced him—would make him look like a giant from well across the ballroom.

With a vague hope that there would be something salvageable in the box, Julian emptied it completely, strewing item after unsuitable item around his bedchamber.

No. He could not wear this atrocious costume to a ball given for the lady he loved.

The lady he loved. Did he just think that? How could such a thing be even remotely true? They'd spoken only a few times. But those times had been warm with shared insights and common interests. Or perhaps he'd made too much of them. Just because Miss Ashcombe understood how to manage Bramble and kept a fascinating bird was hardly enough on which to base such a rash, unaccustomed feeling.

To be honest with himself, it was more than that. A number of small things added up to make him feel that way. She seemed to sense his discomfort when he came to the house and simply and naturally put him at his ease. Her eyes lit up when she saw him in the park, and the way she climbed down from Dawlish's curricle without a second thought was a spontaneous and joyful action. Surely she didn't just do it because Kavi flew to him. She seemed delighted that the bird, in his way, accepted him.

And when she came closer, her eyes. He would never tire of gazing into those wide, intelligent eyes with a glint of humor behind them. In their brief acquaintance he had the impression that she had more varied interests than the majority of *ton* debutantes, that she wasn't even afraid to discuss politics and knew enough to do so sensibly. Julian wished more than anything that he could just spend time with Miss Ashcombe. How extraordinary it would be to sit with her in the same room without ceremony or propriety to get in the way of saying whatever they thought to each other. But he also knew it wasn't just his mind that she engaged. A flood of unfamiliar yet pleasurable feelings washed over him whenever she was near—feelings that nearly robbed him of the ability to speak.

None of this helped him with his immediate conundrum, however. It only made him more convinced that he must find a different solution. This costume would be an insult to her. It lampooned the country that clearly held an important place in her heart. The country of her mother's family.

"Addison!" Julian called.

His valet emerged from the small office he occupied behind Julian's dressing room. "Yes sir?" he said, then cast a horrified eye over the discarded costume elements that littered the room. "I thought you was getting dressed in your costume for the ball. It's late, sir."

"Yes, I know Addison. But I can't wear this! What can I do?"

Addison picked up the coat and held it to the light, his nose wrinkled in disgust. "No indeed, sir. This will never do."

"What can I wear instead? I have no domino and it's too late to procure any other costume. I don't even have a mask."

Addison pursed his lips and stroked the tip of his nose with his finger. Julian waited. His valet never failed to find a solution to a problem when he adopted that expression.

"I believe you have a pair of black stockings that you have worn through. I put them in the basket for rags. But I can easily fashion a simple mask from them." Addison hastened away without waiting for Julian to respond, and returned a minute later with the ruined stockings, a pair of scissors, and a needle and thread.

"I say, Addison. I don't expect you to make anything for me."

Addison shrugged. "It's no more difficult than sewing on a button or mending a cuff."

"I suppose not, but then what?" That would solve only one part of the costume problem. *I can't go,* Julian thought. And then, *but I must, cost what it may.* "That's what I'll do," he said.

Addison looked up expectantly, already having attached the two stockings together and wrapped them around Julian's head to ascertain where to cut the eyeholes.

"Evening dress. Black coat, white waistcoat, black stockings. The plainer the better. I don't want to call attention to myself. But it would be rude to simply stay away."

And so, at five minutes past eleven o'clock that evening, a hackney deposited Julian at the house in Upper Brook Street. Sounds of revelry spilled out as soon as the footman opened the door and ushered him in. He walked up the grand stair and gave his name to another footman at the door of the saloon.

The liveried servant pulled himself up to his full height and said in stentorian accents, "Sir Julian Meredith."

A temporary hush settled over those who were near enough to hear the announcement. Although it wasn't exactly a social solecism to come to a masquerade without a costume of any kind, every single person in that saloon was either dressed as a character or wearing an elegant domino. Julian had assumed he'd be in the minority, but not that he might be the only gentleman who had not entered into the spirit of the evening.

Fortunately, a footman approached with a tray of glasses of champagne, and he took one, wishing it were brandy instead.

Of course, there was no sign of Miss Ashcombe. She was no doubt dancing in the ballroom. Julian had been in this house often before. He and Lewiston were friends who shared a love of music. He'd attended a private performance of *La Clemenza di Tito* with Lady Lewiston singing the soprano role in her glorious voice a few months ago. That evening, however, the theatre was given over to its original purpose. He could tell even from hearing just a few snatches of melodies that Harry had engaged an excellent ensemble, perhaps some of the musicians from the Philharmonic Society. He had an idea of wandering in that direction in the hope of encountering Miss Ashcombe. If nothing else, he could enjoy listening to the music. And somewhere in this crush there must be someone he knew.

CHAPTER 15

At first when he saw the young ladies all wearing saris in such an incongruous place, Thomas worried that his daughter's grand debut would become a travesty, that her parentage would end by being an inconvenient focus of the evening. But he underestimated not only the social skills of these young women, but their bred-in-the-bone air of quality, their unerring instinct for the balance of the remarkable and the tasteful. And when Anjali walked among her improvised court as the embodiment of dawn, he saw in an instant what it was that Lady Mariana achieved with this theatrical flourish, and the tension left his shoulders. Anjali still reminded him forcibly of Shanta. But she did so as an echo, a reminiscence. She was her own unique self.

He took the floor with Caroline for one dance, a cotillion, intending it only to be an expression of respect for all the effort and thought she had put into this important evening. But something about the atmosphere, the ebullient gaiety, took him back thirty years to the first time he saw Lady Caroline, daughter of an earl, at Almack's. How young they both were! He'd been lost from the instant their eyes met.

Thomas looked directly into Caroline's eyes now when the movement of the dance brought them together. Yes. She was still there, that girl, and the knowledge of that touched him somewhere deep in his heart.

Foolish to think of that now, he told himself. Events at the time had proven it to be an illusion and if anything, all that had happened since then only pushed it farther into the distant recesses of his mind.

After their one dance, hostess duties called Caroline away from the ballroom, and Thomas began to meander amongst those who were not dancing. They were mostly older, except for a few very shy young gentlemen and Atherleigh, who did not take the floor because having only one hand made it difficult for him to enter fully into the figures of a dance. Thomas walked over to where the baron, wearing a red domino and a mask that covered only his eyes, stood talking to another man dressed as a highwayman—stained buckskins, a homespun black waistcoat, pistols tucked into a scarlet sash at his waist, and a black mask that covered his face down to his mouth.

Atherleigh said, "Ah! Ashcombe! I was about to come and look for you. This gentleman, whose acquaintance I have made just this evening, says he's a friend of yours."

Thomas stared hard at the face for a moment. He was at a loss as to who it could be and began thinking back to the days before he went to India, to no avail. Then the man broke into a broad grin, and Thomas exclaimed, "Lascelles! How the devil? I beg pardon, I mean, you're the last person I expected to see in London. What brings you here?"

The two men shook hands heartily and Atherleigh wandered discreetly away.

"This is quite the do," Lascelles said, sweeping his arm to encompass the entire room. "And Miss Ashcombe is looking lovelier than ever. Has she already taken the *ton* by storm?"

"Of course, through my eyes she could never fail to. But it's early days yet. I'd forgotten how judgmental the *ton* can be, how one must watch one's step and be so aware of the proprieties."

"Come, Thomas, the British in Calcutta are just as bad. You chose not to make that community the center of your life, that's all."

Thomas snatched two glasses of champagne off the tray of a passing footman and gave one to Lascelles. "Let's find somewhere to sit and you can tell me what's been happening since I left. Of course, you must have boarded the next outbound ship yourself. I don't recall that you had plans to do so. What happened?"

"Oh, one of Hastings's secretaries desired me to carry a letter to India House. He tried to get Gordon to do it, but the fellow came down with a nasty bout of tertian fever."

The two men wandered off in search of a quiet corner where they could talk privately without being thought impolite. Having found two chairs in an alcove in a smaller drawing room where card tables had been set up but were not yet occupied, they continued their conversation.

"So," Thomas said, "I didn't know you were so connected with Hastings. I thought you shared my view of the situation." The two men had polished off the better part of a bottle of fine French brandy one night after dinner in Calcutta where they had spoken frankly and at length about the deteriorating situation there. Deteriorating for the Indians that is. The British were going from strength to strength, getting more and more regions under their administrative control—mostly without armed conflict at that time.

Lascelles said, "Isn't it midnight yet? I'd like to remove this infernal mask. It's deuced hot in here."

"An hour at least until then," Thomas said, noting that

Lascelles had not answered his question. And then he thought of something else. "How is it that you are here this evening? You can't have been invited on your own account. Lady Lewiston does not know you."

"I'm racked up at Vennor's place in Bond Street. He's somewhere hereabouts. He insisted I come, said that no one ever minds an extra gentleman at these things, so long as he's well born and well behaved."

"Vennor … His father went out to India more than fifty years ago, I think." Although Thomas hadn't noticed the name on the list of guests that Caroline showed him, he assumed it had been added later.

In response to the implied question, Lascelles said, "We were at school together. Eton. He's the one who put the idea of India into my head, although I didn't go out for some years after that. I thought I could be of use, do some good."

Victor Lascelles had arrived in India eight years ago as part of the EIC contingent, but unlike many of the officials, he was not interested in exploiting the Indian manufacturers and traders. Younger than Thomas, Lascelles successfully managed to keep one foot in the Company and one in the community of independent traders. That made him a very useful man to know. He was also handsome and charming, a fact that ensured he would be invited to every social occasion in the vicinity of Calcutta.

Aware, as the honoree's father, that he could not sit talking to an acquaintance for any length of time and that he had a duty to perform, Thomas said, "Come! Let me see if Anjali is not dancing. She will be delighted to see you, I'm certain. And I should like to introduce you to Lady Lewiston as well." Thomas had not told Lascelles about his history with Caroline, only claiming her as a friend of the family when he explained to him before leaving Calcutta that he hoped to place his daughter under her chaperonage.

Whatever had brought Lascelles to London and to the ball, Thomas was glad to see the fellow. He'd been so preoccupied with the matters that sent him to London that he failed to realize how much he missed life in Calcutta—being able to talk to someone who was intimately acquainted with the city made him feel a little less stranded in a sea of potentially hostile people.

It also occurred to him that what Lascelles knew about the inner workings of the company could help him channel his information to the most receptive ear in London. But that evening was not for business. The focus must remain on Anjali and her prospects.

Anjali and Dawlish had worked their way to the bottom of the set, and Anjali was heartily glad. Although polite to a fault, Dawlish's conversation appeared limited to the weather and the first Ascot races. In fact, the only subject that truly animated him was horses.

The ensemble played the reverence and Anjali curtsied and allowed Dawlish to take her hand and lead her off the floor. The next dance was to be a waltz, and she had deliberately guarded that particular spot on her dance card, not for any reason, she told herself, except that she'd seen no one at the ball in whose arms she wished to parade around the floor.

"May I fetch you a glass of lemonade?" Dawlish said in his unfailingly pleasant voice.

Just as Anjali was about to answer in the affirmative—eager to send him away without being rude—she spotted a tall figure across the ballroom, remarkable in that he wore no costume. A makeshift travesty of a mask covered his eyes, and he kept touching it to keep it from falling down.

Sir Julian! Without thinking of what anyone would say, Anjali left Dawlish abruptly and flitted across the dance floor to where he stood. She didn't know whether she felt more like scolding him for so flagrantly ignoring the conventions of a costume ball or greeting him with relief. At last, someone she could really talk to about something other than sporting pursuits or fashions.

Sir Julian looked to his left and right as if he thought she must be coming to greet someone standing next to him.

Anjali was less than a yard away from him when she came to a sudden halt, her face warming when she realized she must seem very brazen to have singled Sir Julian out in that manner. Nonetheless, it was done. "Sir Julian! I did not see you earlier," she said, feeling the complete inadequacy of her remark.

He bowed over her extended hand. "I-I'm afraid I was late. Something prevented my arriving sooner." He turned as pink-faced as a maiden at her first party.

"I see you've left Bramble at home," Anjali said and smiled. It was the first thing she could think of that might break through the tension between them.

"What? Oh, yes, of course. Although he would have loved to come. And no Kavi this evening?" Already his high color was beginning to fade.

Anjali laughed. "Kavi would hate this. Too many people, too much noise."

"You look beautiful." Sir Julian blurted out the words as if he'd been bottling them up and all it needed was for him to open his mouth and they would come spilling out.

It was Anjali's turn to blush. "I'm supposed to be Aurora. It was Lady Bridlington's idea." She wanted to say, *so do you look beautiful* to Sir Julian, who—despite his very sober evening dress—inexorably drew her eyes. Was it those dark red curls? Or the fact that among so many outlandish costumes he could not fail to be noticed for his absence of display? No, it had to be the intense gaze of his green eyes, so extraordinary a color with so much depth and complexity. She pulled herself together and said, "I believe at a ball it is customary to dance." She fingered her dance card in supposed absence of mind.

"Forgive me! W-would you care to stand up with me in the next dance, Miss Ashcombe?" Sir Julian said. "If you're not already engaged, that is. I hardly dare hope, at this point—"

"I am not engaged, and would be delighted," Anjali said, just as the master of ceremonies announced the waltz.

Julian's eyes widened and he said, "Are you certain?" which startled Anjali. Did he not want to waltz with her?

"Yes," she said, boldly reaching for his hand to make him lead her out to the floor. His trembled, and Anjali was afraid she had embarrassed him, which was the last thing she wanted to do. But she did, truly, wish to waltz with him. It struck her with almost overwhelming force that, though she had not realized it, she'd been saving the two waltzes and the supper dance for him alone. When there was no sign of Sir Julian for more than an hour, she began to resign herself to having to accept some other gentleman's embrace in that most intimate of socially acceptable dances.

Then it occurred to her that perhaps Sir Julian did not know the steps of the waltz, and she wished she had not been so insistent. But in contrast to his stumbling words, Sir Julian held her with confidence and led her around the floor with all the flourishes and grace the waltz demanded. Anjali wanted to close her eyes and simply feel the movement, feel his hand firmly on her waist, let Sir Julian guide her through the throng of dancers, spinning and swirling in their wildly varied costumes. But of course she could not. She stifled a giggle when she caught sight of a couple nearby, the lady of which was desperately trying to maneuver her wide, old-fashioned panniers so they did not hit anyone else around her. When her partner went to twirl her around, she shook her head vigorously and mouthed, "No!" because of course, that would have been disastrous.

Also on the dance floor were Lady Henrietta and Dawlish. The baron looked down into his partner's eyes with an expression that revealed much more interest than it had when he danced with Anjali. In response, Lady Henrietta quite consciously lowered her eyelids and tipped down her chin so that she could look up at him through her lashes. She must have sensed Anjali watching her for an instant and after a quick glance in her direction, altered her own attitude to be less coquettish.

Ah, Anjali thought. *So why in heaven's name is Dawlish making up to me?*

Unlike the country dance in which Lord Dawlish was her partner, the waltz ended all too quickly for Anjali. Fortunately, the ensemble would take a brief break after it, so she needn't be claimed immediately by Dawlish, whose second dance, a cotillion, was next.

"My papa is here, and I'm certain he would wish to say hello to you," Anjali said to Sir Julian. "Shall we see if we can find him in one of the saloons? This house is enormous though, and I barely know my way around it."

Sir Julian put out his arm and she laid her gloved hand on top of it. "I've been here often. Lewiston is a friend. We have many interests in common."

Before she could lead him away, however, a stranger approached her. At least, she thought he was a stranger. He moved with loose-limbed confidence, as though he had every expectation of a welcome. He was dressed as a highwayman, right to the horse pistols tucked into his belt. It took her a moment because of the disguise, but she finally recognized him. How could it possibly be? He was completely out of context. No wonder she didn't recognize him right away. It was her father's friend from Calcutta, Mr. Lascelles.

"Miss Ashcombe! I have found you at last. I have just been speaking with your father, who was as surprised to see me as I can see by your expression you are as well."

"Mr. Lascelles! What are you doing here?" She turned back to Sir Julian, sending him an apologetic look. "I'm sorry, allow me to present my friend Mr. Victor Lascelles to you. Mr. Lascelles, this is Sir Julian Meredith. Mr. Lascelles and I know each other from Calcutta."

The two men bowed to each other with civility.

Sir Julian said, "I shall leave you to talk of home while I fetch some lemonade for you," and before Anjali could protest, he walked off. She hadn't intended for him to go away, and was aware of feeling intensely disappointed.

"I didn't mean to frighten away an admirer," Lascelles said, with an expression behind his black mask that made her think he, unlike her, wasn't at all sorry Sir Julian had gone away.

"I assure you—" she started to say, when Lascelles interrupted her.

"Who could help but admire you, Miss Ashcombe. I don't think I've ever seen you look so ravishing."

His words of flattery made her vaguely uncomfortable. He never flirted with her in Calcutta. Why did he do so now? She'd known him since she was a girl of twelve. "I'm sure Sir Julian will return shortly. But you haven't answered my question! How is it you are here?"

"Need you ask? Calcutta has been desolate without the vivacious Miss Ashcombe to liven up the tedious entertainments offered by my countrymen." He lifted his mask, although it wasn't yet midnight, and tucked her hand into his arm. "Alas, I am not come on a pleasure visit. It's all business,

I'm afraid. But I won't bore you with such nonsense. I don't suppose you have any spots on your dance card still available?" He snatched it and pulled her wrist toward him before she could lie and say she was fully engaged. "The supper dance! How fortuitous. I would be honored to take you in. Your father can join us, if you like."

He wrote his name in the empty space, and Anjali's disappointment sharpened as she resigned herself to not being able to enjoy a few moments of conversation with Sir Julian during supper. Why Mr. Lascelles should be so determined to dance with her she couldn't imagine. He was much too old to be a potential suitor. In his mid-thirties at least, and not even a score of years younger than her father.

She had little time to ponder the matter, however. Lord Dawlish came back to claim her for his second dance. Anjali introduced them briefly and took note of Lascelles's expression as he eyed the baron in a measuring way.

She placed her gloved hand in Dawlish's so he could lead her into the cotillion, a dance she normally enjoyed, but was now secretly dreading. Anjali couldn't have said exactly why, but she had taken the very-correct peer in aversion, if not outright dislike.

Her reasons, however, crystallized in the course of the dance with him. When they first came together for a few moments, Dawlish said, "You must be quite relieved to be amidst civilized society at last, Miss Ashcombe."

After a sharp intake of breath, she said, "I wasn't aware that the society I left was uncivilized."

He smiled. "What I mean is a Christian society. One based upon the ten commandments and essential decency."

"Forgive me if what I am about to say shocks you. Perhaps you are unaware that my mother, an Indian native, was a Hindu. I was raised to respect all beliefs."

"Of course, I had forgotten that someone as lovely as you

is not wholly English in breeding. But that is of little matter, so long as you are willing to conform." They then separated and engaged in intricate figures, so their conversation ended. When they spoke again it was on trivial subjects, she made sure of that.

Anjali tried not to judge Dawlish too severely. What he said about India showed great ignorance. But it was no more than she believed just about everyone who had never been there would think, based on what made its way back to England through Company channels. He never said anything else to make her uncomfortable, but on their drive in the park, his responses to both Kavi and Sir Julian had not presented him in a favorable light. She could not help thinking that he believed he could purge her of her Indianness in some way. Again, she thought, why on earth would he persist in his suit if she was so clearly defective in his eyes?

Despite the knowledge that her debut was a resounding success—as evidenced by how often she danced and the number of people who seemed eager to make her acquaintance—Anjali had many lingering thoughts that added up to an overall sense of discomfort and disappointment. Discomfort at Dawlish's benighted views and proprietary air. Discomfort at the unexpected appearance of Lascelles, who belonged, in her mind, in Calcutta. Disappointment that she didn't have a second dance with sir Julian, who vanished after their waltz, never returning with the promised glass of lemonade.

Perhaps this last was the primary cause of her low spirits. Or perhaps she was simply fatigued, she thought, looking out of the carriage at the dreary, dawn-lit streets of London gradually coming to life while they, on the other hand, were eager to seek their beds.

CHAPTER 16

The morning after the ball proved to Caroline both that she still possessed social power, and that she was getting old. Old? She was only eight and forty! Yes, that was old in the eyes of society, even if there were so many moments when she still felt young.

Eleven o'clock in the morning after only a few hours' sleep was not one of those moments, however. She breakfasted in her room and it took some time for her to work up the energy to face what she hoped would be a barrage of posies and cards and visitors for Anjali. She'd instructed Falk to tell the kitchen to send a tray up to her, but not before eleven.

When she made her way downstairs at noon, Caroline was a bit surprised to see Anjali not only dressed, but in the breakfast parlor with the remains of a meal around her and in a buzz of astonishment. She sat surrounded by flowers and cards, eyes full of wonder—tinged with confusion. As soon as she saw Caroline, Anjali jumped up and ran to embrace her.

"Lady Lewiston! Last night was remarkable. Thank you for all your hard work."

Although put a little off balance, Caroline couldn't help responding to Anjali's heartfelt gratitude with a broad smile. "You were the shining star of the ball, my dear! Just look at all these tributes. And you had two dances with Lord Dawlish. The other debutantes were quite envious, I imagine."

"Well, I was not the only one so honored. Lady Henrietta Vaughn danced with Lord Dawlish twice as well. She is lovely, and very English. I daresay her mountain of posies and cards fairly dwarfs mine!"

Anjali was still clearly uncertain of her place, of her worth. It was only natural, but it tugged at Caroline's heart. Not just because she was Thomas's beloved daughter but because she had so much to offer in herself, although Caroline couldn't have defined precisely what that was.

"Help me go through the cards, please, My Lady. I've been wracking my brains for hours trying to remember who everyone was."

"For hours?" Caroline said. "I told Millie she wasn't to disturb you before eleven at the earliest."

"I couldn't sleep. So much happened last night. I came down here at nine. I'm afraid the servants weren't expecting me, but they've all been terribly helpful."

Caroline exchanged a glance with Fairing, who stood benevolently by, caught up in Anjali's feverish activity in his own sedate way.

"Well, I shall look through these quickly, but we had better retire to the drawing room soon. If this is anything to go by, I imagine the visits will begin shortly."

"Who do you think will come?" Anjali asked.

"Who do you hope will come?" Caroline responded, making Anjali's cheeks blush a becoming shade of peach.

"To tell the truth I thought that after Lady Allston's party people were simply being polite, that no one really wanted to visit."

Caroline heard the lingering edge of uncertainty in her voice and said, "Nonsense. You are well and truly launched into the *ton* now, my dear."

They had no time to say anything more because the heavy knocker sounded below. Caroline stood and said, "No need to hurry," then turned to Fairing. "See who it is and take a bit of time with his hat and coat so Miss Ashcombe and I can get settled in the drawing room."

They needn't have worried. It was Thomas, who arrived at the first decent hour, his arms full of two dozen magnificent roses. At that time of year, they must have come from a hothouse, Caroline thought. How extravagant!

Anjali ran to him and said, "Papa! You don't have to bring me flowers!"

He accepted her kiss on the cheek and said, "I know. However, it is customary for a gentleman to visit and bring flowers to the lady he danced with the night before."

Caroline met his eyes as he looked toward where she stood in the middle of the room. He brought her flowers! Two dozen red roses. Just as he had done so many years ago. For a moment, she was not Lady Lewiston, standing in her elegant dower house, but a debutante, stomach fluttering with nerves the day after her come-out ball, in the blue saloon of the Holbrook townhouse in Berkeley Square, hoping against hope that the young gentleman she had danced with twice and who had the most beautiful eyes she'd ever seen would be among her callers.

Remembering where she was, she moved forward, arms outstretched to receive the bounteous blooms. Before she reached him, though, Thomas turned away and signaled to

Fairing to relieve him of his burden so he could take Caroline's hands and plant a delicate kiss on each of them.

By now Caroline's heart was pounding. How foolish! She was a grown woman, past the age of falling in love, especially with the man who had forsaken her thirty years ago. She gave a light, flirtatious laugh and turned away, once again taking her seat by the hearth and nodding towards the chair across from her on the other side of the fireplace, which Thomas took.

She looked quickly at Anjali, who stood with a questioning expression in the middle of the room. What must she think? Fortunately, another knock fell on the street door and a moment later Fairing announced, "Lord Dawlish."

Caroline and Thomas rose as Dawlish entered. She smiled at him, out of the corner of her eye watching Anjali. The girl had had an opportunity to meet and dance with many more gentlemen last night. The rout party had been too soon after her arrival for her to feel comfortable with anyone. But at the masquerade ball, whenever Caroline caught sight of Anjali she was surrounded by young gentlemen and laughing and talking gaily. More than one of them appeared enchanted by her spirit and liveliness. The question was whether she distinguished anyone among them with particular regard, but as far as Caroline could tell at the time, she seemed delighted with everyone. Only natural, of course.

Anjali smiled at Dawlish politely and thanked him for the posy he'd sent earlier. She didn't blush, however. She spoke to him calmly and sensibly, the budding hostess greeting a guest she knew slightly, not flirting at all. So that was the way of things, Caroline thought. Apparently, eligible though Dawlish might be, Anjali did not have any feelings for him warmer than friendship. With a rueful smile she recalled his unwise words at his first visit. Although she couldn't have known what he and Anjali spoke about at the masquerade, it appeared that he had yet to redeem himself in her eyes.

In truth, the young baron, although handsome, was not particularly charming, and didn't have an inquiring mind to make up for it. Sadly, Caroline deduced that her first choice for Anjali likely wouldn't do at all, unless he soon revealed a heretofore unsuspected intelligence. Besides, his interest in her protégée puzzled her. If he really felt as he did about India, why had he come forward at all? Although his family was a good one and his fortune respectable, she knew little about why he'd stayed abroad and what he'd done while there. No one did. She began to fear he was more taken with Anjali's fortune than with her person for some reason. Perhaps something had changed for him while he was away that she hadn't heard about. No matter. The way things were going, Anjali was not likely to develop a *tendre* for him so the point was moot.

Not long after Dawlish arrived yet another knock sounded, and in a few minutes Fairing announced "Sir Julian Meredith."

Anjali stood so fast she nearly sent the small cushion at her elbow to the ground. She did not step forward, but Caroline could sense something in her demeanor that took her by surprise. Sir Julian wasn't even what one might describe as handsome. Pleasant looking, and when he smiled he became very engaging, but his red hair—aside from the startling color, its curls, rather than appearing purposeful, could only be described as unruly.

Once greetings were exchanged, Sir Julian said, "I apologize for not bringing flowers, Miss Ashcombe." He looked at Dawlish who had been busy examining a speck of something on his sleeve ever since Sir Julian arrived, and said, "I-I did not do so simply because the last time I visited, well, I had a bit of a mishap and crushed the flowers I brought. I assure you, I chose them very carefully. Today, however, I'm afraid I must beg your pardon for having arrived *not* bearing gifts."

"Apology accepted, although not needed. In fact, if you were Greek, I would be relieved that you have not brought any gifts," Anjali said, provoking him to smile. She moved to a small settee and indicated that Sir Julian should sit next to her there. Dawlish, whose side she had left, simply turned toward Thomas and began quizzing him about whether he owned any hunters and whether, now that he was once again settled in England, he would be establishing a hunting box in the shires. Caroline pretended to be listening politely to this innocuous conversation, thankfully not touching on India, but all the time with her other ear strained to hear what Anjali and Sir Julian were talking about. They seemed animated and engaged, each listening to what the other said as if it was of the greatest interest. Anjali wasn't being coquettish or hanging on Sir Julian's words in the manner of an ingenue who believed he was much smarter than she was, so it was hard to see any evidence of a *tendre*. By turns her brow wrinkled in concentration, and then her eyes widened and she responded with something that made Sir Julian nod and smile.

Caroline supposed she must play the chaperone and insert herself into their exchange, so she rose and took a seat near the settee the two of them occupied. "Sir Julian, I only saw you briefly last night. You chose not to come in costume. I'm curious as to why."

The young man flushed and Caroline instantly regretted asking. Before he could answer, however, Dawlish rose from his seat, sauntered over, and said, "Sir Julian is too serious a man to enter into the gaiety of a masquerade. He must maintain his dignity as a barrister."

Having delivered himself of this observation, which he clearly thought would bring an end to the discussion,

Dawlish continued to the sideboard to pour himself and Thomas each a glass of Madeira. He looked over his shoulder at the trio comprising Caroline, Sir Julian, and Anjali and lifted the decanter inquiringly. All three of them shook their heads no.

Caroline was incensed. Surely Dawlish had better manners than that! To interrupt a conversation with a comment that could only be interpreted as a slight. For someone who appeared to have little genuine interest in Anjali he was behaving as if her attention to Sir Julian piqued him. She must try to smooth things over with the baronet, who had done nothing to deserve Dawlish's derision. So she gave him one of her most gracious smiles and said, "Seeing you here, Sir Julian, laughing and chatting, I imagine Lord Dawlish must have been teasing. You're clearly the opposite of what he described."

Sir Julian flashed her a grateful look and said, "Alas, some of what he told you is true. But the actual story of what happened to cause me to arrive at your glittering party dressed like a schoolmaster—"

"A very elegant schoolmaster!" Anjali said, her eyes alight with mirth.

"But a schoolmaster nonetheless," Sir Julian said, then continued, "The true story is—"

They had been chatting so animatedly that no one heard the knocker this time, so when Fairing announced, "Mr. Lascelles," at the door of the drawing room, he had to raise his voice a little. This silenced everyone instantly.

"Please don't let me interrupt what seems to be a very congenial gathering!" Lascelles said, advancing into the room with his dazzling smile, his left hand tucked behind his back. "How do you do, Lady Lewiston. We met last evening but just briefly." He then focused his attention on Anjali, bringing out from behind his back a small nosegay of Arabian jasmine and orange blossom. "I would have been here earlier, but it took me some time to find a flower seller who could procure these. I thought they might remind you of home."

Anjali buried her nose in the small bouquet and closed her eyes, inhaling deeply. "Thank you," she breathed.

Without being invited, Lascelles dragged a delicate chair over and sat next to Anjali. "I couldn't help thinking that one thing London cannot supply to anyone accustomed to the gardens of Calcutta is the intoxicating aroma of jasmine at this time of year. If I could somehow bring the brilliant sunshine as well, I would have done so."

Anjali's expression softened at his words, and a faraway look came into her eyes. Caroline stole a glance at Sir Julian. He did not look cross or angry at this interruption, only a little sad. Lascelles, although he gestured and looked around at everyone as though eager to bring them into the conversation, confined his remarks to a comparison of Calcutta and London, larded with amusing quips and bon mots that referred to events that had occurred in India—a strategy that effectively left both Sir Julian and Lord Dawlish out of the thread. Thomas, Caroline noted, had the good manners to continue speaking in a low voice to Lord Dawlish, even though he could easily have joined in with Lascelles.

It wasn't as if Lascelles actually flirted with her, Caroline thought, but Anjali was clearly captivated by the pictures he conjured up with his words. And it would take a lot of fortitude to withstand that beguiling smile.

All this time, Sir Julian sat silently by, his eyes never leaving Anjali's face. Caroline couldn't help feeling sorry for him, although she wasn't sure why. He was an intelligent, successful barrister, not a languishing schoolboy. However, despite having been "on the town," as they said, for some years, Sir Julian lacked social assurance. He had little obvious charm, and no small talk. Anjali saw something in him, though, of that she was certain. Caroline decided she should keep her mind open about a match for Anjali. Sir Julian would not be ineligible. Could she do better? Did Thomas expect her to? Or would the girl prefer the older, more experienced, and more familiar Mr. Lascelles? She knew little about his family. Thomas told her he was at Eton and went to India after a number of years among the Corinthian set in the *ton*. Thomas seemed to hold Lascelles in high esteem, so perhaps it wouldn't be a terrible match for his daughter.

What a shame it would be, Caroline thought, if Anjali came all the way to London only to secure a husband she could have found without leaving Calcutta.

DURING THE TWO HOURS WHEN ANJALI AND LADY LEWISTON were receiving callers that afternoon, a dozen of Anjali's dance partners came to Park Street. They extended invitations to go out driving in the park and solicited her for the opportunity to dance with her at upcoming parties. As she hadn't received vouchers for Almack's, this crucible of matchmaking was not a possibility for her, so she must rely upon the private *ton* parties for society. Anjali was perfectly content with that. The lack of vouchers was more disturbing to Lady Lewiston than it was to her.

Flattered by the many flowers and visitors, Anjali recognized that they appealed to her vanity more than her heart. None of the young gentlemen she'd met for the first time at the ball could be considered serious contenders for her hand. In fact, if she were forced to choose among them she found she'd rather remain a spinster. Why was that? They were pleasant enough. One or two were even witty. Several quite handsome. But they felt remote from her. She could not picture herself embracing any of them, let alone sharing her life with them.

That, unfortunately, applied to Lord Dawlish as well. He had done nothing to repair the negative opinion she had of him after his first visit and their drive. Anjali knew he was Lady Lewiston's choice for her, but his handsome face, polished manners, and well-formed figure did not compensate for his lack of intelligence and education. Worse, he seemed entirely unwilling to see that India enriched Anjali's life rather than rendering her in some degree in need of rehabilitation. Still, it was perfectly understandable that Lady Lewiston would think of him as a suitor. He had all the external qualities that made him a suitable candidate. The trouble was that after spending time with him and dancing with him, Anjali was at a loss to discover any appealing internal qualities. She felt certain a life with him—even absent his gothic ideas about the country where she was born—would be dull beyond bearing. Dawlish would make a perfectly satisfactory husband for someone like Lady Henrietta Vaughn, she thought. Did he not see that the girl had spent the whole evening throwing out lures to him? She was pretty and vacuous. Surely she was the kind of wife Dawlish expected to have, *and if he ended up with me, he'd be sorely disappointed.* So why was he courting her?

Anjali stared absently into her dressing table mirror as Millie brushed her hair. So, that crossed Dawlish off the list —if she had one. She would be forced to drive in the park with him again, but she felt confident she would be able to depress his pretensions.

On the other hand, thoughts of doing that to two of her other callers were very far from her mind. The first of these was Sir Julian. He lacked the outward polish of Lord Dawlish, but he had an indefinable something that appealed to her for a reason she could not identify. She didn't know him well, but on some deeper level she understood him. Yet in her heart she knew it was more than that. Anjali suspected that all his best qualities were locked below the surface he presented to the world, where the *ton* would be unlikely to discover them.

Sir Julian's looks were not classically handsome. He was tall and was possessed of a pair of green-gold eyes that were always full of life, never seeming to look at the world with boredom. It was as if he didn't simply look at, but really saw and was affected by everything around him, as if he was well aware that the world he surveyed was not put there for his own amusement. In this he was not very English. Most members of the *ton* whom Anjali had met perceived little beyond their own private spheres. They didn't even seem to notice the servants who enabled every aspect of their privileged lives. Sir Julian's profession of barrister and the fact that he was a baronet anchored him securely in the mainstream of British society. Yet of all the people she'd met here —with the possible exception of Lady Mariana—her instinct told her that Sir Julian was the most liable to step outside the expected mode of behavior. That ridiculous, badly behaved spaniel, for instance. Bramble belonged in a lady's drawing room, not being walked around London's stylish lounges by a gentleman. And to arrive at her come-out ball not wearing a costume and barely a mask also made him singular.

Yet there was a distinct difference between Lady Mariana's singularity and Sir Julian's. Unlike Lady Mariana, Sir Julian didn't appear to revel in what set him apart socially. Either he wasn't aware of it, was embarrassed by it, or didn't care. Not caring would be rather callous and self-centered— which he certainly wasn't. He was too intelligent not to be aware of himself in the world. So Anjali was inclined to think that he was embarrassed, and yet in some sense either powerless to change his behavior or unwilling to conform just for its own sake. She based this on the fact that when he found himself in his element, talking about something that mattered to him, he opened up like one of those blossoms that needed the focused warmth of a direct ray of sunshine to coax them to reveal their full beauty.

She'd experienced just such a moment with him earlier that very day, more so than on any of the other times they'd met. For a few minutes, when they sat next to each other in the drawing room, they spoke in a way that broke down the polite, cool barrier that was supposed to remain in place between a bachelor and an unmarried lady. Moreover, that breach of defenses happened without awkwardness, almost as soon as he took the seat next to her. With no preamble he asked, "Is Kavi the only bit of India you brought with you to London?"

She'd been prepared for yet another conversation about the weather, and this took her aback for a moment before she smiled and said, "No, in fact, he isn't."

"Forgive me, but I expect you're a bit weary of London small talk. I'm not particularly good at it anyway. I hope I'm not being impertinent."

"Not at all! Aside from what you might expect—my mother's jewelry and some beautiful saris—"

"What's a sah-ree?"

"It's what Lady Belinda and the others wore at the ball last night. Oh! But you arrived late and did not see the tableau. You might have noticed them dancing, however."

"I noticed no one other than—" he broke off suddenly, his face coloring, and said, "But you were saying…"

Anjali wished he had continued what he first started to say. Her imagination filled in the missing *you,* and a bubble of something fluttered in her middle. She took a breath and said, "Yes, apart from those things, I brought several volumes of Urdu poetry with me. I'm making a translation into

English, which is challenging because it's not just a question of getting the words right. Urdu poetry is nothing like your English verse. And it's written using a completely different script and orthography, which is read from right to left." She was conscious of offering more information than he actually requested. She was nervous. Perhaps she had said too much.

But to her delight Sir Julian's eyes lit up, and he said, "I love poetry. It's such a balm to the spirit after all the dense legal documents I read for my profession. I find I want to remind myself that words can express love and beauty as well as fear and difficulty and details no one seeking either financial redress or to escape a dire punishment would really like to know."

They shared a quiet laugh, and Anjali unconsciously leaned slightly toward each other, touching shoulders for one brief, electric moment. Anjali cleared her throat and looked down at her hands. "The only English poems I am very familiar with are Shakespeare's sonnets, which I find lovely—once I understand what he's saying. Their meaning can be very subtle, and yet in some sense they far more direct, more linked to real life than the poetry of someone like Mir Taqi Mir."

"Is he your favorite poet?"

She smiled, deciding to risk looking up at Sir Julian again. "Yes. His verses reward reading and rereading." Sir Julian's cheeks still held a faint wash of pink in them. *So he'd noticed it too,* Anjali thought.

"I would be intrigued to know in what way Mr. Mir—do I have that right? —Mr. Mir's poetry is unlike the poetry I know. If you would consider letting me read one of your translations I would be most honored," Sir Julian said.

During the whole of their conversation, to Anjali's amazement, Sir Julian never evinced surprise that she should be engaged in such an intellectually challenging pursuit. He merely accepted it, speaking to her as if what she said was worth hearing. In India, only members of her mother's family showed an interest in her education and erudition. The English there treated her in much the same way as the English in London did: as an ornamental being that was of value only in her ability to bring pleasure to a social occasion.

They had little time to say more, however, because after a too-brief interval Mr. Lascelles arrived. That confident, roguish gentleman entered the drawing room bringing not just the memory of India, but its very atmosphere. Anjali found herself captivated, caught up in the vivid pictures of her Calcutta that Lascelles painted. He didn't *appear* to exclude Sir Julian from the conversation, but how could anyone who had never been to India have found anything to contribute? In retrospect, Anjali thought it was a bit impolite of Mr. Lascelles to monopolize the conversation in that way, but in the moment she felt powerless to stop him. She had the bouquet of jasmine he'd brought to her in a vase on her dressing table, and the heady scent still evoked the garden she had left behind.

Anjali generally liked Mr. Lascelles, whatever his faults of conduct. She was inclined to forgive him because he'd been in India for years. He'd started coming to their house when she was still a schoolgirl. On those occasions he would tease her and bring her gifts of sweetmeats, feed Kavi bits of fruit, and tell her some little-known tidbits of information, such as the one about the mysterious baya weaver bird and its hanging nests.

She was, however, at a loss to imagine what brought him to London just then. He was only staying a month, he said. Some business to do with the traders, no doubt. This gave her an idea she'd been mulling ever since their callers had left. Rather than entrusting her letter to Nalin to a stranger who might lose it, perhaps she could ask Lascelles to take it with him when he returned to Calcutta? The idea had the added advantage that Lascelles knew Nalin. She would have to make up a plausible reason why she would be writing to her father's former clerk, why she wouldn't simply append some message to a letter her father was sending.

I know! she thought. She would say she is asking Nalin to procure a special surprise gift for her father. Something like a carved sandalwood writing box. Yes! Since her father's birthday was not until the autumn there would be time for the message to get there, for the box to be made, and for it to be brought back to London.

Her letter would be sealed, so she had no fear that Lascelles would read it. He was too much the English gentleman to abuse a lady's confidence in that way.

But what if he volunteered to procure the box himself? Perhaps she could say that Nalin had some special knowledge of a craftsman deep in the countryside.

Anjali yawned and stretched out her arms. She'd had little sleep the night before and now she was heartily tired. Her mind whirled with confused thoughts and emotions, but she was too weary to sort them out that night.

"I 'spect you'll sleep like a dormouse, Miss." Millie had long since finished brushing her hair and stood patiently by, waiting Anjali to let her help her into bed and blow out her night candle.

"Thank you, Millie. It's been quite a day." Tired as she was, Anjali was reluctant for it to end.

"Yes, Miss," the abigail said and prodded Anjali in the direction of the waiting four poster. "I 'spect tomorrow'll be just as nice."

CHAPTER 17

*J*ulian read the first page of the first of the documents Griggs left for him on his desk in chambers three times without retaining a single morsel of what it said. Thank heaven the matter wasn't of great urgency. He simply had to assimilate the information the solicitor gave him and write an opinion. Normally this was easy for him. He could read fast and comprehend even more quickly, and once he mastered the content he wrote with fluency an opinion that rarely failed to illuminate some important aspect of a case.

That day, though, his mind kept wandering. It wandered to the masquerade ball and his waltz with Miss Ashcombe. Then it wandered to his visit the next day, and the conversation that increased his admiration for this extraordinary girl. What he had sensed about her was true: she had depth and character. She wasn't a pretty wigeon who beguiled the eye but left the intellect untouched, as so many debutantes were —or at least were trained to be. Not Anjali—Miss Ashcombe —though. He had never met anyone like her.

If he could have, he would have stayed at the Park Street

house talking about poetry and other matters all afternoon. She had beckoned him to sit next to her. She wanted to talk to him. That in itself gave him hope that she didn't view him with indifference.

But it was the way they spoke that mattered. In an unguarded moment before the ball, he had allowed himself to think of her as the woman he loved. He'd had little to base that surge of feeling upon, and until yesterday, he feared perhaps he had been foolish, misguided. That he'd allowed his imagination to find meaning where there was none, simply because she'd been kind.

Now he knew he hadn't. It became very clear in that brief moment of contact, when their bodies had moved involuntarily toward each other and his shoulder had brushed hers, that she felt it too. Miss Ashcombe looked away, but her cheeks glowed, and her voice shook just a little when she began speaking again.

Ironic, really. They'd had a scant fifteen minutes to speak in relative privacy while others were engaged in their own conversations. A scant fifteen minutes to discover threads of connection and start to weave them into something solid and real. A scant fifteen minutes until those threads were broken when Lascelles arrived.

That fellow swept in with his charm, his dashing looks, and his air of the exotic, bringing Miss Ashcombe flowers Julian wouldn't have known to look for. The disruption was painful. Almost violent. The dazzling creature who honored him by trusting him with knowledge of pursuits that would cause many to label her a bluestocking was wrenched away from him by a bunch of flowers. All Julian could do was sit helplessly by while the handsome trader spun tales that brought a look of misty fondness to Miss Ashcombe's eyes— a look that Julian would relinquish his fortune to have trained upon him.

Julian's dislike of Lascelles had its seeds in the night of the masquerade when the confident, adept stranger scooped Miss Ashcombe away and secured the supper dance with her before Julian had worked up the courage to ask her for it himself. He was self-aware enough to know that he did not judge this fellow with indifferent eyes. He must admit to himself that he was jealous. At least, that's what he assumed. He had never felt so before. On the other hand, he was also astute enough, after years of facing very clever criminals at the Old Bailey and in the countryside at quarter sessions, to trust his own judgment when it came to assessing character. He couldn't shed the conviction that there was something vaguely smoky about Lascelles. What exactly that was he couldn't yet say.

Julian pushed away the papers he was reading and took out a blank sheet of foolscap, smoothing it on the desk in front of him. Then he trimmed his quill, opened the standish, and dipped his pen into the ink. After a moment's thought, he wrote, "Victor Lascelles" across the top of the sheet and underlined it. Then he took the ruler he used to guide his pen when underlining important passages in documents and drew a straight line down the center of the page.

This was an exercise Julian often used when something about a case was obscure or he felt he had not quite reached the truth of it. On one side of the line he would write the bare, indisputable facts. On the other, he articulated what it was about each of those facts that raised a question in his mind. Sometimes he was able to reassure himself that everything was indeed as it appeared to be. But in many cases, thinking this way helped him identify the source of his unease and led him to approach the case in a different way. Every time that occurred, he won.

So he began.

Fact: Lascelles is a trader from Calcutta who is a friend of

Thomas Ashcombe. He is in London to deliver some sort of message to someone at India House, so he says.

Question: Who is the message for? What are its contents? Why must this message be delivered exactly now?

Fact: Lascelles is clearly of the upper class, as witnessed by his dress, his mode of speech, and his manners.

Question: Why have I never heard of him before, if he's only been in Calcutta for less than ten years? He has all the marks of a public school education. He did not go to Harrow certainly, or he would be known to me by reputation if nothing else.

Fact: Lascelles is well connected and received in the first circles. Lewiston acknowledged knowing him.

Question: What does Lewiston know about the man? Why did he seem reserved when I mentioned him? And how could I find out without seeming impertinent?

Julian paused, laid down the quill, and rubbed his eyes.

No, he couldn't go to Lewiston and ask questions. It would be ungentlemanly. It would be the act of a petty gossip. In fact, would doing anything at all to find out more about Lascelles be immoral, given his own position?

Julian let that thought roll around in his mind for a while and finally decided that no, it would not be wrong if it preserves Miss Ashcombe and her father from harm. And yet, he had no real reason to think Lascelles meant them any harm. The opposite, in fact.

He was getting nowhere. He didn't know enough to make even a basic judgment of the matter.

"Griggs!" Julian called.

The clerk bustled in, looking typically harassed. "Yes, Sir Julian, what's yer pleasure?"

"I met a gentleman the other evening, an acquaintance of a friend, and we thought we might meet at Brooks's to play cards one evening. Trouble is, I can't for the life of me remember what he said about where he's staying. I don't suppose you know someone who might make some discreet inquiries so that I don't insult the fellow when I fail to arrange the evening?"

Griggs gave Julian a hard stare. "Ye're seeking private information about an individual what has no bearing on a case?"

"That's it exactly," Julian said, an uncomfortable feeling in his heart. "I feel such a fool for not asking him more at the time."

"You tell me 'is name. I'll take care of the rest." Griggs raised one eyebrow and winked.

Julian colored. "It's Lascelles. Victor Lascelles. Just arrived from Calcutta."

"Calcutta…" Griggs said. "Isn't that where the young lady we talked about is from? The one with the masked ball?"

"Yes. They are acquainted. That's how I met him." Griggs saw through him, Julian was certain. One didn't become a chief clerk in chambers without being fly to the time of day. Oh well, he'd done it now. The question was, how would he use any information gathered in this havey-cavey way? There was no use worrying about that until he knew what exactly he was dealing with.

He turned back to the documents he'd been trying to read before. This time he was able to focus on their contents, and in less than an hour had mastered them and outlined his incisive opinion.

THEY'D BEEN IN LONDON FOR MORE THAN A FORTNIGHT AND still Thomas was no closer to discovering a way to put his information into trustworthy hands. He was so frustrated that he needed to do something physical just to release the tension, so he took himself to Jackson's Boxing Academy to spar a bit with the man himself—or more likely one of his associates. The occasional ride on a job horse or long walk from Bloomsbury to Mayfair did nothing to get his blood pumping.

The other potential way to produce that result, rather than helping, was causing him some disturbed nights' sleep. He was becoming aware that the friendly feelings he thought he'd have for Caroline after such a long period of absence and so many life changes for them both were inexorably—and rapidly—heading toward something else altogether. The last thing he wanted was to risk being rejected all over again, so he steeled himself against those feelings as much as he could, and the effort wreaked havoc on his peace.

His one consolation was that where Anjali was concerned things seemed to be going well. She'd *taken*, as Caroline told him, which was a very good thing. Eligible young men were queuing up to squire her at a dance or take her for drives in the park. He did wonder if any of this was enjoyable to Anjali, who was accustomed to pursuits that were more intellectually or physically demanding. But she hadn't complained to him and clearly had made real friends among Caroline's extended family.

Caroline appeared at first to be promoting the interests of Lord Dawlish. He was eligible, certainly. But his views on India were disturbing, and Thomas could see no evidence of particular regard on the part of Anjali. Nonetheless, when the peer came to him the day before and requested permission to make his addresses to her, he saw no reason to deny him that opportunity. He had no doubt the man would be unsuccessful with his suit.

Anjali seemed more taken with that red-headed baronet, a thought that made him smile. How odd a couple they would make! Still, he only wanted for Anjali what would make her happy.

He had to put all those concerns aside for the moment, though. More important just now was resolving the issue at the heart of their flight from Calcutta. And without the name of someone he could trust who knew the right people in the government he was temporarily at a standstill.

He arrived at the famous boxing establishment 13 Old Bond Street at one in the afternoon two days after Anjali's come-out. A neatly dressed porter answered Thomas's knock at the door and asked his name. When Thomas explained that he'd just come from India, but that he'd boxed when younger, seen Jackson in the ring, and hoped to be able to spar for a while, the porter smiled and led him into a dressing room where Thomas divested himself of his hat, coat, waistcoat, and boots, donning the slippers the academy provided along with a pair of leather mufflers.

Thomas walked into the training room and was startled to see not a rough packed dirt floor and an atmosphere of sweat and aggression, but something a great deal more genteel. No torn, blood-stained clothing. Instead, clean knee breeches and stockings, shirtsleeves rolled up—but carefully, as if a valet had assisted in that process. Still, most of the faces wore hard, determined expressions and were flushed with exertion. Those pairs of gentlemen sparring brought back memories of the turbulent months before he left for India, when he was young and heartsick and despairing and looking for any way to distract himself from his frustrated hopes. At that time, Jackson had just won his first prize fight and would go on to win many more, so this academy did not exist. Thomas learned to box in a rougher school, with a private instructor who didn't hold back, sometimes encouraging him to fight bare-knuckled—which suited his mood entirely at the time.

Judging by what he saw, Thomas expected that no one ever got badly hurt at Jackson's rooms. Perhaps a cut lip or a bruised eye worn as a badge of honor might result from a particularly heated contest, but no more.

After the servant who accompanied him to the main room introduced him to the Gentleman Jackson, who paired Thomas with a different fellow he didn't know to test his level of skill. They took their positions and Thomas drove in, landing hits over his partner's guard. The fellow appeared surprised and wasn't quick enough to evade Thomas's assault. It felt like a very unequal match, and Thomas was a little disappointed.

Jackson clearly saw the discrepancy and motioned him over to another corner of the room, opposite where the weigh scale stood. "There's someone else here who might be a better fit for you, although he's younger. You're in decent shape, and I see that you're game for a challenge. He's just gone into the other room to get a drink of water... Here he is now."

Thomas looked over to where Jackson nodded his head and saw a familiar figure emerge from the other changing room. He wanted to laugh aloud. Of course it was Lascelles. He smiled and waved him over. Jackson looked back and forth between them. "So you gents are acquainted I see. Might've guessed. Lascelles here is from India as well. How about you spar a bit?"

Thomas and Lascelles exchanged polite greetings, and Lascelles said, "Are you sure you're game for this, man?"

"Of course." Did he think he wasn't capable? The two of them had never fought in India, but Thomas boxed privately at times with one or two of his British acquaintances there. Boxing was not the pervasive gentlemanly activity in Calcutta that it was in London, so Thomas also stayed fit by training occasionally with some of his native friends, who practiced wrestling and other martial arts in their *akharas.* Old Bond Street was a long way from those dirt floors and the stifling heat of bodies engaged in strenuous physical activity. It seemed that showing obvious strain was not the point for many of the gentlemen in that room.

"Shall we?" Lascelles said.

The two men shook hands, then Thomas took his position opposite Lascelles, one foot slightly advanced, one hand curled near his face, the other poised to strike. And then the dance began.

He thinks I'm old and slow, Thomas thought as they circled each other. *He has a surprise in store for him.* All at once, Thomas thrust himself forward to get Lascelles off balance. But Lascelles anticipated him and slipped aside, not countering, just waiting for Thomas's next move. The fellow was young and agile, but Thomas was larger, and he drove in to put some weight behind his fists, managing to get a hit over Lascelles's guard into his ribs.

Clearly, Lascelles didn't expect him to be so aggressive, and began to pay closer attention to Thomas's every move, dodging and answering neatly once or twice, catching Thomas on the side of his head and one sharp jab to his mouth. Although completely different fighters, they appeared to be well matched, Thomas thought with a degree of admiration for Lascelles, whom he expected to be all flourish and no force.

They continued sparring until they were both breathing heavily and the sweat ran down in rivulets from Thomas's temples. But he was in no way ready to stop, and pressed in to land his left in the pit of Lascelles's stomach with more weight than he intended.

"Gentlemen, I think we can end it here—you've both had some good hits and defended well," Jackson said, standing near enough to them that they were forced to separate.

Lascelles untied his right muffler and held out his hand to Thomas, who did the same so they could shake hands. "You've stayed fit, I see, Ashcombe," Lascelles said through ragged breaths.

"And you've had some clever training," Thomas said, still breathing hard as well.

"What say we go over to Limmer's for a glass or two? If you've nowhere else you have to be, that is."

"It would be my pleasure," Thomas said. Perhaps this would be an opportunity to find out more from Lascelles, maybe get the name of someone he could trust at India House.

HALF AN HOUR LATER, CLEAN AND ONCE MORE ATTIRED LIKE the gentlemen they were, Thomas and Lascelles entered the nearby hotel with its tap room frequented by the Corinthian set. Thomas felt old among all the young men eager to prove themselves on the hunting field or in foolhardy curricle races. But the hotel was near Jackson's academy, and the brandy was good.

"I don't really understand what was so urgent that you had to come all this way," Thomas said to Lascelles as they sat at a small table in the corner of the lively room. "It's a devilish rough journey."

"Oh, you know. Everything seems urgent to those Company men. To be honest, I'm not even certain of the contents of the dispatch I've brought. Fulbright sealed it and just told me who to give it to. I think it has to do with opium imports. And I believe that if a packet was sailing immediately after I reached London he'd have had me turn right around and sail back to India."

Although opium was an essential ingredient in some medicines, Thomas had seen too many men and women become obsessed with it, using it to escape to a dream world far away from real life. The fact that Lascelles's mission in London had a tangential relationship to this shadowy commerce disturbed him. "What do you know of the trade? I fear it has become temptingly profitable for some both in and outside of the Company," Thomas said.

Lascelles nodded. "I believe that Hastings has worked to squash that tendency, however. The board of controllers won't stand for that sort of thing."

And yet, Thomas thought, it went on right under their noses. He didn't say that to Lascelles, however. He trusted the man generally, but he preferred to keep the details of his business with the board of controllers to himself.

"It happens that I have some business I should like to discuss with someone at India House," Thomas said, "Information that concerns the government." It was the closest he'd come yet to telling anyone anything about it.

"Oh? What sort of information? If I knew I could help you make sure it found its way into the right hands—someone who could use it to advantage, perhaps." Although Lascelles effected a relaxed posture in his chair, his eyes narrowed slightly as he spoke.

Careful, Thomas thought. Even if Lascelles bore him no ill will, the fewer people who knew about the explosive intelligence he'd kept closely guarded all the way from Calcutta the better. "It's just something to do with one of my trading partners, a zamindar, who I want to be certain remains a valuable source even though I'm no longer there to do business with him."

"That sounds simple enough," Lascelles said, the minuscule degree of tension in his body visibly lessening. "I should think you could give that to any of the clerks at Leadenhall Street."

"That's as may be, but you see, this is also a family contact of mine. I think he deserves special consideration, and I don't want my letter to get lost in the bureaucratic maelstrom that is The Company." He smiled, hoping this provided Lascelles with enough of an explanation for his caution.

After draining his glass, Lascelles said, "I'll tell you what, old fellow, why don't you give your papers to me and I can use my connections to make sure they find the right pigeon-hole, so to speak."

That was exactly what Thomas did not want to happen. "Oh, it's no bother. I'd like to see some of the officers there anyway, so if you can give me a name, I'll take them myself."

Lascelles shrugged. "Suit yourself. I'll see what I can discover for you."

Thomas had to be content with that for now. Something held him back from being more open with Lascelles about his purpose. That afternoon had given him an opportunity to get the measure of Lascelles in a way he'd never done in Calcutta. The man was easy, charming. But he fought with nuance and agility, and Thomas perceived that the same qualities might be applied to his verbal skills.

As they were leaving Limmer's, Lascelles said, "I'm taking your daughter out for a drive later. I'm afraid it's just a hired curricle and cattle, but we'll have a chance for a comfortable prose at least."

Without saying anything more, he touched the brim of his hat and walked off, leaving Thomas unsure of exactly how he felt about Lascelles paying that kind of attention to Anjali.

CHAPTER 18

*I*t was too early for the usual visiting hours when Fairing entered the drawing room and announced that Lord Dawlish had arrived and wished a private word with Miss Ashcombe.

Lady Lewiston put her embroidery aside and said, "Were you expecting this visit, Anjali?"

Anjali shook her head. "What do you mean? Of course not. Although he has visited before so I am not entirely surprised."

Her chaperone's face lit up with amusement. "My dear, are you aware of what it means when a gentleman asks for a private word with an unmarried lady?"

After an uncomprehending moment, Anjali thought *Oh no!* Was he there to propose? She gulped. "Do I have to see him?"

Caroline rose, sat down next to her, and took her hand in both of hers. "You do not have to do anything you do not want to. However, your papa wrote to me to say he had given Lord Dawlish permission to pay his addresses to you. It takes great courage for a man to risk refusal. I think it only polite that you allow him to present his case."

Anjali saw the sense in Lady Lewiston's words. It would indeed be cowardly and unkind of her not to hear him after he had so assiduously courted her—despite the fact that the more she knew him the less she liked him. Doubtless he was accustomed to being acceptable to all. She sighed.

"Please show Lord Dawlish in, Fairing," Lady Lewiston said, rightly interpreting Anjali's silence as acquiescence.

The peer entered the drawing room, showing no evidence that he was nervous or unsure of himself. After greeting him, Lady Lewiston rose and said, "I shall go and instruct my cook concerning the day's meals. I expect that will take only a quarter of an hour."

Anjali felt as if her only ally was leaving her alone on a hostile battlefield. She suppressed the urge to make an excuse to leave as well, rose, and held her hand out to Dawlish. He took it and raised it to his lips, barely touching her knuckles so that the effect was only to make her shiver.

"Miss Ashcombe," he began, "You can be in no doubt of my reasons for seeking this interview with you. My attentions have been too pointed for you to be unaware of this eventuality."

Anjali wanted to say that she hadn't really noticed his attentions but decided that she should refuse him politely and so nodded and let him continue his declaration.

"Despite the natural scruples I have struggled to overcome because of your breeding and unconventional upbringing, I have found myself enchanted by your myriad charms and undeniable beauty. Therefore, Miss Ashcombe, I humbly ask, would you consent to be my wife?"

Humble would not be the adjective Anjali might have used to describe Dawlish's proposal. He'd implied, in fact, that he considered himself vastly superior to her, and was descending from his Olympian heights to bestow upon her the blessing of being elevated to the ranks of the acceptable.

Anjali drew herself up and looked directly into Dawlish's eyes. "I thank you for the honor of your proposals. I am sorry that I cannot accept them."

A look of astonishment crossed Dawlish's face. "Might I ask, Miss Ashcombe, why you reject me so summarily? I offer you security and acceptance. An unimpeachable name, and estates that date back to the Conquest. These are benefits I cannot believe you expected, given the circumstances of your birth."

Ah, yes. There he was again. "Lord Dawlish, you appear to consider me beneath you. I do not consider myself so. My mother's lineage is not centuries but millennia old and of the highest caste. Forgive me if I am loath to accept an offer from someone who would value me so little. I am sure my mama would not have wanted me to."

"Yet your father, no doubt, understands the importance of eradicating the taint of foreignness from you in order to ensure your success in society."

Anjali's pulse raced, and not with pleasure. "My father, I know, wishes only for my happiness. He was obligated to allow you your chance to present your proposals. But he values me as I am, and I know would wish me to engage myself only to someone who did the same." By this point, Anjali's blood was racing through her veins and it was with difficulty that she kept her voice calm.

Dawlish turned away and walked around the room before returning to stand before her again. "I see. Perhaps you would rather ally yourself with a mere baronet who must pursue a profession. Or someone in trade, who will not disdain the occupation of your father. In that case, I can only be grateful that you have spared me from making a terrible mistake." He made a crisp bow and turned on his heel, nearly colliding with Lady Lewiston as she reentered the drawing room.

Anjali stood where she was and fixed Lady Lewiston with a challenging glare.

"I gather something has upset you," Lady Lewiston said.

Without a word, Anjali ran out of the room and up to her bedchamber. Everything she feared about coming to London had just come to pass. She needed time to regain control of her emotions.

WHEN LASCELLES ARRIVED LATER THAT AFTERNOON TO TAKE Anjali on the promised drive, she greeted him with a sense of profound relief. Here was someone who did not consider himself above her, who knew the world she came from and respected her. She was looking forward to an afternoon that would purge the sour taste in her mouth after Dawlish's insulting proposal. No doubt the baron did not think it insulting, which only made it worse.

Be that as it may, she was still a little vexed with Lascelles for interrupting her conversation with Sir Julian the day before, and vexed with herself for being drawn in by him. He knew just what to say to beguile her. She was homesick, and he must have realized it. She missed so much about Calcutta. Life there—even among the British community—was less regimented, less formal than the sometimes absurd conventions among the *ton* in London. In Calcutta, she had more time for her intellectual pursuits. And in her leisure time, entertainments were more varied and freer. Also, she missed the soulful undercurrent of Indian music and the bazaar with its panoply of colors and scents—not all of them pleasant, but always something to look at and be amazed by. It wasn't that she didn't enjoy many of the activities in London, or the lively tunes they danced to, or the sonatas she played on the pianoforte. But they were all so predictable, so much the same every time. The only variety seemed to be in the locations. Different saloons and drawing rooms, different parks, but still the same people to occupy them. At least Lord and Lady Lewiston—Harry and Olivia—had said they would take her to the opera soon, which was an entertainment that was entirely new to her.

So she was in a mood to be reminded of India when Mr. Lascelles arrived in a hired curricle on that fine afternoon to take her for a jaunt around the park. He'd only left Calcutta a week or so after they had, so not much of interest would have happened before he boarded his ship. Still, he would have been there for *Dol Jatra*, the full-moon festival that always enlivened the city, and she wanted to hear all about it.

They started out heading toward Hyde Park Corner rather than the Stanhope Gate, but Anjali didn't find that so unusual. It was simply another way into the park. It wasn't until they went east and started down Piccadilly that she turned to Lascelles and said, "Where are you taking me?"

"The park is so crowded, and always with the same people. I thought maybe you'd enjoy a different drive this time." He had a mischievous glint in his dark eyes, and Anjali could well understand why the ladies in Calcutta were so susceptible to his charms.

"Yes, but where to?" she asked, glad enough not to be going over the same ground for the fourth or fifth time that week.

After he maneuvered the curricle through a bit of traffic he glanced over at her and said, "You'll see. I promise I'm not abducting you! We shall return to Park Street before you have to dress for dinner."

She wondered if Lascelles had been listening in on her thoughts, or whether he had just guessed based on his familiarity with her that she was beginning to tire of the walks, rides, and drives that had so far been limited to the square mile in the vicinity of Park Street, with a venture into Westminster once or twice. So she settled herself in the curricle and prepared to be entertained by new sights and sounds.

At first, they passed grand houses and public buildings that appeared to be simply more of the same sort of places she'd become familiar with. After they'd left the bustle of Piccadilly she pointed to an imposing building to their right and said, "What is that?"

"That, my dear, is Somerset House. Has no one taken you to see the pictures there yet?"

Yes, she thought. Olivia had mentioned it. She must see about going soon. "How does anyone know that such places exist? Everything is behind closed doors, guarded. Not like the *Dol Jatra* procession. It's out in the open for everyone to see." Another example of what seemed slightly the wrong way around, Anjali thought. She'd become accustomed to riding in an open carriage, but she still felt a bit exposed.

"*Dol Jatra?* Ah. Yes. Much noise and a great deal of disruption—not to mention all the powdered colors the revelers leave behind—makes it a bit difficult to get one's daily work accomplished, and creates more work for the servants."

Anjali sat in shocked silence, feeling a little like a child who had been scolded for something she didn't know was wrong.

Perhaps noticing her sudden stiffening, Lascelles said, softening his voice, "But of course, I realize such things might mean more to you than to the rest of us in the British cantonment."

How very English, Anjali thought, *not to enter into a celebration that required one to act with abandon in front of strangers.*

This surprised her a bit. Lascelles had always been more than willing to attend their evenings of Indian music and dancing. Of course, she herself did not take part in the festivals—not since she was a little girl with her ayah, who would let her trail along behind and be covered in all colors of the rainbow by the time the day was over. The memory tugged at her. There was nothing colorful about London.

As they drove on, rather than thinning out, the traffic—both the vehicles on the street and the pedestrians—became denser, busier, more purposeful. Buildings crowded the street, business establishments were closer together and bore signs that clamored for trade—everything from silk mercers to knife sharpeners, taverns to haberdashers.

"Where are we now?" Anjali asked, shaking herself out of the sulks she'd fallen into because of Lascelles's reaction to the idea of *Dol Jatra.*

"We're on the strand, going toward the district of London known as Cheapside."

It sounded very low. Yet all around were signs of thriving commerce. "This reminds me a little of Calcutta, only not as vivid. No *Dol Purnima* colors here," she said.

He chuckled. "Funny you should say that."

Her dig clearly didn't land. "Shall we go much farther? Would my father wish me to be in this part of London?" It did not seem dangerous. Just different.

Lascelles shrugged, slowing the pair of horses to a walk as they drove down Ludgate Hill. "No more than he would object to your going escorted to the bazaar, I would think."

"Ahead! Look! St. Paul's!" Anjali cried, thinking perhaps he meant all along to take her there. "I know that from the guidebook Papa gave me to divert me on the voyage here. May we go and see it?" she asked, laying her gloved fingers on Lascelles's sleeve.

He looked down at her hand then up at her face, a curious

expression in his eyes. "Perhaps another day. I think you need to persuade your friends to take you to see the sights. Of course, unlike many visitors to London, you would find the menagerie in the Tower of little interest. There's nothing there you haven't seen in far more natural settings in India."

They turned up a street that bordered the Cathedral grounds. So, that hadn't been their destination. Anjali began to feel a little uncomfortable. Why was he taking her so far from Mayfair, and not to any particular famous place? He said they weren't going to the Tower.

They turned again toward the east and continued on that street for a while before a crossroads slowed them and they entered a still narrower thoroughfare. "This is Cheapside, and soon the object of our drive will be apparent," Lascelles said, raising his voice over the clamor and bustle of the street.

Now Anjali's discomfort started to veer into irritation. There was nothing of any particular interest to be seen anywhere. Only more businesses and warehouses. Just as she was about to say so to Lascelles, the street widened again to reveal a massive building occupying a considerable stretch of it on one side. It was newly built in a classical style, with columns and a great portico, and was out of all proportion with the structures around it. Anjali gaped.

Lascelles pulled the horses up right in front of it and stopped. Anjali said, "What is this ugly place?"

He gave a short bark of a laugh. "This, my dear, is East India House."

Home of the infamous Company, Anjali thought. Her father might well be displeased to know she had come here. There was no love lost in his relationship with that monolith. "I think we should return to Park Street now, if this is what you meant to show me."

He shifted the reins to one hand and took hers with the

other. "Aren't you at least curious? The public isn't allowed in, but I have business here so they know me. There's a museum and a library, and an ingenious mechanical device that I'm sure will amuse you." He jumped down from the curricle and called a young lad over, tossing him a coin and instructing him to walk the horses while the two of them went inside for half an hour.

He presumes a great deal, Anjali thought, making no move to descend from the carriage. But she had to confess to some curiosity. And what harm could there be in going into what amounted to an administrative building? They would meet no one who knew her father, or even knew who he was. And she needn't say anything about it to her father either. After some hesitation, she took Lascelles's offered hand and climbed down from the curricle.

The uniformed porter who answered Lascelles's ring on the bell recognized him and bowed politely. "Mr. Lascelles! Are you here to see—"

"I thought I'd take Miss Ashcombe to view Tipu's Tiger."

Anjali thought he was a bit rude to cut the porter's genial greeting short, but she had no time to fret over it. Lascelles ushered her down a corridor to a handsome, carved door that led to a modest-sized hall filled with glass display cases and all manner of curious objects hanging on the walls. The most extraordinary thing, though, right in the center of the hall, was a vividly painted carved wooden tiger, complete with open jaws and lethal-looking teeth, standing over a mauled and bloody carving of a European man. A small legend said it was Tipu's Tiger, and invited the viewer to turn the crank.

"Go ahead," Lascelles said, gesturing toward the handle that extended from the tiger's side.

Both fascinated and repelled, Anjali stepped forward and tentatively turned the crank. When instantly her ears were assaulted by a very loud roar from the tiger and piteous moans from the figure lying on the ground, she jumped back. The unfortunate man's arm lifted a short way as well. Anjali turned her horrified eyes to Lascelles's face.

To her shock, he was covering his mouth to suppress helpless laughter, and his eyes danced with mischief.

"I don't find this funny," Anjali said. "I'm not sure whether the tiger or the man is more disturbing." Tigers were all too real a fact of life in Bengal. To make a spectacle of their menace seemed the height of insensitivity to Anjali.

Lascelles recovered his composure and put his arm out for her to take. "Come, there are much less gruesome exhibits to see here."

They wandered among the glass display cases, which mostly showed captured Indian weapons and domestic objects that were familiar to Anjali but no doubt would seem strange and foreign to any Londoners who might be privileged to come in and look at this odd museum.

"There's a library too. Through here." Lascelles drew her away from a case containing samples of embroidery.

Anjali couldn't imagine what kinds of books would be deemed suitable for a library in that place, and was pleasantly surprised to see several cases of beautifully bound histories and maps. Pride of place, however, went to the manuscripts. These were laid out on a table in the middle of the room. They were mostly on parchment, elaborately illustrated with figures and dainty flourishes, some in vivid colors, others in gold and silver leaf. They were breathtaking.

She approached one that was smaller than the others, on an altogether more personal scale, and not so lavishly decorated. She peered closely at the script and gasped.

"What is it?" Lascelles asked.

"It's Mir!" Anjali whispered. "In his own hand. Poems."

Lascelles wandered over from where he'd been standing

examining a map of India that was affixed to the wall. "Mir? I don't know who that is. How do you know?"

She looked up at him in amazement. "You have never heard of Mir Taqi Mir? The most famous Urdu poet of our time?"

"I find it equally surprising that you *have* heard of the fellow. Surely you don't understand this." He accompanied his words with a dismissive wave at the precious object, written in the Persian-Arabic script that would be immediately identifiable to anyone familiar with the poet's work. "Of course, I know much less about the customs and traditions of the natives than you and your father do."

Anjali had to remind herself that he had not been born in India and had only been there for eight years, and he likely didn't have access to the wealth of literature and art that her mother's family had ensured she be acquainted with. "I do understand it. Isn't the script beautiful? It's like winged, flying things on the page. It looks like poetry even if you don't know what it says. I have an edition of the poems with me in London. I am translating them from Urdu into English."

Lascelles raised a skeptical eyebrow at her and once more took her arm. Anjali looked around her, suddenly becoming aware of the fact that they were the only two people in the library. She was about to hurry away when someone nearby but out of their view cleared his throat. An elderly Indian man stood from where he must have been seated on a leather sofa turned away from them. He came around the sofa and walked forward, put his palms together and bowed. Anjali greeted him in the same manner.

"It is time we were returning," Lascelles said, not acknowledging the intrusion of this stranger, who similarly did not acknowledge him.

"Forgive me, but it is rare for an English lady to take an

interest in our poetry. And to be translating it is a monumental task," the old man said.

An English lady? Anjali was a bit disconcerted by that. "Oh, but I am only half English. My mother's family is from Bengal."

"Ah," the fellow said.

"My father's munshi helped me learn both Urdu and Hindustani, as well as Bengali," Anjali said, recalling the patient scribe's gentle encouragement. She turned to Lascelles, "You remember Hakim."

"That's all very well, but it's time we were leaving."

Anjali resisted for a moment and turned back to the old man. "I am so glad that someone who can appreciate these beautiful things is here to watch over them. What is your name?"

"I am Munshi Abdul Rahman." He bowed to her once more.

Before Anjali could tell him her name, Lascelles tugged harder and she could not with dignity resist. She wanted to wrench herself free of his hand, but also quailed at the thought of making a scene, and so flashed an apologetic smile at the old man as they hastened out of the library.

She said nothing until they were once again seated in the curricle and heading west toward Mayfair. "Mr. Lascelles, I hope you will forgive my impertinence, but why did you treat that poor man so badly?"

"Hm?" he said, distracted by the traffic.

"Mr. Rahman, in the library."

"Yes, very impertinent of him to talk to you like that. But tell me, why did you say you were 'only half English?' I would have thought you would be more inclined to say you were 'only half Indian.'"

"Bengali, to be exact." How revealing. All of it. Now her mind was in a whirl about what she had seen and heard that day and what it could all mean. Why had Lascelles brought her to India House? If he hoped to remind her of Calcutta, he miscalculated badly. Nothing about that place bore any relation to the city she knew and loved. All it called to mind was the British quarter, which always seemed as if it had been dropped in place from the sky.

She looked up from contemplating her folded hands in time to see a large, forbidding-looking building on the left side of the road. "What is that place?" she asked.

"It's Newgate."

Lascelles didn't explain. He didn't have to. It was the fearsome prison Anjali knew of from reading the newspapers and hearing her father speak. She shuddered. "What kind of criminals are in that prison?"

He shrugged. "Mostly thieves, some with more serious, violent crimes. Although I've heard that with this new law they've started putting some of the rebels and political prisoners there as well."

He seemed very well informed. Next time she had an opportunity to talk to Sir Julian she would ask him about it. "Will we be at Park Street soon?" They weren't retracing their route, she noted. But as they were headed west, she was confident that her strange outing would soon be over.

"Soon enough. I'm taking you home via Holborn this time. You'll see where your friend Sir Julian works. He's responsible for getting a number of criminals convicted and imprisoned in Newgate."

This piqued her interest in her surroundings once again, and she followed their progress attentively, revising her increasingly negative opinion of Lascelles as he seemed to recognize that Sir Julian was in some way significant to her, a fact of which she still wasn't certain in herself. She and Sir Julian would have to spend more time together for her to understand it. The thought of seeing the baronet's unruly red hair and kind green eyes revived her spirits still more, and the uncomfortable visit to India House began to fade.

Meanwhile, she would soon be back in the familiar setting of the Park Street dower house. She hoped she would have time for a little private reflection before dressing for dinner.

CHAPTER 19

$\mathcal{C}$aroline yearned for an opportunity to speak privately with Thomas and held out hope that it would be possible at the opera that evening, if for no other reason than to tell him of his daughter's refusal of her first offer of marriage. Somehow, she thought he wouldn't be surprised by that. But the opera party was large, so it might be difficult. Thomas had told her that he would have to arrive separately, saying he had business to transact that wouldn't finish until there was just enough time for him to dress and get from Bloomsbury to the King's Theatre, so she couldn't ask him to come to Park Street early.

Anjali's refusal wasn't the only reason she wanted to talk to him. With the baron out of the picture, that left Sir Julian and Mr. Lascelles—unless someone else came forward with more than passing interest in Anjali. Sir Julian she knew all about, and although she might have wished for a more brilliant match for Thomas's daughter, he was unexceptionable. Mr. Lascelles, however, was harder to pin down. Something about Anjali's mood when she came back from her drive with him raised questions in her mind. The man was certainly handsome and charming, and quite clearly an adept flirt. From what little she'd seen of him with Anjali, he appeared to know just how to ingratiate himself with her by appealing to her nostalgia for India, trading on his familiarity with her and her family. His manners were polished, and Caroline had no misgivings about letting him take Anjali driving, having learned from her son that he'd gone to Eton —although some years before Harry's time—and been assured that his family was a good one.

However, she became a bit uneasy when Anjali and Lascelles remained absent for a very long time. When Anjali finally returned, Caroline asked her if they'd seen some friends in the park and that was why the drive extended until late in the afternoon. Anjali's answer was, "Oh, we didn't drive in the park. Mr. Lascelles took it upon himself to give me something of a tour of London."

A tour of London! She hoped he didn't take her anywhere dangerous. Or take advantage of her in some way—heaven forbid. "Where did you go?" Caroline asked.

When Anjali answered vaguely, claiming not to have paid much attention to the street names, only mentioning that she had seen St. Paul's, Caroline did not press her further. This only reinforced her sense that something Lascelles had shown Anjali on that long drive had disconcerted the girl. She wanted Thomas to see if he could find out what that was.

As they were eleven people, the party that evening was distributed between two boxes. In one box, Olivia sat next to Anjali so she could explain the opera to her—it was Mozart's *Don Giovanni.* Caroline, Belinda, Hector, and Harry sat in the other seats. The other box was occupied by Atherleigh, Antonella, Sir Julian, Lord Jeavons—a friend of both Thomas and Sir Julian—and Thomas. If Caroline had arranged the seating she would have made sure that Sir Julian was nearer Anjali. They naturally did not invite Dawlish to be of the party. She had discreetly let fall to Olivia that Anjali had declined his offer of marriage. And it was Anjali herself who discouraged her from inviting Lascelles. *I'm certain he would not enjoy opera,* was all she'd said by way of explanation.

"I have brought a translation of the libretto for you," Olivia said to Anjali.

Caroline saw Anjali's slightly amused expression and said, "Miss Ashcombe is quite the Italian scholar, my dear. I don't think she'll need to refer to that little book!" Olivia blushed, and Caroline was sorry she had leapt so quickly to Anjali's defense at the expense of her daughter-in-law. "But of course, you weren't to know that. It was extremely kind of you to be so considerate."

"What I can certainly tell you about is the singers. I know all the gossip!" Olivia said, recovering her composure. "You'll hear one of the new stars this evening, Ambrogetti. He has a powerful voice that's also very flexible, and I've seen him perform well in both comic and tragic operas." She spoke for a few minutes about the other members of the cast, adding humorous tidbits about their foibles.

Anjali said, laughing, "I see that performers are performers the world over! Is this opera not very popular? Half the boxes are empty, as well as the benches in the pit."

Caroline entered the conversation at this point. "The fashionable practice is to arrive late and take one's seat with the greatest possible disruption to the people around you."

"That seems very rude!" Anjali said, and they all laughed again.

"Of course, Harry and Olivia insist that we come before the overture even starts—which has the advantage that, besides enjoying the entire opera, we can see everyone who comes into the theatre."

Caroline, reminded of the joys of spying on the other opera goers, peered over the railing of the box and looked into the pit below. The benches were filling up, which meant that at any moment the orchestra would strike up the overture. She was about to turn back to say this to Anjali, when one gentleman's entrance caught her eye, and she gave a tiny gasp.

"What is it, My Lady?" Anjali asked.

"Nothing at all," Caroline said. "I thought I saw someone I knew, but I was mistaken."

What she had seen was Mr. Lascelles entering with a small group of gentlemen—a group that included Lord Dawlish—and a lady decidedly not of the first respectability. He must have sensed her gaze, because he looked up at the box and a slow smile spread across his devilishly attractive face. He turned back to the others who were taking their places just before the orchestra played the dramatic opening chords of the overture, and next to her Anjali jumped, eyes widening.

Unlike many of the spectators in the other boxes, all eleven of them in their party sat in rapt silence listening to the magnificent music—except when they were applauding at the end of a brilliant air. Caroline was glad to see that Anjali leaned slightly forward in her seat, lips parted, as she took in the music. When the first act ended and the audience's applause died down, Anjali turned to her and said, "I never thought music and words could combine to make such a moving whole! I love Indian classical music, but it's very different. It's not made for grand spectacles like this, but to be enjoyed in intimate, private spaces."

Olivia had been listening to her and said, "I should very much like to hear real Indian music someday."

Just as Lady Lewiston was about to agree, a man's voice from behind her said, "If you are so inclined, Lady Lewiston, would you accompany me for a stroll behind the boxes?" raising not-unpleasurable gooseflesh on her neck.

It was Thomas. She had not noticed him enter their box. Caroline had just been wondering how to engineer a private conversation with him, and here he was. He helped her up from her seat and led her out through the box to the corridor, now occupied by other box dwellers wandering and chatting as well as servants with trays of champagne and cakes.

"I'm happy to have a moment to talk to you about Anjali," Caroline said once her hand was hooked through Thomas's strong arm and they'd put a little distance between themselves and the others. It felt so natural to be walking like that, as if no time had intervened to make such contact unusual.

"That is partly what I wished to talk to you about as well. Is she all right? Not unhappy I hope. I got your note about Dawlish. I can't say I'm surprised."

"Nor am I, to be honest," Caroline said. "Now that I know Anjali better, I wonder that I ever thought they could make a match of it."

They both laughed about this, and Thomas said, "I'm sorry I haven't been with you both more, but my business affairs are far from being settled as yet." He pressed her arm closer to his side.

"Please don't worry. I think she's happy. She is certainly occupied! I wish I'd been able to hear what she said to Dawlish. By his expression when he left she must have obliterated his hopes, if he had any." With a start, Caroline realized that she, against her better judgment, had been entertaining hopes of her own—hopes that felt tantalizingly close at times. Especially at times like these.

Thomas smiled down at her. "He'll recover. I judge him to be quite secure in his own worth."

"Indeed. That should enable him to make a very good match elsewhere. He is what the *ton* considers a catch. He arrived this season fully formed after a long sojourn on the

Continent, like Apollo from the head of Zeus." They laughed again. It was so easy to laugh with Thomas. It was one of the things she loved most about him. Loved—past tense? When she recovered she said, "The person I wanted to ask you about was—"

"Sir Julian?" he interrupted. "I like him. A bit of an odd bird, but I can't help admiring him for having a profession. And it's clear he's smart as a whip. A thoughtful man, I think."

Well, it was good to have that insight from Thomas, Caroline thought. It accorded with her own opinion of the gentleman. "I wasn't going to say Sir Julian. I was hoping you could tell me a little more about Mr. Lascelles. Anjali went for a drive with him yesterday and when she returned she seemed … I don't know how to describe it. Not disturbed. Perhaps unsettled?"

"It's hard to imagine how he could have unsettled her during a drive around the park," Thomas said, rubbing his chin thoughtfully.

"That's just it. They didn't drive in Hyde Park. He took her east, toward the city. All she mentioned to me was seeing St. Paul's. She was very vague about the rest of it, but they were gone for quite a long time. I suppose I'm imagining things, but well-mannered and attractive though he is, I can't help vaguely mistrusting Mr. Lascelles. Or perhaps that's why I mistrust him. Forgive me if I'm unfairly judging your friend."

They strolled on in silence for a while until they reached the end of the corridor and turned back—too soon, Caroline thought.

"I know Victor well, and yet not at all," Thomas said, making no sense.

"How is that possible?"

"We have business interests in common—or had—and he

has always been good company. In India we talked at length about many subjects that interest us both, and he was a frequent guest in our house, even when all the other guests were Bengalis. But I never felt he let down his guard or said anything that really revealed his character."

Yes, thought Caroline, she could see how that might be. What little she'd observed of him he always took great care to be agreeable and witty, telling stories that entertained and gave information but no personal insights.

Thomas continued. "I always assumed he, like most of the British in Calcutta, was simply exactly what he seemed to be. A well-born younger son of a family with a genteel competence rather than true wealth, sent out to try to make something of himself. Only he was not so closed minded as most."

"What you're saying," Caroline said, "Is that he presents an acceptable facade but you don't know for certain there's anything of substance behind it."

Thomas pursed his lips in consideration. "What I do know about him is that he makes himself a useful person. His very being here is evidence of that. For no more reason than to oblige someone in a position of influence in the Company he spent three months on a ship to England, and he'll turn around and go back in a week or two. I imagine he is being paid handsomely for this, but he never gives anyone an idea of his circumstances."

They'd arrived back at the door that led into their box, and the musicians were tuning their instruments for the second act. Caroline didn't find what Thomas had to tell her very reassuring, other than confirming that she wasn't alone in thinking Lascelles a rather slippery character.

"Perhaps we can rearrange the seating in our two boxes for the next act. I find I am unwilling to relinquish your company just yet," Thomas said, turning her toward him and searching her eyes with his.

Caroline looked down in confusion and said, "Why, of course. Shall I come and sit in your extra chair?"

"You shall sit next to me and tell me what I am to most admire about this opera. I admit, it is not the entertainment I would choose, all things being equal, but I think if I understood more I would grow to like it better."

Caroline smiled up at him as he led her into the box. "You never did like opera, as I recall. Most gentlemen only come to see the ballets."

"And as I recall, I was quite willing to go wherever you were, whether I liked the entertainment or not."

It was the first time he'd directly referred to any events in their previous acquaintanceship. Caroline had begun to think his love for his late wife had eradicated any tender feelings he might still have been harboring for her. And yet, more and more she sensed warmth from him—warmth that went beyond friendship.

The opera boxes were not capacious. Sitting next to Thomas she would more than likely come into contact with him. It had been such a long time since she'd wanted a man to touch her in any other way than to take her hand in greeting, or to help her in or out of a carriage. She found she very much wished that Thomas would hold her. That was unlikely to happen, but sitting next to him, knowing his solid presence was by her side, was better than nothing.

JULIAN WAS STILL TRYING TO MAKE SENSE OF WHAT HE'D SEEN yesterday when he found himself in a box at the opera with Mr. Ashcombe, Lord and Lady Atherleigh, and Lord Jeavons. He was keenly aware from the first moment he entered it that Miss Ashcombe was sitting in the box next door, along with the other members of the Ambleton family. He was relieved to note that neither Dawlish nor Lascelles were among their company. Indeed, he and Lord Jeavons were the only two who were not related to any of them and he couldn't help wondering why he had been singled out to join this group. He decided he must put it down to Harry, who knew how much he enjoyed opera. In fact, he'd wanted to see *Don Giovanni* ever since he learned that it was being offered this season.

He found Dawlish irritating, but Julian had another reason for not wanting to count Lascelles among the company. That morning, Griggs had come to his chambers for a discreet word with him, saying, "That matter you inquired about? My source discovered this," and slid a folded piece of paper across his desk, not releasing it to allow Julian to pick it up. Correctly interpreting his action, Julian reached into his pocket and placed a sovereign on the desk. The clerk slipped it so quickly into his pocket that if Julian hadn't placed it there himself, he would have assumed he'd been imagining its existence.

It didn't matter, however. Without noticing Griggs leave, Julian unfolded the paper and read. *Well connected, Eton, in the petticoat line. Gaming debts. Awkward situation with a wealthy lady, hushed up and sent abroad.*

None of this surprised him. Lascelles was enough older than Julian that the hushed-up scandal would have long since faded from memory by the time Julian was at the bar. The behavior was too common to inspire more than passing interest.

The note went on to say that Lascelles's father was a country squire of modest fortune, and that Griggs couldn't come by the details of the scandal that had him packed off to India. As to how Lascelles behaved in that country—that could only be conjecture. He was clearly ambitious, as were many men accustomed to living beyond their means. Did his ambition run to basket-scrambling? And was Miss Ashcombe his prey? Julian wouldn't put it past him to be well acquainted with the extent of Mr. Ashcombe's considerable fortune and eager to get his hands on it for himself. Altogether too handsome and charming for most ladies to resist, he thought.

Yet although Lascelles paid assiduous attention to Miss Ashcombe, Julian had the distinct impression that she herself was not the object of his ambition. As to what was, he couldn't say.

Miss Ashcombe's feelings about Lascelles were also hard to discern. The day after the ball she seemed completely enthralled with him. Yesterday—when he glimpsed her seated next to Lascelles in a curricle in the most unlikely part of town—not at all.

He had been about to cross High Holborn to meet a few friends at the Red Lion when the vehicle drove by. There was time for but a fleeting glimpse in which to take in this odd sight, and at first he'd been occupied only with trying to understand why she would be there at all. When he registered the expression on her face, what he saw was not a lady enjoying a pleasurable ride, but someone who appeared as mystified as he was concerning her whereabouts, and perhaps a little vexed. Lascelles, by contrast, wore what could only be described as a smug half smile.

Miss Ashcombe's gaze never deviated from straight in front of her, so Julian was tolerably certain she had no idea he'd seen her. It was possible that Lascelles had caught sight of him, however. The fellow was casting his eyes about, as if trying to discern whether anyone noticed him driving along with the captivating Miss Ashcombe.

His mind occupied with these puzzles, the splendid first act went by in a blur for Julian. He could barely concentrate on the music, he was so distracted. On the one hand, Miss

Ashcombe sat very near him, separated only by a curtain and railing. Very likely, he thought, this was her first experience of opera. On the other, the specter of Lascelles refused to relinquish its hold on his imagination.

"Sir Julian!" Ashcombe's voice called him out of his reverie just before the second act was to start. "I was wondering if you would consider relinquishing your seat to Lady Lewiston."

"Of course." Julian stood and nodded to the dowager, whose glowing countenance told its own story. Jeavons had recounted to him a little of what had happened between Ashcombe and Lady Lewiston as well as the circumstances that led to Ashcombe's departure for Calcutta. It was apparent that the sparks that had existed all those years ago wanted only circumstance to be rekindled. If giving up his seat next to Miss Ashcombe's box would create such a circumstance, Julian was more than willing to acquiesce.

He moved to take the previously empty seat at the back of the box, but Lady Lewiston stopped him. "Wouldn't you prefer to sit where I was in the other box? It's nearer the stage, and I'm sure as a true aficionado you could help Olivia reveal the mysteries of opera to Miss Ashcombe."

He couldn't help smiling, and without a word, went out through the door into the corridor.

His delight at moving closer to Miss Ashcombe was short lived, however. As soon as he closed the door behind him, he saw Lascelles approaching. Lascelles only had a ticket for the pit. Julian had caught sight of him when he rose at the end of the first act. How did he get past the guards? Julian stood still, unwilling to open the door into Miss Ashcombe's box while Lascelles was there.

"Sir Julian! Well met. I was hoping to pay my respects to Lady Lewiston and Ashcombe, as well as Harry and Olivia. And Anjali of course.

Her given name on his lips made something twist in Julian's middle. "Ashcombe and Lewiston are in this box," he said, gesturing toward the door he had just emerged from.

As he said it, Lascelles opened the other door. "I'll say hello to Anjali first, then," and without waiting for an invitation entered the box.

Julian followed him, but Lascelles, seeing the empty chair next to Anjali, immediately sat there. Anjali looked around quickly and spotted Julian, her eyebrows slightly raised. He could do nothing but stand at the back since all the other chairs were occupied as the second act was about to start.

From his vantage point he watched Lascelles lean in to say something in Miss Ashcombe's ear and a faint reddening wash up from the back of her amber velvet gown to the nape of her neck. What was the fellow saying? Julian had no doubt that the man was dangerous. He was just the sort ladies liked. Handsome, witty. He knew how to pay a compliment with address, *unlike me, who can never think of the right thing to say.*

The music started. Surely Lascelles would go to the other box to sit with Harry and Mr. Ashcombe. No one—except the connoisseurs in these two boxes—thought anything of spectators moving around during the performance.

Yet Lascelles showed no sign of leaving and continued to murmur to Miss Ashcombe. She turned to him and put her finger to her lips, signaling that he should not speak, but to no avail. The marchioness—Olivia—reached right across Miss Ashcombe and tapped Lascelles on the arm with her fan. Julian wanted to laugh out loud to see his startled reaction. Rather than excusing himself, however, he settled back into the gilt chair, slightly angled toward Miss Ashcombe. *He'll be bored to death,* Julian thought with satisfaction.

As for himself, he didn't mind standing where he was and listening to the masterly second act of his favorite Mozart opera—a second act where the character of Don Giovanni reveals himself more and more. Don Giovanni cared only for his own pleasure and left a string of scandals and broken hearts all over Europe—*Ma in Ispagna son già mille e tre.* Whatever else he didn't know about Miss Ashcombe, Julian felt certain that—judging by her attitude right now and the day before—she had no interest in succumbing to the charms of her father's beguiling friend.

CHAPTER 20

Please do not invite Lascelles. Anjali had been very clear to Lady Lewiston about that. She needed a day to digest what had happened on their odyssey around London. He had been perfectly polite, not forward or encroaching, but somehow, in London, he didn't seem like the same Mr. Lascelles he was in Calcutta. Still, he would only be there for another sennight or less, and he was still the only channel she could think of to get her letter discreetly to Nalin.

When Lascelles came into the box and boldly sat next to her—leaving Sir Julian standing at the back—she wished she weren't a well-bred lady of quality so that she could have given him an appropriate set down. Her mother would have been able to do it in a way that only the recipient would notice. That was the first time, she thought, that his actions betrayed anything less than good breeding, in her view. But perhaps she was being too sensitive.

He spoke pleasantly, telling her how ravishing she looked, and asked if she was enjoying the opera in a way that made it plain he had little interest in it himself. The second act started and she assumed he'd either go away or remain quietly where he was. Yet he continued to speak to her, as if the music, the action on the stage, was nothing more than background noise for his far more interesting discourse.

Anjali wanted to laugh out loud when Olivia reached across her and tapped him none too gently on the arm with her fan. That silenced him.

And when the opera ended and Don Giovanni descended spectacularly into hell, making the audience erupt into applause and shouts of *bravo!* Lascelles rose, took her hand, and kissed it. "I must leave you to go and fetch a friend whom I wish to introduce to your father. Forgive me for rushing off so suddenly," he said, bowing apologetically to everyone in the box, and then was gone.

Anjali was still recovering from the soul-stirring finale and hardly noticed him leave, so she didn't see Sir Julian make his quiet way forward to take the seat just vacated by Lascelles. When he did, she flashed him a grateful smile, which he returned and said, "I don't want to presume that you are desirous of my company, Miss Ashcombe. But I could just as easily enjoy the ballet from here as from the other box. That is, I believe we planned to remain and watch the ballet."

"Yes. I confess, I feel a bit wrung out after that stirring drama and a little light entertainment would be welcome. So please do stay! Indeed, I wish you had come before this. I had no desire to speak to Mr. Lascelles at this moment. He seems not to be fond of opera."

"What about you? I imagine you've had little opportunity to see it in Calcutta."

She laughed. "I didn't know what to expect exactly. But once I became accustomed to the style, I found myself being drawn into the story."

The relief, the comfort Anjali felt conversing easily with

Sir Julian soothed her ruffled nerves. She needn't attend to anything Mr. Lascelles said and would pretend she hadn't heard him try to bespeak two dances at the upcoming Hartland ball.

Sir Julian's quiet, capable presence—something, Anjali guessed, few outside of his profession were able to witness due to his natural diffidence and anxiety about his outrageously red hair—appealed to her strongly. More than appealed, if she were honest. She found herself recalling how it felt to waltz with him, the touch of his hand, the sureness of his lead. More than once since that evening she had fallen asleep imagining those moments and wishing for them to be repeated.

"Would you like me to get you some champagne?" Sir Julian said.

"No!" The word popped out before she could stop herself. She didn't want him to leave her side. The thought of him going away in that moment was unbearable. "That is to say, I have no need of refreshment at the moment. Unless you…?"

"No," he said, much more softly than she had spoken, and gazed into her eyes, searching them as if he might find the answer to the meaning of life hidden there.

Anjali did not look away.

THOMAS LEFT THE BOX AT THE INTERVAL BETWEEN THE OPERA and the ballet intending to procure a glass of ratafia for Caroline. In truth, sitting next to her, being close enough to inhale the light scent of roses that wafted in his direction every time she moved, affected him powerfully. She was older and wiser, had lived a life of both joy and suffering, but in essence she had not changed. Their time together thirty years ago came back to him in waves of longing, regret, and, yes, passion. He had loved Shanta, deeply. But that did not negate his feelings for Caroline. Although he never expected it, he had to admit that he now found himself inexorably falling in love with that dazzling, beguiling girl—Lady Caroline Holbrooke—all over again. Why had she not tried to communicate with him all those years ago? All he had wanted was a word from her, and he would have stayed, come what might. Now—if he interpreted her feelings correctly—she too was susceptible to him. It was in her every look, her words, her behavior. Had she regretted what she did then?

He was deep in the recesses of his own mind when a voice hailed him from the end of the corridor behind the boxes. "Ashcombe! I want to introduce you to a gentleman I know. I think he could be of assistance to you."

It was Lascelles. Thomas shook himself and straightened his shoulders before striding forward to meet his friend, who was accompanied by a middle-aged man unfamiliar to Thomas. He did not recognize him from any of the *ton* parties he'd been to in these past weeks, so perhaps he was someone with business ties in the city. In any case, he looked like a typical bureaucrat—pale faced, pale eyed, puffy.

"Ashcombe, this is Dobson. He's a senior clerk at India House, and I've told him a little bit about you, that you wanted to tell someone of influence about some financial matters concerning your business—"

"Not directly concerning my business," Thomas said, wanting to steer the conversation to something closer to what he needed to convey, "but deeply concerning that of the EIC."

Lascelles cast a glance around at the other spectators, some leaving before the ballet, others simply wandering and chatting. "I think we should go somewhere a little more private to talk, don't you?"

Dobson said, "I believe there is an anteroom downstairs that is out of the way. If you've no objection? I'm also most interested in any matters to do with the Company in Calcutta. We often do not get the complete picture at India House."

"We must be quick. I've left my party in the boxes and I should rejoin them soon," Thomas said as he followed the two of them down the stairs and through the lobby of the theatre to a room that appeared to be the adjunct to some sort of office with a second door that might have led outside or to another part of the theatre. It was perhaps impolite for him to rush off like that, but he felt he had to take advantage of the opportunity to make a vital connection.

Once the door was closed, Lascelles said, "You haven't told me much about these documents you possess. So they are not simply financial?"

How much should he reveal? If he kept everything to himself, this opportunity might have been for naught. If he revealed too much, it could potentially frighten away someone like Dobson who was associated with the Company. How to strike the right balance? "They are financial, but they touch on much more than simple trade. I have records of transactions that I think the Company ought to be made aware of, as well as first-hand accounts of certain dealings with the zamindars."

Dobson said, "What kind of transactions? We have all the trading documents here. The Board of Control is very scrupulous and demands the most transparent accounting."

Thomas was uneasy about being pressed. Who was this Dobson fellow? Could he really be trusted? Lascelles was a friend, but what did he really know about him, after all? "What is your exact position in the Company, Dobson, if you don't mind me asking?" Thomas suspected he was being a bit over cautious, but he hadn't risked his business and his future without taking great care that those who might have an interest in keeping the misdeeds he uncovered secret did not know what he had.

"I understand your reticence," Dobson said, "But I am chief clerk, appointed by the assistant controller."

The Board of Control was a government rather than an EIC body, so this reassured Thomas a little. "I am most anxious to ensure that the evidence I possess reaches the people with the power to do something about it."

Lascelles said, "I am certain Dobson is your man for that. You refer to financial irregularities, I infer?"

"I wish that were the extent of it. They prove that those who should have the interests of the Crown in India are betraying that trust."

"How so?" Dobson asked.

"They are not presenting the British interests in India in a good light." Thomas wracked his brains for a way to convince Dobson that what he had was explosive without giving anything specific away.

Dobson smiled and said, "My dear Ashcombe, there will always be bad actors in any such situation. We have been made aware of some, and they have been summarily dealt with."

But, Thomas thought, this wasn't about individual bad actors. "No doubt," he said. "But it is not the individuals who are in need of reprimanding. It is the entire operation that is called into question in the evidence I have amassed."

Dobson and Lascelles were silent for a few moments. At last Dobson said, "By the entire operation you mean what exactly?"

"Everything about the British in India. It has been allowed to develop into a system that is rife for abuse of the worst kind." He'd said it now. Surely Dobson must see the urgency of the information he held? "Hastings should be stopped and someone more accountable put in his place. Immediately. Before it is too late."

"So," Dobson said, rubbing his chin, "you would seek to overthrow the individual the government has put in place to manage our interests?"

"Not only that," Thomas said, relieved that his message appeared to be getting through, "it is my belief that the entire system in place in Calcutta should be dismantled and something more accountable to the well-being of those being governed should be instituted." Thomas warmed to his subject. It had been months since the time he first discovered the extent of the extortion and cruelty perpetrated against the Indian landowners by a few at the highest levels of the Company, and he'd thirsted for just such an opportunity as this to share what he knew.

Dobson paced around the room. "So you advocate a complete revolution in the management of the Crown's administrative domain in India?"

"It would be difficult. Conditions on the ground are volatile. I fear that violence might erupt."

"But if the situation could be rectified through such actions you would condone them?" Dobson said.

What was so difficult to understand? Thomas felt as though he could not state anything in plainer terms. Surely Dobson must understand. "Yes, not to put too fine a point on it. I believe extreme measures must be employed."

Lascelles had been listening, looking back and forth between the two men. At last he said, "Of course, you don't really mean to advocate something as drastic as that, Ashcombe. What could possibly justify it?"

Thomas took a deep breath. "If you saw the records I have in my possession, you would agree that the most extreme measures—a complete resetting, if you will, a kind of revolution—would be necessary to stem the corruption."

It was the closest he'd approached to revealing the damning evidence he had hidden away—some in his strongbox, other documents in a place he hoped no one would ever think to look.

At that moment, Dobson's face hardened into a mask. Was he shedding a disguise or putting one on? Thomas hardly had time to register what was happening when two other men entered the room and approached him, each one taking rough hold of one of his arms.

"What—?"

"Mr. Thomas Ashcombe," one of them said, "I apprehend you by warrant of His Majesty's Secretary of State."

After a stunned moment of silence, Lascelles said, "This is outrageous! Dobson, what have you done?"

Dobson said nothing, but the officer who spoke before said, "You are charged upon oath of high treason."

"Treason!" Thomas's voice exploded out of the depths of his body. "It is the very opposite of treason, what I am doing!"

Lascelles said, "Calm yourself. Of course it is, but you can do nothing right now. There must be some mistake. I will get to the bottom of this." He turned to Dobson. "You have the wrong idea entirely. Ashcombe is a loyal servant of the Crown. This is ridiculous!"

Thomas struggled for a moment, but the two burly men had him in a tight grip. The nightmarish quality of the episode was beginning to make him feel dizzy.

"There are people in the theatre, some who know him," Lascelles said. "Surely you can spare Mr. Ashcombe the humiliation of being paraded out in front of them." His voice was acidly bitter. "Thomas, I cannot stop this. It's the new law. I will find out where they have taken you tomorrow."

"Lascelles!" Thomas called over his shoulder as the officers led him out of the anteroom by the other door he'd spied, "Tell Lady Lewiston. And Sir Julian. Try not to frighten Anjali!"

They took him out to an alley where a plain closed coach waited. He didn't know where he would go. How could someone believe he had to do with sedition? With treason?

If only he could go back and tell Caroline and Anjali what had happened. Caroline! Especially now. He was leaving her behind again, although not by his own will. Anjali might perhaps suspect what this was about, except that he'd been careful to tell her as little as possible. She was smart enough to guess, however. She had said things that made him think she knew he had not told her the true reason they had to leave Calcutta. Is she safe? Lascelles will let them know what happened. He must place his trust in that.

Sir Julian—he's a barrister. He might be able to sort this out. He would tell Sir Julian where to find his papers so that the authorities could see the justification for his words, realize that what he wanted them to do was for the good of the Crown, not to undermine it.

And then Thomas thought with a sinking feeling of what he had said to Dobson. *Revolution. Condone. Extreme measures.* His damn passionate nature had led him to be more open about his feelings concerning the Company than he should have been.

Dobson. All at once, the man's face swam in front of his eyes. He'd seen it before. He'd seen it at his club, at Arthur's, that day he met Jeavons.

A chill spread through his veins. Now everything fell into place. Jeavons had been right. He should not have spoken as he did then.

Oh God! How will I ever untangle this?

THOMAS WAS GONE A VERY LONG TIME. THE BALLET WAS HALF over, and still he had not returned with her ratafia. Caroline was a bit distracted—in a pleasant way—by seeing that Anjali and Sir Julian appeared to be enjoying easy conversation, leaning toward each other like old friends. How odd. She would never have matched the two of them. They seemed so very different on the face of it. Clearly they had some kind of connection she could not discern. She must make a point of becoming better acquainted with Sir Julian.

Not long before the ballet was finished, the door of the box opened. Caroline looked around expecting Thomas, but instead, it was Lascelles.

He quietly came forward to where she sat at the front of the box and whispered in her ear. "Thomas asked me to tell you to excuse him. He was taken suddenly ill and had to go home. Nothing serious, but requiring his immediate departure." Lascelles patted his midsection.

"Are you certain he is all right?" Caroline whispered to Lascelles. "Perhaps it was something he ate. The oysters?"

Lascelles said, "Yes, that is likely the case. He said that you should all go home as planned and he would call on you tomorrow—as shall I."

Caroline didn't know whether to be concerned or relieved. Thomas had been used to very different food in India, so perhaps it was just a bit of indigestion. But they were neither of them getting any younger. This reminder was at odds with how she felt in his presence, as if she had returned to a youthful version of herself she'd thought long gone.

The ballet concluded and Anjali looked around, and upon noticing that her father wasn't in the other box said, "Has Papa gone to call for the carriage?"

"No," Caroline said. "He had a bit of indigestion and begged leave to be excused to return home early."

"Indigestion? That's unlike Papa. He has the constitution of an ox!" She rose and let Sir Julian help her into her evening cloak. "However, we'll no doubt discover more tomorrow."

CAROLINE PASSED A RESTLESS NIGHT. WHAT ANJALI HAD SAID made her uneasy. Could Thomas truly have been feeling bilious? Or was he making an excuse to leave before anything more passed between them? For she did not think she imagined that they had taken steps that evening toward a friendship that would become much more than that. And yet, he went away without a word to her. Again. Perhaps he was unwilling at heart. Perhaps his regard for her was superficial, had always been so. His marriage had been a love match, after all, and he had left for India without answering her letter begging him to fight for her. That was the cruelest thing of all. Once she knew he rejected her in the face of her family's opposition, she hardly cared whom she married.

How foolish and self-centered! Likely his leaving the opera had nothing at all to do with her. He was only indisposed. But to be so much so that he would have to leave them like that was worrying in itself.

When Caroline came down to the breakfast parlor that morning, she found Anjali already up, breakfast eaten, and wearing a simple carriage dress. "Good morning dear! Are you going somewhere? It's a bit early for calls."

"I couldn't sleep and woke early. I decided that I must go and call on Papa to make sure he is well. He won't have left for any business meetings or to go to his club as yet, which is why I want to leave right away." Her agitation of spirits was clear. Caroline could hardly blame her.

"If you will wait until I have had some tea, I shall come

with you." She turned to Fairing. "Order the carriage to be here in half an hour."

"Very good, My Lady," he said.

In somewhat less time than that, the two of them were in the barouche tooling towards Bloomsbury. "I'm ashamed to say that I've never been in my father's house," Anjali said. "I realized it this morning. I know it has only been a few weeks, so I don't feel too guilty about it. Besides, he always comes to us or meets us where we're going."

"I expect he doesn't want you to be seen in an unfashionable district," Caroline said, and then, realizing her mistake, said, "Of course, Bloomsbury is perfectly respectable. Many city merchants and professionals live there." She privately thought that perhaps Thomas was unwilling to reveal his less-than-luxurious circumstances to her, as she would of necessity have to accompany Anjali there if she were to visit him.

But when they arrived in Bedford Square, Caroline revised that assumption. Thomas's was a double-fronted mansion of a house that would have been handsome among the grand houses in Mayfair. The difference was only a matter of less than a mile.

A footman came out and opened the door of the carriage, helping each of the ladies out. Standing at the door was a butler in plain but pristine livery trying hard not to look at them with rampant curiosity.

Caroline approached and said, "Is Mr. Ashcombe at home to visitors?"

"I'm afraid not, Madam," the butler said with a deferential nod.

Anjali came forward. "I'm his daughter, Miss Ashcombe, and this is Lady Lewiston, my sponsor. I feel certain he would want to see us."

At that the butler flicked his eyes toward the footman,

then said, "If you will step inside, I shall ask Mrs. Fishgard to come."

This is most odd, Caroline thought, looking around approvingly at the spare yet tasteful furnishings and ornaments, thinking that she would far rather have been invited by Thomas than to arrive unbidden in this way.

Anjali whispered to her, "What do you suppose is wrong?"

Before Caroline could answer, a matronly woman in a starched white cap emerged from a door at the back of the hall behind the staircase. "Good morning My Lady, Miss Ashcombe," she said bobbing two curtsies. "I'll take the liberty of inviting you into the drawing room, if you don't mind."

Stranger and stranger! Caroline thought, but followed the housekeeper up the stairs and into a comfortable first-floor parlor. "Perhaps you would ask Mr. Ashcombe to come down—if he is not unwell, that is," Caroline said, growing a little impatient.

Mrs. Fishgard knotted her hands together and said, "Oh dear," then drew in a long breath and expelled it before saying, "I am afraid I am unable to do so."

"What do you mean?" Anjali said, hackles raised dangerously. "I demand to see my father!"

"We would all like to see him," the housekeeper said. "Unfortunately, he is not here."

Not here? Where could he be?

"Has he gone out already?" Anjali asked in wonder. "I felt sure I would find him still at home at this hour."

The housekeeper looked down at the floor and said, "Normally I would not tell you what I am about to now, except that Mr. Ashcombe is generally most regular in his habits." She paused, looking back and forth between the two ladies, her hands still gripped tightly together. "I am afraid he has not been at home since he left for the opera last evening."

Anjali strode to the window to look out over the square and Caroline sank down on a chair nearby. Not since last night! "Are you certain?" she breathed.

"Where could he have gone?" Anjali said, whirling around, a note of tearful panic in her voice. She ran to Caroline. "My Lady, I am uneasy. I know Papa was trying to keep something from me, something that had to do with why we had to leave Calcutta in such a hurry. He thinks I had no idea, but I suspect ..."

Caroline glared at Anjali and she stopped speaking. It would not do to expose any such fears to the servants. "Perhaps there is a perfectly reasonable explanation." She rose and patted Anjali's shoulder kindly and turned to the housekeeper. "I wonder if you could have a message sent round to Park Street the moment Mr. Ashcombe returns? In the meantime, may I trouble you for a pen and some paper?"

Mrs. Fishgard directed her to an elegant writing desk under one of the windows where she found everything she needed to pen a hasty note to Thomas. There was now no question in her mind that something was very wrong. He would never simply disappear without telling his daughter, or at least causing a message to be sent to her. He must be in a situation where that was not possible. But she wanted to avoid worrying Anjali any more than necessary, so once her note was written she folded it and sealed it with a wafer, wrote Thomas's name on it, and left it atop the desk.

"Come, Anjali. Let us return home. It's possible your papa is there waiting for us at this very moment."

She thanked Mrs. Fishgard and once more begged her to send word the moment they heard anything from Mr. Ashcombe, and then she and Anjali endured a tense ride back to Park Street.

CHAPTER 21

njali fought the urge to scream. How could her father have disappeared? It was completely unlike him. He always took pains to make sure she didn't worry about him. All the way back to Park Street, Lady Lewiston did her best to suggest reasons why he would not have returned to his house. He had felt better and met a friend, and they went to their club for cards and congenial conversation. He remembered a previous engagement and had been invited to stay the night. None of it seemed remotely likely, and the more Lady Lewiston tried to explain away his absence, the more Anjali wanted to leap out of the carriage and scour London for him.

When they arrived back at Park Street, Fairing opened the front door for them and said, "The gentleman is here. Upstairs in the green saloon."

Papa! Anjali thought, and without caring what Lady Lewiston would say, brushed past Fairing, took the stairs two at a time, and ran breathless into the room.

She stopped short. It wasn't her father. It was Mr.

Lascelles. Anjali was too stunned to greet him politely and left that to Lady Lewiston, who was close on her heels.

Lascelles appeared not to have any awareness that an emergency greater than a mere case of indigestion had arisen. "I came hoping to find out from you how Ashcombe is faring after his … indisposition … last night. I hope he is fully recovered." He looked at Anjali and Lady Lewiston in turn, his brow creased in concern. Anjali noticed his hesitation before saying *indisposition.*

Lady Lewiston said with a remarkably calm voice, "We have just been to his house in Bloomsbury. The servants said Mr. Ashcombe did not come home last night."

Anjali expected Lascelles to immediately become as distressed as they were, but to her surprise, he simply said, "I see," and rubbed his chin, then gestured toward a chair and said, "May I?"

He and Lady Lewiston both sat, but Anjali was too overwrought to be still and walked back and forth to the windows, looking out every now and then in the vain hope that her father would come striding down the street.

"You appear to have some thoughts to share with us, Mr. Lascelles," Lady Lewiston said, her voice cool as ice. "Please don't keep us in suspense."

"I don't want to alarm you," he said with a placid smile, "but was Mr. Ashcombe likely to walk back to his house at night?"

Anjali knew this to be entirely plausible. Her father didn't much like being closed in an odiferous and dirty hack. She nodded, not trusting her voice to say anything further.

Lady Lewiston looked at Anjali with alarm. "Would he really have risked doing so? Why, he could have been attacked and robbed and—" She stopped suddenly.

Anjali sank into a chair and put her hands over her face.

"This is very useful to know," said Lascelles, "and by no

means cause for serious alarm. He could have been attacked, or perhaps he was more ill than he thought and collapsed on the flagway, and some good Samaritan might have taken him to a watch house—or even to a hospital. St. George's, for instance."

"My Papa spent thirty years in India making his way through desperately poor districts at times and he knows how to protect himself. I just don't see how a London footpad could have taken him enough by surprise to over-power him." Anjali wanted to believe he had not been robbed —he always made sure he had a roll of soft in his pocket so he could take care of any expenses, as well as a coin purse for dispensing tips and vails. A robber would have reaped a rich haul.

The other possibility, that he was so ill that he collapsed senseless, seemed more plausible, and yet ... She felt the bile rise into her throat and struggled to suppress it.

"Mr. Lascelles is right. We must make inquiries straight away," Lady Lewiston said. "Where should we begin?"

Anjali all at once perceived that Lady Lewiston's calm was beginning to fray at the edges. The normally imperturbable lady was fighting to retain control of her emotions. This was, in its way, more alarming than it would have been had she flown into panic in the first place.

"Please leave this in my hands for now," Lascelles said. "I will make inquiries at the hospitals—St. Georges and The Middlesex would make the most sense—and at the watch-houses between Mayfair and Bloomsbury. I will of course return to you with any discoveries I make, or perhaps even with Ashcombe himself."

His smile was meant to be reassuring, Anjali thought, but it was clear to her that he was treating their concern as a hysterical reaction to something that he thought might be perfectly harmless. "And what if you do not find news of my father in any of those places?"

"Forgive me—" Lascelles said, then cleared his throat. "I didn't want to say anything while you are so agitated. But last night … Thomas begged me to make his excuses and it seemed to me that he was unwell. However—since he did not return home—it might be that … how can I say it without … I don't want to be impertinent, but …"

"What?" Anjali said, her voice sharp. "Just tell us. Anything to put us out of this misery!" She didn't want to look at Lady Lewiston, who was no doubt horrified that she had spoken with so much heat.

"Very well," Lascelles said, "I can only surmise that Mr. Ashcombe had another private reason to leave so precipitately."

Anjali stared hard at Lascelles. "What *private reason* could you mean? My father would not have gone away without telling me for any reason whatsoever, private or not, unless he was very unwell indeed. I thought last night that it was odd, but I trusted what you said. Today, knowing he didn't return home from the theatre, I am persuaded that he is in some peril or other. Perhaps, as you say, he collapsed and is languishing in a hospital. I don't know! What explanation can there be?" Her voice had increased in volume as she spoke, until she uttered her final sentence in such stentorian accents that the crystal drops in the chandelier over their heads tinkled quietly.

Lascelles stood and went to her, taking one of her hands in a strong grip. Anjali wanted to shake him off. Ever since their jaunt into the city, she had been uncomfortable in Lascelles's presence. Although his expression was one of serious concern, his eyes seemed curiously untroubled, almost assessing. "May I beg you to leave this in my hands?

Let us not jump to the worst conclusions. I am certain I can discover what's amiss."

Anjali could stand it no longer and wrenched her hand away. "I should like to consult Sir Julian. He has much greater knowledge of London and of what might have happened to someone like my father. Papa would have come home if he could have, I know that."

Lascelles shook his head and turned to Lady Lewiston. "Please come to my aid, My Lady, and impress upon Miss Ashcombe the unwisdom of taking such a step. I would urge you not to trouble Sir Julian at this juncture. What if it indeed ends up being nothing more than an innocent misunderstanding?"

"You can hardly blame Miss Ashcombe for being concerned for her father's well-being, as am I. Deeply concerned," Lady Lewiston said. "But, perhaps you are right, and we should give you a little time to investigate before taking the matter further."

That was the last thing Anjali wanted to do. Nonetheless, although she was willing to offend Mr. Lascelles, she felt it would not be polite—or politic—to contradict Lady Lewiston. Her chaperone was older and knew the ways of the world, and of men, better than she did, and she was clearly deeply troubled by her father's disappearance. But she was maddeningly content to relinquish the burden of inquiry on Lascelles for now, which Anjali was not. She needed to get out of that room and away from that man right away. She didn't know why exactly, but his presence impeded her ability to breathe. It was not any of his business what had become of her father. Just because he knew them from Calcutta was no reason for him to assume an intimate connection. "I fear I have the headache," Anjali said. "If you will excuse me, I should like to retire to my bedchamber."

"Of course, my dear," Lady Lewiston said, rising and

coming to her. She took Anjali's hand and pressed it, then murmured, "I'm sure Thomas—your papa—is all right. I expect he'll return any time. Let's just see what Mr. Lascelles can discover."

Anjali gave her a wan half smile and without taking her leave of Mr. Lascelles fled up to her bedchamber.

As soon as she opened the door, desperate to fling herself down on her bed and cry with frustration, Kavi gave a great squawk and said, "Namaste!"

It was so unexpected and comical that for a moment Anjali let out a sharp laugh. *How could I?* she asked herself. There was nothing amusing about her father's disappearance. But Kavi's intrusion into her thoughts made her think again about Sir Julian and Bramble. The mere image of his tall, lanky figure walking the ridiculously ebullient spaniel sparked a warm feeling somewhere near her heart. That feeling spread slowly outward until her entire body felt comforted and a little calmed.

In a moment of decision Anjali strode to the desk in front of the window and sat down, taking a sheet of paper out of one of the drawers and placing it on the surface. It didn't matter what Lascelles or Lady Lewiston said. She would write to Sir Julian. He would know what to do. He had much more extensive knowledge of crime and the underworld in his role as a barrister if some mishap of that sort had indeed occurred. And whatever the outcome, Anjali felt instinctively that she could trust him. Which was not how she felt about Lascelles. She didn't quite know why, but everything he said downstairs came across as disingenuous, even if he wasn't actually prevaricating. It was as if he wanted to make himself sound more capable and caring than he actually was.

She wrote a quick note to the baronet. But where did he live? How would she get it to him? And then she recalled that Lascelles told her that Sir Julian's chambers were in Lincoln's

Inn. By this time of day he was likely there. Unlike so many in the *ton*, Sir Julian was conscientious about his work. That was well enough, but who could see that the letter reached him?

Andrew. The footman had a liking not only for Kavi but Anjali guessed he was a little smitten with her as well, and would agree to do whatever she asked of him. She would give him a sovereign for his trouble, because she intended him to wait to put the letter directly into Sir Julian's hands and bring a reply, which he would have to deliver to her without anyone seeing it.

Simply taking some sort of action was a balm to her spirit. She hastily folded and sealed the note then rang the bell for Andrew. It was a step. One step closer to discovering what had happened to her father. Whatever it was, however bad, she must know.

AS SEEMED TO HAPPEN OFTEN EVER SINCE HE'D MET MISS Ashcombe, Julian's mind refused to bend itself to the knotty legal problem buried in the pages spread over his desk. All he could think about were those magical moments sitting next to Miss Ashcombe in the box at the King's Theatre the night before. They were close enough that he could feel the warmth of her body next to him. What had they talked about? Everything and nothing. It was so easy, so natural. At the same time, the deepening attraction he felt for her heightened every sense. He remembered bits and pieces, but mostly he recalled how lively she was, how intelligently she spoke on several subjects, how interested she was in matters that pertained to him. Her subtle scent of spices. The warm tone of the skin on her upper arm, between her puffed sleeve and the top of her evening gloves.

When Griggs ushered a footman in Lady Lewiston's livery into Julian's chambers, he looked up guiltily.

"A message for you, Sir Julian," said the servant, who handed him the folded and sealed letter.

He did not recognize the handwriting. It wasn't Lady Lewiston's copperplate—he knew that from the invitations he'd received. He examined it curiously at first. He'd been planning on paying a call of ceremony in Park Street later after he finished his work. What could this be?

"If you please, sir, my mistress was most insistent that I wait for an answer and bring it to her directly." The young footman blushed as he said this.

Not a simple invitation, then, Julian thought, quickly breaking the seal and spreading the note scrawled across a single sheet open on his desk.

A moment later he jumped to his feet and said, "Tell Miss Ashcombe that I will do as she bids me."

"Very good sir," the footman said, bowed, and left.

Julian, meanwhile, was scrambling into his coat and wildly trying to discover where he had lain down his hat, only to see that it was resting on the table by the window. He snatched it up and hurried out of his chambers, not even bothering to tell Griggs where he was going or when he would be back.

Miss Ashcombe's note awakened all his instincts as a man and a member of the legal profession. It simply said, *My father is missing. Meet me in the Green Park, at the same place.* Since they'd only met there once, anyone would be forgiven for being skeptical that Julian would recall where *the same place* was. Except that the exact location was emblazoned on his heart, and would be until the end of his days. Would that he could fly there. Her father missing? Ashcombe had left rather suddenly the night before, but Lascelles said that was because he was indisposed. What could this mean?

. . .

By the time he strode up to where Anjali stood pacing back and forth, Kavi perched on her shoulder, Julian had rapidly thought through several possible scenarios that would account for Ashcombe's disappearance. But it was no good conjecturing, his practical mind said, before he had all the facts, the relevant information—and he had none of them at present.

When Anjali spotted him she rushed forward, stopping a few feet away as if suddenly recollecting herself. "Thank you, Sir Julian. I am sorry to trouble you, except that I am beside myself with worry!"

Her eyes filled with tears that she blinked away, and he had to suppress the urge to take her in his arms and comfort her. "Tell me everything. Don't leave out the smallest detail," Julian said, leading Anjali to a bench. Only then did he notice a maid standing a short distance away.

Miss Ashcombe's eyes followed his. "It's Millie. She won't come closer. She's afraid of Kavi, which is why I brought him." The ghost of a smile flitted across her face.

After only a few minutes Julian was in possession of the facts as far as Anjali knew them. He said nothing for a while, just sat looking down at his feet and thinking. "You said Lascelles is checking the hospitals and watchhouses."

"Yes, only—I don't know, something made me think he's not as concerned as he ought to be that my father, his good friend, is nowhere to be found."

Julian thought that was significant as well. He did not hold Lascelles in high esteem, and not merely because it appeared he was trying to fix his interest with Miss Ashcombe. Nor was his dislike based solely upon what Griggs had told him about the fellow's past actions. Something about his arrival in London so soon after Ashcombe's seemed too convenient. "What is Lascelles's precise relationship with your father? Are they in business together?"

"No, although they are in similar trade. Mr. Lascelles acts as an intermediary between the East India Company and some of the landowners in Bengal."

Although he had not been told directly, Julian had some idea that Ashcombe was highly critical of the EIC and had come to London in part for a reason tied to this criticism. "Miss Ashcombe, please don't think me inquisitive for any other purpose than my interest in seeing your father safely restored to you. But do you know if he has any enemies in London? Perhaps people associated with the Company who bear him a grudge?"

Anjali knitted her brow. "I don't know for certain about that, but I do know that he has some very valuable papers in his possession, although he has not told me what they concern. Oh Julian—Sir Julian—we left Calcutta in a frightful hurry, almost as if Papa thought someone was after him, but he didn't say a word to me about it. I can't imagine why anyone should dislike him. He is the most honest man I know."

Julian took a long breath and closed his eyes for a moment. His experience told him that honesty was no guarantee of fair treatment, or of respect. Indeed, many dishonest men held those of the opposite stripe in strong aversion. "Of course, it could be that your father suffered an illness or an accident, as Mr. Lascelles has suggested. It happens that I'm acquainted with sources other than the watch where I might be able to find out if that was indeed the case, sources that would be unknown to Lascelles. I fear, though, that his disappearance may be tied to other matters."

"What other matters?" Anjali gripped his arm in a sudden movement, causing Kavi to flap and squawk.

Julian covered her hand with his and looked into her

deep, brown eyes. How he wished he could erase the pain and confusion he saw there! "I am too uncertain to say anything yet. I shall make some inquiries among those with more knowledge of such things. Sometimes a person's actions can be misinterpreted." Or more likely, he thought, willfully misconstrued. "I promise I will visit this evening and tell you everything I have been able to discover, as well as what I intend to do next."

She gave a huff of a laugh. "You're likely to meet Mr. Lascelles there if you do. He has promised much the same thing."

Julian smiled, but said nothing, only bidding Anjali adieu and watching her walk away, head bowed, followed at a distance by her abigail. Julian knew that there was no way Lascelles could discover what he would be able to, even if he wanted to. And he was beginning to doubt that the fellow did so. He knew the type. Lascelles only cared about his own concerns, what would bring him the greatest benefit. It could be that Ashcombe's disappearance would in some way reward Lascelles. It would fit with everything that Griggs communicated to him—none of which did Lascelles very great credit. Julian had not planned to reveal any of the fellow's sordid past to Lady Lewiston or Miss Ashcombe. But if things turned out to warrant it, he would have no hesitation in making them both aware of everything he knew.

CHAPTER 22

Although for Thomas the nightmare began the moment he was apprehended at the theatre, it acquired monstrous proportions as the hours went by. His captors first took him to Bow Street, where he sat in an open office amid the confusion of runners coming and going, miscreants entering under guard, clerks shuffling papers, and the sordid business of apprehending criminals going on around him. If it weren't for the beefy guard stationed next to him, he thought at the time, he could have slipped out unnoticed in the chaos.

Even there he held out hope that he might be charged and released, so he could refute whatever it was Dobson accused him of, explain that his words had been misinterpreted.

But no one asked him anything. And any attempt on his part to tell someone that a terrible mistake had been made was ignored. It must have been around midnight when he arrived, and from the hard bench where he sat he could see the night sky gradually lighten to gray, the men around him leave and be replaced by others, and hear the sound of a distant clock chiming to mark the hours until morning. He didn't think he'd slept at all, only perhaps fading into some dreamlike state for a few moments.

His confused thoughts played the scene at the theatre over and over again. He was tormented by how worried Anjali must be, and what Caroline must be feeling at that moment. Had he proved himself entirely unworthy of her by allowing himself to be apprehended this way? Perhaps she was congratulating herself on her near miss, perhaps thinking her parents had been right about him. A terrible scandal might ensue even if he could somehow be released quickly. His heart sank like a boulder.

At some point while his mind traced over and over paths it couldn't find its way beyond he was bundled into another conveyance that took him to Whitehall. There he sat in an anteroom with several other men of different stations and ages, expressions of combined anger and fear on their faces, hands gripped until their knuckles whitened. If any of them tried to talk they were quickly shut down, so they sat there looking at each other or at the floor, the walls, the high ceiling—anywhere—as one by one they were called into the chamber beyond and never seen again. As he waited, Thomas permitted himself a glimmer of hope that perhaps Sir Julian would have begun to untangle this mess. He knew the law. And he loved Anjali, Thomas was certain of that. Surely he could make everyone see that this was all an enormous mistake.

All that was left was for Thomas to hope that whatever awaited him beyond the door in front of him would give him an opportunity to address the spurious charges that had been brought and defend himself against them so that he could be released.

After what felt like an interminable amount of time it was his turn to go through to the other room. As soon as he entered it his heart sank. Here was no judge. At the single long table covered in papers sat a soberly clad, very correct gentleman Thomas later learned was Lord Sidmouth, the Home Secretary. Two other officials flanked him and a clerk hovered nearby. Sidmouth lifted one of the papers from the table and perused it for a long time before speaking.

"You have been apprehended by warrant on suspicion of treason, I see."

Treason. The word sent a chill down Thomas's spine. "My Lord, I—"

"You may answer my questions, but otherwise remain silent," Sidmouth said. "Who introduced you to Dobson?"

A very odd question to begin with, Thomas thought. "I believe—I saw him some weeks ago, but did not meet him until introduced by my friend, Victor Lascelles."

"Are you acquainted with a certain Mr. Heatherington from Calcutta?"

Where had that come from? What bearing could that man he hardly knew have on whatever this was about? "Only remotely," he answered.

"You entered into a close alliance with a Bengali family during your time in India, I am told. Is this true?"

A *close alliance?* "I assume you are referring to my marriage into one of the foremost landowning families in the region. The father is a zamindar. My wife is now deceased."

Lord Sidmouth examined another paper and the clerk leaned to whisper something into his ear and then noted something down in a small book.

Sidmouth raised his eyes to Thomas again and said, "How long have you known Lascelles?"

Thomas told him. He didn't understand. This was madness. Why ask such a question? Why ask any of these questions?

And then, all at once, everything started to become clear,

as though a noxious breeze was gradually blowing away the poisonous fog in his brain. That was when the questions took a turn that made Thomas's stomach clench.

Sidmouth began asking him about Calcutta, why he had come to London, and whether he possessed any papers or documents related to the conduct of the East India Company or His Majesty's government. When Sidmouth asked whether his wife's family had ever participated in the uprisings in the west of the country, Thomas had to suppress a bitter laugh. Clearly the man had no real idea of Indian politics or geography.

Then the Home Secretary began to ask still more pointed questions about his life in Calcutta, probing about details no one who hadn't known him—and known him well—could possibly be aware of. *Was it true that he was on friendly terms with many natives whom he entertained in his home? Was it true that his daughter could read the Indian script and participated in Hindu rituals?*

Lascelles. He was the only person who would have been able to give Sidmouth such personal details. The Home Secretary could not have come by that information any other way. And now they were twisting perfectly innocuous facts around so that he appeared to be fomenting rebellion in India.

It was not in Thomas's nature to lie, but he saw the murky waters waiting for him to step into and drown and did not want to answer Sidmouth. "I beg pardon, My Lord, but upon what exact charge am I being held? Or am I here based merely on a suspicion?"

"Please answer the questions that have been put to you."

Thomas stood straighter and said, "I know of nothing that could bear upon these unfounded accusations." He had sworn no oath and this wasn't a courtroom. Thomas was not a legal professional but he'd spent thirty years negotiating contracts and knew when it was politic to hold his tongue, to keep information in reserve.

"Did you state at the King's Theatre last evening that you possessed evidence of actions in India that would justify insurrection?" Sidmouth asked.

"I will not answer any further questions until I am shown the charge against me and know the names of my accusers."

The three men seated at the table held a hushed conference, then Sidmouth nodded to the guard who had brought Thomas in. The surly man once more took rough hold of his upper arm and pulled him through another door that led to a stairway down to street level, where he was again bundled into a closed carriage with no windows. He did not know where he was going, only that he was passing through and beyond London traffic for perhaps somewhat less than an hour. All the time his brain worked feverishly to try to think of a way out of his predicament—in the few moments it wasn't agonizing over how Anjali and Caroline must be feeling.

When at last the conveyance came to a halt and he stepped down from the vehicle, Thomas found himself facing a very long, high brick wall with a heavily armored door and no windows that he could see. *A prison.* How could he be in a prison without having had a trial and been convicted of anything?

Then he remembered vaguely what Sir Julian and Anjali had spoken about in Lady Lewiston's drawing room the day after the rout party. Something about a law that enabled anyone to be apprehended and held on suspicion only. He'd not paid close attention. It seemed remote from anything that could possibly have to do with him. What other law, however, would lead to his being imprisoned without having committed a crime and without any legal representation? At that moment a turnkey, stationed in a room just inside the door, let them in and closed, locked, and chained the door behind them. After that, the guard led him through a network of corridors and courtyards with no view outside the walls. Each time he passed into a different enclosure, a door or gate was unlocked and then bolted behind him with a chilling clunk.

At last the guard opened a barred door that led into a square room at the end of a short corridor. One small window set high in the wall gave a view of an implacable gray sky. The room was furnished only with a narrow cot covered by a mouse-eaten blanket, a table, two rough wooden chairs, a chamber pot, and an inadequate coal fire in a soot-blackened hearth. From this, smoke filtered about equally up the chimney and into the room. A sconce with a single tallow candle appeared to be the only light that would illuminate the space once daylight faded.

"You're staying here," the guard said.

"And here is … where? Where am I?" Thomas could barely form the words, his mouth was so dry.

The guard lifted one corner of his lips in a sneer and said, "Ye're at Coldbath Fields."

The only London prisons Thomas knew of were Newgate and King's Bench. What was this place? At least he wasn't in a crowded cell with hardened criminals.

What was he saying? He was locked away! It didn't matter where. All at once, he craved nothing more than the freedom to stride about in the open air. How had this happened? Who was Dobson really, and how did he have the power or influence to instigate this chain of events?

More importantly, why had Lascelles given away the existence of his papers?

Surely his friend couldn't have known what would happen when he introduced him to Dobson. He had been shocked when Thomas was apprehended. Or was he really?

In whose interest has Lascelles truly come to London? Lascelles was the master of playing both sides of an issue, Thomas knew well from their time in Calcutta. Whose side was he on now? Whatever the answer, Lascelles was out there, telling Anjali and Caroline—what was he telling them? Surely as soon as they knew what happened they would have set the wheels in motion for his release. But what if…

It didn't bear thinking about. If Lascelles didn't tell the two most important women in his life what had truly occurred they wouldn't know to raise the necessary questions and set the legal remedy in motion. *I must send them a message.* They must be able to alert someone to come to his aid if Lascelles had failed to do that.

Just before the guard locked the door behind him, Thomas said, "My daughter will be beside herself with worry. I must let her know where I am, what has become of me. Please bring me a quill, ink, and paper."

The guard grinned. "Now how d'ye think I'd come by such as all that?"

Of course, Thomas thought. He would have to pay for anything beyond the barest necessities. "I'm a wealthy man. They took my money at Bow Street, but you will be well rewarded by the recipient of my message. I must not leave my poor daughter to wallow in the misery of not knowing what has happened. I was taken unbeknownst to her." There was no need to mention Caroline at this point, although her reaction, for reasons he had only begun to understand, weighed even more heavily upon him.

The fellow paused, then laughed. "No one's decided nuffing about you, so it's more'n my neck is worth to bring you anyfing. Not til Sidmouf has a say."

Before Thomas could protest, he was gone, whistling merrily as he strolled down the corridor away from him.

WHEN ANJALI RETURNED TO PARK STREET, CAROLINE COULD see that she was still very agitated. Her walk had done little to calm her, which was completely understandable. Caroline could barely stay still herself she was so wracked with worry. With a huge effort to set aside her own anxieties for Anjali's sake, Caroline did her best to get Anjali to occupy her mind with other things. Her efforts were futile. What did Caroline expect when she herself was barely able to set a stitch in her embroidery, and when she picked up a book, the words simply danced on the page and made no sense.

They ate a desultory dinner together, each of them hardly tasing a morsel, starting at every sound from the street. When at last a carriage drew up and was followed by a knock on the front door, Anjali shrieked.

"Calm yourself, my dear. Being in a passion will not help anything," Caroline said, taking Anjali's arm with her own trembling hand and leading her into the drawing room to await the visitor.

But it wasn't just one person entering down below. A babel of happy voices sailed up the stairs, soon to be followed by Fairing opening the door so that Belinda, Antonella, Gainesworth, and Atherleigh could enter. Normally glad to see her family at any time, Caroline thought they could not have come at a worse moment. What could she tell them?

They all greeted one another, Belinda saying, "I hope you don't mind that we invited ourselves to come and drink tea with you!"

Antonella said to Anjali, "I hear you enjoyed the opera! I'm afraid I don't love the entertainment very much. That will likely be the only opera we attend this season—" She stopped speaking abruptly and moved a step closer. "Something is troubling you. Are you ill?"

Belinda heard this and said, "I expect it's her Papa's indisposition. He left before the end of the ballet." Turning to Anjali, "Is he recovered now?"

At that moment Caroline held up her hand, exchanging a speaking glance with Anjali, and all talking in the drawing room ceased."Please, everyone, sit. We have something to tell you. To explain."

For a few unbroken minutes, Caroline tried to give them the gist of what had happened since they were all at the opera together. But she could not keep her voice from shaking slightly. Belinda sat next to her and took her hand.

Shocked silence reigned until Atherleigh stood, adopting the demeanor of an officer surveying his troops before a battle. "What is being done? Who is looking for Ashcombe, and where?"

"Mr. Lascelles said he would ask at the hospitals and watchhouses," Caroline said.

Atherleigh shook his head. "It's not enough. Please allow me—"

Before he could say a word more, the door knocker fell again and Fairing greeted a visitor down below. A man's voice. Not Thomas's. Caroline would know his voice anywhere.

No one spoke. No one even breathed until the door opened and Fairing announced Mr. Lascelles.

Caroline said, "Mr. Lascelles. You find us *en famille*. I have just explained everything to my daughters and their husbands. Have you any news to share?" She tried to read the likely answer in Lascelles's expression, and couldn't.

"I am so sorry," Lascelles said, "to interrupt." He strode to Anjali and took her hands. "I have spent every moment since I left you this morning, Miss Ashcombe, making inquiries throughout London. I have checked hospitals and watchhouses, as well as some other localities … better left unmentioned." He paused and turned his attention to Caroline. "I am afraid I am unable to bring you any definite news, although I found a few tantalizing tidbits that turned out to result in only more confusion."

Atherleigh, who still stood at attention in the center of the room, said, "There is little an individual unfamiliar with London and its ways can accomplish. I have numerous contacts, both military and civil, and will immediately see what I can bring to bear on this distressing occurrence."

Caroline had never witnessed Atherleigh in so magisterial a mood, and was impressed—and a little relieved. No doubt what he said was true. She really only knew him from Cornwall, but he had begun to take an active role in the House of Lords and knew many influential men.

"My Lord," Lascelles said, "I am not certain this warrants any military or government intervention. Surely it's still a private matter, to be dealt with discreetly."

Caroline's brow furrowed. What was Lascelles implying? Did he think Thomas had gone off on a drinking or gambling spree? Or gone whoring on a whim? The Thomas Caroline knew would never have done any of those things and, as far as she could tell, he had not changed fundamentally in his thirty years of absence. It was preposterous.

There was no time for her to react to Lascelle's words, however, because while he was speaking, another visitor arrived and now stood at the door of the drawing room.

Sir Julian!

She didn't know why, but Caroline instinctively felt that in the awkward young barrister lurked a deep well of capability and intelligence—not that Atherleigh was not also capable. But Sir Julian had an altogether different, more subtle view of the world. He had to perceive the myriad shades of gray, to find the chinks that would allow something true to emerge, where Atherleigh, as a soldier, was drilled in the black and white reality of enemy and ally. If Sir Julian could be prevailed upon to turn his mind to the problem, Caroline felt certain it had a chance of being solved.

The baronet first greeted everyone, sweeping the room with an assessing gaze, pausing a little longer first on Anjali, and then on Lascelles, who didn't look at him directly. Then he spoke. "I will not waste any time with meaningless pleasantries. I have some news of Mr. Ashcombe. I should like to share it privately with Miss Ashcombe and Lady Lewiston. I mean no disrespect to others present."

How came Sir Julian to know of their troubles? Caroline fixed Anjali with an inquisitive stare. It could only be she who somehow managed to tell the baronet of Thomas's disappearance. When had she?

On her walk, of course.

Lascelles ambled toward Sir Julian, hand held out as though he expected to be greeted as a friend. "Good fellow! Surely there is nothing so dire as cannot be shared with all who have Ashcombe's well-being at heart? I'm half inclined to believe that your fiery head has been indulging in fantasies! I am most anxious to hear what you have discovered, for I could find nothing."

The icy stare the baronet gave him in return stopped him in his tracks. It seemed that Sir Julian did not like the man. Caroline wondered if that sentiment sprang from the fact that he perceived him as a rival for Anjali's affections, that Lascelles made fun of his remarkable red hair, or for some other cause she was not aware of.

Caroline drew herself up and said, "Of course, Sir Julian. Anjali, let us go down to the library. Fairing will bring wine to the drawing room. I think we all need something stronger than tea."

The three of them descended the stairs in silence. Her heart pounding uncomfortably, Caroline closed the door of the library behind them. "Please, Sir Julian. Tell us what you know."

His expression was serious, but calm. "I do not know where Mr. Ashcombe is. But I do know that he has been apprehended under authority that is linked to the Suspension of Habeas Corpus Act."

CHAPTER 23

*A*njali inhaled sharply. "Why?" She could not think of anything else to say.

Lady Lewiston said, "Apprehended? You mean he has been arrested? Charged? Taken before a magistrate? Whatever for?"

Sir Julian shook his head. "There has been no charge, and no actual arrest. He is being held at His Majesty's pleasure at a place I will discover tomorrow. No magistrate has heard his case, nor will one, until a charge is brought."

Anjali couldn't breathe. The power to inhale simply left her. All she could do was try to gulp air into lungs that felt too small. Tiny dots appeared before her eyes and the room dimmed.

For a few minutes, Anjali was aware only of being steered to a settee, a lady's voice saying, "My vinaigrette! Here!" and firm hands supporting her and then gently pushing her head down between her knees. A calm, lower voice said, "Breathe, Miss Ashcombe. All will be well. I make you a solemn promise."

She clung to the words as if they were a sturdy craft sent to rescue her from a foundering ship.

After a short while, her world rearranged itself before her eyes and she sat up. Sir Julian was next to her, still holding her, and Lady Lewiston knelt by her on the floor. "Oh! I am so sorry," she said. "I don't know … That has never happened before. I'm quite well now. It was just the shock." Anjali lifted her eyes to meet Sir Julian's. Their green-gold depths held a world of care, of longing. No one had ever looked at her like that before. In that instant she knew. He loved her. And, with sudden and complete comprehension she was certain that she loved him too.

She gasped at the unexpected thought, and Sir Julian's grasp tightened. Did she say any of that out loud? "No! I'm all right. I swear. Lady Lewiston, I'm sorry I didn't tell you before. I sent a message to Sir Julian to meet me in the Green Park and I told him all. I couldn't sit here and do nothing."

"Drink this," Lady Caroline said, holding out a glass of wine to Anjali. "I do understand."

"I don't want it. I just want to know. Sir Julian, what has happened to my father? Please tell us everything."

Sir Julian took a deep breath, but he didn't let go of her hands. Perhaps that was because she was holding onto his just as tightly. "I went first to the King's Theatre to see if anyone had seen Thomas leave, and found a porter who did so. The man said he saw him put into a vehicle under restraint and taken somewhere."

"How could you know where?" Anjali said, wanting certainty but fearing its opposite.

"Bow Street would be the only logical place to take someone in that circumstance. I went there. They told me nothing—or very little—which told me everything." He then explained that a simple criminal charge would have been easily tracked down.

When a clerk told him that Ashcombe had been sent on somewhere else, he knew instantly that this was not a case in the usual manner. Only the Home Office had the authority to cause such a procedure, which meant there was a warrant and he was suspected of something that fell under the infamous act.

Anjali felt an odd mixture of calm at the reasonable explanation given by Sir Julian and anguish at her own powerlessness. "What now? What will you do next?"

"I will first go to the likely place of detention."

"Not Newgate!" Anjali cried, a vision of that menacing building rising before her eyes.

Sir Julian's expression softened. "No. He would not be thrown together with cutthroats and villains. There is another prison to the north where those whose crimes are more political than legal are sent."

"Why is it so difficult to clear up this matter? Surely he simply needs to show he is innocent," Caroline said, a sob in her voice.

"Innocent of what exactly?" Sir Julian shook his head. "It's impossible to refute something that has not been officially charged. Therefore it is important that we identify the source of the information and discredit it so that the Home Secretary will withdraw the accusation."

He continued to stare fixedly at Anjali. All at once, she knew. "You suspect Mr. Lascelles, don't you."

Sir Thomas give the slightest nod, and said, "Suspicion is not enough, however. But I think Lascelles will find that if he is indeed involved, he has meddled in something far beyond his ability to control. I believe, as well, that he is likely only the instrument, not the instigator."

Anjali's thoughts whirled. Whatever she thought of him, Lascelles was her father's friend. Could he have done something so heinous?

Caroline sat up very straight and still, lips pressed in a thin line. "Tell me, Sir Julian, what exactly is the accusation?"

"Treason and seditious intent."

The room fell so quiet that the sounds of people passing by outside, no doubt leading untroubled lives where loved ones were not incarcerated on mere suspicion, filtered into the room. Treason. "And if he is charged and convicted?" Anjali's voice sounded strange to her own ears. The punishment for such crimes against the state was death.

"It will never come to that," Sir Julian said, "You must believe me."

"I just don't understand how anyone could—" Anjali was suddenly struck with a terrible notion. "Mr. Lascelles took me to India House on our drive. It was not pleasant, and I didn't know why he did it. I think he wanted me to talk about my father's business perhaps. I can think of no other reason."

Lady Lewiston said, "I can. You are an heiress, Anjali."

"A desirable heiress," Sir Julian said.

Anjali glanced at Sir Julian and looked away, her heart pounding. He had called her desirable. Unfortunately, at the same time the thought that Lascelles could be trying to fix his interest with her because of her fortune filled her with revulsion. "That's not to the purpose," she said, shaking her head. "I believe Papa has some important papers that he brought from India, papers that made him uneasy all through the voyage. He never let his document box out of his sight, and no doubt he has locked it away somewhere safe at his house."

"Do you have any idea what is in these papers?" Julian asked, looking down at their joined hands and then quickly letting them go as if suddenly realizing what he was doing.

The unfortunate thing about people with red hair, Anjali thought, was that they were liable to blush at the slightest provocation. Sir Julian, who had been all barrister a moment before suddenly looked like a schoolboy caught in a misdeed. Her heart ached with longing for him. "Alas, no," she said, making a point of not looking at his reddened cheeks and wishing with all her heart that she could take hold of his hands again. "He didn't talk about such things with me."

Lady Lewiston said, "I, too, have sensed some preoccupation in Thomas these past weeks, as if he was holding himself distant, aloof from the world. Do you think this could all be related to those very papers?"

"I don't know," Julian said, gazing off into the middle distance. "I wish I knew what those documents contained."

Anjali did too. But that was impossible at the moment without her father to tell them where they were. "What will you do now?" Anjali's relief that her father was alive and well had been dampened by the reality of the web he was caught up in and its possible consequences. She could not imagine how Sir Julian could possibly extricate him from this official bind. It appeared to be a monkey puzzle tree of a law, where twisting around would only increase the pain and suffering rather than lead to freedom.

"I will do everything I can, and then more. I promise to get your father back to you with his reputation intact. I am persuaded that he has done nothing that would warrant being detained under this law, and that someone has manipulated it for their own ends."

Anjali opened her mouth to say something, then shut it again. She was about to mention her father's many conferences with Nalin before they left. That brought the clerk to mind in a way that made her very uneasy. If this was happening to her father in London, could Nalin be facing similar peril in Calcutta? It was too much to think about right then.

Lady Lewiston rose, leaning heavily on a nearby chair.

"That man—I will not call him a gentleman—is in my house at present. I would like him to leave. I would like to have him forcibly ejected from the front door so that everyone in the *ton* can see his disgrace."

Sir Julian smiled grimly. "No doubt we would all like to see that. However, I think we would be better advised not to give him any idea that we have uncovered the mechanism by which Thomas was made to legally disappear. Let him pretend to be helpful for a while longer. He may well lead us more quickly to the answers we seek than could any of my shadowy sources."

Anjali also stood and staggered slightly. Sir Julian reached out to steady her, and their eyes locked. A shiver of pleasure passed through her body. Such a complicated day, Anjali thought. "We must go back. They will all wonder what has been keeping us."

"Let me tell them what little I believe they should know," Julian said. "I want to watch Lascelles's reaction."

BUT WHEN THEY REENTERED THE DRAWING ROOM, LASCELLES was not there.

"Mr. Lascelles begged us to say that he recalled a pressing engagement in another part of town, and was sorry not to be able to take his leave of you properly," Belinda said.

Anjali could well imagine the rakishly good looking fellow working his charm on the beautiful Lady Belinda. Perhaps she believed him. She could also imagine that his true reason for leaving was that he had no desire to be subjected to Sir Julian's intelligent scrutiny, and her negative opinion of him hardened.

Sir Julian said, "I have just been telling Miss Ashcombe and Lady Lewiston that Mr. Ashcombe is alive and well."

"Thank heavens!" Antonella said and rushed to grasp Anjali's hand.

"What have you discovered, Meredith?" Atherleigh said.

"It was a legal matter. As far as I can see, he was apprehended by mistake for something which has nothing whatever to do with him. He was simply in the wrong place at the wrong time."

Although this explanation bore little resemblance to what Sir Julian had told them in the library, Anjali had complete trust that he knew what he was doing, and had a good reason for not elaborating.

"Is there any way I can be of help in this matter?" Atherleigh said. "I do have influential friends in the government."

Sir Julian said, "I may well call upon you. But I hope it won't come to that, and we can restore Mr. Ashcombe to his friends and family without ado."

Belinda crossed the room to her mother and laid her hand on the dowager's cheek. "You look worn to the bone. We shall leave now. Please send word if there is anything you need, or any way we can be of help."

The four of them said their goodbyes and left, leaving the three of them alone with their thoughts. Anjali's were torn between icy fear and a warm glow that permeated her body. She could hardly bear to look at Sir Julian, afraid that her expression would reveal too much.

"Won't you take a glass of wine?" Lady Lewiston said to Sir Julian.

He shook his head. "I mustn't delay. It may take a little time to reach the resolution we desire," he said. "But I shall do all that is in my power to bring it about." He bowed to Lady Lewiston, and approached Anjali, who had remained standing.

The thought of Sir Julian leaving tore a little hole in Anjali's heart, as if in doing so he would be removing a part of her that she had never before realized existed. Gathering herself, Anjali put out her hand to shake his. He held it for a moment, then raised it to his lips and pressed a warm, tender kiss on her knuckles. "Thank you," she whispered, and he smiled.

After the door shut behind him, Anjali turned to Lady Lewiston, as if she'd only just become aware she was still in the room. She felt a pang of guilt, partly because she'd been so wrapped up in Sir Julian, partly because she and her father had brought a world of trouble upon her generous sponsor. "I am truly sorry, My Lady. I'm certain my father had no intention of disrupting your household in this unfortunate way."

Lady Lewiston came to her, took both her hands, and said, "I am deeply grateful that your father brought you to me, and that I have become acquainted with him again, trouble or no." A deep pink tinge washed over the dowager's cheeks. "Let us retire and face everything anew in the morning."

ONCE IN THE PRIVACY OF HER ROOM, ANJALI LET MILLIE HELP her out of her clothes and into her night shift, then tuck her into the comfortable bed, leaving only a single candle on the table by her elbow. She felt wrung out, yet relieved. Relieved, and something much deeper. Sir Julian had called her desirable. He had held her hands. He had kept his promise and discovered what Lascelles was no doubt trying to prevent all of them from knowing. Lascelles! She had thought him their friend. What information could her father possess that would set such desperate measures in motion?

And that made her think again of Nalin. Did Nalin have knowledge that would place him in jeopardy in Calcutta? But what use would her letter be, even if she added a warning to what she had already written? He would not receive it for months. Long after the situation with her father was resolved, she felt certain. Sir Julian would see to that.

Anjali marveled that she had ever thought Lascelles would be a trustworthy courier for a letter to her dear friend. Of course, she would not give it to him now.

The letter.

Suddenly wide awake, Anjali sprang out of bed, and, picking up her bedside candle went to her dressing table where her jewel box lay. The letter could do no good now, and it might instead result in harm. She opened the box and took the trinkets out to reach the false bottom where she had hidden it. She read it over. As she suspected, in a certain light, it might be seen as adding weight to the suspicion that her father was somehow involved in seditious activities, even though it said nothing outright. Perhaps she was being foolish. Yet the very fact of its being written in two languages could be deemed suspicious. Still, who would care what a young lady wrote to a friend thousands of miles away?

Nonetheless ... she took the letter to the hearth, which was burning low but held enough heat to create a spark. Just as she was going to reduce the letter to ash, she thought better of it. It was absurd to be so frightened. Her actions might almost make it seem as if she herself believed in her father's nefarious intent. And despite everything, despite her growing feelings for Sir Julian, Anjali was unwilling to relinquish this possible link to her dear friend.

Anjali refolded the letter and hid it away again, taking care to replace all her trinkets so they wouldn't look as though they had been disturbed. She would seek Sir Julian's advice, tell him all she knew about Nalin and her father's business. It may be that the information would be useful to him in his inquiries. The thought made her blush. Was that the only reason she wanted to tell him?

Anjali's bare feet were cold despite the rich carpet beneath them and she scurried back to the warmth of her bed, hoping for rather than expecting sleep. Her mind swirled not only with anxiety for her father, but with something else altogether.

At the end of the evening he kissed her hand. Not just a polite social kiss. She could still feel its soft imprint on her knuckles. She pressed those same knuckles to her own lips, closed her eyes, and imagined it all again. The look he gave her. His bow. None of it was what she thought would happen in London. She'd fully expected to enjoy some light flirtations, go through the motions of courtship perhaps, and ultimately retire to the country and keep house for her father. Perhaps eventually return to India and her family there.

She did not expect her father to disappear because of some new law that gave the government the power to apprehend—without concrete proof—anyone they suspected of seditious actions.

Above all, she did not expect to fall in love with a tall, red-haired, green-eyed, socially awkward yet needle-witted barrister with a spaniel that didn't mind him. She didn't know what would happen next in either case. But she did know that Sir Julian would employ the full force of his knowledge, intelligence, and contacts to bring about a good result on behalf of her father.

He would not have to try so hard to achieve the same good result with her.

~

Julian didn't reveal everything he knew to Miss Ashcombe and Lady Lewiston, just enough so that they would know Ashcombe was not in immediate physical danger and not accused of any actual crime. The political danger, however, was very real. Although the likelihood that it could work its way to the ultimate conclusion and Ashcombe would be charged with treason and executed was very slim, Julian knew that specter was no doubt in the minds of Miss Ashcombe and her chaperone.

There was only one place Thomas would likely have been taken after his interview at Whitehall, but Sir Julian wanted to be sure before he made any more inquiries. Knowing that if he sought to present a very correct appearance when he arrived in a hack at Coldbath Fields he would need some help, Julian allowed Addison free rein to arrange his neck-cloth in one of the fashionable knots, persuade him to wear a striped waistcoat, and ensure that his Hessian boots were polished to an impressive sheen. He also added a fob and a quizzing glass to his master's raiment.

Of course, Julian wore his curly brimmed beaver and tried as best he could to hide his distinctive mop of curls. Apparently among the minor denizens of the legal community, his red hair had earned him more than one pejorative nickname. More pomade than usual darkened the color a bit, so he hoped whoever he met would not instantly recognize him and turn him away.

Legal representatives were not permitted to see those held under warrant, therefore he would present himself as a concerned relative with friends in high places who had given him to understand that he might find Thomas Ashcombe in that location.

The hack drew up in front of the prison in Clerkenwell, north of the city. The forbidding, heavy door by the gatehouse nested in a crook of the high wall gave no indication of life. Not a sound, nothing, but for a mournful north wind whistling around the implacable facade.

He pounded on the door with the side of his elegantly gloved fist. After several minutes, scraping on the other side of the door was soon followed by movement as the turnkey opened it and poked his head out, looking left and right. "Who are you, and what d'you want?" he barked.

"I am here to inquire after a relation of mine, whom I believe has recently taken up residence within."

The turnkey spat on the ground and said, "Oh you is, is you. And who might this *relation* be?"

"One Thomas Ashcombe. He is quite elderly, and we are concerned for his health. I would like to assure myself that he is not unwell." Julian drawled his words in an affected, fop-like manner.

The fellow laughed until he coughed. "Ye're on a fool's errand here. I can't give no name to anyone. And if he was here, I wouldna tell ya."

Julian lifted the quizzing glass and peered at the turnkey. "Why?"

This simple question threw the man off his stride a bit. "Why? Well, uh, 'coz it's on'y the Home Secret'ry can do that. If'n he was here, I mean."

Julian reached into his pocket and drew out his coin purse, which immediately attracted the turnkey's eyes. He slowly teased open the drawstrings and put his fingers inside, pulling out a shilling. Then another. And another. And adding a half a crown to the growing collection of coins.

In a hoarse whisper, the turnkey said, "You ain't heard nuffing from me. There's a cove 'ere that just come, old geezer. Been here since yesterday."

"Might I see him for myself?" Julian asked.

The turnkey snatched the coins Julian held out to him and said, "More'n my life's worth!" And before Julian could ask him anything else, slammed the door shut again.

Julian climbed back into the hack. "Lewiston House, Mount Street," he said, a satisfied smile on his face. He'd learned everything he needed to learn. He didn't honestly think he had a chance of actually being admitted.

Now to get access to the right people. He hoped Atherleigh could help with that. Lewiston was of higher rank, but he was a Whig. It would be harder for him to get an interview with a Tory minister.

Half an hour later Julian was in the library at Lewiston House—the residence maintained by Lewiston for Lord and Lady Atherleigh's use when they were in town—sitting in a comfortable armchair drinking an excellent Mountain with the two peers. He told them both everything he knew.

"Why did you say nothing of this last night?" Atherleigh asked.

"It is important that we not reveal what we have discovered. It would not do Ashcombe or his daughter any good if his apprehension were common knowledge. And I would particularly recommend keeping Lascelles in ignorance of my discoveries. Besides, I wasn't certain where Ashcombe was held until this morning."

Harry shifted a bit uncomfortably in the chair opposite Julian. "Lascelles is older than I am so was gone from Eton by the time I was there. We belonged to the same club in London and he was a congenial chap. But I wasn't quite wild enough to be part of his set. I only knew of the big scandals after he'd been sent to India."

Julian said, "Don't blame yourself for any of this!"

"But I did welcome him to the masquerade ball when I discovered he knew Ashcombe."

"He would have found another way to get to Ashcombe. Such is always the case with men like him." Julian watched the amber liquid of the wine coat the sides of his glass as he idly tipped it this way and that. "But Lascelles is not important right now. Atherleigh, do you know anyone in the Home Office?"

Atherleigh said, "I do. Not the secretary. I believe the fellow is an under secretary or something. What would you like me to do?"

"Since I am not in Parliament I have little excuse for requesting an interview with someone in a position to place the matter before Sidmouth. Do you think you could arrange such an interview for me?"

"Of course, I can try. I don't know how long it will take, however."

Julian stood, removed his pocket watch and looked at it. "While I know you may not have it in your power, it is of the utmost importance that it happen as soon as may be possible. I don't know what the accusers said to get the warrant issued, and I am unable to speak to Ashcombe himself to find out what is in the papers he has in his possession, whether they contain anything that someone might want to bury in bureaucratic limbo."

Harry said, "What sort of papers?"

"I don't know. But Miss Ashcombe said they left Calcutta in haste, and he was closely guarding a box of documents."

"We must obtain those documents!" Harry said, leaping up from his seat.

Julian sighed. "Yes, it would be helpful to have them. But we have no right to go into his house and search for them, even if we knew what we were looking for."

Atherleigh shook his head. "It's all damnably smoky. All hole in the corner. I'll set up that meeting for you, Sir Julian, as soon as I can."

"Thank you," Julian said, downing the last of the wine, placing the glass on a small table, and bowing himself out of the door.

CHAPTER 24

Although he was not incarcerated in a dank, underground, rat-infested cell, Thomas felt every bit a prisoner. Confined to a space he could cross in two strides in either direction, given barely palatable food to eat twice a day, trying to sleep on a thin mattress on a cot that barely supported his weight—and not allowed any visitors or permitted to send so much as an *I am alive* message to anyone—if Thomas didn't know conditions could be much worse, he would think he had descended to the ninth circle of hell.

The hours dragged by, making the days of his captivity feel like weeks, and giving him ample opportunity to curse the circumstances that had once again driven him and Caroline apart. He also had plenty of time to persuade himself that he had only imagined her growing feelings for him, that only his own heart had been touched anew. And then he would remember her expressions, the way she held his arm and leaned into him at the opera, and the memories would awaken even more painful thoughts—that he had ruined his own chances once again.

On the third morning, just after he had forced himself to swallow two mouthfuls of the gluey porridge that served as breakfast, the ring of boots on the stone-flagged hallway made Thomas prick up his ears. It could be someone else coming to be imprisoned, but judging by the obsequious tone of the guard's voice and the cultivated and commanding tone of the other gentleman's, it was definitely a visitor.

The footfalls grew louder and at last, the pair turned the corner of the corridor that ended in his cell. For a fleeting moment, he had allowed himself to think it would be Sir Julian or Atherleigh. But no.

"Dobson," Thomas said through gritted teeth.

"You may safely leave us alone," Dobson said to the guard, slipping a coin into his hand. He waited until the guard's footsteps faded away to say, "I have come to offer you a way to get out of the predicament in which you find yourself."

This was not what Thomas expected him to say.

"You seem surprised. Believe me, no one was more surprised than I was when the officials to whom I report informed me that I might have you released this very day, under certain conditions."

Thomas did not want to give him the satisfaction of seeing any interest on his part. Nothing could justify his having been taken in the first place.

"You do not speak. Very well. After all, it was your words that landed you here. Your words, and certain of your actions. So I will simply tell you what we need from you and you can nod your assent. After that, however, we will require some information."

Here it was. They had done all this to throw him off balance, to make him reveal something he would rather keep secret until he knew it had reached the right ears.

"It appears that you have some papers in your possession that are, shall we say, very inconvenient at this juncture. You may not see them as treasonous or seditious, but their effects could force a very delicate bureaucratic structure to fall to bits—if the information they contain is what we are led to believe it is."

Thomas glared at Dobson, his eyes glittering with rage. Still he said nothing.

"All I ask is that you tell me where to find these papers. Once I have them in my possession, you will immediately be released, no one will be informed of the entire incident, and you may go about your life as if none of this ever happened."

That, thought Thomas, would not be possible. Thank heavens he had not told Lascelles what the papers contained, that they were eye-witness accounts of extortion and cruelty, with the financial ledgers and names to back them up. More than one officer in the Company army would tumble off his perch if all this were known. His hope—albeit a distant one— was that Hastings would also be removed. He smiled.

"Ah, so I see you are willing to be reasonable. I thought you a sensible man. Where are the papers?"

Thomas lifted his chin and said, "I will never tell that to you or anyone you work for. The very fact that you have gone to all this trouble proves to me that by delivering my information into the right hands I would be doing my loyal duty to the Crown."

Dobson, whose expression had been one of a benevolent uncle cajoling a recalcitrant child, narrowed his eyes. "You have made a terrible mistake. It will be easy to persuade the Home Secretary that your loyalties are not with the British in India due to, oh, I don't know, your fraternization with sedi- tious native forces. Or perhaps your marriage and divided loyalties. And of course there is your half-breed daughter."

It took every ounce of Thomas's self control not to hurl obscenities at Dobson. But he did not want to reveal any weakness, to let Dobson know that he had touched him on the raw. "These lack any substance. No one would pay any heed to such accusations."

With a shrug, Dobson said, "You should perhaps have warned your daughter that calling herself 'half English' and refusing the hand of a respected peer of the realm would weigh heavily against your case. It would be such a shame. I understand she created quite the sensation among the curious of the *ton*. Your reputation and that of your daughter will be ruined beyond repair." Dobson turned on his heel and stalked away.

Not just Lascelles then, Thomas thought with a sinking heart. Would Dawlish have given information out of spite for Anjali's refusal? These men had no scruples, to involve an innocent young lady in this. He wished he could reassure her that he was—and would always be—all right. Except he would be lying. If his enemies somehow managed to persuade the Home Office that he was a traitor, punishment would be swift and irrevocable.

And once more that thought intruded that he would be leaving Caroline again, this time for good. His throat tightened and a pain behind his eyes threatened tears. No. He would not cry. All was not lost. He had no doubt that both Anjali and Caroline must be doing everything they could to find out what happened to him. They would use all their ingenuity and influence to do so. And they had the surprising Sir Julian to help them. Sir Julian, whose tender glances at Anjali had not escaped his notice. Her sentiments were harder to determine, but he suspected she was quite ready to lose her heart to someone who truly deserved her.

~

So far, only the immediate family, Sir Julian, and Mr. Lascelles knew of Thomas's incarceration. Lascelles, Caroline assumed, did not know that they knew anything much beyond what he had told them, nor that they knew that *he* knew. Partly for that reason, Sir Julian had impressed upon them the need for secrecy. His object was to get the warrant lifted without any public notice, which he said also required them to keep Lascelles uninformed about Julian's activities. If that could successfully be managed it would leave Thomas's and Anjali's reputations unsullied. Caroline could well understand the importance of that. The *ton* would turn its back as quickly as it had embraced the wealthy, well-born merchant and his beautiful Anglo-Indian daughter. Even a whiff of such a serious charge would render them beyond the pale. And that could have repercussions for others in a similar situation.

It was in the interest of appearing to lead their normal lives that, three days after they learned of Thomas's disappearance, she and Anjali were preparing to attend a ball at the home of the Duke and Duchess of Hartland. It would be a magnificent affair—through her previous marriage the duchess was a Hungarian princess, and acknowledged by all to be the most gorgeous creature in London. The duke had been a notorious rake, who was apparently completely reformed as a husband and stepfather to the duchess's illegitimate offspring, a delightful young fellow by the name of Oscar.

"If ever there were an occasion to wear your mother's jewels, this would be it," Caroline said to Anjali as she half-heartedly completed her toilette. "I know this is the last thing you feel like doing, but we only have to put in an appearance. I can claim to be indisposed at a signal from you, and we will then slip away. You will probably have to dance. But Sir Julian will be there, he assures me."

She did not fail to notice the subtle change in Anjali's complexion when she mentioned the baronet's name. It was completely obvious to Caroline after all that had transpired in the past few days that the two of them were hopelessly in love with each other, whether or not they admitted it to themselves. Of course, Thomas's situation made it inadvisable—if not impossible—for them to declare themselves right now. But clearly Sir Julian's zeal on Thomas's behalf was a result of more than his professional interest. Caroline was inclined to believe that Thomas would look upon the match with favor, but if he had any doubts, they would be swept away in consideration of the baronet's actions ever since his disappearance.

So it was that a little after half-past ten on a mild early-April evening that Lady Lewiston's barouche disgorged the two of them at the Grosvenor Square mansion. Caroline took swift appraisal of Anjali's appearance, saw that she was not only magnificently gowned and bedecked with her mother's emeralds but looking calm and in command of herself. *She would make an excellent barrister's wife,* she thought.

Even in so large a house the ball could already be called a squeeze. The duke and duchess were still at the head of the grand staircase greeting guests, but Lord and Lady Atherleigh, Lady Belinda and Mr. Gainesworth, and the Marquess and Marchioness of Lewiston had all arrived ahead of them.

Of course, Belinda came to them first, tucking her hand in Anjali's elbow and murmuring, "We began to be afraid you wouldn't come. And I would hardly blame you if you didn't. But I'm delighted that you're here."

Caroline let Belinda take Anjali off in the direction of a group of young people who were chatting gaily, and she sighed with relief. She was exhausted. Not just because of having to support Anjali's understandably depressed spirits but because she couldn't help going over and over everything Thomas had said to her that night at the opera, his expressions, how he touched her and sought out her company. Was she wrong to believe he still held her in affection? Perhaps even love? Her feelings for him had not altered through the years. But, then, she had not had a loving marriage since that time, as he had. And thirty years ago he had chosen to ignore her desperate letter, sent to him in secret before he was forced by his parents to board the ship for India. But none of this would matter if the worst happened and he was gone from her for good.

"What are you thinking about, Aunt Caroline? You look so sad." She had not noticed Antonella and Atherleigh approach her.

Although in private Antonella called Caroline *mama*, they had agreed that, since everyone knew they were not related by blood, she would keep to *Aunt Caroline* in public. "Oh, just … things. So much has happened. I hardly know."

Atherleigh drew a little closer so he could speak without being overheard. "I have secured an interview for Julian with someone high up in the Home Office. It is set for tomorrow. He will do his best, but I wish we had some tangible evidence to support his arguments."

Caroline placed her hand on Atherleigh's arm and squeezed gently. "You are so kind to exert yourself in this way. Thomas—Ashcombe—can mean nothing to you."

"But it is quite clear he means a great deal to you, Lady Lewiston. And you mean a great deal to my wife."

She smiled. Was it so obvious? "Don't feel you must stay next to me. I shall seek out the chaperones and no doubt find some of my cronies amongst them. I could do with hearing a bit of idle gossip, something where lives do not hang in the balance."

As she wandered off in the direction of the ballroom, glass of champagne in hand, Caroline swept her gaze around the saloons looking for Sir Julian. His presence would comfort her. He would see that Anjali was not despondent.

Unfortunately, it was not Sir Julian who first met her eyes. Mr. Lascelles walked up to her, a look of false concern on his face. He held out his hand. She could not refuse to take it in public, and so she gave him a two-fingered handshake.

"My Lady, it is so very brave of you to be here."

"We are not making Thomas's situation public. I hope you have not said anything to your friends. Until we know more, Sir Julian advised that we go about our lives as usual. If anyone asks, Mr. Ashcombe has gone out of town on business."

He knitted his brows and nodded. "Very sensible. Can I infer that Miss Ashcombe is here as well?" he looked around and then back at Caroline.

"She is. But I believe she is occupied at present. Her dance card never stays empty for long." She gave him what she hoped was a knowing smile.

"Ah, and so the likes of me—no more than an old family friend—stands little chance of being able to secure her for a quadrille, I expect!" He flashed his dazzling smile at her. A smile that she once thought beguiling, and now thought heartless and calculating.

She made her excuses and walked off, hoping he did not find Anjali before Sir Julian did.

ANJALI WAS GRATEFUL TO BELINDA FOR INTRODUCING HER TO her friends—of whom there were many—and seeing that her dance card was taken up with the names of all the eligible gentlemen she knew. Her hand was solicited for almost every dance, although she'd managed to keep the supper dance free and one of the waltzes. By the time she'd tripped through three country dances and a waltz with a very uncomfortable young man whose face glistened with sweat the entire time, she'd allowed herself to let go of some of her anxiety, to trust that Sir Julian would be able to make everything right, and gradually sank into the pleasure of the moment. It was a relief to be distracted after three interminable days of anxious worry.

Nonetheless, between every set, she cast her eyes around the room, looking for the telltale red curls that would mean Sir Julian had arrived. It was nearly midnight and there was no sign of him yet. The supper dance was after the cotillion, which was next. She had been so convinced that Julian would be there and take her in that she'd pretended to three young gentlemen that she was already spoken for. Why wasn't he there yet?

All around her young people laughed and flirted. Ladies whispered secrets to each other. Gentlemen tried not to make it obvious they were eyeing the beauties. It all seemed so pointless.

"Miss Ashcombe," said a familiar voice behind her.

She turned and found herself face to face with Lord Dawlish. This was definitely not the person she'd hoped to see. Why did he approach her? Surely he could not want to dance.

"If you are free for the next dance, would you stand up with me?"

Anjali looked to left and right. No one was listening. "You want to dance with me? Surely not."

He lifted his chin. "I am afraid I left rather suddenly when we last spoke. As a gentleman, I was not pleased with my response to your refusal."

So, to salve his conscience, he wanted to dance with her?

"All right," she said, and gave him her hand, albeit reluctantly, to lead her out to the dance floor.

They started innocuously enough. Dawlish was a decent dancer. He had little grace, but performed the steps with almost military precision. After a few of the figures, Anjali decided she must initiate some conversation with him. "I trust you have been in good health since I last saw you?"

"I have been remarkably well," he said, just before they were separated by the movement of the dance.

When they came back together, Anjali said, "Remarkably? How so?"

"I have come to the realization that you did me the greatest possible kindness by not accepting my offer."

Anjali was about to revise her opinion of him, thinking that perhaps he was not so petty as she had thought, when he continued by saying, "It would have brought dishonor to my family to marry someone not of pure English lineage. You would have spoiled centuries of breeding. And I saw that our temperaments would not have suited."

They were once again separated by the figure, which gave Anjali time to realize the full effect of what he'd said to her. Was it an intentional insult, or was he simply completely insensible to the feelings of others? When they came together again, she said, "And you have done me a kindness by proving that I made the right decision in refusing you. I based my decision primarily on your lack of intellect and education. Now I see that your essential lack of consideration would also have sufficed."

"Ah, yes. Education. You are a bluestocking, which would have been highly embarrassing for me as well. And you should know, you are unlikely ever to receive another offer of marriage in your situation." He smiled as if he had just said something complimentary to her.

In Anjali's overwrought state, having to maintain the

fiction of being engaged in a pleasant social dance with someone who seemed bent on tearing her down became an almost unbearable burden. She wanted to run screaming from the room. Why did this man think he had the right to insult her this way?

"In the end," he said as he rejoined her for a promenade, "Your fortune was simply not large enough to make it worth the sacrifice."

So, marrying her would have been a sacrifice. And all he wanted was her fortune. Suddenly, it made sense. She could never figure out why, with so little encouragement, he courted her. But Lady Lewiston said he did not need her fortune. Clearly she was wrong.

This dance was unbearable. She was trying to figure out how she could leave the floor without making a spectacle of herself. To do so in the middle of a dance would be the height of impropriety and would disrupt the symmetry of the set. It would also embarrass Lady Lewiston, which was the last thing she wanted. Anjali was thinking so hard about how to get out of that impossible situation before she could no longer hold back her angry, frustrated tears that she became distracted and turned the wrong way. She collided not just with another gentleman in their set, but also with a lady in the neighboring group of eight. Of course it was Lady Henrietta Vaughn, who arched a superior eyebrow at her. "Forgive me," Anjali said, and thinking of the only excuse that made any sense said, "My ankle." She slipped between the whirling couples and fled.

It didn't matter that the supper dance was next and she had hoped to have Sir Julian for a partner. She must find Lady Lewiston and leave. It was a mistake to come at all. *Get me out of here,* Anjali thought, and headed in the direction of the ladies' retiring room. She would collect her wits there and then go to find Lady Lewiston.

She had just turned down a short corridor leading between the saloon and the sanctuary she sought when from behind her she heard, "Anjali! Miss Ashcombe!"

No. The evening couldn't get any worse. She brushed her tears away with the back of her hand before turning around. "Mr. Lascelles. I did not see you come in."

He strode toward her with his easy gait, the wicked smile lurking in his eyes, and put out his hand to her. She let him take it, but seeing that he was preparing to lift it to his lips quickly snatched it away. "Sir! Not here."

He made a show of looking to left and right then said, "But we are alone."

"Precisely," she said.

He took a step nearer to her and she fought the urge to back away from him. She wasn't afraid of this man. "You must be near the end of your time in London, Mr. Lascelles," she said. "I understood you were leaving at the beginning of this month."

"My ship sails in three days. I would be sorry not to have the opportunity to say my farewells to your father." He leaned a little forward and spoke quietly into her ear. "I understand he is not yet restored to you. I can see that you are still distressed."

Anjali stiffened, struggling with all her might not to lash out and slap him. How dare he, when he must know where her father was. But she knew to do so would accomplish nothing. "Yes, although we are hopeful that he will soon be home. If you will excuse me."

She started to walk away but he reached out and took her arm, stopping her. "I have some very powerful, influential friends. I have hesitated to involve anyone else in this matter, out of discretion, you understand." He pulled her closer to him. "But if you were to agree to one little thing, I could ask them to exert their influence to make whatever is detaining your father go away."

"So you say he is being detained? Why? Where is he?" He had not told her that before, and he didn't know that Sir Julian had. What was this now? Was he blackmailing her? Did he want money? The only money she had was through her father, and she couldn't get that while he was confined. "What do you know? And if you know something, why haven't you told us?"

He tsked. "These things are not without complications. I myself know very little. But I am acquainted with those who, shall we say, can exert their authority to bring about desired outcomes."

Anjali pulled and he let her arm go. She turned away from him. She had no desire to gaze upon his duplicitous face. She had some inkling of what Sir Julian was doing in her father's interest, and also that Lascelles had been involved in his detainment. How dare he use her distress to curry favor with her!

"You say nothing, but I interpret that to mean that you would like me to say more. You cannot be unaware of the fact that I hold you in the highest esteem. More than that." He stepped closer still, until she could feel his breath on her exposed shoulder. "You have become a very beautiful woman. You might not be acceptable here, but in India—in India you could reign supreme. You know that's true. If you would consent to return to India with me—"

She whipped her head around and stared at him in open-mouthed horror.

"—as my bride, we could—"

What came next happened so quickly that Anjali couldn't have said later how it transpired that the smiling, elegant gentleman standing too close to her was suddenly lying flat on his back on the ground, his nose bleeding copiously all over his snowy shirt.

She turned to see Sir Julian, his face in a harsh mask of anger unlike any expression she'd ever seen upon it before, rubbing the knuckles of his right hand. A few steps behind him was Atherleigh.

Sir Julian gradually became aware of her gaze and shook his head as if to clear away that version of himself and return to being the kind, thoughtful gentleman she knew he was. "Are you all right, Miss Ashcombe?" he said.

"Did he do anything to you, Anjali?" Atherleigh said in his stern, army major's voice, placing a comforting hand on her shoulder.

"N-no." She didn't know what else to say. It wasn't what he'd done, it was what he said.

"I think you have outstayed your welcome at this party," Atherleigh said, and in two strides, took hold of Lascelles with his one hand and set him on his feet. "Here." He gave him his handkerchief. "Clean yourself up and then we'll walk out without creating a fuss."

Sir Julian just stood there and let Atherleigh take charge. Anjali had to admit that Atherleigh was by far the more imposing man of the two. Although Julian matched him in height, his slighter build made him appear smaller. Yet somehow, the baronet had done enough to demonstrate that someone like Lascelles could not best him. Her heart swelled with pride.

Once the two gentlemen were gone, Sir Julian at last said, "I came to find you for the supper dance. I'm sorry I was late. I was making a plan and lost track of the time." He put out his arm for her to take, as if he hadn't just flattened a gentleman Anjali knew congratulated himself on his athletic prowess.

"Will you tell me about this plan?" she said, almost faint

with relief that Sir Julian was there and hardly able to support herself on her own two feet. She wished he would deal with Dawlish in the same way he had just dealt with Lascelles. But that would accomplish nothing. It was enough for now just to feel the warmth of his arm.

Yet even the thought of taking the floor with him felt beyond her capabilities at the moment. "On second thought, perhaps you could just escort me and Lady Lewiston back to Park Street."

"I will do whatever you wish me to, Miss Ashcombe," Sir Julian said, and Anjali knew he meant it. "But I think your interests would be better served by continuing to keep up the pretense that nothing is wrong, if you can bear it."

"I can bear it so long as you don't leave me alone," Anjali said, tucking her arm more firmly in his.

"Never," Sir Julian said, and put his hand over hers as he escorted her to the supper room.

CHAPTER 25

$\mathcal{A}$therleigh had come through with someone from the home office for Julian to meet, an under-secretary by the name of Higgins. The fellow could only see him before breakfast, so it was a rather tired Julian who waited just inside the Stanhope Gate to accompany Higgins on his morning walk in Hyde Park. Although he'd sent Anjali and Lady Lewiston home not long after the supper dance, he'd gone to his club and remained there until dawn, too disturbed by the events of the evening and the emotions they stirred up to think of retiring. He'd been able to give Lascelles the treatment he deserved, which was deeply satisfying. After that, he danced with Miss Ashcombe and escorted her to supper. His heart twisted at the memory of her trying so hard to pretend all was well. If only he could tell her that what happened to her mattered more to him than it could matter to anyone, that he would do anything to make her world whole.

Before long a gentleman in a dark red coat, striped waistcoat, and fawn pantaloons approached and said, "Sir Julian?"

"Yes, and you must be—"

"Let us not make a gift of my name to anyone beside ourselves just yet," he said, looking around as though ensuring that they were unobserved. "Atherleigh said I couldn't fail to recognize you. He was right." Without actually saying it, Higgins clearly referred to Julian's distinctive head of hair.

"I appreciate you making the time to speak with me," Julian said, thinking that if he was so leery of being seen they might have met indoors somewhere.

"I hope you understand this unconventional setting for our conversation," Higgins said. "But I always walk at this hour because there is almost no one in the park, and I can clear my head before it is barraged with petitions and problems later in the day. To have deviated from this habit would have raised unwanted interest."

Julian inferred that Higgins was not speaking with him in an official capacity, but an advisory one. He had hoped for more, but this was better than nothing.

"Atherleigh tells me you have information about someone who is currently being held under warrant. Do you mind me asking how you discovered this?"

"It was no easy matter, as I'm sure you know. But I have every confidence that the gentleman in question is the victim of false representation by persons not unknown, but as yet unconfirmed. I speak of Thomas Ashcombe, a merchant who arrived from India but—"

"Yes, I know of whom you are speaking. I should tell you that the application for his capture came from the very highest sources."

This merely confirmed Julian's suspicions. "I don't suppose those high sources are associated with India House?"

They walked along for a while in silence. "What makes you assume such a thing?" Higgins asked.

"Come now, sir. A wealthy trader who has managed to

maintain his independence from the EIC is suddenly accused of suspected treason. A trader who has been known throughout his tenure in Calcutta as a man of honor and loyalty, who could well have material detrimental to certain Company officials. You cannot tell me that there are not likely many who might rather he disappeared than that he presented his information to the government." Julian felt he was on shaky ground here. Since he did not have the papers Anjali believed existed, he could only make educated guesses as to what might have made someone uneasy enough to go to such extreme measures to prevent Ashcombe doing whatever it was he intended to do.

"What you are suggesting could be interpreted as criminal malfeasance on the part of the accusers. It is a serious matter to falsely accuse someone of a capital crime. In order to reexamine Ashcombe's case we would need definitive proof that he had no seditious or treasonous intent, or that those who brought the suspicion to our attention were acting with malicious purposes."

Julian gave a cynical laugh. "So it is now a case of guilty until proven innocent. These are not the laws I have been proud to uphold."

Higgins stopped walking and stared at him. "I shall ignore your last statement, assuming it was born of frustration."

It was so easy to let things slip that could be misinterpreted, Julian thought, which only further emphasized the hazards of this sweeping new law. "What evidence have the accusers brought to bear against him?"

"I cannot say, as you well know. But it was compelling enough to justify action."

Compelling and false, Julian thought. "Might I ask if it concerned only things he said since he has been in London?"

After a moment's thought, Higgins said, "The accusation also touches on his life and associations in India."

That would be difficult to refute, Julian thought. No one in India now could be brought forward to corroborate his innocence. However, it was clear that Higgins was unwilling to have Ashcombe's warrant lifted without something more than assurance of his good character. Julian took heart from the fact that the accusers must not have sufficiently damning evidence for him to be charged and tried, which was at least something.

"What would I have to do," Julian asked, "to persuade the Home Office that they have the wrong man in custody?"

Higgins smiled at him. "Bring me something unimpeachable, something that either proves he is not a traitor, or that supports your claim that there are others with an interest in making unfounded accusations. I confess, the charge seems far-fetched to me. What kind of threat can a merchant who has been in India for thirty years pose to those powerful enough to cause the Home Secretary to issue a warrant?"

That effectively ended their meeting. Although Julian hadn't discovered any new information, he did at least learn what he was up against.

He walked out of the park and directly to Park Street, which was quite nearby. A startled Fairing answered his knock on the door.

"I know it's unconscionably early, and I daresay the ladies are not yet down after the ball last night, but I promised them I would come immediately after my meeting this morning."

Fairing bowed and showed him into the hall. "I shall inquire if Miss Ashcombe will see you. She is in the breakfast parlor."

Julian expected to be asked to leave a note, given the unsocial time of day. But Fairing returned after a short while and said, "If you will come this way, sir."

A moment later he was in a small, sunny breakfast parlor,

unable to take his eyes from Miss Ashcombe. She wore a simple muslin day dress cut high to the throat with a lace ruff around her neck. Something about her youthful attire made her even more appealing than she'd been at the ball the night before, clad in opulent silks and wearing precious jewels. He bowed. "Miss Ashcombe."

"Won't you be seated? There is hot coffee. Fairing will get you a cup." She sat at the table again and motioned him to take a seat near her. "I'm sorry Lady Lewiston isn't here to greet you. I believe she will have breakfast in her room a bit later."

"I did not expect to see you down so early after last night," Julian said.

"It was quite an eventful evening." Miss Ashcombe pressed her lips together to suppress a smile, and a dimple formed in one cheek.

He didn't know whether she was referring to his drawing Lascelles's cork, or to the fact that they'd supped together and danced twice, as well as taken every opportunity to converse. If it weren't for what was happening with her father, he might not have been able to prevent himself from making her a declaration then and there. Her force of mind, her command of herself in the face of terrible circumstances, were truly admirable. "Eventful and enjoyable," he said, and she looked away in blushing confusion. "But I am here for a much less pleasant reason this morning, I'm afraid."

Fairing brought the additional coffee cup and Anjali poured for him. The mischievous light that had been in her eyes while they exchanged their mildly flirtatious remarks vanished, to be replaced by the serious expression that seemed her normal state over the last few days. "Have you already seen the secretary?"

He nodded. "He was not dismissive. But I don't think we'll be able to succeed at getting your father freed and cleared unless we can find his papers and they contain something that would explain why someone would want to put him in the greatest possible jeopardy. Unfortunately, we cannot get to him in order to ask him where they are."

Anjali said nothing for a long moment, sipping her coffee and looking blankly out the window. "Nonetheless, find them we must without his help. Although I haven't seen them myself, I believe them to be in a box I would recognize if I saw it. That box has to be in his house. The trouble is, I have no idea where, or even if what it contains will prove to be of any use."

"We can hardly ransack the place to search for it," Julian said. "Loyal servants would be very useful in a case such as this, but his have all been hired recently, I gather."

"You are correct. We did not bring any of the Indian servants with us." Miss Ashcombe paused and tilted her head to the side. "But there may be a way."

"What are you thinking?" Julian asked.

"He is my father. Therefore I am part of his household, so I have every right to be in his house. In fact, a good portion of my possessions are there. I couldn't bring everything I owned here, after all. With that in mind, it would not be unreasonable for me to want to fetch something I needed."

Of course. Why hadn't he thought of that? Where no servant worth the name would allow him free rein to roam around the house and stick his nose in everywhere, Ashcombe's daughter had every right to do so, even if she'd never actually been in residence there. He smiled. "What exactly did you leave behind?"

breakfast on a tray in her room, she didn't expect Sir Julian to be there already. She found him with Anjali still sitting in the breakfast parlor, deep in discussion about a plan to somehow secure Thomas's release.

Sir Julian stood and bowed to her, but Anjali began speaking before pleasantries could be exchanged. "Lady Lewiston, let us tell you what we hope to accomplish this morning."

They explained the problem: that they needed to find and secure the papers Anjali believed must be in the document box her father kept near him on the voyage over. They must do this before anyone else found it so they could give the papers in it to the Home Office.

"And I believe I know how to accomplish that." The girl's eyes shone with hope and fervor. She explained that she would go accompanied only by Millie to her father's house and claim that she wanted some of her personal items that she hadn't brought to Park Street. "Because you see it is my father's house, and therefore I have a right to enter it and go all over it."

It was a bold plan, born of desperation. But Caroline saw one significant flaw in it. "Suppose you find the box you speak of. It might well be locked. Breaking it open would attract the notice of the servants. And even if it isn't—which would surprise me knowing how important the papers are to Thomas—do you think you would be allowed to retain possession of them?" She signaled Fairing to bring her a cup of coffee.

"You are right, Lady Lewiston," Sir Julian said. "We were just trying to figure out a way around that very difficulty. There is also the possibility that someone else has already removed the papers. However, if that were the case, it is my belief that Thomas would have been either released or charged."

Caroline couldn't help thinking that perhaps Lascelles

and the men he worked for would destroy the evidence and not take any steps to alter Thomas's ambiguous position. He could languish in prison until it could be shown that nothing came of whatever suspicion put him there. The thought tormented her. Still, it was hard to think of any other course of action. "Would there be guards around the house?"

"Unlikely," Julian said. "They may have obtained a warrant to search it, but it is not the usual practice to guard a house from which no one is at risk of fleeing."

"After all," Anjali said, "Papers could not get away on their own. And I doubt anyone would expect such a bold step from a mere girl."

Caroline thought that she knew few girls who would be willing to undertake, or even be capable of undertaking such a task. "Fraught as it is with hazards, I see it might be our only hope."

"I must go and prepare right away," Anjali said.

"Perhaps you should bring Kavi for protection," Sir Julian said with a smile and a tender gaze at Anjali.

Anjali returned his smile. *Ah, yes,* Caroline thought. Whatever else has been a disaster, these two souls have found each other.

Before she left the breakfast room, Anjali looked thoughtfully up at the ceiling. "You know, bringing Kavi might not be a bad idea. Servants are generally afraid of him and they might stay away and leave us to roam at will if I take him into the house."

A short while later a nervous Millie and a hopeful Anjali—with Kavi seated docilely on her shoulder—stepped down from Lady Lewiston's barouche outside the house in Bedford Square. A quick glance around did not reveal anyone hovering nearby. Sir Julian said the house would not be guarded, but Anjali couldn't shake the feeling that someone was watching her. There was no time to fret over it, however. She raised the brass door knocker and let it fall twice.

At first there wasn't a sound, except a rustle in the bushes that pressed up against the house. Anjali peered at them, her pulse quickening, and a sparrow hopped out and flew away. She breathed. And waited. What if the servants had all left? That was something they hadn't bargained on. Anjali berated herself for not anticipating that such a thing could well have happened, and was about to turn, defeated, back to the carriage. Then she heard the distinct sound of footsteps approaching on the other side of the door and a moment later she and Millie stood facing the butler.

When that stern-faced man caught sight of Kavi he stepped back reflexively.

"It's all right, he won't hurt you."

"The master has not returned, Miss Ashcombe," the butler said.

"And yet, you are here." She smiled at him, hoping to gain something of an ally.

He nodded and said, "We were paid for the first three months in advance, so it would be dishonorable to leave."

Anjali wasn't certain what to say to the butler. How much did he know? And so she simply asked his name.

"Horton, Miss," he said.

"Well, Horton, may we come in? This is my father's house after all."

He stepped aside and bowed, shutting the door behind them.

Steeling herself to lie shamelessly to this obviously scrupulous servant, Anjali said, "I must retrieve a box that contains my fans and gloves. Somehow it did not arrive at Park Street with the rest of my belongings. I'm not sure where it would be, so I'll just look around. There's no need to accompany me. I'll call you if I need help." She flashed a breezy smile at Horton and climbed the stairs up to the bedroom floor, followed by Millie. She really thought the box she was looking for would be in the library, or the office if there was one. But her excuse would make it odd for her to look first in either of those rooms.

Only two of the dozen bedchambers on two floors were furnished. One was clearly her father's, one just as clearly had been prepared for her to occupy. "Millie, you look around my room. I doubt there's anything hidden there, but we must be seen to be searching for things that would belong to a lady."

Anjali stood in her father's bedchamber and her shoulders sagged. It smelled of him. The lack of him. Kavi said, "Papa!" and it nearly broke her resolve. But she took a few deep breaths, then opened the clothes press, looked underneath the pillows and the mattress, and opened every drawer she could find in the sparsely furnished room. She even peered up into the chimney, gaining an eye full of soot for her trouble. She quickly glanced in the mirror and rubbed away a smudge before deciding that the document box could not be in that room.

She met Millie in the corridor and whispered, "Perhaps you can say the master is forgetful, and he must have tucked the box away somewhere unexpected, or something like that."

Millie nodded, her eyes wide, and did as Anjali said as they descended to the level of the reception rooms. These were likewise devoid of furniture, except for the drawing room she had entered with Lady Lewiston a few days ago. A quick look in the desk beneath the windows revealed nothing, nor did lifting all the unattached cushions.

Now, thought Anjali, it would not seem odd for her to

search the ground floor rooms where business would likely be transacted. She met both Horton and Mrs. Fishgard in the hall. "Alas, I have not found the box! My papa likely didn't realize it contained things that belonged to me and put it with his other boxes. I shall look in his office. Does he have one?"

The two servants exchanged a nervous look. Mrs. Fishgard said, "He did his business in the library, Miss. But—"

Anjali had already opened two doors. One revealing an empty room as yet not assigned its purpose, one clearly a small breakfast parlor.

The third door, toward the back, doubtless with a view over a garden, indeed proved to be a library. At least, that's what Anjali assumed it would be if it had not looked as if a storm had blown through it. Books lay everywhere, along with papers and open crates, the shredded paper stuffing spilling out of them. A porcelain statue of Ganesh lay smashed on the floor. Anjali felt her eyes well up and blinked fast.

"I tried to tell you, Miss. The officers came and searched the house yesterday."

Mrs. Fishgard's kind voice made the tears spill down Anjali's cheeks. She turned and met the housekeeper's concerned gaze. "Did they take anything away with them?" she asked. It was the worst outcome. This would all have been for nothing.

"No, Miss," Horton said, coming to stand next to Mrs. Fishgard. "They was angry when they left. Said we'd be punished if we was hiding something."

Anjali's tears stopped, her sorrow replaced with anger. "You will not be punished if I have anything to say to it!" So the servants must know something was amiss if they had to allow officials in to search the house. "I can't tell you everything now. You have done as you ought to stay here and let them search. I daresay they showed you a paper that gave them permission."

Horton nodded.

"As perhaps you've guessed, I am not searching for fans and gloves. I must locate what those men were looking for. It is vital to secure my father's safety. Will you help me?" She looked back and forth between them. The servants had no cause to be loyal beyond her father's generosity. Yet such actions were rare enough in the *ton* to possibly inspire some gratitude.

"Yes, Miss," Mrs. Fishgard said. "Mr. Ashcombe, much as we knowed him, is a good man. You just tell us what you need."

Together the four of them scoured every inch of space in the house, even going back over places Anjali had already examined. After half an hour of this, they ended up in the dining room. Horton had already turned out all the drawers in the sideboard, the only furniture other than a handsome mahogany dining table and chairs with seats that were thinly cushioned. No box could be hidden within them. Although perhaps individual papers might …

Reluctantly, Horton gave Anjali his pen knife and she slit open all twelve seats of the chairs.

Nothing.

She took a deep breath and let out a long sigh. "It's useless. Thank you both for your help. I shall make certain my father knows of your assistance." She turned away from the scene of fruitless destruction and gazed at the massive silver épergne set atop the sideboard. It was one of the few decorative items her father insisted accompany them on their voyage. It had been a gift from her mother's family, and it was lavishly decorated with tokens of India—palm trees, monkeys, tigers, minarets. It sat on a substantial base of silver engraved with Persian script. How many times in her childhood had she traced those letters and made up stories about the creatures and people in the épergne? Kavi recognized it too, hopped off her shoulder, and perched on the tall minaret at its top.

Of course! she thought, a rush of hope animating her. "Horton, would you lift this up for me?"

"It's very heavy, Miss," he said a bit doubtfully, but started to do as he was bid.

Anjali stepped in to help him. "Lay it down so I can see the bottom," she said.

Kavi squawked in annoyance, but settled on a wall sconce instead. Once the épergne was on its side, Anjali felt all around the bottom and the edges with her fingers. At last, she found what she was looking for. A catch, on a spring. She pressed it in, and the bottom popped open to reveal a wooden box of a size to hold documents. A box she recognized instantly.

She eased it out of its hiding place and shut the bottom of the épergne. "Put it back as it was, please," Anjali said, and turned.

They had all been concentrating so much on what they were doing that they failed to hear the approach of footsteps. Standing in the dining room's doorway was Lascelles, his eyes glittering with triumph. "So very accommodating of you, Miss Ashcombe," he said striding forward.

She was helpless. There was no Julian to plant him a facer this time. The butler was old and weak. The rest of them were females who would never be able to overpower a man accustomed to boxing and other vigorous sports. "What do you want?" she asked, although she knew full well.

"Not what you suppose, I assure you," Lascelles said. "Although this—" he waved his arm around and ended with a gesture that encompassed the two of them, "does not look good, in your father's empty house, with only an abigail and a couple of servants. As things stand right now, you have the prospect of being able to make a respectable marriage—mistake though I think that would be. It would be a shame to change that."

Anjali's breast heaved with indignation. How dare he! The threat was more than implicit. He would think nothing of ruining her reputation. Sir Julian might not care, though. For, she realized with certainty, his was the only opinion that mattered to her. He loved her enough not not care, she was certain, but would being linked to her sully him in the eyes of the world and possibly damage his reputation as a barrister? She could not bear to think it.

"As I said, I have no interest in destroying your reputation, if it can be helped. I would simply like that box you are cradling so protectively in your arms." He reached out his hands to take it, but Anjali turned away, giving him her shoulder.

To her surprise, the butler stepped forward between her and Lascelles, and Mrs. Fishgard pulled the bell rope by the fireplace. A moment later, two burly footmen entered the room. Burly enough to overpower Lascelles.

"I will never give this to you! If you want it, you will have to wrest it from me."

"I think not. Your father's fate is tied to those papers. If you give the box to me, I will make you a solemn vow that your father will be returned to you in a matter of days."

"Hah! Your vow means nothing."

He shrugged. "I can understand you think that. On the other hand, you don't actually know whether those papers will condemn or exonerate your father, even if you place them into what you believe are the right hands. The right course of action is to give them to me. Your reputation will remain intact, and my influential friends will perceive that your father no longer has the power to harm their interests, and thus let the warrant be lifted. Or ..." He stopped speaking and lifted his eyebrows. "Perhaps they will have the opposite effect."

All he said was true. How did she know for certain that, if she sacrificed her good name and kept the box, its contents would have any positive effect on her father's situation? Even if the footmen tossed Lascelles out on his ear before he could force the box out of her hands, Lascelles could still spread malicious gossip. Her heart pounded. *What should I do?*

Anjali felt the weight of an entire life upon her shoulders. She was strong, but she never expected to have to face such terrible burdens. The box was heavy in her arms, which began to shake. To her annoyance, the tears started again. She was caught. She had failed.

She turned back toward Lascelles. Giving him the papers might save her father. *Or, it might destroy him, and I will have sealed his fate.* But surely, if that were to be the outcome, it would not happen right away and they would have time to find another way out. The machinery of the law worked slowly. *What other choice do I have?*

Anjali stepped forward and reluctantly placed the box, which had suddenly become like a lead weight, in Lascelles's outstretched arms.

"I'm truly sorry, Madam," he said. "Believe me, I would rather not have been driven to this expedient. Your father is at heart a good man. Perhaps too good." He gave her a respectful bow then brushed past the footmen and out the door.

As if he sensed Anjali's despair, Kavi flew down from the sconce and settled on her shoulder, making gentle chirping sounds in her ear.

CHAPTER 26

Thomas expected at any moment to learn that Dobson and his cronies had found the papers hidden in the épergne in his house. It might take them a while but eventually, if they kept looking, they would no doubt discover where he'd taken such care to hide them. No doubt they would destroy the documents, and he would have no records that detailed the misdeeds he'd discovered. They would then believe that he was no longer a threat to them, and he hoped that would allow them to take pressure off the Home Office to keep him detained. Perhaps conveniently discrediting some accusation as mere hearsay rather than actually admitting they were wrong. The whole thing was madness.

Given the conditions of his imprisonment, Thomas didn't expect any more visits and on the fifth day of his confinement was lost in contemplation of the days he was not spending in Caroline's company and what might possibly befall him by the time his predicament had run its course. At first he paid no attention to the ring of boots on flagstones approaching his cell, assuming they would continue on to another part of the honeycomb of a prison. With only idle curiosity, Thomas watched the guard round the corner. If anyone came to see him it would likely be Dobson again.

Yet the guard did not have Dobson in his wake. *Lascelles.* Thomas's stomach twisted and he ground his teeth together.

"I trust they are feeding you well," Lascelles said as he walked toward the cell

At least he had the good manners not to smile in triumph, Thomas thought. Still, his fist itched to connect with the fellow's smug chin. He could still remember how it felt to do so through the muffler at Jackson's. How much more satisfying it would be to hit him with his bare knuckles. But Thomas was on one side of the cell's bars and Lascelles stood on the other, too far away for him to reach.

"Why are you here?" Thomas said.

"I wanted to let you know that your papers have been found."

It was as he expected. "Are you satisfied now?"

Lascelles shrugged. "It's not up to me what to do with them. But I have read them. I want you to know that I haven't come to gloat. In fact, I've come to warn you. Dobson tells me they can be interpreted quite differently from the way you no doubt intended."

"Anything can be twisted beyond sense in the wrong hands," Thomas said.

Lascelles crossed his arms and leaned one shoulder against the stone wall. "Unfortunately, there's some damning stuff in them that the Home Office might choose to see in quite an interesting light. A light that does not shine favorably upon you."

Of course, with only the facts, the ledgers, the scribbled notes and names, there was no context. Nothing to place the information in the complex web of malfeasance and cruelty he had uncovered with his munshi's help. In fact, it was that scribe who had first pointed out that the letter from a silk merchant, written in Persian script with details of the shipment he would supply, didn't match what was actually sent. A visit to the merchant and further investigation revealed that the Company—in the person of an unscrupulous officer of middle rank—insisted that, if the merchants and landowners did not want their crops destroyed and their families threatened, they would have to forfeit a portion of every shipment that passed through their hands, whether it was Company business or not.

Thomas was called out of his unpleasant memory by Lascelles, who said, "You might be glad to know that Anjali is in good health."

How dare he even mention her name! "That can be of no interest to you." The idea of this unscrupulous man with his precious daughter sickened him. And to think that only a little over a week ago he'd watched them dance together and felt glad that Anjali had someone from home to talk to.

"I happened to see her this morning. At your house. In fact, it was she who delivered the documents into my hands. What I didn't know at the time—and nor did she—was exactly what the papers contained. So don't judge her too harshly if you get out of here. Which I sincerely hope you do."

Thomas felt as if a stone had dropped into his stomach. Anjali would never betray him. She had been tricked, obviously. "My daughter can do no wrong in my eyes. I could never be harsh with her."

"That's as it should be, of course. I would expect nothing less of you. I too think her an exceptional young lady. She does you great credit. I want you to know that I might not have done what I did yesterday had I known that Dobson would not simply destroy the documents, but use them to have you charged as a traitor. I hope you will at least give me credit for the fact that I have strongly advised destroying the documents rather than using them to destroy you. Please believe me when I say I have no desire for that to happen. We were friends once."

"You don't know what friendship means!" Thomas realized with a shudder that Dobson might reasonably argue that Ashcombe himself had been the one threatening the merchants. There was just enough ambiguity in the papers to leave them open to interpretation.

Lascelles sighed. "Sadly, friendship does not make one wealthy, or even get one out of the river tick. I was up against a wall, truly."

"What did you say to persuade my daughter to give you the documents?"

"I only had to tell her the truth. That she would have to relinquish them if she had any hope of your emerging from this limbo unscathed."

It was a terrible position in which to place a nineteen-year-old girl. She was too trusting, too intelligent, too loving, not to make the decision she thought had the greatest chance of restoring her father to her. Blackguards, all of them. "Get out," Thomas said in a low voice that was almost a growl. "You can have nothing more to say to me."

Lascelles bowed his head. "Neither you nor Anjali will ever see me again, I hope. My ship sails in a few days. Whatever happens to you will take much longer than that to be sorted out. I'm sorry for it, truly. Goodbye."

Lascelles called for the guard, who had been waiting for him just around the corner, and followed the man back the way he'd come.

So like Lascelles, Thomas thought, to believe he could continue to live on both sides of the fence at once. He'd offered what he no doubt considered a flag of truce. But it would never be enough. Thomas's only comfort was that

Lascelles did not know all. Nor did Dobson. The plain truth was that although all the facts had been recorded faithfully by his munshi and hidden away in his document box, the source document, the one that launched Thomas on his investigations, was not among those papers. It was somewhere else entirely, along with another communication that would lend the ring of truth to all Thomas's assertions, and allow for no misrepresentation of the facts.

As to whether Anjali would find those vital morsels of evidence, only fate could decide. Someone else might have invoked God rather than fate. But Thomas was not a praying man. His concept of God and religion had been mixed into a general soup of Hindu deities, Mohammed, and Jesus Christ. His faith, such as it was, existed in the conviction that men were essentially good. He believed in his heart that if he were charged and could argue his case before a jury of his peers, justice would be served.

But that was not possible as things stood. All he could do was wait to see if Anjali and Sir Julian would manage to fit the final puzzle pieces into place. That, he hoped, would lead to a cessation of the illegal activities in India. It would likely not, however, punish those who falsely accused him. He would have to find some other means of doing that.

Despite being reminded forcibly of Anjali by Lascelles, it had not been her face that illuminated his dreams during his scant hours of sleep. These events had made him realize that he was foolish to hold back. Caroline might turn away from him again, as she did before. But he deserved a chance to find happiness, just as everyone did. She did not have a happy marriage. There was still time for her to find love and fulfillment. He would tell Caroline that he still loved her, that in fact he loved her more deeply now after a lifetime without her. And then he would ask her to marry him. Thomas clung to this hopeful dream to keep himself from falling into black despair.

He was not a traitor. He was an honorable man. The truth would prevail.

JULIAN AND LADY LEWISTON SAT IN THE DRAWING ROOM AT Park Street, united in agitation and anxiety. Or rather, they sat and rose and walked around by turns, starting at every noise from the street or other sound that could be Anjali returning from Bloomsbury. Julian had never felt so powerless in his life before. Had he really allowed a young girl—a young girl he loved, no less—to go off by herself to do something that could well be dangerous? She would say, of course, that she wasn't by herself. She had Millie and Kavi. But neither of them could defend her if the need arose. He hoped that, if she were discovered in her pursuit of the documents, her relationship to Ashcombe and her youth would excuse any transgression she might have committed, although he couldn't see how anyone would justifiably accuse her of trespassing or theft.

What seemed like hours but was probably much less time passed in that intolerable anxiety until finally the barouche drew up in front of the house and Anjali, Kavi, and Millie entered the house. Julian didn't wait for her to ascend the stairs to the drawing room but ran down, taking them two at a time to greet her.

He had never seen her look so drawn and despairing. Things had not gone well.

Lady Lewiston stood at the top of the stairs and said, "Come into the drawing room. Fairing will bring us tea."

The footman, Andrew, helped Anjali off with her pelisse and then took Kavi away. Julian offered her his arm and she leaned on it heavily as they climbed up the steps. Still she had said nothing.

Once they were all three in the drawing room and Fairing had closed the door, Julian said to Anjali, "Tell me everything," taking her hands and leading her to a settee by the hearth.

With a shaking voice and wiping away a stray tear now and then, Anjali described the entire episode. Once she was finished, she lost whatever composure was left to her. "I have failed! I have made matters worse! My poor Papa!" She buried her face in her hands and sobs shook her body.

Julian didn't hesitate, not caring that Lady Lewiston would see him. He pulled Anjali into his arms and stroked her head, murmuring to her *hush, it's all right, all is not lost.* What he really wanted to say was, *do not cry, my darling. Please marry me so that I can always be with you to dry your tears.*

A few moments later Lady Lewiston came over to them and took Anjali's hand, pulling her away from him to a stand. Her sympathetic glance assured Julian that she was not angry or scandalized by what he'd done. Perhaps she knew how he felt. If things were different, he would assure her right away that he intended to propose to Anjali. He'd decided he would do that the morning after the opera, before he even knew what had happened to Ashcombe. But all that didn't seem important just then.

"Come, my dear. You are worn to the bone," Lady Lewiston said. "And no wonder. I already asked Millie to prepare a hot bath for you and then you must go to bed. I'll have cook send up a tray." She steered Anjali to the door even as she spoke. Anjali rested her head on Lady Lewiston's shoulder, as if that lady was so much more to her than simply her chaperone.

Julian thought that if only they could get Thomas out of this morass, Lady Lewiston might well end up being much more than a chaperone to Anjali. He had seen Ashcombe and Lady Lewiston together and knew something of their history, although not the particulars. If she had had no feelings for Ashcombe, Lady Lewiston might be sorry about what happened to him, but she would hardly be throwing herself so wholeheartedly into their efforts to exonerate him. Nor would she have agreed at the outset to do so much for his daughter. It was clear to Julian that Ashcombe and Lady Lewiston belonged together, whatever had happened to keep them apart for thirty years.

Julian sat pondering everything that had happened in the last few days for he knew not how long in that quiet, elegant room, watching the afternoon light fade from the sky and the colors of the upholstery and the rug become indistinct, not noticing when the maid came in to light the candles.

At last Lady Lewiston herself returned. "You're still here?" she said.

He shook his head. "Oh, I had no idea it was getting so late." He stood. "I shall go home and put my mind to this problem once again. There must be a way to get Ashcombe out of this terrible fix, even without possessing those papers."

Lady Lewiston walked over to him and took his hand between both of hers. "You have been a true friend. To Ashcombe, to me, and to Anjali. More than that to Anjali, I am certain. I realize you can say nothing until you are able to see Thomas and ask for his permission to make your addresses. If it's any comfort to you, I know he will say yes."

Julian nodded and blushed. "The important question to answer is whether Anjali will also say yes."

"Are you in any doubt of that? I'm not."

Julian went back to his rooms in an odd mixture of despair and elation. He would sleep and hope for inspiration in the morning, as so often happened when he was faced with a difficult case.

But no case in all his years as a barrister had ever touched on his own life so deeply, or mattered so much.

Anjali's dreams were by turns horrifying and beautiful. They began with images of Lascelle's smirking face, his arms like octopus tentacles reaching out to take something away from her, something precious, then faded into lovely swirls of Persian script, dancing across her consciousness from right to left, twisting and twirling. After a time the script whirled into the movement of a waltz, and she found herself in Sir Julian's comforting embrace, looking up into his tender green gaze. A moment later, the eyes became brown, the skin tanned, and the wicked gleam of Lascelles's visage loomed over her, his tentacle arms squeezing the life out of her. Every once in a while, her father's face floated into view, far away, like the moon in a hazy night sky. His mouth was moving and he was trying to say something to her. He was speaking in Hindustani, and then Bengali, and then English.

When she at last awoke, she felt almost as tired as when she went to bed. Nonetheless, the day must be faced. Without knowing what would happen next, how losing the documents would affect her father's future, she needed to find some way to make the hours pass, to occupy her mind.

Of course, Anjali thought. She remembered the old munshi at the India House museum and their conversation about Mir. Perhaps she would be able to lose herself in translating poetry, find solace surrounded by beautiful words and thoughts instead of the ugly reality of a bad law.

It was quite early in the morning. The housemaid had kindled the fire in her bedchamber but Millie had yet to bustle in and draw the curtains open. Anjali pulled on her brocade dressing gown and nestled her toes in her silk slippers, then rose and went to the desk by one of the windows. She opened the curtain to let the early morning sunlight spill across the polished wood and sighed. The English sun was so insipid. By this time of day in Calcutta the light would be blazing and fierce, the air hot and spiced. She would never go back there, she supposed.

Her volume of Mir sat in lonely isolation on top of the desk, where she had placed it a few short weeks ago thinking that she would turn to it every day. Anjali lifted it and traced the ornate, gold engraving on the soft leather cover. A wave of guilt washed over her. She had hardly glanced at the poems since the rout party, since she had become engrossed in her busy schedule of mindless amusements, arriving home nearly at dawn and then rising for visiting hours and shopping. This was all before the day when her father disappeared, of course.

She opened the small book and flipped through some of the pages, looking for where she had tucked the ribbon marking the last poem she translated, when one of the pages came loose. *No!* she thought. The book was so precious to her. Surely it couldn't be falling apart. It was a fine edition, carefully sewn. But there was no denying that something had loosened. Not just a page but a signature somehow seemed not properly bound into the volume.

Anjali idly glanced at it, sighing, and began to read.

Suddenly, everything in her and around her stilled. This was not a poem by Mir. This was something else altogether. It was a message. A warning. Sent to her father by someone. The beautiful Persian script might have been the munshi's, but she couldn't remember it well enough to be certain.

Hands trembling, Anjali smoothed out the paper and began to translate. When she had the meaning of it, she drew a new sheet of paper out of the drawer in the desk and with the stub of a pencil scribbled down what it said.

Beware, Sahib. Your investigations have become known to those with an interest in ensuring you never reveal the crimes you have discovered. They are powerful men who could destroy you and your family. You are no longer safe in Calcutta. I beg you leave India with all haste.

My God! Anjali murmured. She then flipped through the rest of the book, past the familiar pages of flowing poetic lines, until she got to the very end. Then she turned it upside down and shook it, hoping something else would fall out. But she found no other loose signatures or hidden papers and was about to close the volume when something caught her eye. The inside back cover was slit right near the binding, and the tiniest sliver of paper peeked out. With some difficulty, she pinched the edge and teased it out. This was no elegantly scripted letter. It was a hastily scrawled missive in rough, Hindustani writing, as if someone had written it in a state of the greatest agitation. She was a little out of practice with Hindi, but after half an hour's concentrated effort, Anjali managed to translate that note as well.

I beg you, Ashcombe Sahib, to help my family. You are the only British we can trust. They have threatened the lives of my children if I do not agree to their so-called taxes on the opium. I fear these activities will only result in unrest among my people and threaten the equitable arrangements that traders like you have made for the benefit of all. I enclose some accounts that will show you the extent of the wrongdoing.

The note was not from her grandfather. It appeared to be from one of the merchants her father traded with. Duleep Singh.

"Mornin' miss," Millie said as she came in and went immediately to the clothes press without even glancing at Anjali. "What would you like to wear today?"

"Anything! Whatever is easiest. I must dress immediately and go down to Lady Lewiston. Speed is imperative!"

"What is it, miss?" Millie asked, anxiety written across her face.

Naturally, after yesterday—when she helped Anjali find the document box and then witnessed her having to relinquish it—Millie was justified in reacting with uneasiness. "It's all right. It's nothing bad. I think, in fact, it could be something very good. Very, very good."

Anjali trembled with anticipation. These documents alone might be enough to get the warrant lifted, no matter what was in the box she handed over to Lascelles. Sir Julian must be sent for right away! As soon as Millie fastened her corset and slipped the day dress over her head, almost before she had time to tie it closed and put a ribbon around the seam beneath her bust, Anjali pulled the bell to summon Andrew. He arrived quickly, accustomed to being available at that time of day so Anjali could tell him what she needed him to do with Kavi.

"Andrew, wait while I write a very quick note, and then take it right away to Sir Julian's lodgings. They're in St. James's Street. Someone will know!" Her hand was trembling so that the ink dribbled off the quill and she had to take a second sheet of paper to start again.

"Miss Ashcombe," Andrew said, "Whatever's the matter?"

"I can't explain it now, but this is very important. Is Lady Lewiston in her room?"

"I believe so," Millie said, "Although she might have gone down already."

Andrew took the folded note Anjali thrust into his hands and ran from the room.

ANJALI HADN'T EVEN FINISHED HER SECOND CUP OF COFFEE when Sir Julian joined her and Lady Lewiston in the breakfast parlor less than half an hour later. She showed him the original letters and her translations.

"Where did you find these?" he asked, his eyes wide with wonder.

"They were in my poetry book. The Mir. Papa must have hidden them there so that everything wouldn't be found in the same place."

Sir Julian smiled. "You know what this means? It means we have proof. Even without those other documents. We have them. All that remains is to get a meeting with the under secretary I spoke to the other day, Higgins. I'll find Atherleigh and arrange it."

Anjali caught hold of Sir Julian's sleeve before he could dash away. "You are not going without me—to the meeting, I mean."

"They won't let a woman into the office, I'm certain," he said, covering her hand with his and giving it a gentle squeeze.

"Two women, you mean," Lady Lewiston stood. "If we can't be in the room, we will be immediately outside of it so we can know what happens the instant it does."

He promised he would take no action without them, and left a moment later.

CHAPTER 27

*L*ord and Lady Atherleigh were still in their breakfast parlor, each of them absorbed in a newspaper. When Julian came into the small, cozy room, they both lowered the papers at exactly the same time and looked up at him with such similar expressions of curiosity that he was tempted to laugh. He supposed that was what happened with a couple who were so content in each other's company.

"Meredith," Atherleigh said. "Please sit."

"I won't stay, but I wanted to tell you what happened yesterday and what Miss Ashcombe discovered this morning that completely changes the picture, and to ask you to arrange another meeting with Higgins as soon as humanly possible."

He told them the entire story, with only minimal interruptions from Antonella, whose concern was for Anjali and Lady Lewiston, how they were faring in all this turmoil. When he showed them the small bits of paper and the rough translations, Atherleigh said, "It doesn't look like very much.

Do you really think this will tip the balance in Ashcombe's favor? What if the other documents have been destroyed already?"

"Even if that is the case, between Ashcombe's assertions and these desperate communications it will be clear that he was not acting with seditious intent, but only trying to stop an illegal practice at the highest levels of the Company." Julian had to admit to himself that it would be better if these scraps of evidence could be supported by what were clearly detailed records and accounting. But they would simply have to do their best.

"Of course I'll do whatever I can."

ONCE AGAIN, ATHERLEIGH CAME THROUGH. APPARENTLY, Higgins was already scheduled to talk to someone regarding Ashcombe's warrant, and decided that Sir Julian and his friends might as well be included in the discussion.

Later that same afternoon Julian, Lady Lewiston, and Anjali drove to Whitehall to meet with Higgins. Atherleigh and Lewiston agreed to join them there. As Julian suspected, the ladies were not permitted past a semi-public anteroom, so the three gentlemen went into the corridor where the administrative offices were located. Such a pedestrian setting for such a momentous decision, Julian thought. But the law was like that. Sometimes the most important matters were settled in minutes, while the most trivial of disagreements mushroomed into months of fruitless wrangling.

Julian, Atherleigh, and Lewiston entered the office to see Mr. Higgins sitting on one side of the desk. Opposite him were four chairs, two of which were already occupied. *Lascelles,* Julian thought with loathing, recognizing the slightly-too-long wavy brown locks. If he had encountered him in any other setting he would have continued the work he began at the Hartland ball and sent him home to India with a broken jaw and a black eye. But that was not important at that moment. He must not be distracted from the purpose at hand.

The other man was someone he did not recognize, a phlegmatic-looking gentleman with an air of conscious superiority whom Higgins introduced as Mr. Dobson.

Harry's presence required a clerk to procure another chair, which caused some inconvenient shuffling. Still, having a well-respected marquess on their side added some weight, Julian hoped.

Higgins began the meeting with, "Let us settle this expeditiously. We must either charge Mr. Ashcombe or release him. The question is whether evidence exists to support the preponderance of circumstances that caused the warrant on suspicion of high treason to be issued."

Before he could say anything more, Dobson reached into a portfolio by his side and brought out a small collection of documents, which he spread on the desk in front of Higgins. "I believe, sir, that these papers provide ample evidence that the accused was defrauding the Company in India and thereby encouraging dangerous unrest among our trading partners and other natives."

What? What was this man doing? Julian reached for one of the papers and examined it. It certainly appeared very damning, detailing mysterious additional fees and other dubious charges. Surely these couldn't be all the papers from what Anjali had said was a heavy document box. *Of course.* Julian turned and glared at Lascelles, who kept his eyes focused on his hands folded in his lap. So, instead of destroying the papers they decided to use them as weapons against Ashcombe. He should have foreseen that possibility. The thought of what might have resulted were it not for the new evidence he possessed sent a stab of icy dread down Julian's back.

"This certainly does look corroborative," Higgins said.

"One moment, sir," Julian said and stood. He never delivered an argument seated. He was tall as well, so he took command of a room and forced everyone to attend to him. "What Mr. Dobson has furnished does not tell the entire story. There are other documents than these that offer a very different tale."

"Where are these alleged documents?" Higgins asked.

Julian stole a quick look at Dobson. His suppressed smile confirmed what Julian suspected—that he had carefully chosen only some of the papers to arrange them in a way that would mean what he wanted them to mean and likely destroyed the rest of them. Dobson thought it was those missing papers that Julian was referring to and considered himself safe.

"I have them here, Secretary Higgins," Julian said, and withdrew his pocket book from inside his coat and took out the two items Anjali had found. He placed them carefully in front of Higgins. Both Dobson and Lascelles leaned forward to peer at them.

"What do they mean? You cannot offer evidence that is unintelligible." Higgins was slightly irritated.

Julian said, "I also have here translations of these two documents. One of them is in Urdu and the other is Hindustani." Instead of laying them on the table, Julian read them each aloud.

Dobson's face darkened. "This is ridiculous! Who translated these letters? How can they be verified?"

"Miss Ashcombe, who is knowledgeable in both languages—as well as Bengali—discovered these notes and translated them herself." Julian suspected Dobson would not accept this without a fight, but he also knew that

Higgins's attitude had shifted when the translations were read aloud.

"Hah! A schoolgirl. And the man's daughter! Likely she made it up out of whole cloth. A desperate move." Dobson rose as well and faced Julian.

"If you will both be seated," Higgins said. "I take Mr. Dobson's point. Is there a way to verify that these documents are what you claim, and that they have been accurately translated?"

Be calm, Julian exhorted himself. He had faced worse situations in court. His mind worked at its fastest to figure out how they might be able to satisfy this request. There had been no time to find an impartial eye who could both read and accurately translate in these two languages. Another miscalculation. He expected only that the papers from Ashcombe's house would be destroyed. He'd underestimated Lascelles's enmity and fixed a stare brimming with animosity at him.

This time, Lascelles returned his gaze and said, "If I may, I believe we can solve this conundrum fairly easily." He turned to Dobson and said, "We may as well ensure that everything is properly done and expose these papers as unrelated to the case. I know where there is someone who could translate for us, and who knows nothing of the matter at hand and would therefore be impartial."

Now Julian was completely confused. A third party would not undermine the contents of the two letters, but rather support the veracity of Anjali's translations.

Dobson scowled, and then said, "Very well. Who is this person?"

Lascelles said, "There is an old gentleman who cares for the manuscripts at India House, a loyal employee of the Company. If he could be sent for, we will soon be able to know what these little scraps of paper truly say."

"What is his name?" Higgins asked.

Lascelles shrugged. "I do not know. Miss Ashcombe might. She spoke to him the day we visited India House together." He said this to Higgins, but Julian knew he meant it to sting him.

Higgins said to Julian, "Are you agreeable to this expedient?"

Why was Lascelles facilitating something that he must know would expose the flaw in Dobson's so-called evidence? He was undoubtedly aware of Anjali's extensive education and likely able to guess that she knew both of these Indian languages well enough to translate them accurately.

"Yes, we are willing to let the matter rest on an independent translation. Miss Ashcombe is waiting in a nearby room. Perhaps she can furnish a name for the fellow."

Anjali and Lady Lewiston had only been waiting a short while when a harassed-looking clerk rushed in and said, "Miss Ashcombe?"

"I am she," Anjali said. What happened?

"I have been sent to find a native gentleman at India House whose name you apparently know. Could you furnish me with that name?"

At India House? She knew no one there! Her one visit was etched on her memory for its unpleasantness. Unpleasant, that is, except for one distinct moment. "Oh! Yes!" she said, as the elderly man in the library came suddenly to mind. "Could it be that you're looking for Munshi Abdul Rahman? If so, I believe you'll find him in the museum."

The man rushed off without another word.

"You went into India House?" Lady Lewiston said, not really asking.

Anjali smiled ruefully. "I'm sorry I didn't tell you. It was such an awful day, and I hated being there. I've tried to forget it."

"I can well understand. I thought something had happened. But what could they possibly want with that man you mentioned?"

Anjali knit her brows. What indeed? What was it that she and the munshi had talked about? Mir. And the Persian Urdu manuscript. He was surprised she could read it. "I can't think."

"Was there anything there you particularly remember?"

"Manuscripts. Very beautiful. The poems of Mir in his own hand—" She gasped and covered her mouth.

"Anjali?"

"I think they're bringing him here to translate the letters again. They don't believe I've done it correctly." Of course. These men would think she couldn't possibly do a good job at something that required a high degree of skill and knowledge. Did Sir Julian suggest it? She wouldn't have thought it of him, but the possibility nonetheless stung her.

Lady Lewiston reached over and took her hand. "I know what you're thinking. But try not to be offended. It means, at least, that they're considering the letters very carefully."

Helpless tears burned behind Anjali's eyes. Why must it always be so? Her papa would never have doubted her. Nor would Nalin. In India, ladies of high caste were expected to be very educated. Not in England, apparently.

An agonizing hour passed. If the scribe had come, he must have gone in through a different entrance. *A servants' entrance,* Anjali thought with scorn.

Finally, hurried men's steps approached them from the corridor down which Sir Julian and the others had gone. Two men appeared. One of them, the one she did not know, muttered to the other, "I thought you said we had everything! This is a disaster."

Behind him strode none other than Mr. Lascelles. Anjali shrank into herself, wishing he would simply pass by without seeing her. But she and Lady Lewiston were the only two people in the waiting area. Inevitably their eyes met. Lascelles raised one brow in that way he had and nodded slightly before continuing on in the other man's wake. He didn't look so triumphant now, not as he looked when he took the document box away from her in her father's house.

Lady Lewiston gripped her arm hard. "Do you know what this means?" She turned eyes shining with happy tears to Anjali. "I think it worked!"

Anjali didn't want to hope until they knew for certain.

It was a few more minutes before Sir Julian, Atherleigh, and Lewiston emerged, followed by the munshi from India House.

"The secretary was convinced," Julian said, "that not only was your father far from being seditious, but that he had been maliciously accused." Sir Julian, although trying hard to appear dignified and serious, couldn't help the spark of joy that lit his eyes.

Anjali felt weak with relief, although still a bit piqued by having her translation doubted. "When will my father be released?"

"As soon as the paperwork can be completed. Likely tomorrow," Sir Julian said.

"Let us not stand here talking," Lady Lewiston said. "Please come to the dower house for a glass of wine and tell us everything."

They were about to leave the building together when Sir Julian turned to the munshi and said, "Where will you go?"

What did he mean by that? Anjali wondered.

The old man bowed slightly and said, "I do not know, sahib."

Sir Julian took one of his visiting cards out of his pocket book and handed it to Rahman. "Please go here and wait for me. Tell the gentleman who will let you in that Sir Julian said to say he was up to one of his strange starts again. You are not afraid of dogs, I hope?"

The old man smiled, put his palms together, and bowed.

CHAPTER 28

homas rubbed his hand along the stubble on his chin. Doubtless he looked a complete mess. He hadn't so much as drawn a comb through his hair since before the opera—how many days ago was that? His evening wear was rumpled and stained, and his back hurt from trying to sleep on the uncomfortable cot. When he heard the guard's distinctive tread echoing down the corridor he assumed it was some meal on the way—a meal that he'd pick at just to keep himself alive.

But the guard arrived with no tray, no pail of fresh water. Instead, he took out his great ring of keys, fitting one into the lock of the cell door, and swung it open as he stood back.

Thomas stared at him blankly. "What's this?"

"Yer free to go."

What? What had happened? Everything had seemed hopeless after Dobson's and Lascelle's visits. What changed?

"Come along!" the guard said and grabbed his arm none too gently to pull him out of the cell.

After a bemusing quick march through twists and turns of corridors, they arrived at the turnkey's lair and that man shuffled out, unlocked and unchained the main door, and threw it open.

Thomas expected to see an expanse of open fields and the wide, free sky. What he didn't expect was to see Caroline standing there, looking as lovely as ever in a moss green pelisse and a satin straw villager hat, hands clasped in front of her, eyes shining.

At first he just stared. Then he took a step forward and she reached out both her hands and rushed toward him. He took hers in a strong grip. She seemed to want to get closer to him but he held her a little away. "I'm not fit to be seen, let alone anything else," he said, unable to keep himself from smiling. "How is it you are here?" His voice sounded scratchy and uncertain to his own ears, and her smile faded a bit and her brow creased in concern.

"Are you unwell? Have you been mistreated?" Her grip on his hands tightened.

He shook his head. "Only in being locked up in the first place." He tore his eyes away from Caroline's to look around at the sky, the green trees, the ordinary everydayness of the world.

A tear slipped down Caroline's cheek. He freed one hand and brushed it away with his thumb. She leaned into his touch and said, "I thought I'd never see you again."

"It would take more than that to keep me away now," he said. "Let's leave this place. Tell me what happened. How did you manage this?"

"*I* didn't. *We* did."

Caroline led him to the barouche, which was waiting a short way down the road. The footman held the door open and helped them both in. Once they sat in the luxurious comfort of the carriage with its burgundy velvet squabs and well-sprung chassis and had started on their way south to

Mayfair, Thomas said, "Now I need to know what exactly happened to bring this about."

Caroline smiled and angled herself toward him. "Julian will explain it all later. It is enough for now to say that you are no longer under warrant." She lifted her hand to his cheek and said, "There are other things we need to talk about while we can be private."

Yes, Thomas thought. His world had just turned violently on its axis, and he wasn't entirely certain why or how it had come about. Not his freedom—he would wait for the whole story—but Caroline. How was it that she had been the one to collect him from that terrible place? He read more than just affection in her eyes. Or was he seeing what he wished to see? It was very confusing. "Why did you not try to get me to stay all those years ago? I would have. All it would have taken was a single word from you, as I said in my letter."

Caroline's mouth opened and a look of confusion came into her eyes. "What do you mean? I wrote to you! I begged you to keep fighting for me, not to run away. And I never received a letter from you."

The realization dawned on both of them at the same time, and they said, "Mother." "Lady Havering." Caroline's ambitious mama must have intercepted both letters, leaving each of them to believe that the other had abandoned their love.

"Mama told me that you realized your mistake, that you felt you weren't worthy of me, and wanted to go to India to prove yourself," Caroline said, her voice subdued.

"I was given no explanation at all, simply packed off onto a ship bound for Calcutta."

In the half hour it took to drive back to Mayfair, they shared their stories. So much was different, yet there were similarities.

"You don't regret your marriage, surely," Caroline said. "Anjali is a truly wonderful young lady."

"No. I do not regret it. Shanta was extraordinary. I loved her. You would have liked her, too, had circumstances been otherwise," Thomas said, wishing he weren't so bedraggled and could scoop her up in his arms.

Caroline sighed. "I wish I could say the same. But you know the story already, I'm sure. Yet I would not undo any of it either, for much the same reasons. All our children have turned out to be thoughtful, intelligent, and caring. It's as much as a parent could ever ask."

"But not as much as any human being could ask," Thomas said. "Caroline—"

She pressed her gloved index finger against his lips. "Not now. Not yet. When you've heard everything, when you are feeling more like yourself. Then we can talk again."

The barouche stopped at Park Street and Thomas helped Caroline down and then climbed back in. To her questioning gaze he said, "I need a bath, a shave, and a change of clothes. I shall return when I'm in a more civilized state. I don't want Anjali to see me like this. It would upset her."

Caroline nodded, and then said with a wistful smile, "I hardly dare let you out of my sight again. Promise you'll come back later?"

Nothing, and no one, could keep him away, he thought, but he only said, "Of course. Please make all right with Anjali and tell her I shall see her later."

JULIAN HAD HAD TO COMPLETE SOME PAPERWORK ON THOMAS'S behalf the day before his release, so hadn't been able to return to his lodgings until close to dinner time. When he arrived, he found Addison in a state of dignified affront and Abdul Rahman quietly standing in an unobtrusive corner, an expression of bland neutrality on his countenance, Bramble sitting docile at his feet. Julian sighed.

"Do you have any reason to be dissatisfied with my service, Sir Julian?" Addison said in polished, icy tones as he helped him out of his coat.

To Julian's considerable surprise, this activity—which normally caused Bramble to leap about in the mistaken belief that a coat, whether it was being donned or removed, meant that a walk was forthcoming—was unattended by such chaos. He glanced over at Rahman, whose hand rested lightly on an ecstatic Bramble's head.

"No, of course not Addison!" Julian said. "I'm sorry I couldn't get here earlier to explain Mr. Rahman's presence. We have successfully had Mr. Ashcombe released from his confinement, and Rahman was instrumental in enabling that to happen. Unfortunately, what he did on our behalf enraged our opponents—well, one of them at least—who promptly dismissed him from the position he has held for ... how many years is it, Mr. Rahman?" He lifted his chin in the munshi's direction.

Rahman stepped forward and said, "Twenty-five, sahib."

Addison's eyes lost a little of their frostiness.

"Mr. Rahman is with us only until I can find another position for him where his considerable talents will be valued and appreciated. I know I can depend upon you to make him welcome," Julian said, flashing his most winning smile at Addison, who by then had completely reverted to his normal calm, benevolent self.

"Of course, sir," Addison said. "Only ... these lodgings are, shall we say ..."

Yes, there was the issue of where the fellow would sleep, there being only one private alcove for a servant in Julian's rooms. "I have asked Mrs. Morgan to let me hire one of the small extra rooms for as long as is necessary."

"Sahib," Rahman said, "There is no need. I will sleep in this room, on the settee. It is much as I am used to. The sofa in the museum was my only bed for all this time."

Julian looked again at Bramble's docile face and said, "Very well. Do you have any personal items you would like to have brought from India House?"

The munshi owned few things beyond a change of clothes and a prayer rug, he said. Julian swiftly arranged for those to be collected.

JULIAN'S MIND WAS IN TURMOIL, HOWEVER, DESPITE THE HAPPY outcome of the day. After a brief celebratory visit with Anjali, Lady Lewiston, and her family—everyone, it seemed, had been waiting to learn the outcome of that meeting—he had returned home. It appeared that Addison had decided he could tolerate Rahman, if for no other reason than that Bramble took an instant shine to the munshi and instead of following Addison everywhere, cleaved to Rahman as if he held the key to his survival.

When he retired for the night, though, he could not calm his turbulent thoughts and he tossed and turned. As sometimes happened when something wouldn't let go of him, when he was unsure about an argument or feared he had left something important out of an opinion, he awoke in the morning no longer in doubt about what he had to do.

Therefore, on the afternoon of Ashcombe's release, Julian took a hack to the house in Bedford Square. He probably should have given Ashcombe more time to recover, but having made up his mind he couldn't bear the thought of delaying. If the experience had taught him anything, it was that life must be seized by the throat, without fear or hesitation, lest it be wrenched from you unexpectedly.

As he contemplated what was to come on his arrival in

Bloomsbury, he had the sensation of a thousand birds all flapping within his stomach at the same time and several of them simultaneously pecking at his insides. He'd never felt this nervous before even the most consequential case at the Old Bailey. There, he knew his way, understood all, had a clear view of every nuance of the matter, and could be confident of the outcome—barring something no one could foresee. Here, having just let Ashcombe's butler take his coat and lead him to Ashcombe's library, he felt that he might as well be facing a firing squad. Without a wig to cover it, his red hair stood out like a beacon of foolishness. Although he knew Ashcombe was not so petty, Julian couldn't help feeling that this unfortunate feature would prejudice the man against him. He no doubt wanted more than a socially awkward, odd-looking, working barrister for a son-in-law.

"Sit down, Sir Julian," Ashcombe said from behind the large rosewood desk. His expression was serious. Julian thought perhaps it was because of his recent ordeal.

"If you don't mind, sir, I'd prefer to stand."

Ashcombe nodded.

Julian launched into the speech he'd prepared. "Over the course of the last few weeks, I have come to view Miss Ashcombe—your daughter (*of course he knows she's his daughter, you fool!*)—with admiration. Respect. Dare I say affection. No, more than that. Because why else would I—"

"I'll stop you right there," Ashcombe said, rising and coming around to the front of his desk. His face, if anything, had become even more stern. His voice held a harsh note. "I know what you're asking. Do you honestly think that I would give my only child to any man whose efforts freed me from an impossible, possibly life-threatening situation? Or who has treated her with the utmost consideration and clearly values her for all her many qualities and abilities? Do you think that I would be happy knowing I had given her hand to any man who was both scrupulously honest and yet flexible when it was necessary? Any man who has put aside his own needs to undertake a task that was by no means certain of its outcome or likely to result in a single penny of remuneration?"

Ashcombe stopped speaking. Julian hardly knew what to think, and certainly not what to say. This was not at all what he expected. His face went hot and then cold, and he decided he must say something. "Sir, I did not mean to presume—" What next?

Ashcombe paced slowly around the room, circling Julian like a lion tamer testing the temperament of a ferocious beast. "Would you expect me to give my daughter to any man who not only appreciates, but values the ways in which she is different from most of her peers in society? Any man who would not try to change her or take away the rich variety of influences that have shaped her life so far?"

Julian couldn't tell whether it was flinty hardness he saw glinting in Ashcombe's eyes or something else altogether. He didn't know the man well enough to judge, and Ashcombe had just been through a terrible ordeal, so perhaps he was unwilling to bestow his daughter's hand on any man, as he said. "Mr. Ashcombe, what I have to offer your daughter is a comfortable home, an honorable position, and..." He floundered. "...And she would be Lady Meredith." It sounded very hollow. But how could he tell this man he hardly knew how deeply he loved his only daughter?

"Well?" Ashcombe said, pausing in his circuit of the room and fixing Julian with his frank, open gaze. He pursed his lips together in what Julian assumed was disapproval.

This was going terribly. It should have been a mere formality. So said Lady Lewiston. Where had he made his mistake?

So Julian did what he did when a court case was veering

in an unexpected direction. He said nothing. He took some time to think. He thought about what Ashcombe actually said rather than the manner in which he said it. And there was that look in his eyes again.

How could I be so stupid? Julian thought after a moment. What he said was *any man.* He took a deep breath and smiled. It was a brilliant opening statement by the opposition. But now he knew how to answer it. "No, sir, I would not expect you to let your daughter marry any man. I would only hope that you would give her to the one man who loves her more than he is capable of expressing. The one man who would never change her. The one man who cannot imagine his life without her."

Ashcombe stood in front of Julian and his stern face slowly relaxed into a smile. "And you are correct. There is only one man I wish my daughter to marry. I only wonder that you haven't already asked her. But I suppose there were other matters occupying your time."

They both laughed. Then Thomas grew serious. "Don't waste time. Go after what you want in life, come what may. Most people have only one chance at true happiness."

He put out his hand and Julian took it. "I'm heartily grateful that you are not a barrister, Ashcombe. I would never want to come up against you in court."

CHAPTER 29

*J*oyous. That was the only word Anjali could think of to describe how she felt when she saw her father again. He looked thinner, there were dark shadows beneath his normally cheerful eyes, and he didn't have such a ready smile as he had had as little as a week ago. No matter. All that would return. She would nurse him back to health. As far as she was concerned, he must never leave her again. If she could tie an invisible string to him and always know it was there, that all she need do was tug on it and he would come back, that would make her happy.

Their dinner the night before had been calm on the surface, but Anjali sensed something simmering beneath the laughter and teasing, the concern and camaraderie. It wasn't anxiety—not like the overbearing tension visible in everyone's faces from the moment they had realized her father had disappeared. It was more akin to excitement. Perhaps, she thought, it was the thrill of contemplating a future without the nightmare hanging over him that made her father's lips twitch every now and again, as though he was suppressing a smile.

Sir Julian, as well, blushed rosily every time one of them praised him for his efforts on her father's behalf. Then he'd look down and a moment later steal a glance at her. Lady Lewiston sat wreathed in smiles throughout the meal and afterwards like a benevolent goddess surveying her domain. Ganesha, she thought.

After days of little sleep and facing terrible dreams when she did manage to succumb to exhaustion, Anjali sank into bed and surrendered to her body's need for rest. She didn't awaken until the housemaid entered with her breakfast on a tray the next morning. "What time is it?" she asked, sitting bolt upright and swinging her legs out from underneath the blankets.

"Her La'ship says you're not to worry, but have breakfast here and she'll see you when yer ready. It's gone ten, Miss."

But there was so much to do! She wanted to go to her father's house, help him get settled again. Perhaps even persuade him that she should move to Bedford Square. It seemed she was launched in society—although, quite frankly, that didn't matter to her. She was content with her new friends—Lady Lewiston's family—and Sir Julian. Especially, perhaps, Sir Julian, although her feelings for him were in a tumble of chaos. She picked up the cup of tea the maid had poured and gulped it down, then grabbed a slice of bread and butter and ate it as quickly as she could. Her mouth half full, she said, "Tell Millie to come to me now."

It couldn't have taken more than fifteen minutes for Anjali to dress. Millie tutted over her hair, which she only had time to knot into a disheveled cluster at the back of her neck, but Anjali said, "Never mind! He won't care!" and raced down the stairs.

She burst into the drawing room looking for Lady Lewiston, and stopped short.

Lady Lewiston was there, but so was Sir Julian, who rose hastily when she entered and bowed. "My Lady, Sir Julian, I'm so sorry! Is it about my father? Is he well?" her mind immediately going to another disaster. She hastened forward until she stood between them and looked from one to the other, trying to read their expressions.

"Your father is well, Anjali! Please, join us," Lady Lewiston said.

Relief! "But I must go and see Papa, right away."

Lady Lewiston rose and took her hand. "Sir Julian is here to speak to you, dear. And your father is already here, in the library. I shall go down and join him and leave you to have a private chat with Sir Julian."

"He is here? Please take me to him!" Anjali was beginning to be confused. Lady Lewiston was smiling, but asking her to do something unthinkable: to stay away from her father any longer than necessary.

She shook her head. "He does not wish to see you until after you've spoken to Sir Julian." She glared at Anjali, opening her eyes wide.

Anjali turned her attention to Sir Julian, who had not said a word so far. His face was pale, his freckles standing out like points on a map. He had dressed rather more formally than his usual daytime attire. There was a vulnerable, beseeching look in his eyes.

Oh, Anjali thought, and instantly felt her own face heat up.

"I shall return in fifteen minutes," Lady Lewiston said, letting herself out and closing the door behind her.

"Miss Ashcombe," Sir Julian said and strode to her, taking her hands in his. "I think you must know how I feel. I couldn't wait, now that your father is safe. So I ask you, will you consent to be my wife?" By the end of this brief speech, he had taken her in his arms and pressed her to him.

Anjali could feel him trembling. Or was that herself? She was shocked and not shocked. Of course, she was completely in love with Sir Julian, how could she not be? And he was clearly in love with her. His words and actions had proved it in these few weeks. In his arms like that she felt that everything was right, that this was where she belonged. But … "I-I thank you for the honor…" Her voice faltered and tears leaked down her cheeks. "You must understand, I cannot marry you!"

Sir Julian froze. Was he going to let go of her? She didn't want him to and reached up and put her arms around his neck.

He looked down at her in utter confusion. "B-but, I love you! Don't you love me?"

"Yes," she said through her tears. "Yes, more than anything. But I can't say yes. Not now. My papa—he needs me. I must keep house for him, help him to recover from his terrible ordeal. Surely you see that!"

To Anjali's surprise, Sir Julian smiled and let his gaze wander all over her face. His cheeks regained some of their color and his eyes held that expression she particularly loved —a look that betokened intelligence, but with humor and a sense of the ridiculous ready to burst forth. As he looked and looked, he lowered his head to hers. *He is going to kiss me,* Anjali thought, with wonder and anticipation. If she allowed him to do so, it wouldn't be fair to him. But she didn't want to move. Their lips met. Softly at first, than more firmly, until she parted hers and let him kiss her deeply, with passion. It was unlike anything she had ever felt before. She should really not permit him such a liberty, she thought, if she wasn't going to marry him. But stopping him would be cruel at this point, and she was vaguely aware that he wasn't just kissing her, she was kissing him back. She was also aware of pleasant sensations traveling all through her body. Was that what it meant? She wanted to keep feeling it. But it wasn't fair. Not if she couldn't marry him.

She pulled away from him and said, "I mean it. I can't marry you. Please don't make me do this!"

He shook his head, took her hand, and led her to the settee. "Let's talk for a while."

~

"I'VE LEFT THEM TOGETHER IN THE DRAWING ROOM," CAROLINE said as she sat next to Thomas on the tufted leather library sofa.

Thomas laughed. "Poor fellow. I rather teased him when he came to ask my permission last night."

"You must be feeling better," Caroline said. And he certainly looked better even than last night. "I missed that sense of fun. All that was gone from my life when you left." She would never tire of looking at him, at the kindness that poured out of his eyes and the strength in every line of his face. "Are you truly feeling more yourself?"

"No, and yes. Mostly I feel grateful."

They sat together quietly, only the ticking of the mantel clock breaking the silence. After a time Thomas turned to face her. "Caroline, you stopped me from speaking yesterday —and I don't blame you! I looked like a ruffian. I can't imagine how I must have smelled. But please don't stop me now." He slid off the sofa and knelt in front of her, clutching her hand. "If it's not too late, if you still have any feelings left for me after thinking I'd heartlessly abandoned you all those years ago, do you think we could do what our families prevented when we were young? Do you think you could marry me?"

Caroline's breathing became shallow and her heart fluttered in her chest. Was this really happening? After all these years? She searched his eyes. Did he truly mean it? "What about Anjali? and Shanta?" she said, her voice husky and low.

Thomas stood and pulled Caroline up and into his arms. She rested her head against his broad shoulder, listening to his breath, feeling the beat of his heart. His voice said in a comforting murmur, "Anjali will be fine. She is strong and intelligent."

She lifted her head and looked at him again. "But you loved Shanta."

"Yes. I will never forget her. But I loved you first. I want to love you last as well."

Before she knew it, they were locked in an embrace. He kissed her deeply and long. Caroline never wanted it to end. It had been such a long time since she had been this close to a man. Perhaps, in truth, she never had. She wanted it to last forever.

But they separated at last and he whispered, "May I take that as a yes?"

She smiled as she hadn't smiled for what felt like years. "Yes. Yes. I never stopped loving you, even when you were only the ghost of a memory."

"Then kiss me again!" he said.

She was helpless to prevent it, and so she did as she was told.

When the kiss ended, Caroline said, "I told them I would return in fifteen minutes. I should see what transpired in my absence."

"Let's go up together." He took her hand and led her out of the library and up the stairs.

Julian was trying to remain serious, all the while feeling a helpless laugh bubble up in him at this absurd and beguiling creature. Nothing he said could persuade Anjali that she didn't need to become her father's housekeeper. He couldn't tell her what he suspected would happen. It was for Ashcombe to give her the news. Julian felt certain he would marry Lady Lewiston. Without that piece of information, it appeared that nothing he could say would persuade his love that she needn't cling to the idea that without her, her father would be alone. And cling she did, all the time conveying by her actions and her expressions that she was more than willing to marry him.

At that moment, Lady Lewiston and Ashcombe entered the room. They were holding hands.

Anjali started to run to her father, but stopped a few steps away and looked down at their joined hands. "Papa?" she said.

What could Julian say to help her through this moment? Could she really have been so involved in everything she was going through not to perceive the courtship that was right under her nose? Apparently she could. "I am sorry to say that Anjali has refused my offer of marriage."

"Whatever for?" Lady Lewiston said, a laugh in her eyes.

Anjali said, "Don't you see? I can't leave Papa alone. Not yet at least."

Lady Lewiston's mouth formed an astonished O and she said, "I thought you must know, I—"

Thomas motioned her to stop speaking and reached for his daughter. "Anji! Why have you turned your back on your chance for happiness? Your mama would never have wanted that for you."

The tracks of tears still stained Anjali's face despite Julian's earlier efforts to pat them away with his handkerchief. "Because you need me, Papa! Don't you? Who will care for you, keep house for you. I thought … you would be lonely. And I never want to lose you again." She threw her arms around Ashcombe and buried her face in his chest. When she did that, Julian thought, she looked every bit the precocious, persuasive, affectionate young child she must have been. Their children would be just like her, he thought, then reminded himself that she had not yet accepted him, and unless Ashcombe intervened, she likely wouldn't.

"There is no need to worry, *beti*!" Ashcombe murmured. "Lady Lewiston has just agreed to marry me. So you see, I shall not be lonely."

This made Anjali break from Ashcombe as though he suddenly became hot as a burning coal. She looked from one to the other of them. "You have?" Anjali asked, her gaze fixed on Lady Lewiston.

"Yes. Your papa and I were in love very long ago and our families forced us apart. This was meant to be."

Poor Anjali! Surely this news could not come as a complete surprise to her. Julian had seen it more than a week ago. If she hadn't, if she'd truly been ignorant of the current of attraction that flowed between her father and Lady Lewiston, he worried that the shock of this news might send her away from him again. Even telling her that Ashcombe had given him his blessing the night before hadn't swayed her.

Anjali turned. In those few seconds, full comprehension must have flooded through her. Her expression had undergone a complete transformation. Before her father and Lady Lewiston had entered her face was etched with distress and impossibly conflicted feelings. Now—it shone. It shone with joy.

"Is this true? Can it be?" she said.

All three of them said, "Yes" at the same moment.

Anjali clapped her hands together and said, "Oh Papa! Lady Lewiston! I am so very happy for both of you."

Julian was willing to give her some time to absorb this revelation, but not too much. "Miss Ashcombe," he said, "Now, I'm asking you one more time, will you—"

"Yes!"

It was all she said to him, but it was enough. They ran toward each other and Julian lost all sense of time as he kissed her and held her, as he felt her fingers twining through his curls, smelled the spicy scent of her skin, and let overwhelming happiness wash over him.

CHAPTER 30

*O*nce Anjali realized that not only was her father free and under no cloud of suspicion, but that he would be united with the woman he had loved long before her mother, she enthusiastically accepted Sir Julian's offer. How could she not? She felt a bit foolish for even hesitating at all. Looking back, even without a marriage to Lady Lewiston—Caroline—her father would never have wanted her to sacrifice herself to him.

That evening, the four of them sat in the drawing room over tea, an atmosphere of contentment embracing them. But Anjali had questions, questions that still troubled her and prevented her from fully setting her anxieties aside. And this was probably as good a time as any to ask them.

"Papa, what will happen to the men you identified in your papers?"

He shrugged. "Most likely they will quietly be removed from their positions and given other roles within the Company."

"And Mr. Dobson, who accused you so cruelly and whose actions could have got you hung as a traitor?" Her blood still surged when she thought of that man whom she'd seen only once, but whose flabby face was indelibly stamped on her memory.

Julian spoke up. "He has apparently been encouraged to go to Calcutta. His actions did not amount to anything criminal enough to prosecute. The law is worded in such a way that wrongful accusations are not necessarily punished."

Anjali considered this for a moment, then said, "So no one really suffers as a result of the suffering they put us through."

"It is the English way," Thomas said, a tinge of bitterness in his voice.

Apparently, Anjali thought. "And what about Mr. Lascelles? I still don't understand his actions."

Thomas pursed his lips and tapped his finger on the arm of the settee. "Lascelles is a complex man. He looked to his own comfort and benefit, and saw an opportunity to reap rich rewards by undermining me. At the end, though, I believe he couldn't stomach the thought of participating in a scheme that could make me perish. He came to visit me in prison—"

"What?" Anjali, Caroline, and Julian all said at once.

"He has friends everywhere. He came ostensibly to dangle freedom in front of me, but actually to warn me about the way in which Dobson planned to use the papers. He as much as said that had he known of that from the beginning, he would never have acted as he had."

Julian said, "Nonetheless, he did. I shall always think of him as a scoundrel."

"You forget that he gave the final blow to Dobson's machinations by having Rahman summoned to translate the letters. He knew full well that Anjali's translation was correct."

"Do you suppose, Papa, that Lord Dawlish was involved

as well? He said things to me that I couldn't quite interpret. He was very angry when I refused him."

Lady Lewiston spoke. "I found out something about Dawlish that might explain both his courtship and his anger. Falk tells me that while he was on the Continent, Dawlish became a gambler and lost almost all his fortune. He was counting on no one finding that out until he had equipped himself with an heiress for a wife."

Anjali shook her head slowly. "It all fits. And poor Lady Harriett!"

"I wouldn't waste any sympathy on her," Lady Lewiston said. "The other information Falk shared with me was that she and Lord Dawlish were secretly married by special license just yesterday. Her parents were opposed but she's of age, so there was nothing they could do. Her fortune is her own."

They all went quiet until Anjali spoke again. "I have another question, something that has been making me uneasy ever since we arrived in London and I realized that you had reasons I did not know of, reasons associated with your business, for moving us here so hastily."

"Yes, Anji? What do you want to know?"

"I worry about Nalin. I never wanted to mention him to you because, well, because of how we felt about each other at the end. But is he in danger remaining in Calcutta? Will there be retribution for what you caused to be exposed?" She thought about the letter she wrote all those weeks ago and how she never found anyone she could trust to take it to him. It would all have been for nothing in the end anyway.

Her father left Caroline's side and came to sit next to her —there was room on the settee because she was pressed so close to Julian. "You may rest easy, *beti*. I, too, was worried about Nalin's position in Calcutta, which is why I booked him passage on a ship leaving a few weeks after ours. He should have arrived in Southampton by now and be on his way to London. I will employ him to oversee my business here."

Anjali breathed a deep, relieved sigh. Now she knew that everyone she cared about was safe. She stole a glance at Julian, who looked down at her with a piercing, slightly anxious gaze. At another time, she would tell him about Nalin and her girlish infatuation. But not now.

Instead, she leaned her head on his shoulder, drinking in the comforting smell of him, his solid warmth. She would teach him to read and understand Urdu so she could share her love of Mir's poetry with him. He would talk to her about his work, perhaps let her come to watch him argue a case at the Old Bailey. They would live in London. Have children.

Most of all, they would have each other—and Kavi and Bramble, of course.

It promised to be a most remarkable wedding. Because Anjali and Julian wanted a private ceremony, not in any of the *ton* churches, Harry and Olivia immediately volunteered the house on Upper Brook Street as a location. In contrast to Caroline and Thomas's wedding —an intimate ceremony at the dower house by special license—preparations for this one had gone on for weeks. Lady Mariana and Lady Bridlington were in their element, just as they had been when designing costumes for Anjali's come-out ball. And Belinda and Antonella lent their support as well, refusing to allow Caroline to do any of the planning. *A bride shouldn't plan someone else's wedding!* they asserted. Frankly, after all the strain of Thomas's incarceration, Caroline was quite happy to give them free rein.

There was some difficulty over finding an officiant. But Atherleigh knew an army chaplain who had seen service in India and was more than willing to step in for the starched-up vicar of the Anglican church they all attended on Sundays.

As she sat on one of the benches in Olivia's theatre waiting for the ceremony to start, Caroline cast her eye over the guests, each of them extraordinary in their own way. Everyone who mattered, who had a link with her family, was there. Harry and Olivia furnished the setting. Lord and Lady Atherleigh and Lady Belinda and Hector Gainesworth had guided Anjali's immersion in society and supported her through her most difficult trials.

It was wonderful the way Lady Mariana Thorne and Augusta, Countess of Bridlington, joined forces to design Anjali's ensemble, and Madame Pauline herself oversaw the sewing and tailoring.

But even those who had taken no part in the drama that unfolded that season came to give their support, to show that their world could embrace someone like Anjali: the Duke and Duchess of Hartland brought their high rank and social power to the event, and the Earl of Bridlington—who often eschewed public events because of his disability—made one of his rare appearances. The former Persephone Wilkins, now Mrs. James Pentarrant, brought her enterprising husband—he was in trade, just as Thomas was. Their friends, Viscount and Viscountess Axeley, happened to be in town on a visit to his family—another mixed couple: nobility and commoner. Although Caroline wasn't acquainted with them, they were dear to Persephone, and Antonella had become their friend in Cornwall as well.

The young clerk, Nalin, had arrived as well, and she was relieved to see that Julian and he were already deep in conversation about English law as it applied to business.

Of course, there was also the munshi, Abdul Rahman. He stood quietly at the side of the room with the spaniel Bramble, coat brushed to a shine, on a leash at his side and Kavi perched on his shoulder. He would work in Julian and Anjali's household as scribe and tutor helping Anjali with her translations, and would also provide any such help Thomas might need as he wound up his business.

As to the day's events, Caroline didn't know what to expect, quite honestly. The curtain was drawn over the stage so she had no clue concerning what awaited them. A quiet hum of conversation echoed in the high-ceilinged room, a buzz of happy anticipation.

As the hour of the wedding grew near, music of a kind Caroline had never heard before began to sound from behind the guests. Everyone craned their necks to look back. A small group of instrumentalists dressed in what Caroline assumed was native Indian costume sat cross-legged on a carpet. One held a long-necked stringed instrument with frets, like a guitar, but not positioned like one. The neck slashed diagonally across his body and the player plucked out a haunting melody on it. Another's hand loosely wrapped around the even longer neck of a different instrument with a gourd-like bottom resting on the ground. This one was like a drone, creating the constant thrum of a single note. The third musician leaned the most remarkable bowed instrument against his body—nothing like a cello—while he delicately touched the strings and brought the bow across them to create a plaintive counter melody. The fourth sat with two drums in front of him, one small and wooden, one larger and made of dull metal, which he played by means of the clever use of the different parts of his hands.

The squeal of the curtains being drawn to reveal the stage drew everyone's attention back to the front. The guests gasped and a murmur of wonder arose. So, Anjali wasn't going to process in like a traditional English bride. Which was appropriate. Instead, she stood in front of a backdrop painted to look like a fanciful Indian landscape dressed in what Caroline assumed was a wedding sari, its rich red silk embroidered all over with gold—from the close-fitting bodice, to the sweeping skirt with its draped shawl, to the veil that cascaded down from her head over her back. Her arms were adorned with a quantity of thin gold bangles, and she wore gold filigree earrings and beads and a jewel that hung down right in the middle of her forehead. She looked magnificent.

Behind her stood her father in a knee-length, deep blue silk jacket with a wide red embroidered sash and close-fitting cloth trousers, his feet bare in his jeweled slippers, and a modest turban on his head.

And opposite Anjali was Julian, his face aglow. He could barely suppress his smile. He was dressed like Thomas, but all in cream with gold embroidery. Caroline chuckled to herself: he was no doubt happy to wear a turban that covered his famous red curls.

The chaplain stood behind and facing the congregation, speaking the familiar words of the Christian wedding rite.

As they reached the critical moment when the bride made her vows, Anjali proclaimed a confident "I do." A moment later, from the side of the room, another voice said "I do" in exactly the same tone as Anjali. Heads swiveled and a whisper started. But Caroline knew exactly who it was.

Kavi.

Anjali pinched her lips together, trying to suppress a laugh, but gave up when everyone in the congregation began to laugh as well.

The ceremony ended, and they all adjourned to the blue saloon for a wedding breakfast that included both English and Indian dishes.

Conversation ebbed and flowed and the couple accepted the congratulations and felicitations of all their guests. A superfluity of love, Caroline thought, her heart swelling with pride.

Thomas came over to Caroline where she stood surveying the joyous scene. "I hope you don't mind that we imported a bit of India for this day. Anjali insisted, and Julian was just as adamant."

"Mind! Oh Thomas, I could never have envisioned a day like this in all my life. What did I do to deserve such happiness?"

He stepped back and looked at her, astonished. "I don't know how you can ask that. You have brought us all together. You kept faith with me for thirty years. You welcomed a half-Indian girl into your home and helped her navigate the perils of society. You threw the entire weight of your family behind rescuing me from a false imprisonment. You allowed your daughter Belinda to have a love match that your parents would have considered unworthy of her. You embraced your husband's illegitimate offspring, Antonella, and helped her achieve her own happiness. You have become friends with the governess who taught your daughters, even after you discovered that her late sister had been your husband's lover. It's more than most women in the *ton* would do. What did you do? All this. This is all your triumph, my love," Thomas said, putting his arm around her waist and pulling her to him.

Caroline sighed and realized that he was right. She deserved her happiness. She deserved him.

And, she thought, as he bent his head to kiss her—slowly, tenderly, passionately—no one would ever be able to take any of it away from her again.

THANK YOU!

This book marks the end of this series. I so appreciate you coming along with me on this romantic journey. I hope you enjoyed the time you spent with these characters. I certainly loved writing them.

If you want to be the first to hear what's coming next (another Regency romance series!) click here to join my newsletter, or scan this code:

Looking for another historical world to step into?

My Double-Dilemma Romance series may be complete, but if you enjoy richly imagined historical settings, strong heroines, dangerous choices, and love tested by the unique demands of past times, you may also like my trilogy set in Medieval Languedoc, beginning with Listen to the Wind.

It's a different time period, but it shares many of the things I love most as a novelist: women with courage, complicated loyalties, and hearts that refuse to be easily ruled.

A note for Double-Dilemma Romance readers:

My medieval trilogy is set in a rougher, more dangerous world than Regency drawing rooms and country manors. The romance remains emotionally driven, but the books include somewhat more mature themes and historical realities, including franker references to sexuality and women's vulnerability in the period.

HISTORICAL NOTE

Although the pursuit of true love is at the heart of all my romance novels, I am first of all a historian who loves to bring real historical events to the page. For this novel, that included the infamous Suspension of Habeas Corpus Act of 1817.

The Napoleonic Wars ended in 1815, but much to the distress of the British population, peace did not bring immediate prosperity. Demobilized soldiers and sailors flooded the country. Industries that had flourished during wartime saw a downturn. Trade patterns shifted as previously unavailable markets and sources opened again. Many working people faced unemployment or falling wages. The distress was especially sharp in manufacturing districts.

Bread was also at a historically high price because of the Corn Laws of 1815. These laws protected the merchants, but made it difficult for many working families to afford to feed their families. Then 1816, the "Year Without a Summer," brought terrible weather and poor harvests, worsening scarcity and hardship through the winter of 1816–1817.

This was all a recipe for widespread unrest. Reformers argued that ordinary people had no meaningful voice in government, and that giving them one would help create more equitable laws. This was true especially in the rapidly growing industrial towns that saw no corresponding increase in parliamentary districts. Public meetings, petitions, radical clubs, pamphlets, and newspapers became part of a wider reform movement. Although many reformers sought only to increase representation in the government to include new districts, to Lord Liverpool's government and Home Secretary Lord Sidmouth, this reform agitation looked dangerously close to sedition.

Add to all this the fact that the French Revolution still loomed large in the imaginations of the ruling class. Protesters asking for bread, work, or parliamentary reform were reminiscent of 1790s radicalism and continental revolution. Sidmouth, introducing the measure in the Lords, described reform as a possible mask for conspiracy against the government.

Their fears were seemingly confirmed in the Spa Fields meetings in London in late 1816. These began as reform gatherings, but the December meeting was followed by attempts by a radical minority to seize weapons and cause an uprising.

Perhaps the most immediate cause of Parliament's action was the attack on the Prince Regent's carriage on 28 January 1817, as he returned from the State Opening of Parliament. Whether the incident was truly part of a revolutionary conspiracy or merely an outburst by an angry public, it intensified official fear and was used to justify emergency measures.

At this time, the government relied on underground reports of radical plots, some gathered through informers and spies. Documents, private meetings, foreign connections, and suspected "correspondence" could be made to look ominous. Secret committees examined these alarming reports and ministers argued that extraordinary powers were needed to prevent conspiracy before it broke into open rebellion.

The Spa Fields disturbances, the attack on the Prince Regent's carriage, and reports of radical conspiracies persuaded Lord Liverpool's ministry that ordinary legal safeguards should be temporarily set aside. The Habeas Corpus Suspension Act, passed in March 1817, allowed the government to detain suspected conspirators without the usual requirement that they be brought promptly before a court. Ministers saw it as a necessary precaution against rebellion. Critics saw it as a dangerous infringement of one of Britain's most cherished liberties.

This, of course, is what led to Thomas's incarceration in this story.

While the specific events imagined in this novel are fictional, they are set against a real historical backdrop: the East India Company's transformation from commercial enterprise into imperial power. By the early nineteenth century, Company rule in India had been achieved by military conquest, political manipulation, aggressive treaty-making, and the extraction of revenue from conquered territories. Thomas's suspicions are therefore invented, but the atmosphere that gives rise to them is not.

Also grounded in history is the circumstance that Thomas married an upper-class Indian woman. There is much documentary evidence of this practice, including extant wills written by some of these women. However, I have not found reliable population figures for Anglo-Indians in Britain in 1817. People of mixed British and Indian ancestry were not always recorded as such. But South Asians and British-Indian families were part of Britain's imperial world for generations. Anjali's story is fictional. Nonetheless, her presence in Regency England is entirely plausible.

ACKNOWLEDGMENTS

I am so grateful to my community of supporters, all of whom take a role in bringing my books to readers. This includes my coach and brainstorming partner, Julie Artz; my beta readers Margaret McNellis and Kayli Larkin; numerous friends and family who continue to believe in me; and my team of ARC readers who provide much-needed advance reviews.

I would also like to thank, once again, my ever-patient proofreader, Susan Babcock. She keeps me honest and her eagle eyes save me from many embarrassing mitsakes.